# BACK IN HUSBAND'S ARMS

BY

## SUSANNE HAMPTON

MILLS &
BOON

Published in Great Britain 2014
by Mills & Boon, an imprint of Harlequin (UK) Limited,
Eton House, 18-24 Paradise Road, Richmond, Surrey, TW9 1SR

© 2014 Susanne Panagaris

ISBN: 978 0 263 90773 5

Harlequin (UK) Limited's policy is to use papers that are natural,
renewable and recyclable products and made from wood grown in
sustainable forests. The logging and manufacturing processes conform
to the legal environmental regulations of the country of origin.

Printed and bound in Spain
by Blackprint CPI, Barcelona

**Dear Reader**

I am so happy to bring you this story of love the second time around.

Tom and Sara are two very dedicated doctors who fell in love but have been driven apart by a secret in Tom's past that has prevented him from fulfilling Sara's dream for their future. Sara has walked away from their marriage still deeply in love but not willing to sacrifice her needs. For the first time in her life she's made a stand—even though it has broken her heart.

Fate brings them together three years later, and they quickly discover the passion they shared is still very much present. But so are their differences.

Circumstance finds them spending four weeks working together, and they must make a choice: to fight their desire and continue on different paths leading away from each other or to surrender to their longings and find a way forward in each other's arms.

Tom and Sara are two wonderfully strong characters, and I hope you enjoy reading about their journey to find happiness as much as I loved writing this second chapter to their special love story.

Love really can be rekindled…it just takes faith, honesty and two pure hearts.

*Susanne Hampton*

## Dedication

To the very special women in my life
who have helped me through life's challenging times
and made me stronger.

*Your friendship is more precious than diamonds
and a treasure greater than gold.*

And to Charlotte for being the most amazing editor…
thank you for your unlimited patience
and encouragement.

**A recent title by Susanne Hampton:**

UNLOCKING THE DOCTOR'S HEART

**This book is also available in eBook format
from www.millsandboon.co.uk**

# CHAPTER ONE

SARA FIELDING MADE her way along the wet footpath, dodging the small potholes that had filled with water from the overnight rain, her feet tucked inside flat knee-high boots. It was eight in the morning and bitterly cold. She tugged her collar up against the breeze that was cutting through her heavy overcoat, wishing she had worn her woollen tights.

Winter mornings in Melbourne were brutal, she remembered, and today was no exception. It had been thundering down when her plane had landed only an hour before and she had caught a cab straight into the city. The rain had paused momentarily but the overcast sky promised another downpour at any moment. Her favourite pair of brown leather gloves were only just preventing her fingers from freezing around the handle of her briefcase, so she quickly picked up her pace. She didn't want to arrive at the hospital soaked to the bone.

Sara had been living in Adelaide for the last three years and this was only her second trip back to Melbourne in all that time. The first had been four weeks ago when she'd travelled over to finalise her visa at the American embassy. Sara had had serious reservations about returning to Melbourne at all. She would have preferred any other city, but it was the United States embassy that processed South Australian visa applications. She'd had no choice.

Melbourne held wonderful memories but also a sadness that she really didn't want to face. She had told herself it was only an overnight stay. A quick trip. Nothing to worry about. But now, looking back, she realised she should have listened to her intuition and stayed far away from the town where Tom Fielding still lived. She was already planning a new life in Texas. So much further from Melbourne. So much further from the temptation of Tom Fielding.

She now knew that she couldn't trust her heart, or her body for that matter, around the man. He wasn't a bad man, quite the opposite, in fact, but he was definitely the wrong man for her. Against her will, Sara's thoughts were dragged back to that brief trip and how terribly wrong it had all gone.

Day one had been fine. The visa application had been processed without any hiccups. It had been day two when Sara had found herself sitting alone at Vue de Monde on the fifty-fifth floor of the historic Rialto building. She had ordered her meal and had been in high spirits, sipping her white wine and thinking about her impending trip to Texas.

She had been offered a position at a large teaching hospital in San Antonio. It was going to be a fresh start, a chance to move on and find a life that might just fulfil her dreams. Sara had finally grown tired of her life revolving around what everyone else wanted. Sacrificing her dreams, her hopes, for the needs of everyone else had become a pattern until three years ago. That fateful day when she'd decided she couldn't give up on one particular dream. She hoped this move would give her the chance to realise that dream. The dream of becoming a mother. She knew she had the packing, the shipping and all that a move of that distance entailed, but it would be worth every bit of effort. She would be free to live her life on her terms.

Suddenly her thoughts were stolen. As was her breath. Both taken by the vision of a man she'd thought she would never see again.

Sara did a double take. *Could it be?* She shook her head a little. *Could it really be him?*

He walked into the restaurant and took a seat at a table by the window. It had been three years since she had last seen him. They hadn't contacted each other since she'd left. No telephone calls. No letters. Nothing.

Perhaps it was her imagination. Perhaps it was someone who looked just like him.

Then she reminded herself there was really no other man who came close to his looks, his stature, his charisma. It was definitely Tom Fielding. All six foot two inches of him had crossed the room and had turned every woman's head as he'd done so.

Sara's heart raced a little as she watched him take the wine list from the waitress. She saw the waitress attempt to flirt, it was subtle, but enough for another woman to notice. Tom was unmoved. He didn't appear to notice or, if he did, he didn't respond. The flustered waitress placed the napkin in his lap and hovered, a little longer than necessary.

Sara felt a tightening in her chest and butterflies awakening in the pit of her stomach as the reality of being this close to Tom hit home. She had forgotten the effect he had on her. And apparently still did. Her emotions began playing havoc, sending her mind into a tailspin. She looked away. Swallowing hard, she began to play with her cutlery absent-mindedly.

She hadn't expected so many mixed emotions to come in to play. Attraction, regret, melancholy, guilt, even a hint of lust. This was not supposed to happen. This was a bad dream playing out. Sharing the same restaurant as Tom was not in the plan, and her options to escape the uncomfortable situation were limited. She could hardly leave the restaurant after ordering her dinner. Most likely it would draw even more attention to her. She didn't want to look back in Tom's direction but she was drawn to him. Drawn to him just like the conflicting desire to gaze at an open wound.

Tom chose a wine and handed the waitress back the wine list. He looked out the window across the sweeping views of the Melbourne skyline. The panorama of lights all twinkling against the black sky. Then he turned in his seat, just a little, but enough to see Sara.

He didn't move. He froze in his chair, staring in silence. Sara did the same. She had no idea what he was thinking. She barely knew what she was thinking as she looked at the handsome curves of his face and the generous sweep of his broad shoulders in his tailored black jacket. The ultra-modern restaurant was dimly lit and combined with the dark charcoal and earthy brown tones of the sleek decor it was difficult to make out very much. Except that he was still handsome. So very handsome.

It wasn't cocky good looks he possessed. It was as if he just didn't know how appealing he was to women. He had always been that way. He obviously knew on some level that he was attractive but he never took advantage of it or seemed impressed by the gift nature had bestowed on him. Tom Fielding was a lot deeper than skin alone.

He stood up then hesitated for a moment, as if to seek some sort of approval to approach. But he did anyway. Her stomach was a tangled mess of nerves as she watched him drop his napkin on the table and cross over to her. His eyes didn't leave her face for an instant.

'Sara,' he began, as he bent down to kiss her cheek. The scent of his cologne filled her senses. It wasn't overpowering, it was subtle and sensual. It was Tom.

'It's so good to see you,' he continued.

Sara was momentarily speechless. She knew she was in Melbourne, it wasn't as if they had bumped into each other in an isolated town on the other side of the world. Perhaps she shouldn't have even been surprised, but it was still overwhelming.

'Lovely to see you too, Tom,' she finally breathed in reply. It was a struggle as she felt her heart cramp.

'May I?' he asked, as his hand rested on the empty chair.

Sara nodded and he pulled out the chair and sat down at her table. Out of habit, he reached across and touched her hand.

Looking back in the harsh light of day, Sara realised that had been her first mistake. She should have kept Tom Fielding at arm's length. It had begun to rain, and Sara regretted not asking her cab from the airport to drop her at the nearest coffee shop to the hospital. She needed a short black to wake herself up after the early flight and couldn't bear the thought of cafeteria coffee. She was in search of the strength only a barista could provide.

Picking up her steps even more, her mind raced back to that night. That silly, stupid night four weeks ago.

Dinner alone had turned into dinner for two, then a stroll, and then drinks at a bar in the city. Scars had a way of fading a little in the soft lights of the evening, particularly when wine was involved. Old times, old feelings, old reasons for falling in love replaced the wounds and hurt. Her defences became shaky and, against her will, they finally fell.

Reason didn't have a chance. Just before midnight, they were alone in her hotel room. Tom looked more appealing than any man she had ever seen. Sitting on the edge of her bed in his long black jeans, his suede boots a little dusty, his dark blond hair pushed back in waves that brushed the collar of his white linen shirt. His jacket was flung over the small sofa by the window.

He looked like a cowboy. *Her cowboy for tonight.*

And it could only be for tonight. For old times' sake, she reasoned silently. There was no chance of anything more. They had tried that and it didn't work. She wasn't going there again. She wasn't giving up her dreams for this man. But she knew her heart was finally out of harm's way. It was safely protected inside the walls that she had carefully erected when she had walked out and left him, so she gave in to her desires. It's only one night, she reassured herself.

He was staring straight at her with his bedroom eyes. Despite wondering if she was about to make one of life's bad decisions and one she might just regret, she seemed too powerless to stop herself. Was it lust or was it love? She wasn't sure but it was going to happen.

'Don't tell me to stop, I know what I'm about to do…' she started.

Suddenly her words were cut short by his lips pressing against hers. His hands gently cupped her face as his mouth captured her sigh. She didn't fight him. She didn't want to talk any more. Her hands instinctively reached up and pulled him closer. Her body arched with desire. She was aflame with the heat in his fingers as his hands slid under her clothing to stroke her bare skin. His kisses became more urgent and she opened her mouth to him. She wanted to feel him, to have him, just once more. To feel his body next to hers and to taste him. He unbuttoned her blouse and slid it from her warm skin, tossing it on the floor as he trailed moist kisses down her neck.

'I want you, Sara, and I'm going to have you tonight,' he breathed low and heavy with desire as his fingers traced gentle lines along the bare skin of her thigh.

His hands moved to the curve of her spine and he pulled her even closer to his hard body. She felt her pulse racing as her fingers threaded through his hair and she kissed him more deeply than before. They fell back onto the bed, discarding the last remnants of clothing before their bodies became one.

Sara Fielding had woken in her hotel room the next morning more confused than she thought possible. It had all seemed so clear the night before. Just two people sharing a night of pleasure. Two consenting adults needing each other. Nothing more. But now it was anything but clear. She realised just how vulnerable she still was with Tom. She pulled the sheets up to her chin like a flimsy shield. A feeling of dread hit the pit of her stomach.

As daylight slipped through the gap in the heavy curtains she could see the fine stubble on his chin. The satin sheet was barely covering him, and his tanned chest was sculpted like a statue. They had made love all night and he was still the caring, amazing lover she remembered. But she should never have done it. She looked up at the ceiling of the room, wondering what possessed her to be so stupid and impulsive. It was not like her.

She had spent the last three years trying to push past the hurt and disappointment and then, in a few passionate hours, she had ignored her own logic and risked opening up old wounds. She couldn't blame it on the wine, she hadn't even finished her drink at the restaurant and had hardly touched the martini at the bar.

Hormones, memories, melancholy, maybe even the remnants of the love they had once shared, had overridden the voice of reason and they had returned to her room together.

Now, in the light of morning, she wanted to scream at herself. *Why?*

In a few short weeks he would officially become her ex-husband. The divorce would be finalised. She had managed to stay away for all those years, finally finding the resolve to ask for a divorce, and then, just before it became official, she'd slept with him.

She rolled her eyes in disappointment and confusion. Her lawyer had told her that Tom wasn't contesting the divorce. He had signed the papers. It was just a matter of legal processes being completed.

Perhaps it was knowing that the divorce would be

finalised that made her feel safe. That was crazy, she knew, but it was the only explanation she could muster. The divorce was a piece of paper. It wasn't a shield. It couldn't protect her heart.

Tom began to stir. She closed her eyes and feigned sleep. She wasn't sure what to say. Was it *Thank you for a lovely evening* or *I know we slept together but just so you know, I'm not in love with you any more?*

She needed time. Perhaps he would wake up and leave. She felt her stomach knot, not unlike the night before when he'd walked towards her at the restaurant. All those old feelings, the good and the bad, were sitting heavily in her chest.

She wasn't sure if she had imagined it, but as she'd been falling asleep in Tom's arms the night before, she thought she had heard him whisper, *I love you*. She didn't want to go there. She wasn't about to get involved with Tom again. It would be too easy to fall back into his arms. She had taken so long to not need him in her life. To finally realise that she had a right to live her life the way she wanted, whatever it might cost her.

She lay as still as she could. Her breathing was light but laboured as her nerves played with her anxiety level. Last night they had given in to the chemistry they had always shared. But their differences were still there. That hadn't changed and they would never be able to move past what had torn them apart. Sara watched Tom slip from the bed and collect his clothes from all over the room. She wondered if he felt the same. A little part wished he had tried to wake her, to hold her and to talk through their differences. To solve the issues they had and to make love again.

Reason reminded her that it would never happen, so

leaving without a word would be best. She hoped he'd leave a note on the hotel stationery. That's all she should expect. All she wanted, she tried to convince herself.

She had loved every minute of his hands and his body on hers. The tenderness and sense of belonging had been undeniable but now, hearing him dressing in the other room, she knew it had been wrong. It had been a lapse in judgement for both of them.

The door of the bathroom opened and Tom emerged fully dressed. Sara closed her eyes again. She didn't want him to catch her awake, thinking about what might have been. He fumbled for his boots then slipped on his jacket. She watched through half-open eyes as he made his way to the desk and scribbled something on the hotel notepad. Quietly, he crossed to the door of her room, opened it and left quietly. He was gone.

As the door shut, Sara sat bolt upright. She was so grateful he was gone. *Or was she?* She felt horribly confused. There was nothing sweeter than falling asleep wrapped in Tom's arms, the heat of his naked body pressed against hers.

But she had to move on. He wouldn't change. He couldn't change. And she was tired of changing for everyone else. She almost had the divorce. She would be free. They would be free of each other. They were two very different people with very different priorities.

She wanted children.

He didn't.

And this time she was walking away to live her life, her way.

She remembered climbing from the warm bed and heading to the shower. Trying to make sense of the night was pointless, she decided as the warm water ran over her back and shoulders. Images of Tom making love to her came rushing back. She closed her eyes and turned to face the water head-on. The water soaked her hair and ran down her face. She was leaving for Texas in eight short weeks. And she would never see Tom Fielding again.

She turned off the water and wrapped herself in a fluffy white bath towel and returned to the scene of the crime. There was a wrapper or two that she didn't want the hotel staff to find, so she picked them up and put them in the bin. Tom was so very good at being bad but he was always very careful.

She crossed to the desk and picked up the note.

*Dear Sara,*
*Lovely to spend time with you. All the very best*
*for Texas.*
*Always,*
*Tom x*

She smiled, a bittersweet smile at the sadness of the situation. Two people who loved each other but who both had to accept it could never be.

Sara hadn't really pushed for divorce at first but now, with a new life in America awaiting her, she no longer wanted to be Dr Sara Fielding, wife of Dr Tom Fielding. She needed to be single. To have a chance at happiness and a family.

She had only filed for the divorce six months before. She had held onto the idea he would change his mind for too long and she knew it. But Tom had finally agreed to sign the papers. He too had accepted they were over.

The way he'd left this morning showed that. Last night had been like two friends who had given in to their emotions for just one night. But her rationale was fragile in the early morning light.

The sudden sound of an ambulance siren brought Sara back from her reverie. She was beside the tall red-brick hospital walls of Augustine General Hospital and quite close to the front doors and the hospital office of her good friend Stu Anderson. Just after she'd returned from her first trip to Melbourne, Stu had mentioned he was in need of a locum oral surgeon to oversee his private practice while he was away. Sara had had the time and had wanted to help out so she had agreed to work the four weeks before she left for the US.

She was aware returning to Melbourne could hold some difficulties but she also knew she had to push past the hurt and accept the shortfalls of the city. The shortfalls being her failed marriage and the sadness that weighed down her memories of the time she had spent there. She'd studied, she'd fallen in love and she'd left. Now, all these years later she thought she needed to accept that life wasn't perfect here but she didn't need to stay away any longer. She just needed to keep her emotions in check.

With this new resolve, it hadn't seemed such a bad idea when she had agreed to help out but now, being back in the city, memories of the night she had spent with Tom came charging back, and she was a little more anxious about her stay.

She tried to remind herself that Melbourne was a big city. She could avoid the Vue de Monde, and the martini bar. That wouldn't be too difficult as there were many more restaurants and she wasn't that fond of vermouth anyway. And luckily Tom consulted at a hospital the other side of the city.

Mindful of the hospital traffic, Sara kept to the pedestrian pathway as she made her way to the entrance. The ambulance had pulled up in the emergency parking bay and the paramedics, now joined by two hospital staff, were already removing the gurney from the back of the vehicle.

She walked around to the automatic sliding doors of the visitors' entrance. At least she was finally under shelter. Removing her heavy overcoat, she shook the excess water out over the large grey rubber mat before she placed the coat over her arm and stepped inside. Thankfully, inside the hospital was much warmer than outside. She slipped off her gloves and placed them into the pocket of her coat. Crossing to the information counter, she ran her fingers through her damp hair and wiped the moisture from her face.

'Hello, I'm here to see Dr Anderson. Oral maxillofacial surgery.'

The receptionist smiled, although the second glances Sara was receiving from the other administration staff made her think her appearance was a little battered by the weather. She quickly realised her hair was more than just damp when she felt trickles run down her temples and into her left ear.

The young woman picked up a box of tissues from behind the high grey and white panelled counter and offered them to Sara. 'It's really coming down out there, isn't it?'

With an embarrassed smile she took a few tissues and mopped her wet forehead, cheeks and ear.

'You need to take the elevator at the end of this corridor up to the fourth floor and you'll find the oral surgery consulting rooms on the left as you step out.'

'Thanks,' Sara replied, trying to stifle a yawn. The effect of a long night of surgery, combined with an early morning flight, was starting to show. Sara had tried to keep busy since her last trip to Melbourne; she hadn't wanted any time to think about what she had done. Unfortunately, returning to Melbourne was rapidly bringing it all back.

Tom Fielding sat in his office on the fourth floor of Augustine General Hospital, thinking back to the night he'd spent with Sara, the way he had thought about it every day for the last four weeks. Each day since that fateful night vivid, unwanted memories had reminded him of how much he still loved his soon-to-be-ex-wife. Still wanted her but couldn't have her. He had decided to give her the divorce, hand her back her life and return to his alone. But that one night together had destroyed the solace he had finally found; it ate away at his core that there was no future for them. They had different goals, different plans for their lives, and there was no common ground any more.

Except in a hotel room at midnight.

Tom remembered his surprise and elation when he'd spied his beautiful ex-wife sitting alone across from him in the restaurant. In his eyes she was still the most gorgeous, captivating woman in the world. She was intelligent, kind, caring, strong willed and the most giving lover a man could want. A shared dinner had led to drinks and then to her hotel.

Once he had been inside her room, Tom hadn't been

able to control himself any longer. Sara had made it very clear that she wanted him just as much. He had been risking everything, including his sanity, but he'd wanted this woman more than life itself. Even if it was for just one last time.

In the morning Tom had opened his eyes to see his wife lying beside him. Ex-wife, reasoning reminded him. She was sleeping so soundly. She was so beautiful. Her short blonde hair had been a mess, a beautiful mess. A mess he had created when he'd been making love to her all night. The curves of her naked body had been softly lit by the rays that had peeped through the curtain break.

He'd resisted the urge to stroke her soft, tempting skin. She was such a sound sleeper, he knew that from the time they'd spent as husband and wife, but he hadn't wanted to risk waking her. He'd known he had to slip from the bed and leave. It would be best for both of them. Trying to make sense of what they'd done would be impossible. Sara had made it very clear that she was heading overseas. She was starting a new life and he had to do the same. He had to give her the divorce. He had to give her the freedom she needed and return to his life without her.

He loved her, and maybe she still loved him a little at least, but in a few weeks they would be divorced. She had reminded him of that fact last night in the restaurant. She was moving on, she had told him at the bar where they'd enjoyed a martini together. Leaving for the US in a few weeks to start afresh in a new country, she had told him at the door of her hotel room at midnight.

They hadn't talked about their past, they hadn't talked about their work. And they hadn't spoken about their differences. They'd spoken about the present, about light-hearted subjects. It was as if they had been two strangers who hadn't wanted to know anything too deep about each other.

It was an unspoken agreement; each knowing they would only share one last night. Tom didn't want to hold up his end of that unspoken agreement. He wanted his wife back. He wanted to wake up every morning with her in his arms. But he was a logical man and he accepted that could never be.

Before he'd left the room he had paused to take one last look at Sara still asleep in the rumpled bed sheets. She'd looked like an angel. *His angel for one last night.*

# CHAPTER TWO

'SLOW DOWN…AND tell me how exactly you came to misplace a patient?'

'I'm not sure, Dr Fielding. His name was…oh, what was his name again? That's right…Kowalski…Joseph Kowalski. I can't believe he's gone. I messed up big time. I'm so sorry, Dr Fielding. I'm really sorry. I'm such an idiot.'

'Johnson, take a breath. I examined Mr Kowalski in my ward a little over an hour ago. He had multiple mandibular fractures and if I'm not mistaken a blood alcohol close to point two. He was in a hospital gown and hooked up to an IV. I can't see him travelling very far without being noticed.'

Sara Fielding stepped back from the open doorway to where she couldn't be seen. *Dr Fielding?* What was he doing here? He didn't consult at this hospital. He was the oral and maxillofacial consultant at Lower North Eastern on the other side of the city. It was where she had done her training. It was where they met. Why was he here? He must be visiting Stu to say goodbye, as they were friends. They had all been friends once, she reminded herself.

'I know, right, how far could he get?' the young voice

returned in varying pitch, trying to convince himself of a good outcome. But his struggle showed when his voice gave in to a nervous stutter. 'I—I spoke with Security at the b-back and front gates and he hasn't left the grounds.'

'Well, that's comforting, I'd hate to see footage of our escapee on television tonight. We don't want to see our director's face on the six p.m. news if they splash shots of the bare backside of an inebriated elderly man, still attached to an IV stand, walking down Swan Street. I can only imagine the paperwork involved with that Ministerial inquiry.'

Stunned, Sara collapsed back against the wall out of the view of Tom and the young man she assumed was either a final year undergraduate or an intern. *Our director?* Her heart was racing and her stomach had tied itself in a knot. She didn't hear any of what he was telling the young man after those two words, she just heard the thumping of the blood in her temples. Tom Fielding must now be consulting at this hospital. *Her hospital.*

'Security, please.' Tom spoke into the phone then, while waiting for the connection, he began skimming through the unread emails on his computer screen. After a moment, he continued. 'It's Tom Fielding, I'm just checking on the status of a missing patient. Joseph Kowalski. Admitted to the oral surgery ward about two hours ago, apparently did a runner out of the ward… Oh, okay. The cafeteria—poor man's probably hungry. So where is he now? Right, that's unfortunate. I'll send the intern to collect him promptly. Thanks.' With that he hung up the phone.

'Well, Johnson, I suggest you head to the florist on the ground floor. Kowalski's in there, trying to purchase a bouquet, and apparently while searching for his imaginary wallet underneath his hospital gown he has managed to show the family jewels to the volunteers. They're a little disturbed, so you need to calmly head down and collect him. But remember, you're no good to anyone, and particularly not Mr Kowalski, if you beat yourself up about it. You followed hospital procedure. You notified Security, and me, and they have him. Good outcome, so just head off and take him back to the ward pronto.'

Sara clenched her eyes closed. Her mind was struggling to process what was happening. It made no sense to her. Stu had set up the appointment at the hospital to discuss his caseload and show her around the operating theatres. Then he was going to take her to his practice, which was apparently only a few blocks away. There had definitely been no mention of Tom in the conversation. If there had been she wouldn't have agreed to come. Nervously, she smoothed her skirt and tugged her jacket back into position.

More than anything, she wanted to run. To disappear and not face Tom again. But she couldn't. She had made a promise to Stu to locum for him for the month. A promise she couldn't break.

The heat began rising in her cheeks. Her heart began beating a little faster. Elevating anxiety was threatening her composure but she was fighting back. She tried to put the situation into perspective quickly. She had limited time to find a solution, a tidy way to process this.

The practice would occupy most of her time. There would be Theatre two days a week or perhaps only one and a half. She would be consulting at the private practice at least three days, maybe even three and a half.

Thoughts of their recent night together, their romantic whirlwind engagement and their year as husband and wife had to be replaced hurriedly with a professional demeanour. She needed to rebuild those walls that had protected her for the last three years and which would once again be her saviour when she walked into the office to face Tom.

Clearly his presence at the hospital would complicate things but she wouldn't run and hide. She needed to face this head-on. She was thirty-two years old now with a respected medical career. The fact that they had spent one crazy night together couldn't affect their work, they had to put it behind them.

Perhaps he already had done that, she told herself. He had left the hotel room without a word and he hadn't contacted her since, so he must be feeling the same way. She desperately needed to freeze her heart before she saw his face.

Reaching down for her briefcase, she waited a moment for the young man to leave. With her head held high, she would walk into Tom's office and behave as if nothing had ever happened.

Unfortunately, she assumed the young man would be walking, not running, and not straight into her.

His full weight met with her tiny frame, sending her crashing back into the wall and her briefcase tumbling down to the ground.

'Oh, no, I'm so sorry. I didn't see you there,' he gasped, as he reached out to steady Sara. 'Are you okay?'

Sara was stunned into silence for a moment. Finally she managed to mutter, 'I'm fine, really.' She was a little shaken but didn't want to make a fuss. Bending down to gather her belongings, she didn't think the day could get any worse.

'No, you're not. You're bleeding. You've cut your leg!'

Sara spied the gash on her knee. The open lock on her briefcase must have cut her before it hit the ground.

'Come with me. You'll have to sit down while I get some antiseptic and gauze.' The young man directed Sara into the office he had just left. Tom's office. This was not the entrance she had hoped to make, which had been walking in confidently and meeting Tom on an equal footing. Now, limping in, she wasn't going to meet him on any footing.

Tom didn't lift his eyes from the papers he was reading on his desk. Sara noticed his white exam coat was still thrown over the chair. He had always hated wearing it, and apparently he still did. The top button of his blue striped shirt was undone and there was no sign of a tie.

'They're waiting downstairs, Johnson…you need to get there stat.' His voice was stern but not abrasive.

Sara stood in the doorway supported by her apologetic assailant. Across the room she watched the man who had captured her heart all those years ago and who had made love to her only a few short weeks ago. For the briefest moment time seemed to stand still. Her resolve to forget their history vanished and she found herself wondering how it would be if things had been different between them.

She hated feeling this way. It wasn't fair and she couldn't allow her feelings to cloud her future. The chemistry they shared had allowed the anger and frustration to dissipate over dinner and drinks. But here in the hospital she would fight it. Her biological clock was ticking louder than her heart and she was determined that Tom Fielding would not rob her of the chance to have a family. She would not make that sacrifice. Letting him leave the hotel room had proved to Sara that she had the reserves to do it. To walk away a second time, and to let him do the same.

Tom's eyes were shadowed by a slight frown before he lifted his head and met her gaze. Abruptly the frown vanished and he stood to his feet.

'Sara, I thought you were in San Antonio. What are you doing here?' Suddenly Tom's eyes dropped to the injury on her leg. 'Are you hurt? What on earth happened?' Concern etched his voice as he crossed the room with long purposeful strides. He drew her into his arms and pulled her close to his firm body as Johnson released his support.

Sara resisted Tom's hold. She tried to pull away but his strong arms held her still.

'I crashed into her, Dr Fielding. I didn't see her. I'm sorry. She was waiting outside but I was in a hurry and *boof*—I hit her.' The young man re-enacted the collision with his hands.

'Grab that chair,' Tom said, motioning towards the large armchair that sat by the window. 'Bring it here quickly.'

The young man dragged the chair across the room and Tom gently lowered Sara onto the cushioned leather.

'There's a first-aid kit in the cupboard to the right of the bookcase.'

Sara heard the instructions Tom gave to Johnson but her eyes were transfixed on Tom as he crossed the room to retrieve a small footstool by the bookcase.

He looked every bit as gorgeous in the daylight as he had that night just a month ago. His lean, angular face was slightly tanned and his grey eyes were luminous beneath his sandy brows.

He smiled at her as he carried the footstool back, his wide sensual mouth slowly curving upwards. But she would not reciprocate.

Tom had no place in her life any more. In fact, he should never have been there. They were two very different people with completely different priorities in life.

Sara swallowed hard. 'It's just a little scratch, honestly. It's nothing...' Her words were cut short when she felt the warmth of his hands on her bare skin. He looked into her eyes as he knelt on the floor beside her, gently lifting her leg and placing it on the stool. He moved the hem of her skirt slightly to assess the damage to her knee. She swallowed hard. She hated that the feel of his fingers lightly touching her skin sent shivers down her spine. Again she wished she had worn heavy woollen tights, but this time it wasn't because of the cold.

Johnson handed him an antiseptic wipe and some gauze.

'It's just a superficial wound. I'll clean it up but I think a plaster will suffice.'

'I'm so glad and I'm so sorry, I mean it. I can't believe what a day I've had and now this—'

'We'll be fine here, Johnson,' Tom interrupted. 'Go and collect your patient but this time just take it a little slower.'

'Are you sure? You don't need anything?'

'Positive,' Tom replied, not taking his eyes off Sara.

Sara watched from the corner of her eye as the young man put the first-aid kit back on Tom's desk, picked up her briefcase and overcoat from the doorway, put them by her chair and left the room.

And left them alone.

Tom's hands were still cradling her leg. The plaster was securely attached to the clean wound but he didn't want to release her. He had forgotten how good it felt to have Sara this close. He had no idea why she was in his office but for the briefest moment he didn't care. She was with him again. Near him again. And he could touch her soft, warm skin. Her perfume was invading his senses. It was the same fragrance she had always worn. So little had changed and yet so much had changed for ever.

Finally he came to his senses and reluctantly released his hold, standing up and moving back to his desk. He looked at the woman before him. She was as beautiful as the day they'd met, the day they'd married and the day she'd left him. But she *had* left him.

'What brings you back to Melbourne and my office?' he asked, as he rested back against the wooden frame and folded his arms across his chest. 'I thought you'd be in Texas by now.' He suddenly felt the need to protect himself. Then the realisation of why she had come to the hospital hit him. She must have grown tired of waiting for the divorce papers to make the return trip to her, so she had made the visit to collect them herself.

'The documents are with my lawyer. No doubt they'll be with yours tomorrow.'

Sara suddenly realised that Tom had no idea either. He was obviously equally clueless that they would be working at the same hospital.

'I'm not here for the papers, Tom. Although I'm glad

to hear that's progressing,' she announced. 'No, actually, I'm here to work for a month, filling in for Stu.'

'You're filling in for Stu?' Tom was gobsmacked.

'You never said anything that night when we…' He hesitated for a minute. He didn't want to allude to what he knew they were both thinking. He cleared his throat. 'When we bumped into each other. I'm surprised you didn't say anything.'

Sara just stared at him for a moment, trying desperately to push the vivid snapshots of the evening from her mind.

'I didn't know back then, when we…' She paused. It was becoming more awkward and uncomfortable by the minute. 'That night, well, I hadn't spoken with Stu and I had no idea you consulted here. But even if I had known, if you remember, we didn't talk work at all.'

Tom nodded in silence.

Sara knew she would never have accepted Stu's proposal to fill in for him if she had known Tom worked at the hospital where she would be operating. She had assumed he was safely ensconced at the other side of town. But she had to deal with the situation. There was no other choice. Stu would never find another oral surgeon on short notice and she would never leave him high and dry like that. She just had to deal with Tom.

'So, what are you doing at this hospital?'

'I'm the associate professor of oral surgery.'

Sara was taken aback. Tom hadn't said a word that night. With a title like that, and the extraordinary workload and dedication to achieve such a position, he had certainly earned some bragging rights. But he had said nothing about it. She wanted to say how proud she was of him, but of course pride carried ownership or at the very least attachment, and she couldn't afford either.

'Congratulations, Tom,' she finally decided, keeping it simple. 'That must have been a lot of work. You must be the youngest associate professor on staff.'

'So they say. But I'd completed my PhD, and had a year post-doctoral experience so I met the selection criteria. The board approved my appointment for three years and I'm only six months into it,' he responded. The PhD had kept his mind from missing Sara after she left. It had provided him with a focus and purpose in getting up each day.

'I still operate on private patients but I'm more involved with the teaching and rotation programme in the undergraduate, graduate and professional curricula and the development of post-qualifying modules. But enough about me. I'm still in shock that you are Stu's mysterious replacement.'

'What do you mean, mysterious?' Sara replied, giving him a puzzled look.

'I mean he hadn't told me who was filling in at the practice. Stu told me that he had it covered but not that you were his replacement.'

Sara was even more confused. Stu's private practice was not his concern. 'Why do you discuss his practice? Don't you still have your own?'

Tom gave her a wry look. 'Because we're partners, Stu's a partner now in my old practice—he bought in a few months ago. I only consult there one day a week now. The hospital consumes most of my time, but I still wanted to maintain some patient contact.'

Sara was completely flustered for a moment. Not only was Tom consulting at the hospital where she would be operating but he was also a partner at the practice where she would be consulting for the next month. She would be working at Tom's old practice. This was quickly spiralling into a disaster.

'Oh, well, at least this will be uncomfortable for both of us,' she said honestly.

Tom stood watching her carefully, looking for clues as to what she was thinking and, more importantly, feeling. He wanted some signs that would let him into her head. There was nothing. She really had shut him out. That night had been nothing but a moment of passion between two lonely people in a big city. Nothing more.

He knew then and there what he had to do. He had to keep his ex-wife away from his heart. Or he'd go mad. It was crazy and he knew it but he still loved the woman sitting there, so close but emotionally so distant. The woman who had captured his heart all those years ago still held it quite firmly in her hands. He had to push her away. Or, more to the point, he had to push her out of his reach.

He didn't need a reminder of why she'd left. Or why she'd had to leave. They had shared that discussion too many times to recall.

Any feelings she'd once had for him were clearly gone. He had to accept it. And so he adopted the same detached demeanour. A demeanour very far from his true feelings.

'There really shouldn't be any problems. That night...' He paused. 'Let's just say old habits, reminiscing, we crossed the line, both of us. It won't happen again. But, hey, we got it out of our systems. Like an itch that needed a good scratch, and now it's done we can both move on.'

Sara was thrown by his response. It was cold. He really was over them. An *itch*? That sounded so unlike the Tom she had known. Still, three years had passed and he had obviously changed. Or, just like her, was he putting on a façade to make the arrangement they found themselves in a little less awkward? It didn't matter. They both knew and understood the rules.

Without answering, Tom crossed back to her and reached for her leg. Sara jumped as his hand gently lifted her leg down from the stool and placed her foot back on the floor.

'We're good, Sara…we're good.'

Sara wasn't so sure. She was going to be operating at the hospital for a month. That meant bumping into each other, on ward rounds, near the OR. There were too many opportunities where they would see each other.

The way her body had reacted to Tom made her realise only too quickly that the chemistry she shared with him wasn't just a memory. She suddenly worried if her love for him would ever truly be over. But they had no future. She would not give up on the idea of bringing children into the world. Being a mother was a dream she wanted to hold onto but Tom never wanted to be a father. That was written in stone.

She had spent too long getting him out of her head and her heart.

Sara looked at him, and even through her tired eyes she could see the man who won her love was still as handsome and charismatic as ever. *It's four short weeks. It can't be that difficult.*

'I'm a little tired—can we discuss the work schedule later? We can sort out the personal arrangements

too over the next few days. I'm happy with the financial separation the way it is. It won't change after we
divorce. You won't need to support me, so it should be
done very quickly.'

There was an uncomfortable silence between them.
She had no idea what was going on in Tom's mind but
he clearly wasn't about to share anything. She had said
her piece and cleared the air.

'Quick and painless, like an extraction of an upper
molar,' he said matter-of-factly.

Sara knew when Tom became uncomfortable he always used dark humour. It was how he masked his
emotions.

'Not quite,' she replied, then chose to change the subject. 'After the four weeks here, I'm off. I don't know a
lot about Texas but the position sounded exciting and I
jumped at it,' she told him as she crossed to one of the
floor-to-ceiling bookcases that lined the room. Part of
her didn't want to go to the US. Part of her still wanted
Tom. But she also wanted more.

Sara lightly ran her fingers over a row of leather-
bound medical books standing next to one another on
the shelf and thought back to all of the nights she had
spent poring over books just like them as a postgraduate
student at the university library, hoping to come close to
Tom's knowledge and skill. But it wasn't just his ability and compassion as a doctor that had her in awe, it
was his commanding presence as a man that had drawn
her to him. He had been her lecturer and her mentor
but more than that, she had wished he was her lover.

She had felt on some level there was chemistry that
ran between them. She would watch him standing at
the lectern, speaking to all the medical students, and

she had hoped, as his eyes had scanned the lecture hall, that he had seen her as more than just his student. She had wanted him to see her as a woman. A woman who respected his knowledge, admired his skills but wanted to know more about him as a man.

Sara would daydream in the tram on the way home, a bag full of handwritten notes at her feet and a laptop in her backpack, about the two of them driving home together. She had pictured them talking about their days, comparing notes on cases and discussing surgical procedures. Sara remembered back to the long nights when she would lie in twisted sheets staring at the ceiling in the darkness of her university bedroom. She would picture the curves of his handsome face, the skin wrinkling softly around his grey eyes when he laughed, and the warm, masculine scent of his body.

Not being able to say how she felt during those many months of study was at times almost impossible. But she knew better than to say anything to her incredibly handsome tutor. It was more than likely that her romantic musings were one-sided. She didn't want her imagination to steer her into attracting more of his attention. He was almost seven years older, infinitely wiser and often intimidating. And she was his student. Capable and willing to learn, passing with distinctions, but still his student.

She thought he would be more interested in dating one of his peers, yet there were moments when she felt there was something more. She would ask a question, or answer one that he had posed, and he would appear genuinely impressed.

There were times when his eyes seemed to linger on her a little longer. His mouth would curve ever so slightly and his eyes seemed to be smiling. Her heart would skip a beat, and she hoped she didn't blush. Sometimes he would ask her to stay late with a small number of postgraduates to discuss a topic or alternate prognosis in greater depths. On more than one occasion he bumped into her in the university cafeteria and they shared a table and talked of things other than work.

She wanted more than anything for his interest to be more than just academic, and these chats led her to believe it was, but he was a complicated man. She decided that until her training was over and he made his feelings clear she would keep her own locked safely inside her heart.

Sara never regretted that decision. Soon after she graduated and found a role in a private practice based in Brighton, Tom invited her to a celebratory dinner. She was so surprised and happy. It was a dinner for two. Standing at the door of the restaurant as they waited for their table, his soft hands cupped her face and gently turned her towards him. Tenderly, he reached down and kissed her.

It took Sara's breath away. Her intuition about his feelings had been right all along. The man of her dreams, of all her late-night fantasies, was kissing her. And not caring who saw them.

She remembered every wonderful warm feeling that rushed through her body when, with love in his eyes and a wicked grin, he whispered huskily that given the chance he would never let her out of his sight again. He told her he wanted to keep her in his arms for ever.

It was a whirlwind romance. Every second weekend they spent away at different cosy bed and breakfasts all over Victoria and then, three months after their first

date, Tom surprised Sara with a trip to Paris. Winter
had set in and they had planned on heading to the ski
slopes of Mount Hotham. The night before they were
due to leave for the snow, sitting by the heater in Sara's
apartment eating raisin toast and sipping on hot chocolate, Tom told Sara there was a slight change in plans
but one he hoped she would like. He suggested that she
should pack some summer clothes and her passport instead of thermal underwear. As Sara frantically emptied
her suitcase of her sweaters, ski pants and thick socks,
hurriedly replacing them with cotton dresses, shorts
and T-shirts, she told him that he was crazy.

And he told her that he loved her.

Tom managed to keep the new holiday destination a
secret until the cab arrived at Tullamarine airport and
he carried their luggage to the Air France check-in. Sara
was so excited that she felt her eyes brimming with
tears as she took her boarding pass, destination Paris.

Together, they spent a blissful week at Hotel Man-
sart on Paris's Right Bank. They strolled hand in hand
around the Tuileries Garden and along the pathways
lined with tulips. Tom was the most romantic, wonderful lover and Sara knew without doubt that she was
totally and completely in love. She couldn't help but
smile with happiness as they sat together by the spar-
kling pools in the warmth of a perfect summer day. A
perfect day with her perfect man and Sara thought life
couldn't be any more wonderful.

But it could. And a short time later it did. As they
stood admiring the Maillol sculptures in the soft light
of sunset, Tom fell to one knee and slipped a diamond
solitaire ring on Sara's finger. She gasped and nodded
before she kissed the man of her dreams and fell into

his arms. She knew with all of her heart it was where she belonged.

After years of study to qualify as an oral and maxillofacial surgeon, Sara was twenty-eight years of age and Tom was about to turn thirty-five so they decided to have a very short engagement and that night as they lay in each other's arms they set a wedding date only three months away.

Sara was going to spend her life with a man she completely and utterly adored and she had never been so happy in her life...

'Sara. Yoo-hoo, I asked you when exactly you're leaving for cattle country?'

# CHAPTER THREE

SARA RAISED HER chin and turned around to face Tom. She looked across the room to see him sitting back down in his high-backed leather chair. She thanked the heavens that, no matter how extraordinarily talented her estranged husband was, at least he wasn't a mind-reader.

She was angry with herself for the way she was reacting to him again. She was so distracted. Closing her eyes for a moment, she took a deep, calming breath. She had to get her emotions under control. Tom was bringing back feelings that she couldn't afford to entertain. She had other plans.

But now, seeing Tom again, her heart began questioning her head.

Would she ever find a man she loved as much as Tom?

She had dated a few men over the past three years but not one of them had ever matched up. She always compared her dates to Tom. She hated that she did it. And she hated that they never came close.

She cursed silently as she studied him. He wasn't going to ruin her life. She could be happy one day and have the big messy family that she'd always wanted.

She deserved a man in her life who was willing to give her that family.

'Listen, Tom, I think that it's best I head to the hotel and put my feet up for a while.'

There was a knock on the door, forcing Sara to step back. A tall, well-dressed woman entered, a clipboard in hand. She was very attractive and Sara guessed her to be in her late twenties. Her hair was short and dark in a Cleopatra cut, which suited her almond shaped eyes and Mediterranean features.

'Tom, I'm sorry to interrupt but I thought you should know that tomorrow afternoon's list has an alteration. The mandibular advancement, Troy Reeves, has cancelled. Influenza. I've rescheduled him for the twentieth of the month. With any luck you'll finish surgery by six tomorrow night.'

'Christina, this is Sara,' Tom said, as he reached for the amended list. 'Sara, this is Christina, my secretary.'

Both women smiled courteously.

'Christina, if you've done your bit, go on home,' Tom told her. 'I really appreciate you coming in on a weekend. I'll make it up to you.'

'Don't be silly, Tom. I'm happy to help out under the circumstances and I'll see you around seven.' With that she headed back to the open door. 'Nice to meet you, Sara.'

Sara smiled and with equal grace said goodbye before the door closed.

'Don't know what I'd do without her,' Tom remarked casually. 'She's a remarkable woman.'

Sara felt an unexpected ache in her heart when she heard him talk that way about another woman. And they had plans at seven. They had a date. It was ridiculous to be feeling anything other than elation. But she didn't. She felt jealous. It was insane. Why should she care what he thought of or, for that matter, did with other women? Tom could date other women. And now he'd signed the divorce papers he could marry another woman. *As long as she didn't want children.* It wasn't her concern what he did.

You wanted a divorce and now you have it within your reach. And don't forget it, she reminded herself as she tried to pull her thoughts back to the situation at hand.

Before Sara had a chance to open her mouth, the door burst open again. She spun around and found herself being hauled into the arms of a tall, rather robust man with a bushy beard. She felt dwarfed by his stature. He hugged her ferociously and then stepped back.

Sara had to steady herself. It took a moment for her to register just who was on the giving end of the exuberant embrace.

'Sara,' he said. 'You're looking great. How long has it been?'

'Stuart!' she managed to return, realising it was her old friend hiding beneath the thick facial hair. His trademark mop of russet curls hadn't changed at all, now she took stock of him, neither had his twinkling brown eyes in rimless glasses. 'Gosh, it must be three years or more. Last time I saw you would've been…at…um…your…' She stumbled over her words.

A cough echoed from across the room. 'I think Sara's trying to say it was at your anniversary party just before we went our different ways,' Tom interjected. 'And by the way, Stu, it would've been nice of you to let me in on the fact Sara was filling in for you. I had no idea.'

Stuart just shrugged his shoulders. 'Should've read the memo I left on your desk in the office.'

'Maybe you should have just told me.'

'I'm not your secretary, Dr Fielding. We're partners!'

Sara smiled at the banter. They were like bickering children.

'It's lovely to see you again, Stu,' she cut in, to change the subject before it escalated further.

'Just wonderful to see you, gorgeous. You haven't changed a bit. Stunning as always,' he said, stepping back. 'I'm sorry I was delayed in ICU. I wanted to be here when you arrived and talk through everything but since Tom is here I'm sure he can run you through my caseload and his as well. He's going to take over my day at the hospital and you will cover his day there. It's easier than trying to have you cover at the hospital for me. Way too much paperwork in this place,' he said, rolling his eyes.

'Okay, I'm happy to fit in where I can,' Sara said after hearing the update. She'd had no idea she would be covering for anyone else, let alone Tom, but it did make sense.

'I'm glad I got to thank you in person before I leave. You're a trouper. Dana and I can't tell you how much it means to us.'

'It's my pleasure. Are you looking forward to your time off?'

'It's not exactly time off for the sake of it. I'm taking time out to be with Bonny. She was hurt in an accident up on the farm. The tractor lost its grip on an embankment. It rolled into a ditch where Bonny was playing.'

'Oh, my...' Sara's hand instinctively covered her mouth. 'When did that happen?'

'A few weeks back. She's okay. She's out of hospital now. I mean, all things considered, she's doing really well. It was a dirty great tractor and she's so tiny and it could have been much worse. Thankfully there were huge great boulders that took the full weight of the tractor. It fell sideways and Bonny got injured when the metal toolbox lost its moorings and landed on her. She was knocked unconscious and her leg was pinned underneath the exhaust pipe.' The pain in his eyes couldn't mask the distress he was feeling at retelling the story.

Sara was horrified at the thought of Bonny pinned beneath the tractor. She felt her own spine rush with cold and then tears begin to build. She blinked them away.

'I didn't want to guilt you into coming so I didn't mention Bonny when you offered to fill in. It would've been unfair to put that sort of pressure on you.'

'It wouldn't have been pressure. You know I would do anything for you and Dana. I'm just so incredibly sorry to hear about all of this,' Sara told him truthfully. 'I'm glad I'm here, and I hope you can just focus on Bonny and get her better even sooner.'

'She's up and walking but still in a frame,' Stuart told her. 'But she's determined to get back on those little feet of hers. I know she can do it and I think she's going to get better that much sooner with me home full time to help her through the physio. I'm usually home three days a week then here in Melbourne, consulting, the other four.'

Sara watched as Stuart looked pensively down toward his hands and nervously twisted his wedding band back and forth. She felt helpless to ease the almost tangible pain he was suffering.

'She hasn't regained her speech yet,' he began, in little more than a dying whisper.

Sara reached for his hands and encircled them in her own.

'If she's anything like you, little Bonny will be back on her feet and telling you off before you know it.'

He coughed to clear his throat and slowly pulled his hands free of hers and stepped away from her. Sara suspected it was some sort of male strategy he was using to keep his emotions in check.

'I know she will. It's Dana that needs convincing. The specialists have told us with family around her full time she'll be racing ahead. I originally organised a nurse to help out with the twins so Dana could spend time with Bonny, but now, thanks to you taking over for the next month, we can keep it just the family and I know it will make all the difference to her recovery.'

Stuart wrapped one arm around her shoulder and pulled her close again in a bear hug. 'Dana sends her love and hopes you can visit us at the farm soon. We've had it for two years now. Dana really wants you to meet the twins. They're nearly one and, of course, Bonny's almost seven now.'

Sara felt a twinge of guilt for not returning to Melbourne to visit Stuart and Dana. The four of them had shared some wonderful times together, but after the separation Sara had felt the need to stay away from risk of seeing Tom. She'd emailed often and called occasionally. She'd sent them a basket filled with toys and baby gifts when the twins were born. But for the last few months she had been too focused on planning the trip and hadn't spoken to them. Obviously because of the accident and their priority being Bonny, they hadn't reached out to her either.

'It has been far too long since I saw you,' she began. 'I really would love to visit you and Dana on the farm when Bonny is up to it.'

'Of course, Dana would love it,' he responded. 'Sars, some things never change, you know, like you and Tom. Good friends you can always rely on in times of need.'

Sara was having trouble concentrating. Her mind was spinning with images of helpless little Bonny lying in the ditch beneath the tractor. She could only imagine how devastating it had been for the family.

She was deep in terrible, vivid thoughts she didn't want to have filling her head, when Stuart's prickly beard brushed against her neck as he kissed her cheek to thank her yet again.

'I won't forget this, kiddo,' Stuart told her. 'If there's ever anything I can ever do for you, just ask.'

'Don't you think twice about it,' she returned. 'Just get Bonny well—that's enough for me.'

'Well, I expect to see you up on the farm the first break you get.' He smiled and was gone, leaving her alone in the office with Tom.

The atmosphere in the office changed within moments.

With calm composure Sara walked to the door and softly closed it. Her hand quietly released the handle before she turned on her heel and marched over to his desk. 'Why didn't you tell me about Bonny when we caught up the other night?'

'I hadn't seen you for three years, we were keeping it light and I didn't see the point. You said you were leaving to live in Texas. What could you have done? I had no idea that you were coming here to work with me...'

'Neither did I, but surely something as serious as that would rate a mention.' Sara was angry with Tom and not afraid to let him know it.

'Sara, you walked out on me. You walked out on our life together and everything we shared. You never brought up Stu or Dana that night. What right do you have to question me about my actions or what I do and don't tell you? We shared a few hours together. I don't know what's been happening in your life any more than you know what's been happening in mine. We kept it light, Sara, so don't lecture me about what I should and shouldn't have shared with you.' His lips were tight and his mouth formed a hard line.

Sara stepped back. She was acutely aware that Tom was right. She had walked away and she had no right to criticise him. She hadn't asked about Stu and Dana during the evening they'd spent together. That night she had purposely steered the conversation away from anything and anyone that linked her back to their life together.

'You're right. I'm sorry,' she said, regret tainting her voice. 'I guess it wasn't your job to bring me up to speed that night. It's just that we were so close to Stu and Dana and I wish I'd known. I wish they'd called me or I'd called them.'

Sara realised that she had only herself to blame. It wasn't Tom's fault. Her lack of sleep was finally taking its toll and she could feel that her eyes were becoming heavy.

'Tom, I've had a long night and I need to get some sleep, maybe just a short nap.' She reached for a pen and began writing on a small message pad on his desk. 'This is the name of my hotel. I'll call you in a few hours after I take a nap and perhaps we can sort out the working arrangements for the next month over a late lunch.'

Sara woke to the sound of a knock at her door.

She lifted her head from the pillow, surprised to find the room dark. She sat bolt upright and could see the bright lights of the city skyline through her window. A muted glow from the corridor was creeping under the narrow gap below her door.

Fumbling a little, she reached for the lamp beside the bed. Her blurry eyes tried to focus on her watch. *It couldn't be. Seven o'clock, in the evening?* She must have slept for almost ten hours. She looked down to find she was still dressed in her suit and lying on top of the bed covers.

'Who is it?' she called out, as she climbed from the bed.

'Tom,' his husky voice returned. 'I thought we'd go out for a late lunch. It's nearly eight here but it has to be lunchtime somewhere in the world. Maybe in Texas they're tucking into buffalo wings.'

Sara smiled but she felt uncomfortable knowing that he was at the door of her hotel room. She remembered only too well what had happened last time.

She ran the brush through her hair once more, quickly looked in the mirror and cleared the smudges of mascara from under her eyes, then crossed the room. Her hands ran over her crinkled skirt and, as respectable as she could look under the circumstances, she opened the door.

Tom stood before her, dressed in a fine grey polo knit and black trousers. His hair was swept back from his forehead in gentle, still-damp waves. He looked as if he had just climbed from the shower. It only took seconds for his subtle cologne to penetrate her senses.

'Hello, Tom,' she managed, glad that her tone was cool, despite how nervous she felt or how handsome he looked, standing in her doorway. 'Just to let you know it's not eight, it's only seven.'

He grinned ruefully. 'No, it's nearly eight, you're on Victorian time now, you're not in Adelaide anymore. You must be tired,' he said, tilting his head to one side. 'Are you up to grabbing a bite to eat?'

She glanced down at her watch. He was right on both counts. It was eight and she definitely wasn't in Adelaide anymore. She was in Melbourne and she was uncomfortably close to her far too handsome and soon to be ex-husband.

'I suppose I am a little peckish,' she began trying to push away how he was making her feel. She looked down and saw again how crumpled her clothes were after flying and then sleeping in them. 'Can you give me fifteen minutes to freshen up?'

'Not a problem. I'll wait downstairs.' With that he walked off down the corridor to the lift.

She watched him. The way he swayed just slightly as he walked. The way his clothes fit his masculine body. The perfect silhouette of his broad shoulders and slim waist.

'I'll be in the bar,' he called back, turning around too quickly for her to pretend she wasn't watching him.

She slammed the door shut with her foot, angry with herself once again.

* * *

The hot water over her body felt good and she wished she could stay there longer but she knew she had to get downstairs. Quickly, she applied light make-up and then searched through her suitcase for something that didn't need ironing.

She chose a salmon knitted top and cream slacks, casually draping a soft pastel scarf around her neck and slipping on her kitten heel sling-backs before she left her room.

On the trip down in the elevator Sara tried to remind herself that she was doing this for Stu and now for Bonny. There was no backing out.

The lift reached the ground floor and Sara walked across the foyer and up a few steps into the raised bar area. She spied Tom at a table but he wasn't alone. Christina, his secretary, was with him. Of course, she suddenly remembered, they had a date.

Sara unexpectedly felt a tug at her heart. It was ridiculous. Why shouldn't Tom move on? The divorce papers were on their way to the lawyer. But even so, seeing Tom with another woman made her feel unreasonably possessive.

Suddenly, as she approached the couple, a little voice inside her head demanded to be heard. *Sara Fielding, this will make it so much easier. He is taken. He's not available so keep your emotions in check.*

Sara watched the way Christina was looking at Tom. Her heart wasn't thrilled at what she saw, but her mind was elated with the couple's body language. They were at ease and relaxed with each other. So relaxed Sara felt sure they must be lovers. She swallowed hard with that thought.

'Tom, Sara's here,' Christina prompted, in little more than a whisper.

Tom turned and his eyes met Sara's. For a split second she felt as if they were the only two people in the room. It wasn't right, she knew it. Perhaps he didn't realise the effect he had on her. But she did and she had to take responsibility for her own thoughts. Right here and right now. She would never step back into Tom's life.

'Sara,' he said, as he stood and pulled out a chair for her. 'I thought you must have fallen asleep, again.'

'I wasn't that long,' she replied brightly, trying to set a light-hearted mood as she sat down. 'In fact, if I wasn't so hungry I'd probably still be in the shower.'

'Speaking of food,' Christina interrupted, 'I'd better be getting home. I want to prepare something special for tomorrow night's dinner with Robert.' She bent down and kissed Tom on the cheek. 'Thanks for the drink and thanks for listening.'

Tom patted her hand. 'Any time.'

'Sorry I can't stop, Sara,' she said, with a smile. 'Perhaps next time we'll be able to chat.'

'That would be nice,' Sara replied, with a curious frown. She watched as Christina slipped her bag over her shoulder and left.

Sara waited until Christina was out of sight before she asked the questions niggling her to distraction.

'Who's Robert? And have I just interrupted your date?'

'Date? With Christina?' he said, glancing over to see his secretary leaving the hotel. 'No, she just wanted to chat about a problem over a drink and get my take on it—some male advice, you could say. But why do you want to know about Robert?'

'No reason,' she lied. 'Just curious.' She hoped Robert was Christina's brother or friend. It meant there was still room for Tom in Christina's life.

'Well, to answer your question, he's her husband. He's been away on business for a fortnight,' Tom replied, quite happy that Sara cared.

Sara's face fell with disappointment. 'So she has a husband yet she needs you to listen to her problems…?'

Tom shot her a wry look. 'She didn't know how to break the news to her husband that she'd written off his uninsured Audi. But, come on, Sara, what's prompted the twenty questions? This isn't like you.'

'Sorry, maybe I'm a bit stressed. I've got a lot on my mind.'

'Then let's talk over dinner. What would you like? Chinese, Italian, seafood?'

*What would I like? I'd like Christina to be single. I'd like you and Christina to be having an affair. And I'd like her to want to marry you and, more importantly, you to want to marry her, giving me some perspective. I'd like to be able to say, and actually believe, that being around you for the next month will be easy. I'd like to rewind to a month ago and leave you outside my hotel room. I'd like my life to be as simple as it has been in Adelaide for the last three years.*

'Italian,' Sara replied.

# CHAPTER FOUR

THE WOOD OVEN baked pizza was delicious. Sara hadn't realised how hungry she was until she found herself picking up the lonely mushrooms from the empty pizza tray.

'I can order another one,' Tom said drily. 'And then maybe I'll get a look-in.'

Sara wiped the corners of her mouth with the napkin and sat back in the padded booth. She didn't bother answering him. She had seen his hands moving as fast as hers back and forth from the tray.

With a good sleep behind her and now a full stomach, Sara felt ready to sort out the working arrangements so they discussed the rosters, the patient load, the surgical amenities at the hospital and the general planning for the following month.

When they had covered everything, Tom sat back in silence and sipped his drink. His eyes were focused on a spot somewhere in the distance. A place that was taking all his attention.

Slowly he turned his face to hers. 'I know I disappointed you, Sara. As a husband, that is, but I never misled you. I was upfront about the subject of children. I'm sorry that I can't change my mind or give you the all the reasons for my decision. But I've never lied. I just needed to tell you that.'

His sudden statement took her by surprise and added to the emotional see-saw that coming to Melbourne had created.

'I'm sure you had your reasons, just as I have mine. I suppose we should have discussed it all before we married, not after.'

Sara drew breath and with it came a calmer and more resigned disposition. She had to keep emotion out of the equation. She wanted more than Tom would ever be prepared to give. And it had hurt her that he had never been prepared to consider children. She wanted all the joy a family brought, and that money and a career could never replace. The happiness of a child being given a puppy, the first artwork they brought home from school, the cuddle at the end of a day just before they fell asleep. She felt a maternal longing that with each passing year became more difficult to fight.

'I want to hear their laughter, to feel their hugs, to tuck them into bed at night. We're two people with very different priorities. You and your brother have so much in common. You both choose a career over having children. Clearly you have goals you wanted to reach. Becoming associate professor is a huge step and probably not one that would have been easy to achieve with a house full of children. I get it. Really, I do. Your career is your focus and there's no room for anything else.'

'Having a child is not the be-all and end-all…' He faltered, then dropped his gaze without finishing the sentence.

'Not to you, but to me it is,' she said with conviction. 'I couldn't give up on that dream.'

Tom lifted his eyes again to study her face. He had always wondered what drove this need for children. He understood that the maternal instinct might kick in at a certain age. But it seemed more than this.

Finishing his drink, he decided to ask that very question.

'You know, I really do understand that most women like the idea of having babies and planning big Christmas dinners with the family and all of that,' he said. 'But with you it has always seemed like more. Am I reading too much into it, or am I right in thinking there is something else that drove you to walk away when I wouldn't see it your way?'

Sara wondered why it had taken Tom this long to ask that question. But she sensed it was that he hadn't wanted to know before now. When they had been married and the subject of children had come up, he'd changed it very quickly. Knowing the truth behind her motivations, she suspected, may have put additional pressure on him to consider her reasons and, in turn, her feelings.

'I just love children, I always have and always will,' Sara began slowly. 'And the idea of having to give that up would just mean that history was repeating itself. You already know the number of times in the past that I have had to give in to my parents' wishes. Do what they wanted. Become who they wanted me to be. I do love them, but I had to put my life on hold so many times. It wasn't always obvious, and I'm not sure if was even conscious on their behalf, but I would always end up feeling guilty if I forged ahead without their consent.

'Even as a young child, I frequently had to give up on my own dreams to live theirs. Every time I showed free will, and they thought I might make a decision for myself, they had a way of making me think I was being selfish. But I take responsibility for my feelings. I should have stood up to them and told them I was my own person. It was almost like having my spirit killed with kindness. They were so protective but it was so stifling.'

Tom listened intently. He suddenly felt guilty that he hadn't asked this question before. It had clearly formed a huge part of her childhood.

'So was medicine their dream or yours?'

'No, fortunately my career was a mutual vision. I'm not sure what I would have done if they had wanted me to walk away from that. Perhaps it might have persuaded me to take a stand much earlier.'

'This stand?' Tom cut in, interrupting the story.

'Yes, not to back down and feel guilty about wanting something for myself. I had always done what they expected, I think being an only child made me feel as if I owed them a great debt for bringing me into this world and I had to repay them. To be who they wanted me to be. At least, it always felt that way.'

'I'm sorry to hear that. I had no idea.' Tom looked at his hands absentmindedly and wondered what else he didn't know about his wife.

'In high school I was offered the opportunity to go to Germany for a six-month cultural exchange but my father told me that my mother was about to have more tests and he needed me at home to help take care of her in case the news wasn't good.'

Tom looked surprised to hear this. 'But your mother is fine. Well, she was when we visited her a few years ago. Is she okay now?'

'She's perfectly healthy now but she suffered from benign fibroids and the doctor decided on a myomectomy to remove them. They knew it wasn't a permanent solution in the sense that fibroids can grow back after the procedure. I felt an enormous pressure on me to cancel my trip. I knew they needed me, I couldn't abandon them…could I? The doctor did reassure them both that the condition and surgery wasn't life-threatening but there was more going on than that.

'I remember I wanted to head off with two girlfriends and backpack around Australia and maybe travel over to Italy and Greece after my final year at school. Well, let's just say my friends had a wonderful time but all I saw of the outback and the Mediterranean was on their postcards. My mother's hysterectomy had been scheduled during that time. Apparently my mother was one of the ten per cent that needed a second surgery. The trip had meant so much to me but I felt as if I had to give it up to keep them happy. Honestly, looking back, I don't regret what I gave up, it meant starting my medical study early, but I do wish I had drawn a line in the sand a little earlier.'

'But you all seemed to get on so well whenever I was there.'

'By the time you met them, I'd achieved everything they wanted for me, and during my training I gained back some level of independence. I had proved that I could cope without them and, of course, that they could cope without me. Plus, they loved you, so they were happy with my choice. If they hadn't liked you then I probably would have felt pressured to break up with you.'

'And would you?' he asked, looking intensely into her eyes.

Sara swallowed. 'They loved you, so that question is irrelevant.'

Tom wasn't satisfied. 'That's not an answer to my question, Sara.'

Sara could feel her heart racing. She answered him honestly. 'No, I wouldn't have. I would have told them that being with you was something I wanted more than anything in the world, that it was my dream to spend the rest of my life with you and they would have to live with it.'

Tom felt unashamedly happy with her answer but also immensely guilty. She would have fought for him. He shifted uncomfortably in his seat as he realised what he had done to her. It was her dream to be a mother and she had been fighting him for that right. He had added to the conflicts of her childhood and tried to prevent her right to choose her own path.

'So I was asking the same of you, to give up your dream of children.'

Sara nodded, her heart heavy as she thought back to the sadness of their situation.

'I suppose you thought I would soften to the idea,' he told her. 'Just as I hoped you would move on and be happy with only the two of us.'

'I guess we rushed into our marriage and we paid for the mistake later,' Sara replied.

He sipped his drink and looked thoughtfully at Sara. 'Perhaps we're both still paying.'

The early morning wake-up call had Sara up and about by six. But it wasn't a chore considering how many hours sleep she'd enjoyed. Probably more in the last twenty-four-hour period than in any other since she had chosen a career in oral surgery. And she had needed every minute of it.

Tom had dropped her back at the hotel just before ten-thirty. They had gone by the practice and he had picked up the notes for the next day's patients. Then, downstairs in a booth near the bar, he had gone over his major surgical list and explained the treatment plans. His work was as accurate and thorough as ever. Sara appreciated the long hours he must have spent to cover the caseload at his practice for both himself and Stu, to oversee the hospital in his new role as associate professor and still have such clear and precise details recorded. She was going to be able to take over without any disruption to the patients at all.

Thankfully there were only consultations and minor surgical cases scheduled for the next two days, so she had time to familiarise herself with everything.

After Tom had left, Sara had reviewed the next day's patients, made her notes and finally given in to sleep at about twelve.

Living in the hotel was not a viable situation. Later in the day she would have to make some calls and arrange a comfortable place that was a little more affordable. She would also have to arrange for someone to pack up the last of her belongings in Adelaide and have them sent on to Texas.

As she pulled underwear from her suitcase and shuffled into the bathroom, her thoughts then wandered to Bonny. She prayed the child's recovery would be easier now her father was with her. She'd often thought that she and Tom would one day have a daughter just like

Bonny, and a son…or maybe two of each. Tom was right, she had tried to convince herself that in time he would change his mind about children and realise that they did have the capacity, in terms of time and love, required to raise a family. That their careers were important but the joy they would experience bringing up a child of their own was incomparable.

But you were wrong, Sara admonished herself. He never wanted a child. He reiterated that tonight. So forget the past.

She turned the shower taps on full and enjoyed the very long shower she had wanted the night before as she tried to put outdated dreams from her mind. And know that she was doing what was right for her.


'George Andrews was due at nine. Impressions for his wafer splint. His surgery is in just under two weeks,' Marjorie, the receptionist, informed Sara. 'But his mother just called. They've had car trouble and she's called a taxi. They should be about another fifteen minutes.'

'Thanks,' Sara replied with a smile.

Marjorie was in her early sixties. Her hair was a deep auburn and cut short at the back with flattering soft curls around her forehead. She had a pretty face, with gold rimmed glasses perched on her bob nose. She was about the same height as Sara, just a little bigger in build.

The pair had introduced themselves and as far as Sara could make out, she and Marjorie would get along just fine. The woman did not appear to be the prying type and, with everything on Sara's mind, that was a huge relief.

Sara asked Marjorie not to call her Dr Fielding. Her first name was fine and made her feel more relaxed. But the reason was two-fold. She thought it might also avoid a barrage of questions from patients about her relationship to the other Dr Fielding.

Looking around the rooms, Sara couldn't help but notice that everything had been completely revamped since she had left three years ago.

She absentmindedly ran her finger over the frame of a painting that hung nearby. A beautiful watercolour of a blue kingfisher. It was new. Everything was new. There was no sign that she had ever been there. It was as if anything she had brought into the practice had disappeared and something else now stood in its place. She wondered if their marital home had been gutted in a similar manner. Had Tom sold her favourite pieces to the highest bidder? She blinked away her unanswered questions and turned her attention back to her surroundings. It was not her business. She had left and Tom did what he wanted. She knew she had no right to judge his actions.

The decor was modern, painted in pastel tones and decorated with light-coloured wooden furniture that had a Scandinavian feel. The spacious waiting room had a large, low pine table covered in magazines, a mix of wooden and chrome chairs lined two walls and there was a wicker basket brimming with toys in the corner of the room. Something to keep little hands amused. Stu's idea, no doubt, Sara surmised. Definitely not Tom's.

Overlooking the waiting room, Marjorie's office was filled with enough computer equipment to run a small NASA project. Sara gently opened the adjoining door to find the fully equipped surgery for minor surgical procedures not needing a general anaesthetic.

She knew that the kitchen and bathroom were located at the back of the rooms. The practice was on the first floor of a quaint old two-storey building that had been totally modernised inside, whilst retaining its exterior character. It was in South Yarra, overlooking the Yarra River. Sara had always loved the calming effect of the scenery.

Melancholy drew her back to the view and she crossed in earnest to the large picture window. Sara sighed as she took in the vista. The day was cold but the sun was shining down and it was a nice change after the gale the day before. The gentle breeze played with the last of the red-gold leaves of autumn. Weeping branches of the willows dipped in the rippling water near the riverbank. The brown-speckled ducks swam around the row of paddleboats, which were tied together and bobbing with the current at the riverbank.

She closed her eyes for a moment and recalled how a few years ago she and Tom had often stood at the same window. Sometimes they had been so immersed in each other's presence they would barely notice the view. They would hold each other tightly and discuss their days. They understood and respected each other's needs. Two tired bodies moulding as one…

'Penny for your thoughts.'

Sara jumped. She hadn't realised how far her thoughts had travelled until the deep voice broke through.

Tom's voice.

'Um, nothing, nothing at all,' she returned, nervously straightening the lapels of her short navy trench coat and brushing imaginary lint from her matching skirt.

'So, what brings you here? Don't you have a hospital to take care of?'

'Board meeting. I hate those damned things. It's always the same old bickering about increased funding cuts, meaning fewer beds and fewer staff. So I sent Johnson to take notes. That should be eye-opening for everyone, Johnson *and* the board members.' He smiled.

Sara smiled back at him in silence then he noticed the softness suddenly turn to something more professional and reserved as she adjusted her jacket and moved away to the other side of the room.

Tom looked at her, wishing things had been different. Wishing he was able to give her what she wanted and what she deserved in life. She wasn't asking for the world and to any other man it would seem fair and natural to want children. But Tom couldn't provide that. Fatherhood would never be a part of his life. He could accept it but it wouldn't be fair to keep Sara in his self-imposed childless life so he had to keep his distance.

Stirring up old feelings again would only delay the inevitable. Even if they rekindled their love, she would leave and turn his life upside down all over again for the very same reason.

Marjorie walked in from the kitchen. 'I've put the kettle on. Will you both have a cup of tea or coffee?'

'Yes, that would be lovely,' Sara answered hurriedly.

'Not for me,' Tom replied. 'I was just leaving. I'm needed back at the hospital—it was just a quick visit.' His sentence was cut short when the door opened. Tom took this cue and left. It had been a short visit, with no purpose other than to spend a few minutes with Sara. He knew he couldn't change their fate. The divorce would seal that but he had a month to enjoy her company, as a doctor he admired and a woman he desired. He was torturing himself just being near her, but he was unable to stop.

Sara watched him leave then turned her attention to a boy in his late teens and the older woman who had entered the office.

'George, Mrs Andrews,' Marjorie greeted them cheerily. 'Please, take a seat. Dr Fielding, I mean Sara, will be right with you.'

'Where's Dr Anderson?' George asked anxiously. The metal braces on his teeth caught the light. 'Isn't he seeing me today?'

Sara stepped forward. 'No, George. Dr Anderson won't be seeing you today,' she began. 'He had to spend some time with his family. His little girl isn't very well and he asked me to step in and look after you and all of his patients. I'll be carrying out your operation.'

George had looked a little anxious when he walked in but now his worries seemed to escalate to distress. Surgery for anyone was a stressful time but Sara was aware that for an adolescent it was doubly so.

'Don't worry, George,' Sara told him. 'I won't do anything without first explaining it to you and if you have any questions, please, ask me. In a moment we'll go and take some moulds of your teeth, which will be sent off to a lab. The technician will use these moulds to make a special splint, called a wafer, and I will use this to position your jaws during surgery. I'm sure you've had impressions before.'

The boy nodded but his expression was guarded.

'I know they're a bit mucky but they don't hurt. Your orthodontist has put special pins in your braces in preparation for this. We call them high hats, and they make it easier for me to do my job.'

'Yeah, and they stick out a bit,' George complained, and pulled his lips down over the braces.

'How long will it take today?' Mrs Andrews cut in.

'Not very long at all,' Sara replied, turning her attention to the woman. 'You're most welcome to come in.'

'I'm not a child, Mum,' George growled. 'Just wait out here.'

Mrs Andrews raised her eyebrows and sat down. She clearly knew it was pointless to argue with a teenager. Sara smiled to herself. She doubted that George's bravado would hold up just prior to surgery. Then without doubt he would want his mother close by.

'Well, let's go and get started,' Sara said, and led George off towards the consulting room. Marjorie followed closely behind, leaving Mrs Andrews sifting through the magazines. The appointment didn't take much longer than twenty minutes. George didn't ask too many questions but with a mouthful of impression material that would have been difficult. After the impressions were checked by Sara, then packed and taken to Reception to be collected by the laboratory courier, Sara asked Mrs Andrews to come in.

Sara clipped the X-rays onto the wall viewer and studied them for a moment. 'Are there any questions?'

'Are there lots of guys with this problem?' George asked, rubbing his very pronounced lower jaw.

'Guys and girls,' Sara reassured him. 'You have what we call a skeletal class-three malocclusion. This means that your lower jaw is forward in relation to your upper jaw. I'm sure Dr Anderson has gone over this with you but it happened because your mandible, or lower jaw, has grown more than your upper. It's a case of one didn't grow enough and the other grew too much.'

'So you're going to pull my jaw back?'

'Not exactly.' Sara looked at the X-ray viewer, where a profile of George's skull was illuminated. 'You have a skeletal discrepancy. So Dr Anderson had planned on surgery to advance the upper jaw.' Sara pointed to the relevant facial features on the X-ray as she spoke. She moved the tiny mouth ruler she used as a pointer down to the lower jaw area as she continued. 'And set back the lower jaw. Just think of your lower jaw coming back and your upper jaw moving forward about the same amount until they sort of meet halfway and then surgery on your chin to make it a little less angular or severe.'

'I think I kind of get it,' George said. 'But I told Dr Anderson that I didn't like my nose much and he said he could fix that too.'

Sara thought it best to keep clear of decisions that were purely cosmetic. 'George, I think it's best if you and the family make that decision at home. Just call Marjorie next week if you want me to proceed with a rhinoplasty at the same time—that's the name we give to the nose operation.'

'But what do you think?' George asked, giving unexpected value to Sara's opinion on the matter.

Sara was flattered that he had asked her but she had to remain impartial. 'To be honest, George, it is a cosmetic improvement and therefore has to be a family decision. No surgeon can tell you what you should or shouldn't look like when it comes to nose shape or chin shape.'

'But if he was your son, what would you advise us to do?' George's mother asked.

Sara was taken aback by the question. *If he was my son?* She stared down at her hands clasped tightly in her lap. If I ever have a son, she thought, I would want only the best for him. I would want him to grow into a strong, perceptive individual just like Tom. Her stomach tightened a little at her reaction. Day one and Tom Fielding had safely tucked himself into her subconscious. Just where she didn't need him.

She swallowed as she looked at Mrs Andrews and George, then thoughtfully she answered, 'I wouldn't rush into any surgery on a whim. I would think it through, discuss it at home and be very sure it was something George felt very strongly about undertaking.'

She blinked away her other thoughts. It was going to be long month in Melbourne.

Sara switched off the X-ray viewer, slipped the X-rays inside the case notes and then escorted the young man and his mother back into the waiting room.

'Sara, your nine-thirty appointment, Mollie Hatcher, is here,' Marjorie said as the three approached the front desk.

Sara remembered reading Mollie's referral notes and when the child smiled nervously, Sara could see the large fleshy membrane that ran between her front teeth, giving her a gap large enough to hold a gold coin. The referring doctor had recommended a frenectomy to remove it, and even before the consultation, Sara had judged that to be the right treatment plan.

Looking over the medical history, Sara ushered in the little girl and her mother.

It was another half hour consultation, which ended

with Mrs Hatcher booking a time for Mollie's minor surgery in the rooms the following week.

The day continued, with Sara seeing a steady load of Stu's patients. Most of them were new patient referrals and there were three post-operative check-ups. Tom had stepped in to cover Stu's consulting role at the hospital and Sara would be picking up Tom's private patients. It was a sensible arrangement for the weeks ahead.

She knew the next day it would be Tom's patients and a minor surgical list in the afternoon. Both men were professional and skilled surgeons and Sara hadn't disagreed with any treatment plan either had suggested for their patients. She knew the next day would be no exception. When it came to work, that was the one area that she and Tom would never come to loggerheads. He had taught her well and she would never doubt his decision. His knowledge as a consultant and his dexterity as a surgeon were second to none.

Sara was quietly honoured he had approved her stepping into the practice that he had built over many years and had then invited Stu to join. And she was pleased to be doing it without any intervention from him. He did trust her. From someone with a reputation of being one of the finest surgeons in the country, that was a huge accolade for her.

It was about six o'clock when Sara realised she had done nothing about accommodation. She would have to spend another night at the hotel and then tomorrow she had to organise something else.

Marjorie said goodnight, locked up and left for the day. Sara was tidying up the last of the case notes when she heard a key in the front door. It didn't take her long to realise who it was.

'I'm in the office, Tom. Just a few bits and pieces to tidy up.'

She heard his footsteps draw nearer and looked up to find him framed in the doorway. His face was a little drawn but still unbelievably handsome. His jaw was darkened by the first signs of fine stubble.

'I'm here to take you home.'

'That's very sweet of you,' Sara remarked. 'But I've already booked a taxi to my hotel.'

Tom crossed the room in silence. His dark eyes didn't stray from her face for a moment. 'I wasn't talking about the hotel, Sara. I'm taking you to our home.'

# CHAPTER FIVE

Sara was stunned into silence.

She swallowed a lump of emotions that had converged in her throat. *Our home.* There was no 'our' anything any more. She chewed nervously on the inside of her cheek. What on earth was Tom thinking? She felt herself falling into the deep, grey eyes that were focused solely upon her. She wanted to pull away, she had to, but she couldn't pull away far enough. Her gaze dropped only to his wide, soft mouth.

A mouth that her heart could suddenly remember giving her the most tender of kisses. Sara felt so confused. Confused about her own feelings. Even more confused about Tom's. She thought they had set the parameters. She was not about to move back in with him on either a short-term or long-term basis.

Did he think by her staying in Melbourne that she would throw away her new life and come back to him? He must know after their talk the night before that she wouldn't back down. She wanted children, and it was not negotiable. Then was he looking for another few nights of passion for old times' sake? She couldn't, and she wouldn't allow him to change her plans. Her mind had to take over. Calculated logic had to kick in. She had to control her body's desire for him. If she didn't, Sara was terrified of where it all might lead. Heartbreak, no doubt, for both of them.

'There is no *our* any more, Tom.'

'You can call it my house if it makes you feel any better.'

'It does,' she returned. 'Because it's the truth. I don't belong in Melbourne. I don't have any ties here any more.' Sara closed the file of paperwork she was completing.

'I'm just trying to help,' he argued. 'Unless, of course, you'd rather pay for accommodation at the hotel for the next month.'

'So moving in with you is the best solution? I hardly think so.'

'Not with me exactly. The other half of the maisonette, the part that belonged to Mrs Vandercroft, is now mine. She moved into a nursing home only a month after you...' Tom hesitated, not wanting to make her feel that he was blaming her for their separation.

'Well, just after we parted, so I bought it. You remember how she had one or two falls, well, they increased and finally she really injured herself on a coffee table she just didn't see. Her eyesight was failing, and she was unsteady on her feet. Her family didn't want her living alone any more and, as you know, they all lived interstate. Anyway, she had just turned ninety-eight and didn't want to haul herself up to Sydney so she moved into a nursing home not too far away. I just use the place for storage, so you can have it for the month. I was going to offer it to the locum anyway. I had no idea it would be you.'

Sara considered him suspiciously then felt a little

silly for overreacting. Perhaps it was an offer with no strings. After all, he had signed the divorce papers. And he had an empty place.

She shook herself mentally. He definitely appeared to have his emotions in check.

'Well, does this silence mean you're considering my offer?' he asked, jolting her out of her thoughts.

Sara closed her eyes for a split second. She had no logical argument for refusing his offer. Only her irrational thoughts. Against her better judgement she made a decision and prayed for everyone's sake that she was doing the right thing.

'I suppose it's a sensible idea.'

But even as the words passed over her lips, weighty doubts rang alarm bells loudly in her mind. But that was her problem, not his.

Tom smiled. He knew their time together would be short-lived but apart from the great love life they had shared, he enjoyed spending time with Sara. He always had. She challenged him. She was his equal on so many levels. He just wanted a few more weeks with her and then he knew he would let her go. Let her start her new life and not make her think twice about her decision. He hoped this time when she left it might be easier. He hoped his heart wouldn't shatter this time.

As they pulled into the driveway Sara felt a tightening in her chest. They had collected her things from the hotel and made their way to his home about twenty minutes from the city. It was a corner property in a suburb filled with double-fronted cottages and bungalows.

Lit by the headlights of the car, the house looked the same as it did the day she had left. It had been one of the hardest days of her life. She had walked away from her home and her marriage, even though she had still been very much in love with her husband.

The cream stucco walls and shiny gunmetal-grey roof with green gutters hadn't changed. She and Tom had planned to have the front facade steamed-cleaned to reveal the bluestone lying beneath the thick paint but their schedules had never given them the time. It had been something they'd always put off, thinking they had plenty of time in the future.

The roses were in bloom, the way they had been that day in June three years ago. Huge open cabbage roses in deep reds and pastel pinks lined the gravel path to the front door.

Tears welled in the back of her eyes and threatened to spill over.

'Let me get that,' Tom said, as Sara reached into the boot of his late-model Lexus. Their hands touched as they tried to retrieve her luggage. His soft skin brushed against hers. Sara released her hold on the bag immediately and turned away. His touch was unsettling.

'I've got a key for you somewhere in my pocket,' he told her, as he closed the boot and followed behind her, his footsteps crunching on the gravel all the way up to the front door.

Sara's mind was anywhere but in the present and she struggled to keep on track.

'Here it is.' He handed her a key chained to a small crystal slipper. It was the one she had bought when they'd first moved into the house. She couldn't believe he had kept it all this time.

'You know, I always thought this was a little kitsch considering your good taste.'

She held the keyring in her open palm and stared at it in silence.

She remembered back to the day she had bought it. It had been the day before they'd left Prague, where they had spent three days of their four-week honeymoon. Strolling along a cobbled street, they had stumbled upon a little shop that was filled with the most beautiful crystal. Sara had spied the slipper and had known she had to have it. Tom had wanted to buy a beautifully cut crystal vase but she bought the slipper, never telling him the reason.

It was because their romance had been like a fairytale. Having the crystal keyring ensured she was never going to lose her keys, or her Prince Charming. But she knew better than to tell Tom. The logical man that he was, he never would have understood. His diagnosis would have been to tell her she was completely crazy.

Of course, he could have no idea what she was going through now. The memories, the guilt of leaving, it all came flooding back and she wanted so desperately to fall into his arms and pretend that the three years they spent apart were all a bad dream. But she couldn't. Standing there together, she knew she still did have strong feelings for him but that they weren't enough to build a life upon. She wanted more and she knew she had every right to ask for more.

'It's getting mighty cold, standing here while you admire the keyring, Sara.'

Sara looked up and him and wished she could brush aside her feelings and offer a witty retort, but she couldn't. She had agreed in the car on the way home that they would eat their takeaway dinner together, but suddenly she felt too fragile to honour her promise.

The house, the keyring, they had brought too many memories to the surface and she needed time alone to sort through these feelings and put them away. Time without Tom.

'I'm sorry,' she began, rubbing her temples in a circular motion, 'but I have this splitting headache. Would you mind terribly if we didn't have dinner together? I wouldn't be very good company.'

Tom considered her for a moment in the soft light from the streetlamp. She felt that his silence hinted at disbelief but he didn't confirm it with his words.

'Of course not,' he finally uttered, and handed her the box with her dinner inside.

Sara graciously took the warm package and unlocked the front door then felt along the wall for the light switch.

'I'll call over if I need anything,' she called back, before wheeling her luggage inside and closing the door on the cold night air. And on Tom. She just wished her heart could do the same.

The maisonette was the reverse floor plan of the one that she and Tom had shared next door. Dropping her case to the floor, Sara's steps echoed down the polished hallway as she made her way into the sitting room.

The maisonette was furnished nicely but it was the antithesis of the home they had shared. It lacked the character of the home they had decorated together. With modern furniture not unlike that in the waiting room at the practice, she would be comfortable and it would be more than adequate for the month.

Tom closed the door to his maisonette, wondering what Sara was doing. Was she eating, unpacking or had she

collapsed from the first day on the job? She was actually staying in his side of the maisonette. He had been
living there for the last three years as he couldn't live
amongst the memories of the furniture that surrounded
him tonight.

This was actually the house he had intended to offer
the locum but he couldn't let Sara stay there. It was still
furnished with all their belongings. For the next four
weeks he would be staying in the home he used for storage. He couldn't let her know that he had kept everything. He didn't want her to know that he hadn't been
able to give it away but he also couldn't live amongst
it. Not yet. She had moved on…he hadn't.

He loved everything they had bought together but
that was the problem—they had bought it together.
When they had been happy and in love and planning
their future. Tom had called his cleaning lady to move
his clothes and toiletries and books from one side to
the other when he'd found out Sara was working for
the month.

He went to the kitchen to find a fork and then ate his
dinner on his lap. He could hear Sara moving about and
unpacking through the thin walls.

Even though it would only be for a few short weeks
it felt like she was home. But he knew neither of them
had the power to do the slightest thing about changing
the paths that would eventually lead them away from
one another for ever.

Half an hour later Sara threw the remains of her dinner in the bin. She was hungry and she had picked at
the pasta but her churning stomach hadn't allowed her
to finish it.

She worried about how she would deal with the proximity of Tom. She still loved him. She wondered if he knew it too.

'Damn you,' she cursed under her breath.

Why couldn't he talk about their differences? Tell her the reason he didn't want children in his life? Was he really that selfish or was there something that made him hate the thought of children? She had tried so hard to understand when they had been married but he'd shut the conversation down every time she'd brought it up.

She knew his brother, Heath an ENT specialist, hadn't had any children either. Sara hadn't spent much time with him as he had lived in Los Angeles with his wife until they'd divorced. It hadn't appeared to be an unhappy marriage but, like Sara, his wife had wanted children. Sara wasn't sure if that had been the precursor to her leaving or not. Shortly after the split, Heath had moved to San Francisco to practise. Although she'd seen him with Tom both times he had visited Melbourne, the subject of children had never been discussed. It was like both brothers had decided not to have children and that was final. It was a taboo subject. The elephant in the room.

Was there something in their past that stopped them from wanting a family? Sara doubted that. Whenever Tom had spoken of his parents, both of whom had passed away before Tom and Sara had begun dating, the memories he'd relayed of his childhood had been happy. He and his brother had shared a love of BMX bikes as teenagers and had then dropped that sport to both study medicine. It appeared a happy upbringing.

Sara had wanted more than a blanket refusal to discuss the idea of children. She wanted to know the truth but instead came up against his stubborn refusal to talk. She was forced to accept that his stubbornness went hand in hand with selfishness. She still wondered if there was more to it.

Despite how difficult it was to fight her feelings, Sara knew nothing could happen between them. Tom's timing was all wrong. She was leaving to start a new life.

*Don't ruin it, Sara, don't put your life back on hold*, she told herself as she finished unpacking. She knew it would lead to resentment, that she would be sacrificing what she wanted and needed to keep him happy.

*It won't work with Tom and you know it*, she told herself. Then why did she have to feel so at home? A feeling she hadn't experienced since she had left the same house three years ago. A sense of belonging.

She put a little hot water in the sink and washed her cutlery and glass. As she dried and put them away in the drawer she decided to take a nice long soak in a bath.

There was no point in analysing her curious feelings towards Tom, she decided as she slipped into the steamy bubbles and tried to soak away her troubles. It was just reverie and lost love playing games with her emotions. It was over and they both knew it. It was an *itch*, that was all. Some time later, after almost drifting off to sleep, she stepped from the deep tub, towel-dried her warm body and slipped into her pyjamas and dressing gown.

It wouldn't take long to regain control of her feelings, she resolved. She lay back on the sofa and pulled a patterned rug over herself. It was so cold. She looked over at the heater. It was the same old gas style they had next door. And she knew she could never light it. She didn't want to call Tom and ask for his assistance but she also didn't want to wake up with chilblains in her toes.

'It's just me.'

'Hi, me.'

Sara wished for a moment that she hadn't called. Running her fingers through her short, damp hair, she worried about depending upon him for anything. She pulled the rug and her knees up under her chin, perhaps it wasn't *that* cold. She'd felt unexpectedly awkward talking to him on the phone, knowing he was next door. It was odd. She felt so at home, knowing Tom was only the other side of the wall.

Finally, she mustered her thoughts and asked him to come over and help her light the heater. It sounded like a call to a repairman. Businesslike and distant.

Her fingers and toes were quickly becoming icicles, but two minutes later she heard Tom's speedy knock.

'Hello, Sara,' he muttered, as she opened the door. He smiled wryly. 'How's the headache?'

Sara frowned at the question. The way he looked made her fumble over her words and forget momentarily that she had used the headache as an excuse to get away from him. He was standing on her porch in a dark blue dressing gown. It wrapped over low down and exposed his bare, toned chest. His hair was dishevelled and his face was shadowed with fine stubble. His legs were naked and his feet were inside leather slippers.

'Hello…Tom,' she replied, dragging her eyes back to his. She was so angry with herself. It wasn't as if she hadn't been around good-looking men over the years. In fact, she'd dated one or two handsome men. But her reaction was more than that. She suspected that it was being aware, very aware of what lay beneath Tom's loosened robe that made her feel this way.

He began shivering, pulled his robe tighter and started to rub his arms vigorously. 'Could I come inside and light the gas heater before they have to cart me away suffering from frostbite to the extremities?'

Sara nodded. 'Oh, God, I'm sorry,' she said, and stepped away from the door, allowing Tom to move past her.

'So you're feeling okay, then?'

She closed the door on the frozen night air. 'I'm fine, truly…actually, I haven't felt better. The headache's gone. I just needed to soak in a tub for…' She paused and glanced nervously down at her watch. 'Gosh, absolutely ages. But I'm glad I did. I'll need a clear head tomorrow, I've got a full day with minor surgery. Two sets of wisdom teeth to be removed, an exposure of a canine and a few others that I can't recall off the top of my head.' She felt her heart racing and couldn't believe how she had prattled on like a nervous teenager. Why did he do this to her? It wasn't fair. She just wanted him to light the fire and leave.

Tom's mouth curved to a smile. 'They're all my patients. So make sure you do a good job, won't you?'

Sara was grateful that he had chosen to ignore her ramblings and she took his sarcastic cue. 'I'll try really hard not to lose any of them for you,' she returned drily.

He walked over to the heater, catching some creaking floorboards on the way. Standing with his back to her, he reached for the box of matches on the mantelpiece. He squatted on the ground and lit the heater. It was old but Sara remembered how quickly it heated the room. She blinked and looked away before she had time to admire his broad-shouldered physique for too long.

'Thank you, Tom,' she said, as she walked over to warm her hands by the heater. 'I'm sorry that you had to come over to do that. I never did get the hang of lighting the old heater.'

'Just what a good landlord does.'

'Of course, I forgot to ask how much you would like in rent for the place while I'm here.'

Tom looked at Sara in silence. She was trying to turn every part of their lives into a business arrangement. He knew why. And he understood she would be leaving when Stu returned. He wouldn't fight it. But he was glad to have her living close. It was almost like old times. She was all rugged up in flannelette pyjamas and fluffy slippers, her face scrubbed bare of make-up, and she was still the most desirable woman in the world.

'What figure are you looking at?' she asked. 'Three hundred, three fifty?'

Money was the furthest thing from his mind. She was a part of the house and his heart and if she had nowhere else she needed to be, she could stay for ever.

'I'm happy to pay four hundred, if that's closer to the mark…'

'Sara, I don't want anything for the place. You are doing me a favour, filling in for Stu…'

'And you are reimbursing me well,' she cut in.

'I know but that's immaterial. You can have the place…for a coffee. I need to stay awake to go over some reports so I could do with a short—'

'Short black, no sugar,' she finished his order. She smiled. It was so easy. It was like the three years had never passed. Here they were together in the house, in their pyjamas. She hated the fact that she wanted so badly to reach out and feel his arms around her. To cuddle up in front of the fire with the sound of the rain on the metal roof. To hold each other till they fell asleep, just like they'd used to.

She snapped out of it and headed for the kitchen and turned on the coffee machine. She looked back at Tom, standing by the fire. Looking so good. It wasn't fair. He was almost the perfect man. And he *was* the perfect lover.

# CHAPTER SIX

MORNING CAME QUICKLY AGAIN. Sara thought she might find it difficult to sleep with Tom only on the other side of the wall but she'd fallen into a deep and restful sleep quickly. Almost the moment her head had hit the pillow.

Climbing out of bed, she showered, applied light make-up and dressed in camel-coloured trousers and a striped black and camel fine-knit sweater. She intended to throw her overcoat on top before she left. The number to call for a cab to the practice was already on her phone. Unexpectedly, there was a knock at the door.

As she opened the door, she saw Tom, dressed in dark woollen slacks, a black sweater and heavy grey overcoat, his keys in his hand.

'I trust you slept well.'

'Very,' she told him, as she took a step backwards and held the door open for him to come inside.

Tom walked in, swinging the keys around his finger playfully.

'Do you intend telling me what the keys are for?' she asked.

'Mrs Vanderbilt sold me the house and her car. At ninety-eight, she thought it was better to get off the road. I didn't argue with her—in fact, I told her it was a wise decision considering all the idiots out there now. And that's how I came to be the owner of the 1967 Austin Healey in your driveway.'

Sara forgot about everything as she crossed the room excitedly. She knelt on the armchair and pulled back the lace drapes. With her sweater sleeve she wiped a small circle of fog from the window. There in the driveway was a mint-green Austin Healey, its duco and chrome shining in the dappled morning sun. She hadn't seen it the night before as it had been too dark when they'd arrived home. Sara adored old cars, old houses and old furniture. They had so much character and history to offer.

She turned around and beamed. 'Tom, it's so sweet of you to let me drive it. I swear I'll be so careful.'

'You can't be serious,' he said with a smirk, as he threw the keys across the room to her. 'You can drive my Lexus. I'm the only one who drives the Healey!'

A little after eight o'clock Sara pulled into the car park of the surgery in Tom's late-model Lexus. She'd had a light breakfast of cereal and toast from the contents of the fridge and pantry that she assumed Tom had stocked for her. Marjorie had just arrived and they walked into the building together.

'Not that it's any of my business, Sara, but tell me, did you decide to move in to Tom's house?'

Sara didn't try to hide her surprise. 'How on earth did you know about that?'

'Then you did?' Marjorie smiled broadly as she slipped her car keys inside her bag and patted it closed. 'Very sensible idea, Sara, very sensible. I think everything will work out quite nicely.'

Sara wasn't too sure if she should read anything in to Marjorie's comments but decided to let it go. 'It will save me a considerable amount of money over the month.'

'Lisa, his cleaning lady, dusted and polished everything, moved his things and stocked the fridge and pantry for you. Tom certainly makes our lives hectic, but we manage.'

'Moved *his* things?'

Marjorie realised that she had said too much. 'Just some boxes and bits and bobs he stored there.'

The cover-up worked and Sara didn't bother asking the woman any more questions. She picked up her pace and headed towards the door.

'I bet you were busy,' Sara said. 'Almost as busy as we'll be today.' She changed the subject as they rode up in the lift. To move further from the subject of Tom and her living arrangements, Sara asked about the fantastic network of linked computers that occupied most of the front office. Thankfully, Marjorie obliged with a lengthy discussion about her big toys and dropped the subject of her employer.

Sara had consultations with new patients all morning and was looking forward to the afternoon surgery. Being so busy kept her mind on track and most importantly off Tom.

She and Marjorie both chose something nice and light from the assorted sandwiches that the lunch delivery girl brought around. The anaesthetist, William North, arrived about one o'clock and so did the part-time nurse, Laura, whom Tom and Stu employed for the days of surgical procedures. After introductions and a friendly chat they were ready to begin the afternoon list.

'Melanie Sanders,' Marjorie called softly across the waiting room. 'The doctors are ready now if you would like to follow me.'

Melanie was seventeen years old and needed her impacted wisdom teeth removed. She had been sitting nervously with her mother.

'Hi, Melanie, I'm Sara and I'm filling in for Dr Fielding for a few weeks while he is at the hospital. So if it's all right with you, let's get started and remove those teeth that have been giving you trouble.'

While Melanie climbed into the operating chair, Sara scrubbed in, slipped on her latex gloves and a pale yellow disposable gown.

'Melanie, Dr North will give you a little shot in the hand, which will make you feel a bit drowsy. You will still be awake and able to follow instructions but you won't feel any pain, and as a bonus the amnesiac properties of the anaesthetic means you won't remember anything about this operation when you get home.'

Laura pinned a surgical bib around Melanie and then William began the sedation. It quickly took effect and Sara was able to begin the removal of the offending teeth. The X-rays were illuminated on the wall beside the chair. The procedure went well and forty-five minutes, and numerous sutures later, the four teeth had been removed and Laura escorted the patient to the recovery room.

William and Sara scrubbed and prepared for the next patient while Marjorie prepared the small surgery again.

The next patient was booked in for a similar removal of wisdom teeth. Luckily, this one was straightforward and he was soon in the recovery room.

Sara and William took a short break and were about

to prepare for their third patient when Marjorie asked her to take a telephone call. It was George Andrews' mother. And it was urgent.

'It's Sara Fielding, Mrs Andrews. How can I help?'

'Sara, it's about George, he's refusing to have the operation. The other boys he mixes with have filled his head with worries. He's convinced he could die on the operating table or end up with brain damage or a jaw that has no feeling.'

Sara rubbed her forehead with the inside of her wrist. It wasn't the first time she had encountered friends throwing in their unwanted advice and worrying a patient unnecessarily.

'Don't worry, Mrs Andrews. I'm more than happy to talk to George. I'm sure between the two of us we can convince him he needs to finish his orthodontic treatment and have the operation.'

'I'm not so sure but, Sara, if he doesn't have the surgery now, I know he'll never do it. His friends have persuaded him to move up north and work as a jackaroo.'

'You leave it to me, Mrs Andrews. But it's important for George to undergo the surgery because he wants to. He'll be an adult in a few months and he should be making his own decisions. Even so, they should be informed decisions not something based on the imaginary fears of his friends.'

'I hope you can convince him because, goodness knows, we've tried everything,' Mrs Andrews confided.

Sara flipped open the appointment book. Her eyes scanned over the pages. There wasn't a time free during surgery hours for nearly three weeks and that would be too late. She would have to stay late one evening.

'Friday at seven,' Sara told her. 'Can you both be here then?'

'I'll do my best.'

Sara hung up the telephone. At that moment she wished she had the counselling skills of Tom. She knew that she was more than competent, but Tom seemed to have the edge when it came to handling patient anxieties.

With a sigh, Sara pursed her lips and returned to the surgery, where she scrubbed and prepared for the next patient. She studied the X-rays while Laura popped the young girl in the reclining chair. The patient's canine tooth had developed in the palate, so it needed to be exposed and brought into position.

'I'm Sara and I will be doing your minor operation today. Has Dr Fielding explained it to you?'

The young girl nodded and opened her mouth. She clearly wanted to get it over and done with. Sara explained what the anaesthetist would be doing and then they were ready to begin.

William started sedation while Sara checked the trays had everything ready for both the surgical procedure and then the bonding of the attachment. When she was quite sure that Josie would be free of pain, she began the procedure of exposing the tooth. Laura was an experienced nurse in oral surgery procedures and assisted Sara to attach the bracket to the exposed tooth. A fine surgical chain was attached to the bracket before being linked to the metal braces.

The bracket held well and Sara was happy that the tooth should move down into position over a few months. It wasn't long before the patient was resting comfortably in Recovery.

There were four more patients on the afternoon list and it had just passed six o'clock when the final patient left for home. Sara had enjoyed working with William and Laura and thanked them for their work.

'Any time,' William said.

'Ditto,' agreed Laura, and they both headed off.

Closing the door on the pair, Sara remembered she still had to make some calls about George Andrews.

'Marjorie,' she called aloud, trying to determine her location in the rooms.

'I'm tidying up the recovery room, Sara.'

Sara walked quickly in her direction, talking as she went.

'Do you recall any young male adolescent, class-three malocclusions who underwent surgical correc-tion around twelve months ago?' Sara entered the small room as she finished her question.

After fluffing up the last of the generously propor-tioned cushions that rested on the sofa in the recovery room, Marjorie stood upright. She tilted her head to one side, thinking.

'I'd have to check. Why do you ask?'

'The phone call from Mrs Andrews. Her son George now has reservations about the surgery and I thought if he could have a word with boys around his own age who had undergone the operation, then he might feel better about it.'

'Seems like a swimming idea to me. Are you going to check with Tom before you contact them?'

'No,' Sara told her bluntly. 'I am here in place of Dr Anderson. So any decision I choose to make does not have to be seconded by Dr Fielding. He's far too busy at the hospital to ask for his opinion on something like this.'

'Whatever you think is best,' Marjorie remarked as she slipped past and made her way into the office.

Sara didn't reply. She knew it had come out a little too assertively but she needed to let Marjorie know that she was running the practice. And she needed to keep Tom as far away as humanly possible. To ensure their contact was limited to the absolute minimum. She had hoped it would be easier by now. But it wasn't. And now she doubted it ever would be.

She followed in silence and waited for Marjorie to produce the patient's records.

'I do know what you to are up to,' Marjorie said matter-of-factly.

Sara stopped in her tracks. 'I'm sorry, what did you just say?'

'That you are trying to be all independent and keep Dr Fielding at bay. But if you need to keep him at bay, that says enough for me.'

'Not dragging Dr Fielding back here doesn't explain anything other than the need to allow him to stay focused on his busy schedule at the hospital. He is associate professor after all.'

'I know how important Tom is to the hospital, Sara, but I think he's also very important to you. Perhaps you don't like being too close because you still have feelings for him,' she said, as she sat down in front of her office desk. 'Take some advice from me and don't leave it too late.'

'Too late for what?'

'To start living life again,' Marjorie began, swivelling on her chair to face Sara. 'I know for a fact that

Tom hasn't been. He's been cooped up here or, according to Christina, making up any excuse to stay late at the hospital. He has no sign of a social or romantic life. It's just such a waste when a young person forgets to actually enjoy life.'

Sara was stunned. Perhaps it was his workload and, of course, the PhD would have consumed his time along, with maintaining the practice and keeping up his hours at the hospital. He had probably been doing fourteen-hour days.

She didn't want to believe that perhaps he was still hurting over the separation. Because if that was the case, surely he would have contacted her during the last three years? Reached out and said he wanted to discuss the unresolved issues in their marriage? But he hadn't. He was a stubborn man who would not change his mind and negotiate. Neither could she on something so important. Her days of backing down, of putting her needs last were over.

'Tom's social life has nothing to do with me, Marjorie. Now, if I could have those records, please. I have some calls to make.'

Marjorie's smile didn't mask her doubt at Sara's remarks as she handed over the patient's charts in silence. But something about Marjorie's disposition made Sara realise that the subject was not finished, at least not in the other woman's eyes. But a busybody receptionist was still the least of Sara's concerns.

It was around seven by the time Sara had spoken to both the boys and their families and explained the reason for her call. Thankfully they both agreed and Sara set a date for them to come in near the end of the week. She then called George's home and confirmed with his mother that he would attend one last consultation.

In allowing the boys to speak with George and for him to see their successful surgical outcomes, Sara hoped it would convince him that the results of the operation outweighed the risks.

After locking up the practice, Sara headed off to pick up dinner from a Mexican takeaway she had spied on the way to work. She vowed to get out to the supermarket the next day. The front porch light was on when Sara pulled into the driveway. It was a welcoming sight. But she could never admit it. Not to Tom. Not really even to herself.

With her takeaway in one hand and her briefcase in the other, Sara made her way up the gravel path. It was cold outside and the warm breath of her yawn made a fine steam in the crisp night air.

'Hello, there, Doc. Need some help?' Tom's familiar voice came closer with each word until he was upon her.

'No I'm fine, really I—' she started to say, before she felt him tugging at her briefcase. She struggled to retain ownership and suddenly a warm hand encircled her wrist. It was a powerful grip but tender enough to not bruise her skin. She froze. She didn't want to have these confusing feelings. His touch was unsettling. It was like a burning torch on her skin that spread a dangerous heat through her body. As much as Sara valued her imported leather briefcase, she didn't want to feel any part of Tom's body touching hers.

Her fingers purposely slipped from the handle. The briefcase fell heavily to the ground with a thud and then a crunch as it skidded across the loose gravel. Sara cringed as she imagined the scratches and tears across the fine surface but it was worth the toll to feel his hand finally release its hold on her wrist.

'What just happened?' he asked sharply. 'Do you dislike me touching you that much, Sara?'

*No. I like it too much*, she thought. Time had not dimmed her body's response to him and that was what she hated.

'It's nothing to do with you,' she lied. 'I'm tired and I want to eat this…' she held up the paper bag '…before it goes cold and soggy.'

'Well, why not just say so?' he demanded.

'You'd manacled me like a prisoner. You didn't give me much choice.' It wasn't true but she couldn't help her reaction.

Tom didn't reply. He just shook his head and walked away in silence. Sara wanted to run after him and apologise. She had overreacted and her behaviour had been rude. She realised what she'd done and what she'd said had been wrong. Tom certainly couldn't be held responsible for how her heart was feeling. Or for the desire he was stirring in her soul. But apologising would only bring him back and she needed to keep her distance. She needed time to sort out her feelings. Sara pulled up the collar of her coat against the cold breeze as Tom slammed his front door shut.

Sara realised she would have to work harder at controlling her feelings if she was going to get through the next month. Without doubt it was going to be the longest four weeks of her life.

# CHAPTER SEVEN

MARJORIE HANDED SARA the mail. 'There's one addressed to you and it's from the country,' she said in an enthusiastic tone.

Sara was surprised. All of the correspondence that she had been dealing with was addressed to either Tom or Stu and all related to patient referrals or reports. But this large envelope was addressed to her.

Curiosity made her reach for the letter opener and open this one first. Out fell a beautiful painting of the sun in glorious shades of yellow and orange. It had a huge toothy smile and the eyes were large blue pools of paint with glitter twinkles.

Sara read the words at the bottom.

*To Aunty Sara,*
*Thank you for giving me my daddy for a whole month.*
*Love, Bonny*
*XXX*

A few simple, heartfelt words of a child quickly brought a smile to Sara's face. Dear little Bonny with all her problems had thought to send such a beautiful painting to say thank you.

'Marjorie, isn't this the most wonderful picture you've ever seen?' Sara asked, proudly holding up the brightly coloured sheet of paper.

'Magnificent, Sara. Simply magnificent. We'll have to put it on the pinboard in the waiting room.'

'Just be careful how you attach it to the wall,' she warned. 'I'll be taking this masterpiece with me when I go and I don't want it to tear.'

It took some time rearranging the other notices to accommodate such a big painting but finally it was done.

'Bonny's painting is like taking the sun out of the sky and having it in the room with us. It's just glorious,' Marjorie commented, stepping away to admire the decoration.

'Lucky she doesn't have her father's artistic ability.'

The voice made both women spin around in surprise. They hadn't heard the door open.

'Stu couldn't paint to save his life,' Tom added, before leaving both women and walking into his office.

There had been no 'Hello' or 'How are you?' No greeting whatsoever. Sara thought he must have decided to keep his distance after their words the previous night. She had such mixed emotions. She was upset with herself for being so rude but justified her lack of manners as a necessity to keep Tom at bay.

'What are you doing here, Tom?' she called as she followed after him.

He looked her up and down in an irritated silence. 'No food going cold? So you have time to talk today?' His eyes dropped down to the drawer of the filing cabinet that he was rummaging through.

'I was tired and cold—' she began.

'And just a little rude,' he continued for her.

Sara closed the office door and crossed to him. 'Fine, I'm sorry. But, be fair, you've had bad days in the past and been less than gracious.'

'When?'

It was an honest question as Tom had never been rude to her in that way. They had disagreed, heaven knows how many times, but he had never been cruel or cold the way she had been to him.

'Point taken. I'm sorry for the way I behaved.' She walked to the window and stared outside in silence. She didn't want to tell him about her feelings as it wouldn't change anything. She just had to hope they would fade in time.

Suddenly she felt his warm hands kneading the soft flesh of her shoulders. She flinched and had to stifle a gasp. He stood so close behind her, his supple fingers finding the knots of tension and working them into putty. His masculine scent invaded her senses, sending red heat rushing to her cheeks and then flowing through her entire body.

'I can understand. I guess I threw you in at the deep end here, you must be exhausted.'

His hands on her body felt so good but she had no intention of letting him know that. She mustered a laugh, 'I never liked that briefcase anyway and you did ambush me somewhat.'

Tom smiled in spite of himself and gently turned her around to face him. They were so close. His soft lips, only inches from hers, were so inviting. She hated it that she wanted to taste him and hold him like she had that night a few weeks ago, and all those years before.

'I'd better be going,' he told her huskily, pulling his own feelings into check. 'You've got a full afternoon at the hospital.'

Without saying another word, Tom left.

Relieved that he had gone, Sara collapsed into the chair. She was so glad that she hadn't given in to her desire to kiss him. Just being near him and not reacting to him was so difficult, but she was determined to break through those feelings. She just wasn't sure how.

Taking a deep breath, Sara walked back into her office and gathered up her notes and X-rays for the afternoon's surgery at the hospital.

As Tom left the building he rushed to fill his lungs with the cold air. He had not realised touching Sara would stir feelings so quickly. He was doing his best to remind himself she was leaving and he needed to accept that they had no future together. There was no reason for her to stay. Nothing had changed. They both saw their lives laid out so differently. Sara saw the picket fence and a house filled with children, and he saw his life filled with work. Having children was not in his plans. He couldn't change and she shouldn't change. He loved her for being the loving, caring woman she was and it would be wrong to tie her to a life that gave her less than everything she wanted. Everything she deserved.

Sara drove to the hospital and then parked her car in the doctors' car park and made her way to the doctors' lounge on the fourth floor. It was adjacent to the oral and maxillofacial ward. She placed some groceries she had bought at the market on the way to the hospital in the refrigerator, relieved she would have a nice home-cooked meal for that evening. Fresh King George whiting and some vegetables to steam. She couldn't stomach the thought of takeaway again.

With her dinner safely tucked away, she headed up to Theatre. She scrubbed and gowned and entered to find her drowsy patient already prepared for surgery.

'Hi, David, I'm Sara and, as Marjorie informed you over the phone, I will be carrying out today's procedure. If things go as smoothly as I envisage, you will be in Recovery in a little under two and a half hours with a brand-new-looking jaw but a bit of a sore hip for a few days.'

David smiled limply and tried to nod.

'After that you will be in ICU overnight and then off to a ward for another few days.'

'We're ready, Sara,' the theatre sister told her.

'Count slowly back from ten, David,' the anaesthetist said, and after a few moments David drifted off to sleep under the brilliant theatre lights. The nurse draped David in sterile green sheeting and prepared the surgical sites with antiseptic solution.

Sara checked the X-rays again on the viewer and then looked over towards the surgical trays nearby. 'Today we'll be undertaking a chin augmentation of this young man. We start with an intra-oral incision extending from canine to canine.' There was a first-year intern present so she briefed him on the procedure. 'I am aware of the risk to the long root apexes of the canine teeth and the associated nerve so will move cautiously.'

The operation took just over three hours. There was a short break when David was taken off to Recovery. The staff then rescrubbed and in fresh gowns and caps they returned for another three operations. The first was the release of an adult tongue-tie, followed by re-moval of the remaining upper and lower teeth of an el-derly patient in preparation for full dentures, and the last was a complicated lower-jaw reduction and rhino-plasty. It was almost seven o'clock when they finished and the last young woman was wheeled into Recovery.

Sara thanked the staff for their skilled assistance. She then changed into her street clothes and visited the two patients in ICU, before dropping into the wards and checking the two other less serious cases. They were all progressing well. Sara reassured the concerned families that the patients all looked bruised and swollen but they were fine and then she decided to have a quick cup of coffee before heading home. She was almost dead on her feet after seven straight hours of surgery.

She had just sat down in the doctors' lounge, savour-ing the wonderful aroma of steaming coffee in her mug, when Tom and another doctor appeared, apparently in search of similar refreshment.

'Jake, have you met Sara? She's been kind enough to fill in for Stu while he's up on the farm.'

Sara watched as the man shook his head and walked towards her with his hand outstretched. She purposely avoided eye contact with Tom. She also noted that he hadn't referred to their relationship or history at all. She was just there to help out.

'Jake Manning, I'm in reconstructive surgery,' he told her. 'Pleased to meet you.'

'Likewise,' she told him, as she met his handshake. 'Please forgive me not standing up, but I'm done in. I've just finished a killer of an afternoon list.'

'I can appreciate how you're feeling,' he answered, and collapsed into the chair beside her, throwing his feet onto the low coffee table. 'I've had it for the day and I've only been on rounds.'

'I suppose this means I have to get the coffee,' Tom complained in jest.

Sara's eyes darted to and from Tom as he made his way to the percolator. She tried not to stare, but the sight of his lithe body in form-fitting black linen trousers and an apricot-coloured cotton shirt was more appealing than ever.

'Sugar and white?' he enquired of his colleague.

'No, black and strong. I have a long drive home and I'll need something to keep me awake.'

'Why were the rounds so difficult today?' Sara asked as she lifted her feet up and curled them inside the chair and took another sip of her coffee. 'Heavy load or difficult patients?'

'No, that nervy intern by the name of—'

'Johnson!' Tom cut in smiling, as he crossed the room and placed the mugs heavily on the low table. 'I wondered where he'd turn up. Not that I made any enquiries, mind you.'

'That guy can talk,' Jake continued, reaching for his cup and cradling it in his hands. 'Actually, that's all he did. Talk and talk and—' Jake suddenly started slinking down in his seat. 'Don't look now, but speaking of the devil.'

The door was pushed open by a dishevelled Johnson. He looked around the room and then spied the three of them in the far corner.

'Dr Fielding, I'm sorry to bother you, I know you've finished for the day but your patient Mr Kowalski, the one who went missing and then we located him inadvertently exposing himself to the florists...'

Sara's eyes widened as she heard him recall the story. She watched him fidget nervously and then dig his hands into his white examination-coat pockets. He drew closer and sat down on the edge of the seat. 'You don't mind if I sit, do you?'

Sara leant forward and placed her mug on the table. 'Not at all. And by the way, I'm Sara, I'm filling in for Stu Anderson.'

'Oh, hi. I remember you from the other day in Dr Fielding's office. I hope your knee's okay. I'm so sorry about that. I guess I came across like a bit of a twit, I mean losing a patient and then crashing into you. I mean, it doesn't happen all that often. Actually, only twice this year, and the other one wasn't really missing, I mean, Mrs Summers died and she was taken to the morgue but no one told me. One of those admin types of problems, well, actually it was a heart problem, but then Admin didn't tell me...'

Tom dropped his cup onto the table. 'Johnson, please get to the point, it's getting late and we all want to go home. Is our patient all right?'

'Yes, Dr Fielding. It's just that Mr Kowalski doesn't have any family. He told me that his wife died about ten years ago and then the business went under. They never had any children and he lost contact with his brother, Alexander. I guess he was too embarrassed to admit that he had lost everything. He's been living in shelters on and off for the last nine years. So I would like to refer him to the social worker tomorrow, if that's okay.'

'That sounds like a good idea.'

He stood up, smiling, and backed out of the room. 'Thank you, Dr Fielding. I'll arrange it now.' And with that he was gone.

'Glad he's in your ward more often than mine,' Jake said with a smirk. 'He tries so hard I'd go mad!'

Tom leant forward and tapped his knees like a drum kit. 'He's a good kid but I think he could talk underwater. Some days it does wear thin.'

Sara stood up, smoothed her skirt and self-consciously made her way to the sink. She wasn't sure if Tom was watching her but she felt like she was on show.

'So, Tom,' Jake began. 'I'm not giving up on the whole double-dating idea. I know you keep refusing but I have this amazing woman for you, and I can set it up on Saturday if you'd like. She's Bella's friend over from Adelaide. Pretty girl, radiologist, single….'

The sound of Sara's cup crashing onto the sink and sliding into the soapy water cut short Jake's words.

'Are you okay?' he asked.

'Tired, that's all. Like I said, it was a tough day.'

Sara wiped the suds from her clothes and concentrated on quickly washing and drying her cup. Tom lowered his voice and Sara was grateful that he did. She didn't need to hear his response but she heard Jake's answer.

'Think you're making a huge mistake, Tom. She's a great girl. Maybe next time, then.'

Sara was relieved. She wanted Tom to date, she really did, but she just wanted him to do it after she left Melbourne. When she was living in San Antonio, not now, not while she was still living next door. That would be too much to deal with.

Everything put away, she went to the fridge to collect her groceries.

'Oh, no! Where's it gone?' she exclaimed.

'Where's what?' Tom asked bluntly.

'My shopping bag, everything I bought for dinner. It's gone. Someone's walked off with it!'

Sara wasn't sure she was doing the right thing accepting Tom's dinner invitation but she was too tired to argue. He had offered to cook her a steak and she wasn't about to refuse. In fact, she was so hungry and exhausted that she would have eaten drive-through hamburgers and fries if Tom hadn't offered to cook dinner at her place.

She'd followed him home and on the way they had picked up some fresh bread from the continental deli. Tom had clinched the dinner deal with the promise of ice cream and hot chocolate sauce for dessert. He had run into his place and picked up the steaks while Sara unlocked her door and turned the lights on.

She told herself that she would simply enjoy Tom's company and, more particularly, the meal. To refuse would appear rude and also admit to both of them that she perhaps didn't trust herself to be alone with him.

'I'll throw the steaks under the grill,' he told her. 'Won't take too long. Why don't you turn the heater on and make yourself comfortable in the sitting room.'

'Because I can't turn the heater on.'

Tom gave a wry smile as he popped his head around the kitchen door. 'That's right, I forgot. I'll be right there.'

The bright light from the kitchen filtered through so she didn't bother to switch on a lamp. Tom lit the heater and they both returned to the kitchen to cook the steaks. Sara noticed how he knew where everything was, almost as if it was his kitchen. It was an odd level of familiarity, she thought, then she reminded herself that it was the reverse of their old home so it made sense that the kitchens would be the same.

Tom finished seasoning the steaks and put them on to cook. Together they prepared their meal and Sara felt so happy. She was enjoying Tom's company and trying her best to find a way to define their relationship in her mind. To find a suitable box in which to put them. Unfortunately she couldn't find a label to fit. Nothing came to mind with the feelings she still had.

The meal was wonderful and Tom had opened a nice Cabernet Sauvignon from the Hunter Valley. It was a smooth red wine that complemented the food but Sara declined, preferring a mineral water. Wine made her feel tired and she was already struggling to stay awake.

They talked about work and the cases she had seen over the last few days while they ate their ice cream, sitting together on the comfy sofa. Hours passed like minutes and they both relaxed like old times, each choosing to avoid the subject of children. They accepted in that area they would simply never agree. Then the subject of Bonny arose.

'Isn't Bonny's painting beautiful?'

Tom nodded as he took his last sip of wine and put the empty glass on the coffee table. 'Stu rang yesterday, actually, and apparently Bonny's coming along well. Better than anyone expected. She's not talking yet, she's still using a board to point to the letters of simple words, but they're confident her speech will return in a short while.'

Sara thoughtfully fingered the rim of her empty water glass. 'It must be terrible for them. I know how I would feel if she were mine. I'd be devastated—'

'Yes, I suppose you would,' he cut in. There was

no bitterness in his voice, a touch of melancholy perhaps, but none of his signature hostility on the subject of children.

Tom reached across the table and affectionately brushed away the wisps of hair that were threatening to cover Sara's eyes. Her beautiful eyes. He felt sure that if they had children, they would all have those beautiful big blue eyes…

She flinched and bit the inside of her cheek. With his hand so close it was making her pulse quicken again.

Tom looked into her eyes. He needed to be honest with Sara. He knew that in order for them to find some sort of closure as their marriage ended, there should be no more unanswered questions between them. She had been honest with him about her parents and now she deserved the same. He decided it was the right time to share something with her. To let her know why he would never have children and that his decision was final. He suddenly felt safe to tell her now. To open up to her, secure in the knowledge that she would not try to change his mind. Her new life was waiting and their life together had ended a long time ago.

'Sara,' he began, 'I want to share something with you. I need you to finally understand why we are where we are. Why you're moving on and I choose to devote my life to work and not a family. You need to know. I owe it to you and I owe it to us and what we had together. I should have told you a long time ago.'

Sara was taken aback and her surprise wasn't masked. Her body shifted a little on her chair and she gently pulled her hands free from his. His desire to open up seemed so sudden. This was what she had wanted all along but he had never been prepared to do so. She was confused why he had decided to open up now. She suddenly felt the need to protect herself from what she was about to hear. She didn't know why.

'Go on,' she said, looking at Tom and his new serious expression.

'My brother Heath and I...' Tom started, then he stopped, choking on his words momentarily. 'Well, when we were young, and through until teenagers, we were mad keen on BMX bikes. It was our obsession but he was so much better than I was. He was an extremely skilled rider.'

Sara nodded. This information was nothing new. She was aware that Heath had been the under sixteen BMX state champion for Victoria at one time.

Tom cleared his throat. This was as difficult as he'd imagined. The guilt he felt was still so raw. So many years had passed and yet he could picture it all as if it were yesterday. Each time he thought about his actions it was the same regret that filled his mind and ripped at his heart. He wished he could travel back in time and change it all. Change everything. Relive his life and not be the irresponsible kid who had made a bad decision and ruined his brother's life. And consequently ruined his own chance of happiness with Sara.

'Heath was almost sixteen and I was fourteen,' he started with a sigh. 'He was at the qualifying event for the UCI BMX world championships. He just had to beat the last rider from the Gold Coast in order to win the top spot. I suggested a move that would set him apart. It was called a tail whip. It was risky but I urged him on and told him if he pulled it off he would be on his way to the next world championships. Only he didn't pull it off. He fell. And he was badly injured.'

'Oh, no.' Sara sat up. 'What happened to him?'

'Along with the broken collar bone and multiple abrasions, he suffered testicular trauma or, to be specific, testicular torsion. Long story short, no fatherhood for him.' Tom's face was contorted with guilt as he looked down at the floor. 'So how can I just go ahead and have a big happy family while he is left alone?'

Sara felt so sorry for Heath and for Tom. Both brothers' lives had been changed for ever by normal teenage behaviour that had gone wrong. It hadn't been malicious or even reckless. Sara thought adventurous was a better description. But she felt Tom was carrying a burden that wasn't his to carry.

'But accidents happen to good people every day, Tom, you know that as a doctor. Sometimes no one's to blame.'

'In this case there was. Me.'

'I know what you're saying and I feel desperately sorry for your brother but you were fourteen and you couldn't have known the repercussions.' Sara could see the pain in Tom's eyes and hear the sadness in his voice. It ripped at her heart to see his burden and to know he had been carrying this for so long. She wished he had confided in her before.

'Maybe not, but why should I walk away scot free?'

'You choosing not to have children is not going to change anything for your brother except rob him of the chance to be an uncle. And you are punishing yourself for something that happened decades ago,' she said, reaching for his hands. 'I wish you hadn't kept it from me. I wish you'd told me this years ago.'

'I couldn't because I knew you would try to make me see things your way.'

'Did you ever tell Heath about your decision?' she asked. 'I don't know him that well, we only spent a short time together, but he seemed so lovely. He's a kind, intelligent man who wouldn't expect you to give up your chance for a family. Does he even know that you made this sacrifice, and are continuing to make it years later?'

Tom looked away. 'There's no need for him to know. We're just two brothers who didn't have kids. That's it. He's never questioned me and I haven't seen the need to discuss it with him. He's still paying the price. Why should I be any different?'

'Because you're hurting more than just yourself in the process.' Sara hesitated and then decided to be more honest than she'd thought she ever would. 'You're hurting me and the children that we will never bring into this world because of your decision.'

Tom lips tightened. He knew she was right. And he didn't want to hurt her. He hated it that he couldn't give her everything in the world she wanted. But he couldn't. He knew she would be better off without him.

'This is exactly why I didn't tell you.'

'But you were a child, you were fourteen. You can't own that guilt for ever. It's not fair to you. And I don't think Heath would want you to own it for ever,' Sara argued.

'Heath's marriage ended because of the accident. They tried IVF for years unsuccessfully and it wore them down. He never told anyone but me. How can I look past that? I caused that pain. I wrecked his chance for a happy marriage and children of his own. That's not something that happened when we were kids, Sara, it happened three years ago.'

Sara looked at the man sitting opposite her and she

suddenly saw a very different man. He wasn't a selfish, career-driven man who disliked children at all. He was a man who had put his needs last. It was so sad and ironic that she finally putting her needs first and Tom's decision to place his needs last was what had driven them apart. And yet she had never suspected anything even close to that. She had thought the very opposite for more than three years.

She knew more than ever that he would always own her heart and now she needed to somehow get through to him. To make him see that he was throwing away a future with his own children and this sacrifice, however noble, wouldn't change anything. It would only seal their fate.

# CHAPTER EIGHT

SARA AWOKE AND rubbed her eyes as she slowly rose
from the softness of her warm pillow. She thought back
to the night before. They had talked for hours. She had
tried desperately to change Tom's mindset. She had
pleaded with him to talk to Heath. To be honest about
wanting children and apologise again for what happened
but explain that they all needed to move on. Move past
the hurt and the blame and find a way to be in each
other's lives and accept the past.

Although Tom had seen how it was hurting Sara too,
he felt in his heart he had made the right decision. It
was in his eyes the only course of action. He had made
a decision over twenty years ago and he wasn't going
back on it. Sara had felt helpless to change his mind
when he'd finally left in the early hours of the morning.

She realised she must have fallen into the deepest
sleep when she turned and looked at the clock beside
the bed. It was seven-thirty. She remembered talking
and trying to make Tom see the situation from the outside. She remembered crying a few times too. The accident was a secret that Tom and Heath had kept from
her. She had never met her brother-in-law's wife—both
times she had stayed in the US while Heath had headed

out to Australia to visit. Perhaps it was because she had been undergoing the IVF treatments or perhaps because they had been struggling within the marriage. Sara realised she would never know.

Tom had decided he had a cross to bear for something he'd innocently done as a child, something he felt he had to take responsibility for the rest of his life. She wished there was a way she could get through to him. Sara knew she loved Tom and even though their marriage was over she knew she would never stop caring.

She hoped, not for her sake but for Tom's, that he would one day see it differently. At fourteen, she knew only too well that boys thought they were invincible. She imagined Tom and Heath thought the same way. The idea that one adventurous BMX trick could go horribly wrong and affect the rest of their lives would have been incomprehensible to both of them.

Sara knew it was going to be almost impossible to try to sway Tom's opinion at this time. It was strange but she finally felt now, with this understanding of Tom's attitude and behaviour, that she knew him more intimately than she had ever known him before. This was the real Tom. The caring man who would not turn his back on what he perceived as the permanent scars he had inflicted on his brother. He was a hero, but unfortunately he was a misguided hero. And she had no idea how, or even if, she could change his direction.

She still felt a little tired. Her eyes had been so heavy the night before and they were no different this morning. It was out of character for her to be this exhausted and if it continued, she decided she would have some blood work done. It had been a struggle to get through the day and she'd slept so soundly when her head had hit the pillow. This level of tiredness had occurred once before and it had been anaemia. An iron supplement, spinach or red meat, she decided, might be the order of the day until her count was back up again.

Sara rolled on her back, drawing in a deep breath before she slowly exhaled. In silence, she studied the pattern of the pressed iron ceiling, not really seeing it. The night before had been as enlightening as it had been frustrating. The conversation they had shared had been the most honest they had ever been with each other. Tom had finally opened up to her, and she assumed he found it easier now they were close to finalising the divorce. It was too late for both of them and perhaps it made it less painful for him. She knew his deepest secret but was almost powerless to sway him to choose with his heart. His misguided conscience had ruled his head for far too long.

'Hello…anyone awake?'

Sara jumped at the sound of Tom's voice from the other side of the wall.

'I'm awake and just getting up,' she called back loudly.

'I made breakfast. I've just eaten mine but I have some for you if you'd like to unlock the door. The key's on the dresser.'

Sara had noticed the internal door that linked the two homes but assumed it had been locked for years. She climbed from bed and searched the dresser.

'Not here, I'm afraid,' she called back, slightly pleased there was no key and no way for Tom to be in her bedroom.

'Try the top drawer on the left, it might be in there.'

Sara sighed. He wasn't giving up. How did he know where everything was? She decided not to think too much of it. He was an organised person. She pulled the drawer open and found a neat stack of men's summer T-shirts. She assumed they were Tom's. Then she felt at the bottom of the drawer and found a set of keys.

'Got them.' She couldn't lie. She also had to let him in. With reservations, Sara unlocked the door and opened it to see Tom, still in his dressing gown, smiling at her with a breakfast tray held high. She stepped back, allowing him to enter.

'After the last fall Mrs Vanderbilt had, just before she had to be admitted to the nursing home, she wanted to know I could get through to help in an emergency. So she gave me the key,' he said. 'Made her feel more secure knowing she had someone close by to help in an emergency.'

It didn't give Sara anywhere near the same feeling as she eyed the doorway suspiciously. Her version of ground rules for their working relationship did not extend to her soon-to-be-ex-husband being able to access her bedroom day and night. It may have been a comforting thought for Mrs Vanderbilt but it was definitely was not a comforting thought for *her*.

'Anyway, I thought you might like this to start the day.' He crossed the room and placed a tray of hot coffee and a piece of toast on the bedside table. 'Don't want you feeling bad on your day off because I kept you up talking way too late last night.'

Feeling chilly, Sara climbed back into bed and pulled the covers up.

Tom was feeling anxious about the conversation they'd shared and he wanted to see firsthand that in

the light of day Sara accepted his decision was not negotiable. Her newfound knowledge of the reason why he
would not consider having children would never change
it. His mind was made up. He took full responsibility
for the accident and equally the end of his brother's
marriage.

There was no other way to see it. And nothing she
could say would change anything.

'You have a full day of surgery tomorrow, so rest up.'
He walked over to open the curtains and thought better
of it. 'Maybe we'll leave these closed and you can stay
in bed for a while after breakfast. Take your time and
read a book or something.'

'Tom,' Sara began, 'about last night.'

'Sara, let's not go there,' he said, turning back to face
her. 'I said what I should have told you before we married. It was my fault for thinking children wouldn't be
an issue. We never talked seriously about having them
or not having them. I guess I assumed being just the
two of us for ever would be okay with you. No doubt
you, on the other hand, thought I would warm to the
idea of having kids. It's my fault completely for rushing you to the altar.'

Sara's lips curved to a melancholy smile. It had
been a crazy courtship. She had been excited and had
never really thought too far ahead. She had been marrying the man she loved. The man she admired and
respected and thought would naturally be the father
of her children.

'I'm sad that now I know the truth I still can't change
your mind, Tom. I think you would be the most wonderful father and I feel certain that you and Heath could
work through everything if only you would speak with

your brother. Tell him how you feel and see how he feels. He may have no idea that you are still carrying this guilt. He may even have moved on and assumed you've done the same. I know he would want you to be happy.'

'And I want you to be happy, Sara. It's all I've ever wanted, but talking to my brother won't change anything. What's done is done.'

Tom swallowed hard and asked her to leave the subject alone. He was glad he had finally opened up but he didn't want to go over the past any more. Sara just had to accept his decision and he would accept her decision to each travel a different path. He wanted with all of his heart for the ending to be different but it couldn't be. They might be heading in opposite directions but there were another few weeks yet to spend together and that made him happy in a bittersweet way. He leant down and helped to plump up her pillow before he picked up the breakfast tray and placed it on her lap.

'I'll get ready and head off to the hospital, but you should enjoy your day off. I have lectures all day at the university and then marking to do at the hospital tonight so I'll be late home and probably won't see you till tomorrow. Oh, and by the way, the local grocery store down the road is still there. You might like to stock the fridge if you're low on anything. Still the same old family business it was when you were here and they still make the best rock cakes ever.'

Tom smiled and left the room the way he had come in, shutting the door behind him. He felt like a weight had lifted from him. Although he also recognised that when Sara did move on, marry and have a family, it would be difficult to stay in contact. The thought of her waking in another man's arms and sharing a life with her new husband and children would be too much for him to handle.

While Sara sat and ate her breakfast she tried to process all that Tom had told her. After a night to think about it, she felt no less frustrated. At least she now knew the man she had married a little better. She knew now that Tom wasn't selfish. In fact, he was a man of great principles. Although principles wouldn't keep him warm at night or throw their arms around his neck when they came rushing home from school. He was certainly sacrificing a lot for his brother.

Short of a miracle and Tom seeing the light, there wasn't a lot she could do but accept Tom's decision. Thankfully the day went by smoothly. She had made a few phone calls and organised for some of the boxes of clothes she had packed for Texas to be forwarded to Melbourne. She walked down to the local grocer's and stocked the refrigerator and pantry, picking up some rock cakes as well.

Sara left one in a bag by Tom's front door.

She spent the afternoon with her feet up, reading through some notes for the next day's surgical cases. Then she watched some daytime television, cooked an omelette for dinner and soaked in a long bubble bath.

Once she was snug back in her own pyjamas, she locked the door between the adjoining houses, slipped back under the covers and drifted into a restful sleep.

On Friday she arrived early at the hospital. She had a long day's surgical list. The morning was filled with two of Tom's private patients. The afternoon with Stu's.

They were all straightforward and she was keen to start. That evening she had an appointment at the practice with George and his mother, so she wanted to get away on time.

There was a break at around one, between lists, so Sara went up to the doctors' lounge to close her eyes and put her feet up for a bit.

'Hello, Sara.'

Sara opened her eyes to see Tom standing in front of her. 'Hi, there, stranger,' she managed in a cool tone. 'On your lunch break?'

He sat down. 'No, I've finished up for the day. It's the first day of the mid-year break for the students so no lectures or rotations to organise for the rest of the week. Although I'm not a great believer in the current lecture model anyway,' he announced with a frustrated sigh. 'I think we need to bring changes to medical student education, bring it up to speed by actually reducing the number of lectures.'

Sara could see he felt quite passionate about this subject. 'Go on,' she urged him, as she sipped her chocolate milk.

He turned and faced her. She couldn't help but notice his eyes light up as he spoke. He was so animated. She remembered he always was when he felt strongly about something. 'Let's face it, there have been huge changes in the world of medicine but medical education has remained the same. We're in a time warp and I don't think we're keeping up with student needs or expectations. There's been growth in information and research in all facets of medicine. Yet we keep delivering the traditional lecture style of teaching, despite class attendance falling and complaints that we're failing to produce compassionate, well-trained medicos.'

Sara nodded, agreeing with Tom's valid argument for change.

'We need to make better use of the time we're given to train doctors. I'd like to see lecture content delivered differently. Perhaps in short videos that are watched by the students in their own time, and as often as they need, to ensure they grasp the concepts and really understand the material. Class time is then freed up for focusing on patients' clinical stories as a way to apply this medical information.'

Sara was impressed as always with Tom's knowledge and passion. She knew his new role as associate professor was well deserved. He was no doubt going to make a difference at the hospital. She only wished she could be there to see the changes he made and the real outcomes for the students and the patients. She was so proud of the man she'd married and the man, she knew in her heart, she would always love.

'And now I will climb down from my soapbox,' he said with a laugh, sitting back a little and relaxing. 'I have papers to assess but other than that this week is a good one for me. I get to take a breather.'

'Some people get all the luck,' Sara sighed. 'I've got a full list for Stu and then an appointment back at the practice at about seven.'

'What if I assist?' Tom suggested, as he sat upright again and rubbed his chin thoughtfully. 'Then you can get through it even quicker.'

Sara considered Tom's suggestion for a moment. In the past, working with Tom had always been the highlight of her day. Watching the skill of the man who had inspired her and taught her so much had always been an honour, so with a nod of her head she agreed to share the operating theatre for one last time. She knew she hadn't forgotten his operating style—in fact, it was almost hers. He had been the best teacher and mentor she could have asked for as a student. If she wanted to move past their lives as husband and wife and begin again as colleagues, she needed to start now.

'I'd like that.' She smiled.

Sara was ready and waiting in Theatre when Tom appeared in the scrub room.

'Afternoon, people,' he said, as he crossed to the operating table. He looked down at the teenage boy who was at this stage already a little groggy. 'I bet you're feeling more than a bit nervous, Matt, but listen, mate, there's absolutely nothing to worry about. During the surgery we're going to bring that jaw of yours into a respectable position, and while we're at it reshape your chin a bit. You won't be able to keep the girls away after we've finished with you. But don't worry, before you leave the hospital we'll provide you with a large stick to beat them away!'

Sara smiled to herself. He was incorrigible. But that was part of his charm.

She loved the way he communicated so naturally with patients of any age. He never played the academic with his patients. He was so down to earth. She also noticed that in Theatre she was an equal. He paid her no special attention.

'Any questions before we start?' he asked. 'That's not just from you, Matt. Any questions from the crew?'

They all shook their heads as they went about their respective jobs within the operating theatre.

'Okay, Matt, you're off to sleep, mate. See you in a few hours.'

The anaesthetist took over and Matt drifted out of consciousness.

Sara and Tom worked well together. Neither had changed their approach to the operation and four skilled hands made it a relatively easy procedure.

Sara screwed the first titanium plate in place.

'Damn, I taught you well,' Tom commented lightheartedly to Sara, but all the while appreciating her level of skill. He felt a sense of pride as he watched her dexterity with the complex surgical procedure.

She smiled but didn't raise her eyes. They completed fifteen minutes ahead of time. Tom left promptly to read up on the next patient.

The entire afternoon went as smoothly. Working with Tom, Sara remembered why she had chosen oral and maxillofacial surgery as her specialty. She had watched his fingers perform magic in the operating theatre and she had been mesmerised. Not just by the tall, handsome tutor—it was his talent and love of his work that had inspired her to follow the same path.

They finished the last of the patients around five-thirty, which gave Sara plenty of time to change, pick up something to eat and be at the practice to meet with the other post-operative patients before George arrived. She crossed her fingers that George would show up and be prepared to listen to the other boys.

As she buttoned up her coat, her mobile phone began ringing.

'Hello, Sara Fielding.'

'Sara, it's Marjorie. I'm afraid I have some bad news.'

Sara frowned as she slipped her hair behind her ear to hear better. 'What is it, Marjorie?'

'Both boys who were coming along to talk to George. They've cancelled.'

'What, both of them?'

'Yes, apparently some heavy steel band, Slayer, I think she called them, has stayed on in Melbourne for a second concert and they're going. Neither were prepared to miss out.'

Sara collapsed back into the chair despondently. 'They're a heavy *metal* band, but what am I going to do now? If I don't have those boys there by seven o'clock, George will never agree to his surgery. Stu's patient will be living on a sheep station in the middle of nowhere by this time next week.'

Sara knew there was only one other person who could convince George to go ahead with the surgery. That would be Tom. She had wanted so desperately to handle the practice on her own and to prove that she was capable and had the capacity to deal with any issues that arose. But George had already shown signs of disapproving of her. More than likely, it was the general dismissive attitude of a sixteen-year-old boy. His mother had been on the receiving end too, as Sara had witnessed firsthand.

Sara knew this was no time for pride. This was Stu's patient and she needed to exhaust all avenues before she accepted that George would cancel his surgery, a decision she knew for certain he would regret as an adult.

Sara had only an hour and a quarter now to be at the practice. There was no point turning up alone. George would not listen to her.

Sara dialled Tom's mobile. George might listen to a man. Sometimes teenage boys thought more of another male's opinion. And Tom certainly had a way with patients. It was worth trying.

She wasn't sure if Tom was still in the hospital or if he had left.

Damn, he had switched his phone to voice mail. Sara left a message and asked him to meet her at the practice. She briefly explained the situation and its urgency because of George's plans to move up north to the sheep station. She hoped he would make it in time.

She grabbed her case and rushed out to the lift. With her head down, and in a hurry, she turned the corner and almost ran straight into Johnson.

'That was close,' he said, smiling. 'Almost *déjà vu*! Seems like you're in a hurry this time.'

'You have no idea. I don't have a spare minute. I've got a surgical patient due in a little over an hour at the practice—'

'But that's only fifteen minutes from here,' he cut in, reaching down to pick up her briefcase. 'You don't have to rush, unless of course you haven't eaten, then I suppose you would need the extra time, but there's a hospital cafeteria—'

'Johnson,' Sara cut in tersely, 'I'm afraid I don't even know your first name.'

'Nigel.'

'Thank you, Nigel,' Sara said, more than a little anxious about the unfolding situation. 'But I need to find Dr Fielding.'

'He's up in the lecture theatre, tidying up, I think. If you don't know where that is, I can show you.'

'That'd be great.'

Sara followed Nigel as he led her to another floor. 'Excuse me asking,' Nigel began, through a mouthful of muesli bar, 'but are you married to Dr Fielding or are you his sister?'

'No, we're married but separated. It's all very amicable,' she added.

Nigel nodded. 'I asked, because they were all talking about it in Theatre today. With your names, they didn't know if he was on his best behaviour for his sister or his wife.'

Sara gave a wry smile, knowing she and Tom were already the topic of hospital gossip. She followed Nigel till they reached the lecture theatre, where he left her at the open double doors.

Tom lifted his head, as if he sensed her near.

'You have more patients for me?' he asked with a smile.

'Not exactly, well, not at the hospital. This is one of Stu's private patients,' she answered, as she climbed down the stairs towards Tom at the front of the large tiered room.

'My skeletal class-three malocclusion, George Andrews, has cancelled his surgery for a number of reasons. But not one of them is valid,' Sara explained, as she drew closer. 'His friends have made him worried about the possibility of death or brain damage on the operating table and on top of that Mrs Andrews informs me that they've convinced him to head up north and work as a jackeroo, where his bite won't offend the sheep!'

Tom shook his head. 'Crazy kids.'

Sara smiled as he said it.

'And what can I do?'

Sara looked thoughtfully at Tom. 'I hoped you might be able to explain to him the repercussion of not proceeding with the surgery. I honestly think he's at that age when a man-to-man talk might serve him better.'

'I'm happy to tell it like it is to George and let him weigh up his choices and let him make his decision. I think it's our best shot.'

'Sounds like a plan.'

Tom stacked the last of the papers he had been gathering, put them in a large folder and scooped it under his arm. 'Let's do it, shall we?'

There was a knock on the practice door and Sara looked up to see Mrs Andrews in the waiting room with a very surly-looking George.

'Would you like to have a subtle word with George out there while I keep his mother busy?' she whispered to Tom. 'I think the waiting room is less formal and intimidating.'

Tom took his cue and stood up and walked out into the waiting room. Casually he picked a car racing magazine before flopping into a chair.

'And what am I supposed to do?' George growled. 'Sit around while you both moan about me behind my back? I can't see why I even had to come. Complete waste of time, if you ask me!'

'Actually, George, I have to discuss a few things with your mother and I would like you to have a chat with Dr Fielding.'

Mrs Andrews anxiously entered the office and George sat down in the waiting room with an annoyed expression upon his face.

'I almost had to drag him here kicking and screaming,' Mrs Andrews confessed. 'There was some free concert thing on tonight—'

'And don't I know it,' Sara told her with a sigh as she closed the door on Tom and George.

'George, I'm Dr Fielding,' Tom said, as he dropped the magazine on the seat beside him. 'I thought we could have a chat about the surgery. I heard you've cancelled,' Tom went on as he moved to a chair closer to the young man.

George just looked up with a disinterested expression. 'Do you know how long my mum is gonna be? I wanna go already.'

'She's in there, talking to Sara, so I'm not sure. But I'd like to chat to you about your decision—'

'I'm not having it done any more,' he cut in rudely.

Tom lifted one eyebrow and rubbed the back of his neck. 'Absolutely your choice, mate. But I'm not sure you're cancelling for the right reasons.'

'What do you mean?'

'Well, unless you have much older and wiser friends with medical backgrounds, then they're not qualified to discuss the risks or advantages of the surgery.'

'But I could die on the table.'

'You could die bungee-jumping or doing doughnuts in your car on a dirt road up north, but you'll probably do both with your friends.'

'Probably.' George was eyeing Tom suspiciously but now seemed to be listening. Clearly the doughnuts on the dirt road had rung true.

'Listen, George, the operation is not for the faint-hearted. I won't lie to you, but without it you will have much bigger problems in the long run. It's not about appearance. Even chewing will become more difficult with a jaw discrepancy like yours.'

'So I won't be able to eat a steak?'

'George, as you get older everything will become more difficult. You have to think down the track, not just today. Your long-term health needs to be considered. Even your nutritional needs and the effect on your digestive system needs to be considered. This might not mean a lot now but later you will find it difficult. Your friends won't be there then.'

'So it's not just for looks.'

'Absolutely not, George, although that is a bonus,' Tom said with a wink. 'Never hurts to look good for the ladies.'

Tom noticed George's body language relax and become less defensive.

'Maybe I'll think about it, then,' he announced.

'Can't ask you to do more than that. But don't go to your friends for medical advice. I'm sure they know loads about the latest apps and games, but definitely not about surgical procedures.'

'Can you tell the doctor in with my mum that I'll think about it? I'll make up my mind in a couple of days.'

# CHAPTER NINE

After George and Mrs Andrews left the office, Sara thanked Tom for his successful intervention. She knew he had a way with patients, particularly teenagers, and his inroads with George proved it. As they made their way to the car park, she asked Tom about an invitation she had received in the mail a few days earlier.

'By the way, have you rung Dana and Stu with your answer yet?' she asked as she opened her car door.

He paused with her door ajar. 'Answer to what? I haven't heard from them.'

'They sent us both letters asking us to be godparents to the twins. The christening is in two weeks.'

Tom didn't mask his confusion as he hopped into the Healey and wound down the old-fashioned window. 'Honestly, Sara, I have no idea what you're talking about. I'm aware there's the christening coming up but I haven't received anything from them. Typical of Stu, he probably just left it on my desk somewhere for me to find. I'll look tomorrow and get back to you. But I have to be honest, I'm not sure how I feel about being a godparent. All things considered, I don't think it's a good idea.'

'Tom, they're not asking us to adopt them. I think it's

a wonderful idea.' Sara thought it was an honour and she was sorry that they had all drifted apart over the last few years. She was determined that would not happen again and she couldn't wait to catch up with Dana again. The prospect of being the boys' godmother made her happy. It meant that she would have strong links to their family for ever. This time in Melbourne had made her realise she didn't want to leave it all behind. She loved her friends and wanted to be a part of their lives.

'I'll think about it,' he told her flatly, before starting the car to drive home. *Think long and hard about it*, he told himself. Sara's car was soon an illuminated speck in his rear-vision mirror.

The next day went along steadily. Tom told her he would be working late at Augustine's. It was about one o'clock when Sara received a telephone call from the country. She had finished with the morning's patients and was enjoying a break with a hot mug of minestrone soup when the call came through.

'Sara, hi, it's Dana. How are you?'

Sara rested the cup down on the coaster Marjorie had given her. 'Dana, I'm well, really well,' she said, leaning forward onto the desk. 'But how are things going with you? How's Bonny coming along? It was just such a beautiful painting she sent me.'

'Thanks, I'll tell her you liked it. She's coming along so well, I can't tell you how grateful we are to you for stepping in and taking over.'

'Don't worry about that. I'm just glad I could help out.'

'We'll never forget it,' Dana said softly. 'It's made all the difference. And that's why I'm ringing. We hadn't heard back from you. Sara, Stu and I really want you to be their godmother. Bonny's done so well in only a week that we've decided to have a big party for Henry and Phillip's christening. We had planned on something low key but now practically the whole town is coming.

'Sara,' Dana's voice called down the line, 'please, don't feel pressured. I understand if you're too busy. Really, I don't want you to feel that you have to. We'd love to have you up for the party just as our guest. I'm sure Stu could ask someone else.'

'I'm not feeling pressured. Not at all. I'd be thrilled to be the boys' godmother, it's just that I'm not sure if Tom will agree. He's a bit hesitant—'

'That's wonderful!' Dana cut in. 'And don't worry about Tom. Stu spoke to him today and he's on board too. Gosh it's going to be so great to see you again. It's been so long and we have so much to catch up on.'

Sara nodded into the telephone. 'Yes, it will be great, really great,' she managed to reply, totally surprised at Tom's shift in attitude. What had made him change his mind? Was he coming round on some level to the idea of children after all? She realised every day just how complex Tom was and how he could still astonish her.

The afternoon was as steady as the morning. There were new patient consultations and a couple of post-operative checks.

'You certainly like to be busy, Sara,' Marjorie commented late in the day, as she placed the last of the typed reports on Sara's desk for her signature. 'You've booked a hectic surgical schedule for the next few weeks.'

'Marjorie, I'm fine. I'm not being paid to sit around and do nothing.'

'I know, but you must also look after yourself,' she said firmly. 'What about we close up and head off home? Your minor surgical list tomorrow is a long one. Starts at eight o'clock and we won't finish much before six tomorrow evening. Laura and William North will be with us for the entire day.'

Sara agreed it was a good idea and gathered up her case notes for the next day's patients. She intended to read them briefly during the evening to refresh her memory. Locking the door, she headed downstairs.

Wistfully, Sara looked across the reflections in the river and for a moment her imagination took over and convinced her that she was heading home to spend the evening curled up with Tom instead of a pile of cold case notes. With the gas fire warming the room, she pictured Tom cuddling her as they sat together on the sofa, his arms wrapped tightly around her. But her fantasy slowly faded in the cold night air.

She came back to reality and the overwhelming loneliness of the deserted car park. Absent-mindedly, she rubbed her arms and shivered.

She knew she shouldn't allow her thoughts to wander to Tom. But thinking about him wasn't a conscious decision. No matter how hard she tried to block him from her mind, something would always remind her of him. And when she was by herself she needed no prompting to find his image creeping back in. He had unlocked the key to her heart many years ago and now, despite her protests, it appeared he had subtly crept back in.

Mollie Hatcher was on time the next morning and more than a little apprehensive about losing the gap between her front teeth.

'But my grandma says it's good luck to have a gap,' Mollie told them, her big brown eyes wide with worry.

Sara smiled understandingly. 'You know, Mollie, my grandma told me exactly the same story, and you never know—it might just be true. But it doesn't mean you have to keep the gap to keep the good luck! Especially not if it makes it hard to fit the rest of your teeth in and it stops them from meeting together properly.'

'I don't understand.'

'Well, your teeth came through with a gap. Now, if your grandma's story is true, then the good luck has already been decided for you. So there's no need to keep the gap.'

'I suppose,' she said, with a frown wrinkling the spattering of freckles on her nose. 'But will it hurt?'

'Mollie,' the anaesthetist interrupted softly, 'do you like butterflies?'

'Oh, yes, I love the big, bright coloured ones.'

William smiled. 'That's good, because I'm going to rub some special cream onto your hand and a butterfly is going to sit there and make you feel a bit sleepy. You'll still be awake and able to hear Sara and help her but you won't feel anything she does, so it won't hurt at all.'

The neuroleptanagesia quickly took effect, and Sara was able to remove the fleshy frenum that ran between Mollie's upper front teeth. She carefully sutured and then packed the site with a dressing before Laura helped the child into Recovery.

Following her appointment with Mollie, Sara's morning passed without incident—the minor surgical cases were straightforward and uneventful.

Sara's mind strayed to Tom. She hadn't seen much of him for a few days—the mid-year break was over and the hospital was monopolising his time. She had heard his car come and go at odd hours, but she had resisted the urge to pull back the drapes and peer out at him from the window. They had bumped into each other leaving for work, and Sara suggested shopping together for christening presents on the weekend. Tom seemed hesitant at first but then agreed and made a time for Saturday.

Sara had worried the day shopping would be fraught with tension but it was lovely and so far from her initial concerns. She had assumed the idea of buying presents for children would make Tom feel uncomfortable. But it didn't. Tom seemed happy enough to be looking at silver frames and other keepsakes but he had his own ideas too.

He suggested a large antique train set or racing cars as an alternative, then humoured Sara as she wandered around the delicate ornaments for about half an hour. After she asked the salesperson to reserve two stunning silver frames while she wandered a little more just to be sure of her purchase, he took Sara off to the toy department. She watched him for the first time roam around like a kid himself. He was wide-eyed and enthusiastic about what the boys would love now, and as they grew older. Which toys would be the most exciting, and how Stu could enjoy playing with the toys with his sons.

Sara felt a tug at her heart as she saw the genuine interest he had in finding something the children would love.

Finally he saw them. Two six-foot, enormous brown teddy bears.

'I'm not sure,' she said, looking up at the huge furry creatures. 'They're so big. I don't know where Dana would put them. Wouldn't it be nice to have something to keep?'

Tom nodded. 'If that's what you want, I guess you're right. We should be practical. Let's get the silver frames.'

Sara smiled. Shopping with Tom wasn't difficult at all but it was sad seeing his reaction to the toys he would never share with his own children. She had the frames gift-wrapped and they headed off to enjoy lunch at a café before they left the city. Sara felt sure Dana would love the frames. Tom didn't say anything more but he really did love the bears.

Sara had less than two weeks left on her locum assignment for Stu.

George's surgery came around very quickly. She had called in to see him that night on the way home and gone over the procedure. He wanted the rhinoplasty as well and his mother was happy with that decision. Sara explained to George that he would be wearing anti-embolism stockings prior to his surgery and following the operation to reduce the possibility of deep vein thrombosis.

'Now, on top of everything else, I've gotta wear pantyhose?'

Sara smiled, 'No, George, not pantyhose. These are like thin white socks that compress your legs to increase the blood flow, preventing your leg veins from expanding. It stops blood pooling in your legs and forming a clot.'

He turned to his mother. 'Just make sure no one takes photos of me in the pantyhose-sock things. If that gets online I am so totally screwed.'

* * *

Sara slept well and was ready for a full day when she arrived at the hospital.

'Good morning, Rosalie.'

'Hi, Sara. Good to see you again,' the theatre nurse said, as Sara entered the scrub room. 'Long list again today.'

'Certainly is. Starts with George Andrews. He's understandably nervous. It's a long op he's looking at.' Dressed in her green theatre scrubs, with her hair secured under a surgical cap, Sara began lathering her hands and arms.

'If it goes as smoothly as last week,' Rosalie replied as she rinsed the lather from her hands and forearms, 'it'll be a dream for everyone.'

'Unfortunately we don't have Dr Fielding helping out, if that's what you mean—'

'Oh, yes, you do.' Tom's deep voice came from the other side of the small room.

Sara spun on her surgically booted heels to find him also dressed in theatre garb and scrubbing in at the opposite trough. He turned to face her at that exact moment.

'What are you doing here?' she asked. 'I have an assisting surgeon already confirmed.'

She soon found herself facing his broad back as he turned back round to rinse his hands. She watched in astonishment as he casually dried them and slipped into his latex gloves.

'Fran Burton, your assisting surgeon, just called Marjorie, who in turn called my office to say she had been held up and would be late. Great excuse to take a break from paperwork, so I'll help with the first patient and she'll be here to take over in time for number two.'

Tom had more than enough to occupy his time but he'd jumped at the opportunity to work with Sara again.

'Great,' she replied, a little surprised he hadn't just sent another resident surgeon to help. 'Let's get going.'

George was prepped and already in Theatre. The anaesthetist and two nurses were also waiting under the bright lights.

'Hi, George,' Sara greeted his anxious face. 'I won't ask you how you're feeling. I can pretty much guess the answer. But everything will be fine—'

'You don't happen to have a hip flask in your pocket now, do you? I could really do with something to take the nerves away.'

Tom laughed. 'Dr North has something even stronger planned for you. So, if you're ready, let's get started.'

George nodded and William administered the anaesthetic. The patient, groggier by the moment, began slowly counting backwards from ten. By seven he was asleep.

Tom let Sara lead the operation. He backed her up and anticipated each of her moves. She was so happy to have him working with her.

Once she had freed George's lower jaw, she removed an equal portion from the right and left sides. Tom assisted by securing the newly sized jaw with titanium plates. They worked steadily and advanced the mid-section of his upper jaw. Next was the reshaping of the chin, and then they moved up to his nose. The bump was removed and after three hours the operation was complete. By all indications it was a success.

Sara had felt like she was in possession of four hands.

Their chatter was minimal as each knew the other's next move, both equally skilled in the operating theatre.

Sara wished Tom would stay for the entire day. Fran was a more than capable surgeon but Tom just happened to be extraordinary. Yet professional courtesy wouldn't have her decline Fran's assistance.

'Thanks for your help,' she said to Tom as they watched George wheeled away into Intensive Care. 'It went extremely well.'

Tom considered her in silence. She felt uncomfortable as his eyes lingered on her face. She wondered what he was thinking. Was he considering her surgical skills or looking at her as a woman?

'We make an outstanding team, Sara,' he finally said. 'Texas is lucky to be getting you.' With that he bent down and tenderly kissed her cheek. He smiled sadly at her as he tugged the surgical gloves from his hands and walked away, leaving Sara standing alone in the empty theatre.

# CHAPTER TEN

ICU's BUSTLING AMBIENCE of sterile efficiency was un-
usually sombre when Sara visited after finishing her
surgical list for that day. It was around seven o'clock.
All but one of her patients had been admitted to a high-
dependency ward after Recovery. But it was policy for
the more complicated cases to spend a night in ICU.

Each of the critical care patients had an attending
nurse but the faces of their carers showed little emotion
as they efficiently went about their work.

The silence was broken only by mechanical sounds:
the unrelenting and regular high-pitched beeps of mon-
itors; the constant buzzers; and the deep swooshing
sound of the ventilators.

Pale blue curtains separated the patients whose acute
medical conditions made their lives dependent upon so-
phisticated monitoring equipment and round-the-clock
nursing. Each curtain was drawn open at the foot of the
bed and the senior nurse at the desk had a clear view
of each cubicle.

'Good evening, Vanda.' Sara's voice was little more
than a whisper. 'I'm here to see George Andrews.'

'Evening, Sara,' the pretty nurse replied softly, before she drew a deep sigh and checked her list. 'George

is in bed nine. He's doing very well. Debbie is looking after him tonight.'

'Has his mother been in?'

'She just left. Pretty horrified, by the look on her face. But Debbie and Dr Fielding put her at ease a bit and told her it looked a lot worse than it was.'

'Dr Fielding was here?'

'Yes,' the young nurse replied. 'He's still with him now.'

Sara wasn't surprised. Tom always treated his patients like family while they were in his care. The best care for each and every one of them. That obviously had not changed. Sara made her way over to George. He was sleeping. As expected, his jaw and cheeks were a harsh blend of bruises and quite swollen. His darkened eyes looked sunken in the puffiness of his face. He had been connected to a cardiac monitor and lines from intravenous bottles providing fluid, antibiotics and pain relief fed into his veins.

'Hello, Debbie, hello, Tom,' Sara said. 'I hear our patient is doing very well.'

'Hi, Sara,' Debbie replied. 'Yes, he's fine, but, then, we never expected any problems. His chart says his op was a reasonable length but straightforward. There's no reason to think we'll have anything untoward happen.'

'Mum was in and pretty worried I hear,' Sara said quietly, as she picked up the chart and began looking over it.

'She was okay tonight. Let's face it, it's pretty scary to see a patient for the first time after oral surgery, or any surgery for that matter,' Tom replied, as he watched Sara checking the notes. 'Sometimes we just forget that we're all hard nuts after so many years. Nothing much fazes us.'

After they had checked on George and the other patients, who were settled into the wards, Sara accepted Tom's offer of a lift home. She had left the Lexus at home and walked to the hospital that morning to get some exercise but had no intention of walking home at night. He put the heater on high and Sara snuggled into the seat. She rested her face against the crinkled leather and took deep breaths. Secretly she luxuriated in the scent of his aftershave. It was all through the car. It was like old times.

Tom turned his head and smiled. He knew he had so little time with her he had decided to enjoy every minute. It was hard to be this close when he knew these were the last weeks they would ever spend together. This was it. They would part and he would never see her beautiful face again.

Sara was enjoying Tom's company. There was no tension. No animosity. It was like a truce before they parted ways for ever. The city looked extraordinarily pretty through the fogged glass. Sara knew that her relaxed mood and contentment gave her an appreciation of the normally overlooked sights. The cityscape of high-rise buildings sparkled like brightly coloured fairy-lights against the black sky.

A tram trundled along beside them, the 1920s-style red carriage lit up, and Sara watched the people inside. Businessmen in coloured suits, young women in office attire, a few teenagers and an old lady with a strange feathered hat all sat facing forward as it made its way down Collins Street, rocking a little from side to side.

In the silence of the car Sara wondered for a moment about where they were all going, and if anyone was waiting for them.

It was very cold outside and she was so grateful to be with Tom.

It was like old times. Almost. He walked her to her door and she asked him in for coffee.

'I'll take a raincheck. It's late and I've got a killer of a day tomorrow.' Tom sensed her vulnerability and didn't want to risk a repeat of that night they'd shared not too long ago. He wasn't only protecting Sara from being hurt. He knew he was vulnerable himself.

Sara felt both relief and disappointment when he turned her down. She knew it was best, because she knew she was losing her heart to Tom all over again. It was in both of their best interests that he take control before she lost hers and headed down the right path with the wrong man again.

'Mine's hectic too,' she answered with a short sigh, as she watched him cross the softly lit porch and step onto the loose gravel. 'But being so busy the week is just flying by. I can't believe the weekend's so close.'

He paused and the crunching noise beneath his feet stopped. 'Are you happy for me to drive you to our country christening this weekend?'

'That'd be lovely,' she said. 'I'm so excited to see Dana and Stu, not to mention Bonny and the boys.'

She watched as Tom crossed to his own porch and unlocked the front door. He smiled at her and they stepped inside their respective houses and closed their doors in unison.

On Saturday morning her overnight bag was packed and waiting by the front door ready for the early start, the silver frames tucked safely inside. Unfortunately it wasn't an early start. It was after eleven-thirty before they finally left for the country.

A and E was flat out from the Friday night and Tom had been called in at about six in the morning to help out with an emergency jaw reconstruction.

Tom told Sara about the operation as they drove north along the Hume highway towards Seymour. The sky above them was a clear blue, although soft grey clouds were gathering over the hills in the distance. Sara wound down the window and enjoyed the cool breeze on her face. She had wrapped a light scarf around her hair but the loose wisps were tickling her face.

'What are you smiling about?' Tom asked her. His gaze stayed on her for only a moment before he turned it back to the road.

Sara brushed away the hair, trying to tuck it behind her ears. It was no use. The wind was too strong as Tom increased the speed of the car to climb to the Victorian state limit.

'Nothing, really. I've just got hair all over the place.'

'Then wind up the window.'

She shook her head, sending more of her hair flying about. She couldn't contain her smile. 'No, I'm enjoying it. It feels so good to get away from everything. No pagers, no day lists, no…no schedules to keep!'

Her happiness was contagious and Tom's mouth broke into a broad smile as he put his foot down and took off down the highway.

An hour later they pulled into a roadhouse. It wasn't situated in a town. It was just a petrol station and restaurant on the side of the highway, in the middle of nowhere. There was flat dry scrub for as far as Sara could see. Low bushes and an occasional eucalypt dotted the pale green and brown landscape.

'How about an all-day breakfast?' he asked as he pulled up beside a petrol pump.

'Is it safe to eat here?' She made a wry face as she watched a burly truck driver jump down from his rig. The shiny red cabin door was decorated with a painting of a scantily clad woman. Suddenly the loud noise of another huge semi-trailer pulling in made her jump in her seat. The brakes squealed and then whooshed with the release of air as the huge beast came to a halt behind them.

'It wasn't that I wasn't expecting the Ritz,' Sara shouted over the noise. 'But this looks a little, well, rough around the edges.'

Tom grinned. 'You can guarantee, Sara, if the buses and trucks stop here, then the food will be the best. They can't afford to get gut problems on long interstate hauls. They'll only eat where they know the places are clean and the food is fresh.'

Hesitantly, Sara made her way inside.

Tom was right. The bacon was crisp, the scrambled eggs were deliciously fluffy and the coffee was freshly brewed.

'Dana and Stu's place is only about an hour down the road,' Tom said as he paid the bill and gave his compliments to the chef. He held the door open for Sara. 'I still don't know how he manages to drive in every week for four days and then come home for a long weekend. I like city living and country visiting…once or twice a year.'

Sara nodded in agreement. She was looking forward to spending the next two days on the farm but she couldn't stand the thought of driving that far every week, like Stu did.

'I suppose you can't take the country out of a country boy, can you?' she said as she climbed into the car and pull the door closed. 'Or the city out of us city folk.'

He didn't start the car until the last semi-trailer had pulled out onto the road. There was no point leaving first. The vintage car would only get in the way and force the semis to overtake.

They drove while chatting happily about the practice and the hospital. Soon the town sign appeared. Seymour. It was at the junction of the Hume highway and Goulburn Valley and Sara knew it would be a picturesque part of the country.

Tom turned off the highway into Seymour. The farm was outside of the main town so they headed down Station Street and stopped at the Railway Club Hotel.

'I didn't have time to get any wine for tomorrow,' Tom said, as he climbed out of the car. 'I'll just grab a bottle or two. Would you like anything?'

Sara shook her head. She was still full from their lunch. She looked around as she waited for Tom. It was a typical country town where everyone took their time and knew their neighbours. Sara watched as a group made their way to the river with their fishing gear. It wasn't long before Tom emerged with his purchases and reversed the car and continued down the street.

'How long since you were here?' Sara asked him, as she looked at the heritage buildings dotted along the main road. As they made their way through the town she admired the gorgeous gardens.

'I was only here just over six weeks ago,' Tom answered as he left the town and headed along the Goulburn Valley Highway to the farm. 'I came down with Stu when Bonny was released from hospital.'

'That must have been a dreadful time.' Sara paused for a moment and looked across the huge vineyards that surrounded the township. She was searching for the right words. 'I think seeing Bonny so badly injured and yet being unable to do anything more would have made me feel so helpless. It's so hard when only time can heal someone you care about.'

Tom said nothing but the emotion that poured into his face told Sara everything she needed to know. He still felt the pain of Bonny's injuries, that was obvious. And he still carried those of his brother.

Her heart aching with sadness at what might have been, she turned her gaze away from Tom and back to the scenery. They turned left onto a dirt road and the car bumped along the uneven surface for a half a mile before they found the entrance to the farm.

As they travelled up the last part of the potholed road to the house, Tom filled Sara in about the property. Stu and Dana had bought the house when they'd returned from Queensland. It was more of a hobby farm and a rural escape than a money-making venture.

They had bought a small number of sheep to graze over the few hectares of bush land that had been cleared and a couple of alpacas roamed around to protect the sheep from foxes. In another paddock were some grape vines but these were grown only on a small scale. Selling the grapes to local wine producers made just enough to fund the farm. There was no huge profit in this venture. Dana tended to the general running of the property and had needed to employ only one farmhand, Adrian, who also helped out with any odd jobs that Stu was too busy to deal with.

Sara stepped out in the driveway to hear a kookaburra's call from top of the lofty eucalypts.

'Did you have a good trip?' Stu asked the pair as he approached them enthusiastically. He had heard them coming up the long driveway and was already outside, waiting for them.

'Tops,' Tom replied, as he closed the car door.

'What about you, Sara? Did you enjoy the bumpy ride in the old Austin Healey?'

'It was great, and it's even better to see you again,' she said, before she wrapped her arms around Stu and hugged his huge bear-like body.

'Dana's in the kitchen,' he told her, patting her back affectionately and walking her to the house. He opened the front door and stepped back, smiling. 'Those godsons of yours have made one hell of a mess in their highchairs. Food all over the place. Looks like a war zone. I was lucky to get out alive the way they were throwing stewed pears and cereal about.'

Dana was as thrilled to see Sara as she was to be there. The pair embraced affectionately.

Sara couldn't believe it had been three years—it felt like yesterday. Dana hadn't changed a bit. Her brown eyes sparkled and her long red hair was still a mass of curls tied back from her pretty face with an antique clasp. She was about Sara's height, which meant she was dwarfed by her husband. Her petite frame was dressed in jeans and a canary yellow overshirt.

The kitchen was big with a true country feel to it.

Rows of saucepans and utensils hung down from the ceiling within reach of the workbench and beautiful floral curtains draped the windows. The cupboards and drawers were oak and so was the big kitchen table and chairs. The floor was tiled in aged terracotta and a pot-belly stove in the far corner warmed the large room.

Henry was the bigger twin. His brother Phillip was slightly smaller framed, though both had had a shock of red hair. Sara was thrilled to finally see them, and she could hardly wait to see Bonny.

'Where is she?' Sara finally asked, after giving both Henry and Phillip kisses on the tops of their heads. It was the only part of them not covered in food. 'Where's Bonny?'

Dana smiled so widely at the question that Sara was afraid her hostess for the weekend would burst before she told her.

'Dana, what is it? Tell me. Where is she?'

'Horseriding.'

Sara felt the colour drain from her previously flushed face. 'She's what? You can't be serious?'

Dana climbed down from the footstool after wiping the last of the pears and rice cereal from the wall. 'I'm deadly serious. Bonny's out riding her pony, Sheba, with Adrian. And she can talk again. She started speaking only two days ago.'

Sara couldn't believe what she was hearing. Bonny had still been critically ill only a month ago and now she was horseriding and her voice was back.

Dana hurriedly rinsed the checked cloth under running water and hung it over the dish drainer before she sat down at the table with Sara. But her work wasn't done and she reached over and began cleaning Phillip's face. Sara took another facecloth and busied herself with cleaning up Henry.

'It was meant to be a surprise. Bonny didn't want anyone to know she was walking or talking again until the boys' christening party. My mother and father still think she needs a frame to walk and a board to spell the words, and so do Stu's parents. Bonny thought she'd surprise both sets of grandparents by walking into church and singing the hymns.'

'That's wonderful,' Sara told her friend as she finished wiping the last of the sticky mess from Henry's chubby little fingers. He gurgled and gave a toothless grin that immediately brought a smile to Sara.

'Good,' Stu's deep voice called through the wire screen door. 'It's cleaned up. We can get something to eat.'

Dana shook her head as she looked over at Sara. 'Isn't it amazing what impeccable timing men have? It always saves them from the worst scrapes.'

Sara couldn't agree more. After Stu and Tom brought in the bags, putting Sara's in the spare room and leaving Tom's by the door to be taken out later to the guest-house, the four of them ate lunch with the boys safely placed in a nearby playpen. Dana had prepared open sandwiches, with Sara's help.

'Savour the ones with egg filling,' Stu mumbled cheerily with a mouthful of sandwich. 'Thomasina's laying about one a week, and that's only in a good week!'

They all laughed. They cleaned up and put the boys to sleep before the four of them went out to find Bonny and Adrian. The air smelt good and fresh but the sky was almost covered with ominous-looking clouds.

Although a downpour was a while off, the breeze was quite cold and the ground was still heavy from recent rainfall. Sara had worn jeans and a hand-knitted jumper on the car trip so she needed only to grab her scarf, throw her waterproof jacket over the top and slip into some knee-length rubber boots that Dana gave her.

Before they left the farmhouse, Tom took his bag to the guesthouse, not far from the main house, and changed into similar country clothing.

After a few minutes of walking they had reached the small shearing shed near the riding track.

'Uncle Tom, Uncle Tom!' came the excited cry. 'Look at me!'

Sara spun round to see Bonny, all grown up and sitting high in the saddle with her brown riding hat firmly in place, her curly auburn hair tied in long plaits and a yellow raincoat buttoned up against the breeze. Sara felt pure joy as she watched Bonny parade around them on her chestnut coloured pony.

Stu coughed to clear his throat. 'Excuse me, missy. We have another guest.'

Bonny peered down in Sara's direction and pulled Sheba's reins to a halt. 'Aunty Sara?'

'Yes, it's me, Bonny. I'm sorry I've been away so long. Too long.' Sara's throat was choked by emotion. 'It's…it's so good to see you up there. I can hardly believe it.'

Bonny's pretty face was aglow as she began a slow canter around the foursome. 'I'm walking into church tomorrow. Did Mummy tell you?'

Sara nodded. 'She certainly did, Bonny, and I know it's a secret so I won't say a word to anyone.'

'Adrian,' Stu called to the young man who followed

closely behind Bonny on a glistening black mare, 'I'd like you to meet a friend of ours.'

Sara watched as he carefully turned the cantering horse and rode over to her.

'Sara, I'd like you to meet Adrian Gorden. Adrian, this is Sara Fielding.'

'Pleased to meet you, Sara,' the boy said politely, but his eyes didn't stray from Bonny for too long. Before Sara had a chance to respond, Sheba moved her head suddenly and Adrian instantly cantered back over to Bonny.

'We'd better head back as there's lots to do before tomorrow,' Dana told them. 'And that includes you, Bonny. You've got some more physio and then a hot bath. You can spend the afternoon inside with the boys.'

'What size boys are we talking about, darling?' Stu asked light-heartedly. 'Have Tom and I been grounded too?'

Dana laughed as she gently reached for Sheba's reins and turned the pony in the direction of the farmhouse. 'No. I guess you two can have the afternoon off. But don't forget you've got lots to do this evening and first thing in the morning.'

Stu saluted his wife and then bent down and kissed her. Sara looked away. The love they shared was almost palpable and it made her feel a little uncomfortable. It used not to, all those years ago, but back then circumstances had been different. That had been when she and Tom had also shared those tender moments and so much more.

'Okay, Tom, looks like we've got a few hours free. How about a trip into town and a pint with some of the locals?'

* * *

Sara spent the afternoon chatting with Bonny and helping with preparations for the next day's festivities. Dana's parents would be arriving the day of the christening
but spending the night. Stu's family wouldn't stay at all
because they only lived in the next town.

Sara's room was already prepared but she helped
Dana ready another guest room, putting fresh sheets on
the queen-sized bed. This would be for Dana's parents.

Sara offered to go out and prepare Tom's bed in the
guesthouse by herself, leaving Dana free to begin another. It was a small, self-contained unit with its own
kitchen, bathroom and bedroom. Dana gave her fresh
flowers to put on the table and extra blankets for the
bed. It was an odd feeling and she had butterflies in
her stomach as she made the bed Tom would be lying
in that night. She had to push the feelings away as she
tucked in the last blanket corner.

'It's lucky you have such a big place to hold us all,'
she said, when she finally came back into the kitchen,
where Dana was busily decorating the christening cake.
It was a fruit cake in the shape of two booties and iced
in the palest powder blue.

The afternoon raced by. Sara was happy to follow Dana's instructions and roll the three dozen chocolate-
dipped lamingtons in coconut, blend the cream cheese
and salmon for the dip and carefully fold the huge pile
of blue and white serviettes. Bonny joined in and helped
with the serviettes after her bath. They had decided,
with all the party preparations, to leave the physiother-
apy until her father returned home.

'How many guests are you expecting, Dana?'

Dana had her head in the fridge looking for the carrots to grate into the coleslaw. 'We've planned on sixty,' she said, as she stood up and crossed back to the sink with the bunch of carrots in her hand. As Sara watched Dana cut off the leafy, green tops and discard them into the bin, she couldn't help but wonder if one day she would be knee deep in preparing a family function for her own children.

The men came home around six o'clock, just in time for dinner. After the delicious meal of roast pork and vegetables, Tom chose to spend some quiet time with Bonny while the others finished their bread-and-butter pudding. He had excused himself before dessert and headed off to play a board game with the excited little girl in the family room.

Sara noticed how much he loved spending time with Bonny and how his self-imposed sentence would rob him of the opportunity to do the same with his own child. But that was his choice, she reminded herself, although it made her sad to think she could do nothing to change it. She couldn't find a way to get through to him and make him see that he was denying himself something so precious.

'It's not like Tom to refuse dessert,' Dana commented as she stacked the emptied bowls. 'He usually eats like a Mallee bull.'

'That's okay. If he doesn't come back for it, I'm happy to eat his tonight. This country air is giving me an appetite,' Sara said, helping Dana to clear the table.

The two women made quick work of cleaning up the dinner dishes, while Stu gave the boys a bottle each and

Tom remained out of sight with Bonny. They could all hear the laughter coming from the other room as Tom and Bonny played card game after card game.

'I think we should all play cards tonight. What about bridge or poker?' Dana suggested, as Stu took the two drained bottles away from Henry and Phillip.

'Sounds like a great idea to me,' Stu replied. 'I'll just change my little men here, and then get the children up to bed. Give me ten minutes and then I will clean the lot of you up in a game of poker. Bridge is for sissies.'

Sara smiled. 'Poker it is.'

They were about forty minutes into poker when Stu felt a headache coming on and thought he might call it a night. Dana said she thought she might head to bed early as well, since it was going to be a big day tomorrow.

'Why don't you two head back into town and get a drink or something? I mean, you are welcome to stay here and watch television, but we are a bit boring in our old age and tend to settle down quite early.'

'We may just do that. What do you think, Sara? Up for a big night on the town?'

Sara was a little tired but thought it might be fun to head into town and see what the locals were up to.

'Sure, why not?' she replied.

'Then that's settled. You will see us later,' Tom announced, as he stood up and slipped his warm jacket on.

Stu reached into his pocket, pulled out his keys and tossed them across the room. 'Take the four-wheel drive. It's safer on the roads out here at night than that antique toy car you drive, not to mention a lot warmer.'

Tom caught the keys and nodded in agreement. Sara

went quickly to her room and grabbed a warm coat and scarf.

'I'll drive,' she said with a smile, as she took the keys from Tom's hand and headed outside. The air was freezing as they climbed into the huge four-wheel drive. It took only moments to realise she wouldn't be driving anywhere.

'Change of mind, you can drive after all,' she told Tom, and then climbed out of the car. With a puzzled expression Tom stepped out of his side, walked around to the driver's door and climbed in. They both shut their doors at the same time.

'Of course,' he said, with laughter in his voice. 'You can't drive anything with a manual gearbox!'

Sara nodded sheepishly.

'You know, Sara, it has always amazed me how you can perform complex surgical procedures but can't co-ordinate your feet and hands to use a clutch and gear-stick!' He chuckled to himself and Sara rolled her eyes as they took off down the dirt road, the headlights on high beam.

It didn't take long before they pulled up outside the Royal Hotel.

'Someone told me this was the subject of a Drysdale painting. Is that right?' Sara asked as they quickly made their way to the entrance. It was so cold. There was no breeze but it was like standing inside a cold room and it was chilling them both to the bone.

'I don't know, to be honest, but I'm sure Stu would. You can ask him in the morning,' Tom said, as he held the hotel door open for Sara. He added, 'Not sure about you but I think I would prefer a hot chocolate to a wine tonight.'

Sara nodded in agreement as she blew warm air on her hands and crossed to a table near the fire.

They both enjoyed a warm drink and a light-hearted chat about Stu and Dana and their wonderful property and how amazing Bonny's progress was, considering her injuries.

Sara suddenly realised that she had forgotten to take the spare key Dana had placed in her room, and it was only when Tom looked at his watch that they saw how late it was.

As they pulled back into the driveway ten minutes later, they saw that the main house lights were turned off.

'Looks like they've locked you out,' he said.

'I don't want to wake them, that wouldn't be fair.'

'There's nothing for you to do but spend the night in the guesthouse with me.'

Sara swallowed nervously as Tom unlocked the guesthouse and she followed him inside. It was lovely and warm and Sara guessed the either Dana or Stu had put on the heater for Tom before they went to bed. He turned on the lamps and she could see into the bedroom. She had made the bed earlier in the day, thinking that Tom would be lying between the sheets. That had been hard enough to think about.

She'd never dreamt that she would be lying in the same bed. Or that they would fall asleep together and she would wake in the morning to find his gorgeous face on the pillow next to hers.

Her stomach began tying itself in small knots as Tom removed his coat and slipped his heavy shoes off. When he undid his shirt and told her he was taking a shower, the knots turned to churning and her heart started to pound. She didn't know where to look as he casually dropped his shirt on the chair and slipped his belt from his jeans.

She quickly reached for a book, any book on the coffee table, as his trousers hit the ground and he disappeared in to the small bathroom. She knew there was nowhere in there to place his clothes but removing them in front of her was far too unsettling. Sara put the book back down on the table, completely unaware of what was even on the cover. Her mind was spinning as she went into the bedroom and turned down the bed. She was waiting for Tom to finish his shower when she heard him call out.

'Sara, take my pyjama top to stay warm in bed tonight. I'll wear the bottoms. You'll find it in my overnight bag. And there's a spare toothbrush in there as well.'

Sara felt uncomfortable searching in his belongings but decided if she got the top while he was in the shower then she could change without him seeing her naked. She unzipped the bag and found the top and the toothbrush. Hastily, she slipped off her winter clothes and put on his warm pyjama top. Then she put the pyjama pants on the end of the bed for Tom.

'You can come in and brush your teeth, you know. There's a shower curtain.'

Sara wished she hadn't heard. 'I can wait,' she called back.

'You know I take for ever,' he called over the sound of the running water. 'You could be in bed in five minutes if you can ignore my singing while you floss.'

Sara cringed with the thought. Not at his singing

but of him standing naked behind the shower curtain only inches from her. Tentatively, and with an enormous amount of trepidation, Sara opened the door and stepped inside the steam-filled room. Her bare feet crossed the tiles to the sink.

'Almost like old times,' came Tom's voice from behind the curtain.

'Almost,' she muttered, as she squeezed some toothpaste on her brush and bent forward over the basin, beginning to brush her teeth. It was the most disconcerting tooth-brushing experience she could recall.

The curtain suddenly moved back, revealing Tom's head and very naked upper torso. 'Sorry, I couldn't hear you.'

Sara instinctively closed her eyes. Tight. She didn't want to see what she knew was in front of her. The vision of her naked and extremely handsome soon-to-be-ex-husband was not something she could easily, if ever, forget.

She pointed her hand at her toothbrush already in her mouth, hoping he would understand that she couldn't talk. He did and the curtain was pulled back again.

Sara breathed a sigh of relief and finished brushing and flossing in record time. She left the bathroom, calling out goodnight before she closed the door on her way out.

Snug in her oversized nightwear, she climbed into bed. She pulled the blankets up to her chin and tried to push any thoughts of the last time she'd shared a bed with Tom from her mind. She closed her eyes and prayed she would fall asleep quickly. But that didn't happen. Tom stepped from the bathroom with his towel hung low. She didn't want to look at him but she did. In the soft light creeping from under the bathroom door she watched his perfectly sculpted body cross the room to where his overnight bag lay.

'Your pyjama pants are on the end of the bed,' she whispered softly, and again she closed her eyes very quickly and very tightly before he dropped his towel.

She heard Tom thank her before he turned off the heater and the light and slipped into bed.

'Goodnight, Sara.'

She felt his weight on the other side of the bed and the fresh scent of soap as she lay so close to the man she knew she still loved.

She was so confused that it felt so right, so good and so comforting to be sharing Tom's bed. She didn't want to feel that way. She may not have any intention of acting on it, but there was no denying she felt at home and safe in a strange bed because Tom was in it with her.

'Goodnight, Tom.'

It was about two in the morning when she woke up, feeling a little hungry. There were some cookies that she had spied earlier in the kitchen so she made her way out there quietly. Without making too much noise, she heated some milk on the stove and sat at the small kitchen table, dipping her cookies into the cup. Then she made her way back to the bedroom. The moonlight was shining though the gaps in the curtains, faintly illuminating the room. She noticed he had kicked his covers off. Without thinking too much about it, she instinctively moved to cover him.

Gently she pulled the covers up and over his bare back. He had sacrificed the warmth of his top for her. The room was now cold and she suspected his back would be icy to touch. A bittersweet smile tugged at her mouth as she remembered back to when they had been married and how she would always have to cover him during the night. His shoulders would be so cold to touch but he would be sleeping peacefully, perhaps in the knowledge that she would keep him warm.

He gave a deep throaty moan and startled her. She reeled back on tiptoe, holding her breath. His thick lashes flickered and he scratched his head.

Sara's pulse was racing. What would she say to him if he woke to find her leaning over him?

Thankfully she didn't have to find a hasty excuse. He didn't wake up. He just rolled over, tossing the blankets aside and uncovering himself again. Her breathing became steady but quite loud. For a moment she stood in silence, trying not to make a sound in case she woke him. Sara didn't dare to try covering him again. Instead, she crept back to her side of the bed.

There was a tug in her chest as she quietly slipped under the covers, knowing she would be spending the rest of her life without him.

In ten short days she would walk away, again. Gone from Tom's life for ever. She would never be there to cover his back.

# CHAPTER ELEVEN

DANA AND STU were eating breakfast with Bonny and the boys when Tom and Sara entered the kitchen.

'Morning, guys,' Tom greeted them cheerfully. 'I can tell it's going to be a great day.'

'Morning to you two,' Stu said, swallowing a mouthful of porridge and ignoring the change to sleeping arrangements. 'There's plenty of this on the stove. Unless you'd prefer cold cereal.'

'No. Porridge is lovely,' Sara said, climbing to her feet and getting two bowls from the kitchen dresser. Tom followed behind, taking two spoons from the drawer. They smiled at each other when they realised what they had done. It was like old times.

'Church is at—' Dana cut her words short when she saw the arrival of a huge delivery truck in the driveway. 'What on earth is that?'

Bonny ran to the window to look out as Stu and Dana crossed to open the door.

A uniformed man climbed down from the truck, its side emblazoned with the impressive logo of a large department store in Melbourne.

'I have a delivery for Henry, Phillip and Bonny Anderson,' the driver announced, as he neared the open door. 'I need a signature before I can get the parcel from the truck.'

'There's something for me too?' Bonny screamed excitedly, and hobbled to the door. 'But it's not my birthday or anything.'

Sara shot Tom a puzzled look and then leant over to him. 'You got the boys the bears, didn't you?' she whispered in his ear.

He nodded and smiled as he looked straight ahead. 'And one for Bonny.'

Bonny was bursting with excitement. 'Mummy, can I go out and help?'

Dana ruffled her daughter's mass of auburn curls. 'I don't think the gentleman will need too much help, sweetheart.'

The young man coughed. 'Don't believe it. I could do with some help but definitely adult size for this delivery.'

Stu and Tom followed him outside. It was only a matter of minutes before three chocolate brown, six-foot teddy bears with rotund tummies marched their way down the ramp from the truck.

Sara smiled at the sight of the first two with their checked bow-ties and then the third with a string of pale pink pearls around its enormous neck. The men were all struggling to keep their balance as they carried the trio inside.

Bonny was ecstatic and the boys' little faces lit up and they started gurgling at the sight of their huge furry presents.

'But I'm not being christened,' Bonny said, as she hugged the bear now sitting on the floor. She stood possessively beside it, running her fingers over the monstrous pearls.

'It's a get-well present from Aunty Sara and me.'

'You shouldn't have,' Stu and Dana said in unison.

'I'm glad they did!' Bonny said.

The morning went well. Dana's parents arrived at the same time as Stu's mother and father. The church service was at one o'clock and afterwards everyone came back to the house. Adrian had offered to stay behind to put out the food and see to any last-minute preparations. Dana had organised more than enough food and Stu had seen to the alcohol, so there was no shortage in that department.

'Didn't the boys behave beautifully for the minister?' Sara said, as she offered the plate of sandwiches to Dana's parents. 'Not even a whimper.'

'It was wonderful. I had tears in my eyes the moment I saw Bonny walk into the church and they stayed with me for the entire service.'

'You're too sentimental,' her husband told her. 'I knew our Bonny would pull through. She's a fighter, that's what she is.'

Sara smiled and moved on around the room with the sandwiches and then with the dips and other finger food. Finally, she carried platters of cakes and before too long it was coffee. At around five o'clock the guests started to leave.

Henry and Phillip were fast asleep, unaware of all the fuss for them. Two huge bears sat in the corner of the room, watching over them.

'I almost forgot,' Sara said, carrying a present into

the room. 'Tom and I wanted the boys to have something to keep for when they are older.'

Dana unwrapped the parcel with its layers of noisy tissue paper. She gasped. 'They're absolutely beautiful.' Lying in her lap were the two ornate silver picture frames. The family members all gathered around to admire them while Sara started to clean up.

It was about nine o'clock when the mess was under control. They had all picked on the delicious leftovers and were quite full.

'I hate to ruin a nice evening,' Tom said, as he climbed to his feet from the comfortable chair by the pot-belly stove, 'but I'm afraid Sara and I have to head back to Melbourne.'

Tom didn't want to risk anything happening and he was afraid one more night together might cause him to cross the line. He knew Sara had covered him during the night. There had been no need to open his eyes. The warmth in her touch had radiated through his body as she'd pulled the covers gently over him.

It had taken every ounce of his strength not to reach up and pull her into his arms and make love to her. He didn't trust himself. He needed to head back to Melbourne where the boundaries were more defined. Being here with old friends made it even more difficult to remember that he and Sara would soon be divorced.

It would be unfair to both of them, he reasoned, for anything to happen. Sara would be leaving for Texas soon and he would once again be alone with his work.

Sara had made an appointment to see the local general practitioner the next day after work, so she didn't mind heading back early. The tiredness wasn't subsiding so she thought it would be great to have some tests to confirm whether her anaemia had returned.

The next day's patients were straightforward consultations and she left on time to get through the Melbourne peak-hour traffic to the doctor's rooms. She felt great after the two days away but still thought it was prudent to have bloodwork done to rule out anything more serious.

The doctor was a lovely older man and after Sara explained her symptoms he agreed they should do a routine blood test as well as checking her blood pressure and vitals.

'Mrs...I mean, Dr Fielding,' he began, as he undid the blood-pressure sleeve on her arm and folded it back into the pouch on his desk. 'Just run by me your symptoms again.'

'Tired, mostly, and a better appetite than usual. I was up one night recently eating at two in the morning.'

'This may seem obvious but you couldn't by any chance be pregnant could you?'

*Pregnant?* Sara froze. Of course not. She'd only had sex once in the last eighteen months—the night she'd spent with Tom just over six weeks ago—but they'd been careful.

'Definitely not.'

The doctor eyed her with some degree of doubt. 'So you've not had sex recently?'

'Yes, once more than six weeks ago, in fact, almost seven now, but it was safe, we took precautions. I can't be pregnant.'

'My dear, you're a medical specialist. You know as

well as I do that the only one hundred per cent safe sex is no sex.'

Sara was incensed by what he'd said. But it wasn't his tone, it was the fact she knew he was speaking the truth.

*Could she actually be pregnant?* No, it's not possible, she told herself.

'But there's been no nausea. Nothing. I'm eating well. I think it's more likely my haemoglobin has dropped a little. I've had it happen in the past.'

'Well, I will definitely test for that,' he replied as he completed the pathology request form. 'Is your period late?'

'Maybe a couple of weeks but that's not unusual, I'm not always regular when I'm under stress. I'm moving to live in the US and it's been quite a busy time. As I said, my only complaint is being tired,' Sara said matter-of-factly, not completely sure of who she was trying to convince.

'Not everyone suffers from nausea. Some women go through the entire pregnancy without ever feeling sick, some only feel tired and have an increased appetite, so what if we go ahead and do a simple urine test to rule out pregnancy anyway?'

Sara was unimpressed with the idea. Part of her was suddenly very scared of the result. Part of her already knew the answer. But reluctantly she agreed.

He handed her a specimen jar and walked her to the door. 'The bathroom is the second on the left. Take your time.'

Sara sighed as she walked to the bathroom at the end of the corridor. It was the most nerve-racking walk she had made in her life. Her head was spinning as she thought back to that night. She knew they'd been careful, there had been wrappers on the floor to prove it. She couldn't be pregnant. *Could she?*

Sara already knew the answer. Of course she could. She and Tom made love and now she was taking a pregnancy test.

Sara returned to the consulting room with the sample. The doctor inserted the indicator strip into the jar and they both watched the strip.

It changed colour. It was very clearly blue. There was no doubting it.

Sara's head collapsed into her hands. 'How could this happen?'

The doctor turned and looked in earnest at Sara. 'A baby is not the end of the world, you know, but to make doubly sure I will request the qualitative HCG blood pregnancy test.'

Sara knew that was merely a formality. The strip result was very clear and this type of test was close to ninety-seven per cent accurate.

*She was pregnant with Tom's baby.*

'We have a pathology unit on hand in the practice to take your blood sample so you can have it done now and the result will come back tomorrow, but as you are already ten days late and with this positive urine analysis I think we can be quite positive that you are indeed pregnant. Although by your reaction I assume this is not something you are going to celebrate,' the doctor said with a sombre tone in his voice. 'There are options. You don't have to proceed with the pregnancy.'

Sara shook her head. 'No,' she answered. 'It's not how I had planned for it to happen but I will be having this baby.' She already loved her unborn child. It had been instantaneous. She loved the child because she loved its father. She knew that, no matter what happened, no matter how Tom reacted to this child, to his child, she would love it for ever and completely.

After the blood test was done, Sara left the consulting rooms in shock. Her heart was beating so fast she could barely breathe. *A baby?* It was a dream come true and terrifying at the same time.

How would she tell Tom? She knew he would be as shocked as her but, unlike her, he wouldn't find any joy in the news at all. Her heart began to beat a little faster and her stomach churned low with anticipation and dread. She knew she needed to tell him. She owed it to him. She paused her racing thoughts and realised it was perhaps not to him but more to the memory of what they had shared. And to finally make a stand. To stop hiding things from each other, no matter the consequences, and no matter what the state of their relationship. It might not be welcome news but he needed to be told the truth.

She also knew she needed time to adjust to the news. A few hours, a day, whatever it took to absorb the enormity of her situation. Her life would never be the same again. And Tom's life would be changed for ever when she told him. Wish as she might for Tom to be overjoyed at her news, there was really no question mark hanging over his reaction. He had made it clear he did not want a child under any circumstances, ever. He was adamant that he would never change his mind.

Sara was so confused. Her thoughts about the pregnancy, her new job in the US and, of course, Tom threatened to overwhelm her on the short trip home. There was so much to consider. Not just her feelings or Tom's, but this child had rights too. The right to know his or her father. Sara pulled into the driveway with her heart still racing.

Her mind was spinning with clashing thoughts as she climbed from the car. She suddenly felt quite faint.

'Sara, wake up,' Tom urged as he stroked her face with a damp hand towel.

Sara's eyes flickered open. She realised she was in her bed.

'What happened?' she asked.

'You tell me. I was inside and heard a thud and went outside to find you collapsed beside the car,' he told her, with his voice filled with concern. 'Are you okay now?' He carefully placed the hand towel on her forehead.

Sara stared at Tom in silence. The reason she'd fainted was not something she intended to share with Tom right now. She needed a little more time. It would only complicate his life and nothing positive would come from it, so she needed to plan how to break the news. She needed to let him know she would be okay no matter what his decision was. Sara knew he would see her pregnancy in a very different light from her.

She reached up for the hand towel, pulled it from her forehead and dropped it onto the bed as she sat up.

'I'm fine,' she replied. 'I did a lot of running around and probably didn't drink enough water. You know me, I have the world's lowest blood pressure on the best of days.'

Tom didn't know what to think but accepted her explanation. 'I'll get you a glass of water.'

'How did I get in here?' she called out. 'I thought you said I passed out by the car.'

Tom reappeared with tall glass of water. 'I carried you inside.' His face was completely serious as he handed her the water to drink. 'You should have a check-up, what with being so tired and now this. You need to get to the bottom of it. I appreciate you've always had low blood pressure, you function on a level that would have most people lying flat out in bed, but please get yourself looked at.'

Sara could see that the concern on his face and in his voice was genuine. But the real reason for her fainting would be too much for Tom to handle so abruptly. They had only just sorted through their complicated past and finally established a relationship free from blame or resentment. An announcement of her pregnancy, she suspected, would probably create both.

She would tell him about the baby. But now definitely wasn't the time.

Sara worked at the practice for the next two days, keeping busy and keeping her distance from Tom. It wasn't hard as his workload had increased steadily with the new student intake.

Sara lay in bed that night thinking about what could have been and the reality of what the pregnancy would mean in her life. She made plans in her mind. She would travel to Paris before she returned to Adelaide to live. When she returned, she would buy a small place in the eastern suburbs of Adelaide to be near to her family. She would work in the hospital or private practice and when she began to show she could say the baby was a result of a holiday romance. A fling with a handsome medico she'd met abroad.

Well, part of it was true at least. Tom was a handsome medico and they had shared a fling. It just hadn't happened in Paris this time.

It was about eight o'clock on Friday night when Sara realised she didn't have any milk. She was still exhausted and didn't want to drive to the grocery store so she thought she would ask Tom if she could borrow some. Warm milk before bed helped her to sleep through the night. She looked out into the drive but there was no sign of his car. Remembering the door between the houses, she found the key in the drawer and unlocked it from her side. She could replace the milk tomorrow.

Sara opened the door and stepped inside Tom's house, reaching for the light switch as she did so.

Immediately, she froze, her gaze falling upon all their old possessions. Everything they'd lived amongst as a married couple. Everything she'd assumed he'd discarded.

The chintz sofa and two matching armchairs. The Persian rug, another honeymoon purchase. The oval card table that was the centrepiece of his living room, an extravagant purchase that had been too lovely to leave in the antique shop in Ballarat on a weekend they'd spent in the country. Sara spun round in shock, her heart racing as she struggled to take in the whole room. Above the fireplace was the beautifully framed triptych print that Stu and Dana had given them for a wedding present, *The Pioneer* by Frederick McCubbin.

Sara roamed dumbfounded through the rest of the house and she found that nothing was missing. When her emotions got the better of her she collapsed into the soft depths of one of the armchairs. She picked up a small hand-painted vase from the tray mobile. Tears blurred her vision as she studied the delicate piece in her hand.

Never in her wildest dreams had she imagined that Tom would be so sentimental.

Being in the house was like stepping back in time.

Sara hadn't taken her belongings when she'd left. She'd thought it would have been too hard to live with pieces of furniture or ornaments that she and Tom had picked out together. Seeing it all now, she knew she had been right. The tears that had pricked at her eyes now flowed freely. It was a strange combination of sadness and regret. And unexpectedly a quiet happiness at being alone with the precious pieces that meant so very much to her and Tom. But, then, she realised, she wasn't alone. She was carrying their child.

Tom was mortified when he unlocked the door and found Sara sitting in the armchair, her head on her hand, as he walked inside.

Embarrassment fuelled his defence. 'What are you doing here?'

Sara quickly wiped her eyes on her sleeve in an attempt to hide her tears. 'I just wanted to borrow some milk.' Her voice was shaky as she felt swept back to the life they had once shared.

'I'm sorry, I didn't mean to upset you.'

After that neither said anything for a few moments.

Tom was trying not to see the sadness in Sara's eyes. He knew she would feel emotional being surrounded by all their past possessions. He had never expected her to see the house.

Sara just sat staring at Tom. There was so much she wanted to tell him, but so much she couldn't.

'Sara…' He broke off for a moment and tried to summon his thoughts. 'I haven't been living with all of this,' he said, gesturing to the furniture.

Her expression was puzzled as he spoke because she didn't understand.

He settled himself into the armchair opposite her and ran his hands nervously over the huge padded armrests. 'I don't live here. This is my spare place. This is where I store everything. For the last three years I've been living the other side, where you are now.'

Sara was even more confused. 'Then why didn't you say so earlier? Why didn't you let me move in here?'

'I felt embarrassed,' he admitted. 'I'd held onto all of this and you'd moved on. I thought you might think it peculiar of me to have kept everything, even after we were over. You didn't want anything when you left and for some strange reason I couldn't part with it.'

Sara sighed as she gently stroked the arms of the chair and then surveyed the room again.

'If you've changed your mind and want anything, please take it. It's yours to have, anything at all,' Tom said, interrupting her thoughts.

Sara bit her lip as she stopped herself from telling him that all she wanted in that room was him. Not furniture, or paintings or ornaments. Tom Fielding, the man, was all she ever wanted.

Tom wasn't sure how Sara felt. He knew she had plans he couldn't change but he hoped that for a while at least they could still keep in touch. He loved every minute he spent with her. That would never change. And until she met someone else, perhaps they could share more time together.

'I was thinking,' he began, as the awkwardness subsided. 'Maybe I could visit you in Texas over Christmas. That is, if you're not flying back to be with your family. But if you're over in a new country and wanting some company, I could check out America for a week or so. I'd have to renew my passport, but if you'd like to spend Christmas with me—'

'Stop it,' she cried out. 'Just stop.'

Sara felt her mind whirling very fast. The thought of Tom visiting and finding her six or seven months pregnant was too much to deal with. The room, Tom, the baby, it was all crashing in around her.

'You can't visit me.'

'Okay, okay,' he replied, in shock at her terse response. 'I just thought...'

Sara couldn't hold it in any longer. She hadn't wanted to tell him but everything came rushing out, and she found herself close to tears.

'You can't come over because I won't be in Texas at Christmas or ever. I'm not going there any more. I'm going back to Adelaide to be with my family. I'm moving home to live, permanently.'

Tom looked confused and worried. 'Are they all right? Is there something I should know?'

'Yes, Tom, there is something you should know...' Sara paused for a moment. Her heart was pounding, her stomach tightening by the second. Her world was suddenly and completely out of control as the words rushed from her lips. 'I'm pregnant, Tom. I'm having your baby.'

Tom slumped back in stunned silence. He had never thought he would hear those words from Sara. He had never thought he would hear those words from any woman. He had resigned himself to never being a father. His whole world had just changed in an instant. He was shocked to the core. Sara was having a baby. His baby. She was carrying their child. And he knew it would be a beautiful child if it was anything like Sara.

He wanted to rush over and pull her into his arms and kiss her and tell her it was the most wonderful news. But he couldn't. He had to fight his natural instinct, to resist the strongest desire to be with the mother of his child and to protect and love her. He couldn't do either. It wasn't wonderful news. Not to him.

'Aren't you going to say anything?' she asked, not totally surprised by his silence.

He walked over to the window and pulled back the curtains. He was shaking inside. From the moment he'd seen Sara in the restaurant that fateful night, he'd wanted to be with her more than anything he had ever wanted. And now, knowing she was having his baby, he wanted that even more. But he couldn't.

He wouldn't allow himself to share that joy, knowing Heath would never feel the same happiness. Now it wasn't just Sara he had to turn away from, he had to turn away from two people he loved more than life itself. And he hated it that he could never know his own child. They would never meet.

The street was lit by the amber lights and it gave a strange hue to the living room. Sara could see his hand clenching the curtain but still he said nothing.

'Tom, I'm not asking anything from you,' she said honestly, and in not much more than a whisper. 'I know how you feel and I can do this alone. You asked if there was something you should know. Well, there is and this is it. We're going to be parents but I can do it alone. I will move back to Adelaide and get a place near my family. I'll be fine. You don't have to have any part in our child's life, unless you want to.' She rested her hands protectively across her stomach.

He turned to look at her in silence. She was even more beautiful. Perhaps because she was pregnant, perhaps because it was just because he knew she was carrying *his* child.

Tom fought the urge to pull her to him. To wrap his arms around her and tell her that he would protect her for ever. To tell her that he would take care of her, and their baby. But he looked across at the woman who would hold his heart for ever and he knew it would go against everything he believed in. He needed to take responsibility for what he had done to his brother. That would never go away. It was the price he had to pay. And now it was the price they all had to pay. It wasn't fair. Sara and the baby were innocent of any wrongdoing.

His silence was making her feel more uncomfortable by the minute.

Finally he opened up. His soul was being ripped apart but his answer was unwavering. He was steeling himself to push her away. 'You know how I feel about having a child. I explained everything the other night, I opened up about Heath, about the accident, about everything, and you never said a word? Why not then? Why now? Why here in this room?'

Sara was taken aback by the barrage of questions. 'Because I didn't know.'

'And you're absolutely sure you're pregnant?'

'The HCG blood pregnancy test results came back positive three days ago.'

'And you waited this long to tell me?' he asked with confusion in his eyes. 'Three days and you said nothing. There were plenty of opportunities to let me know, Sara. What's different now?'

'Nothing, absolutely nothing. In fact, I wish I hadn't told you at all!'

Sara ran from his house into her bedroom, slamming the adjoining door shut and locking it behind her.

Tom stood in stunned silence. Alone. He was angry. So very angry with himself. For what he was doing to Sara. For the accident with Heath all those years ago. And now for being careless and allowing Sara to fall pregnant. For putting her in the position of having a child that he would never raise.

He knocked on her door.

'We need to talk about this properly. I can't talk to you from the other side of a door.'

He could hear the sound of muffled crying.

'Sara, we can work it out. I will cover the costs of raising the child, I will help in whatever way I can but I can't live with you and raise this child with you. I just can't be the child's father.'

Sara lay there, listening to the sound of Tom walking away. An overwhelming feeling of sadness engulfed her. One fateful night, when serendipity had brought them together, was now tearing them apart.

The next morning, without saying another word to Sara, Tom left for work early. He needed to keep his distance until Sara left. It was for the best.

He loved Sara with all of his heart. His feelings for

her were not in question. But he also knew he wanted more than anything to be the man she needed. To be the father of her child. Not just in name, or financial assistance, but to be the one holding her hand and wiping her brow when their child came into the world. The one to get up in the night and rock their restless baby back to sleep. To take him or her to their first day at school, to sport, to music lessons and everything that Sara had talked about. But he couldn't.

He knew that Sara would be a good mother. And he would ensure the child was provided for financially. The best school, the best medical care if it was needed, the best of everything. But nothing more. He could not be the father she wanted him to be.

He knew he had to let her go. In a few days she would be on a plane and starting a new life with their child. Without him.

# CHAPTER TWELVE

SARA DID NOT see or hear from Tom over the next two days. They had managed to avoid each other. She ate her dinner alone. She was leaving on an early evening flight the next day and this was the last night she would be in the house. Sara thought back to the times they had spent together, the tears and passion, the shared memories and professional admiration. The love. She had enjoyed being back in Tom's life, even though it had been only for a little while.

Tom's attitude was noble but cold. Telling her that he would take care of her financially. She didn't want any money from him. She would take care of herself and the baby very well on her own. Financial assistance wasn't what she needed.

But his skewed sense of responsibility wouldn't allow him to be a part of his child's life. The child they had created. The child she would carry for the next eight months. She was pregnant by the man she had loved for so very long and it should have been the happiest time in her life, but instead she was planning her life as a single mother.

But she didn't have time to throw a pity party for herself. She had to move on. And this time for good. No looking back. It would be months before she started to show. She could work until she was six months or even longer. She couldn't tell Marjorie about the pregnancy. She didn't want to explain any of it. She had one more day to work and then she'd be gone. One day of surgery. She had a short morning list and nothing scheduled for the afternoon. The theatre staff were clearly worried when she entered the scrub room.

'Is he operating with you?' the younger of the nurses asked, with wide eyes.

'Do you mean the other Dr Fielding?'

The girl nodded.

Sara shook her head.

The whole operating team gave a sigh of relief and started chatting happily.

'He was like a bull with a sore backside yesterday,' the senior nurse whispered into her ear, as she held the surgical gloves for Sara to slide her hands into. 'We've never seen him like this. No one wants to work with him.'

Sara looked over her shoulder but there was no sign of the man. She knew in her heart that there wouldn't be. Tom didn't want to see her again, let alone work with her.

'Hi,' came a friendly voice. 'Guess what? I get to assist you today. If that's all right with you? I mean, if you'd rather someone—'

Sara didn't have to turn round to know that Nigel was her assisting intern. 'Welcome to the team, Nigel,' she said, as they entered the theatre. For Sara it would be the last time.

The first patient on the list had impacted wisdom teeth. Confident her patient was under the effects of the anaesthetic, Sara began the routine procedure to remove the offending teeth and to suture and pack the sockets. Nigel assisted and took direction well. Sara considered him a competent young surgeon but working with Nigel couldn't come close to being in the surgery with Tom. She knew the comparison was unfair.

Tom had years of experience and Nigel was just beginning his medical career. But it was the way they knew each other's next move. The way Tom's skilled hands would work alongside hers as if their fingers were conversing. As if they shared a single thought. She pulled her gloves and cap free as she took a break following the first patient, just sitting quietly for a few moments. She felt tired but knew after the first trimester the fatigue would be more than likely to pass.

The morning went by without any problems. The cases were all straightforward and Sara was pleased with each and every result. Nigel was chirpy and eager to learn from her. They had finished the last by twelve and after changing into her street clothes and checking her patients in the high-dependency wards she said goodbye to the staff and was gone by one-thirty, heading home to collect her bags and catch her early evening flight in just over four hours' time.

With tears threatening to fall, Sara locked the front door to her home. Her eyes dropped to the crystal slipper in her trembling hand. With one foot nervously placed in front of the other, she took slow steps to his front door. Her chin quivered as she put the slipper and keys in a white envelope and laid it beside his doormat.

With knees bent, she broke down and slumped in tears at his door.

The sound of the taxi's horn brought her to her

senses. She wiped her eyes and slipped on her dark sunglasses. The sky was clear blue and, although it was cold, it was bright enough to warrant this disguise.

Sara had planned one stop before she left. She thought she owed Marjorie a goodbye and a thank you.

'I'll miss you,' Marjorie told her. 'Are you sure we can't change your mind about staying?'

Sara had managed to bring her breathing to a steady pace and control her emotions. She wanted to keep it that way.

'No. I'm afraid not. You see, I've made plans to see Paris and then set up a practice back in Adelaide. I miss my family and I think it's the right time to be with them.'

'I suppose Melbourne can't compete with the sights and sounds of Paris,' the woman conceded. 'When do you leave?'

'The plane leaves in just over four hours so I must go—'

'Have a good flight.' Tom's husky voice cut in.

Sara spun round to find him standing very close to her. She wanted to reach out and hold him, to touch his face and feel his arms around her. But he kept a distance between them and she did the same.

'I went home and found you'd left so I thought I'd come in and tidy up.' He took a step back as she turned and she knew better than to close the even bigger space he had created.

With tears moistening her cheeks, she looked across at the man she loved. Marjorie left them alone and busied herself in her office, closing the door behind her to give them privacy to say goodbye.

'I hope I've left everything in order.'

'I'm sure you have.' He said nothing about the tears, which he couldn't have missed.

'Take care, Tom.'

'You too, Sara, and if you need anything just call.' Tom wanted to hold her but he knew that it would break him. He would make a promise he couldn't keep, just so she would stay a little while longer. That would be selfish. 'I'll stay in touch and when the time comes I will provide you with whatever you need or want. I promise you.'

'I'll be fine,' she reassured him. But she wouldn't turn to face him. She didn't want to look into his deep grey eyes. It was over. Finally over. He clearly had no problem with her leaving.

She had no idea what she would be doing in a month. Except trying to start a life somewhere without him.

'Sara, you will never want for anything.'

*Except for a husband and a father*, she thought as she walked away.

Squaring her shoulders the way she had when she'd first arrived, Sara made her way to the door. She knew Tom was watching her. She willed him to chase after her and ask her to stay.

He didn't.

He let her go.

Tom stood by the window of his office, thinking about nothing but Sara. He had tried to distract himself with paperwork. It hadn't worked. So he'd walked to the window where he had been standing staring at the same static view for the best part of an hour.

It was worse, much worse, he decided, losing Sara

a second time. And now he wasn't just losing Sara. He was losing much more.

Sara would be raising a child who was a part of him. It tore at his heart that he wouldn't be there with them both.

Tom paced in front of the office window. He didn't want to think about Sara raising the child alone. He wanted to be with her. To hold her and their child every day for the rest of his life. He felt an aching regret for all he had said, and all he hadn't. How he had just let her leave. He couldn't live without her. But his brother weighed heavily on his mind too. He felt trapped.

Standing there alone in his office, Tom suddenly realised he couldn't do it. His heart was breaking. She deserved so much more. She deserved to be loved.

He had to stop her.

He couldn't and wouldn't let her go. Not this time.

He had to tell his brother. He had to face those demons from his past and apologise for the hurt he had inflicted. He had to admit his responsibility but tell Heath that now, after all these years, he had another responsibility that he would not walk away from. A far greater responsibility.

Tom finally realised that nothing he did would reverse the result of their actions as teenagers. Sara was right. He would let Heath know he was about to become an uncle and accept whatever Heath wanted to say, good or bad. He couldn't sacrifice Sara and the baby for the sake of a few brief moments that had gone terribly wrong so many years ago. Sara had told him she wouldn't make any more sacrifices, and he wouldn't let her.

He had too much to lose by letting Sara leave again.

He wouldn't do it. Not today or ever. He would tell Heath how very sorry he was about what had happened but that he refused to lose the love of his life because of his own unwillingness to put the past behind him.

Tom reached for the phone. He had to do it for his child, and for his wife. He was hurting the woman he loved. And he would hurt the child she was carrying if he didn't stop it now.

With trepidation he dialled the number in San Francisco. He knew it was late at night but he couldn't wait for a better time. There would never be a better time than now.

'Hello,' came Heath's voice down the line.

'Hi, brother, it's Tom.'

'Since I don't have any other brothers I'd guessed that one, old man,' Heath responded in a light-hearted tone. 'What can I do for you? Must be urgent to be calling at this hour.'

Tom didn't know where to start. His brother's joviality unnerved him further. He knew he was going to be delivering a blow and he wasn't sure how to begin. It was the hardest call he had ever made. The culmination of years of guilt and blame. Tom felt his chest tighten. He was about to tell a man who had been robbed of the chance of ever being a father that he was going to have a child with a woman he had always loved and would love for ever. A woman he could not let go. Tom's throat went dry before he spoke.

'Sara's pregnant.'

There was silence on the phone. Tom felt a cold sweat rush over him.

'God, that's got to hurt. I know you still love her, so

who's the lucky guy?' Heath said. 'Do you want me to help you take him out?'

'No, you don't need to take anyone out. It's me. I'm the father.'

There was silence again. Tom felt his stomach knot. He wasn't sure what reaction would follow.

'Awesome news. So you two are back together, then, I assume. I'm happy for you both. Congratulations!' Heath answered with elation colouring his sleepy voice. 'Sorry, Tom, I had to leave the bedroom. I'm not alone. Tory's here and I didn't want to wake her.'

Tom was surprised. Not that Heath had a woman there but that he'd never mentioned in previous calls that he was seeing anyone.

'It was one of those rare nights Tory's parents take the children so we get an uninterrupted night together and a lie-in tomorrow morning. That's a hint…don't call again unless it's an emergency.'

'Tory?'

'I'm sure I've mentioned her. We've been seeing each other for almost five months now.' Heath dropped his voice to not much more than a whisper. 'I'm going to ask her to marry me.'

Tom was stunned into silence. Happy for his brother but stunned into a mute.

'I'm the luckiest guy in the world!'

'I'm happy for you,' Tom began. 'But I never thought of you as lucky. Particularly after the accident…that I caused.'

'Tom, don't tell me you're not still harping on about that? For God's sake, man, that wasn't your fault. It was me, a bike and an asphalt BMX run.'

'I know what you're saying but I caused it.'

Heath's voice became a little louder. 'You can stop taking credit right here and now. I had, and still have, the power to exercise free will. I used it that day and I continue to use it every day. I chose a risky trick and it went wrong, but...' he paused '...that was my fault, with maybe some assistance from the universe. Just all-round bad timing.'

Tom felt the tightening in his chest loosen a little. 'But when the IVF didn't work...'

'And now you think you're to blame for my marriage breakdown?'

Tom nodded into the phone.

'You have been thinking way too much, little brother. I can't believe you've been stewing over all this. The marriage broke down because we were unhappy, unsuited and unhappy. We were trying to have a baby as a solution to a marriage with a million flaws. We stupidly thought a baby would be the glue to hold us together. That would have been the biggest mistake. I am so grateful it never happened. It would have been the child who paid the price in the end, living with two unhappy parents.'

Tom had had no idea. This was not what he'd expected to hear.

'And then I met Tory. The most wonderful woman in the world. Her husband was a marine. He was killed on a tour of duty in Iraq about three years ago. She's the best mother and just the most caring soul I could ever meet. And she doesn't want any more children. She had four. And it's a bonus that I don't have to have the vasectomy that she was going to ask me to undergo, until I broke the news about my fertility issues.'

Tom was elated beyond belief. Knowing his brother

was in a great place made his decision so much simpler. They were both in love with wonderful women.

'As much as I would love to chat, it's after midnight here so I am going to say goodnight now and call you tomorrow. We rarely get a night to ourselves so I'm not about to spend it on you,' he laughed. 'Please say big congrats to Sara and can't wait for you guys to meet Tory and the girls. I did tell you I'm going to be the step-father of four daughters, didn't I? I'm going to need a shotgun to keep the boys away if they are as gorgeous as their mum.'

With that he hung up, leaving Tom looking at the phone and wondering why he had wasted all this time.

He wasn't about to waste one minute more.

'I've been such a fool. An idiot of grand proportions,' he said to Marjorie as he rushed into the office and grabbed his car keys. 'You don't happen to know Sara's flight details, do you?'

'You're in luck. I overheard her call to the travel agent the other day and, being the busybody I am, I jotted it down,' she answered with a huge smile, as she pulled a scrap of paper from her pocket. 'It's flight three-five-two, gate seven, and hurry.'

He leant over, grabbed the paper and kissed her forehead on the way. 'Thank God you're a busybody.'

'Your ticket or booking confirmation, please, and your passport, Dr Fielding.'

Sara took a deep breath and reached for both from her carry-on luggage. Her travel agent had secured her a first-class ticket to Paris. *The city of love?* Sara knew that wouldn't be the case this time but it would fit her story perfectly. A fling that had resulted in a baby.

Perhaps she would say her lover was a diplomat and he'd been forced to return to his homeland; or a politician; or...or... Sara couldn't think properly.

She would make up a story that wouldn't cause a scandal or embarrass her child. Also one that wouldn't have her child hurting for a father who didn't want to be in their lives. She never wanted her child to know that Tom had let her go. He'd let the two of them leave his life. No child deserved to think they weren't wanted and loved.

Sara rubbed her temples as she waited for her boarding pass to be issued. There was so much to plan and consider.

Tom raced through the traffic, rechecking his watch every few minutes, hoping that he would make it before Sara boarded the plane.

'Last call for passengers on Qantas flight three-five-two for Paris. Now boarding at gate seven.' The voice echoed across the international airport lounge. It was Sara's flight. This was it. For the last two hours she had sat alone in the terminal, thinking about the last six weeks. It was supposed to be a quick trip to the embassy, then a month taking care of Stu's practice. How was she supposed to know that she was already pregnant with Tom's baby when she'd arrived?

Sadness wasn't consuming her any more. The ache in her heart was lessening. She had a new life to cherish and she was in love with the baby she was carrying. She felt blessed to be having a child by the man she loved, even if he wasn't going to be a part of their lives.

Although it wasn't sadness she felt for herself—she

felt sorry for Tom. He would never have any part in the life of the child she was carrying. None. He would miss out on so much joy. And love.

But she couldn't spend her life thinking about Tom Fielding. Not even another day. She had to accept what had happened and pretend that she didn't love Tom with all her heart. Until it was true. Until she had no feelings for him. She had to move on and raise their child.

There was no turning back. She knew it would be a very long time before she returned to Melbourne. She would visit Stu and Dana one day in the future but it would take time. Time to heal the wounds. Time to build a new life…with her child.

Her head down, she made her way slowly to the departure gate. Her boarding pass was in her hand, although her heart was still nowhere to be found.

'Sara,' a familiar voice called out across the departure lounge. 'Stop, don't get on the plane!'

Sara swung her head round but there was only a sea of unfamiliar faces. No one she recognised…until he appeared. Jostling his tall frame though the throng of people. It was Tom. Desperation in his eyes, he made his way over and pulled her into his strong arms.

'I'm so sorry,' he whispered. 'I love you and I was stupid for so long. But not stupid enough to let you go again.'

Sara was dazed. She had no more tears left.

'I want you and our child more than you can ever know. I've been a fool.'

He kissed her mouth and pulled her closer still.

'There's so much I need to tell you, but the most important thing is to ask you for forgiveness for the pain I have put you through. I have been so caught up in doing what I thought was right I've made even bigger mistakes. In trying to right an injustice to Heath, I committed an even greater injustice to you. I was a fool of the biggest kind.'

Suddenly Sara pulled herself free from his arms and stepped back away from him. She closed her eyes for a moment to try and gain some composure. 'Am I dreaming this? What are you doing, Tom? You chase me down and a minute before I fly away you tell me that you want me and our baby. Why? What's changed?'

'Me,' he said, with the conviction of man who knew where he wanted and needed to be. 'I've changed, Sara. I know I was stupid, putting principles before us. Before our happiness and the happiness of our child. I said that I needed to take responsibility for something that happened decades ago but I was letting you leave to bring up our child alone. That's not taking responsibility.

'What I did as a kid was reckless but to let you walk away, to never hold my child and tell him or her that they were wanted and loved would be far more irresponsible. I want you, Sara, I've always wanted you. And I want this baby, our baby, with all my heart.'

She looked at Tom and wanted so much to believe him but she didn't trust her heart. It had led her down the wrong path before.

'I've been living with a misplaced sense of guilt, and hurting you in the process. I was turning my back on the woman I love. I was driving you away. Please forgive me.'

She sat motionless for a minute, thinking about everything he had said, before she finally reached her hand across to his and nodded.

Sara looked into the eyes of the man she loved and

knew he was telling her the truth. He kissed her again, and again and again, and held her in his arms for the longest time. He was happier than he had ever thought possible.

Finally he picked up her carry-on luggage and holding her hand tightly in his own, they walked away from the departure gate.

Sara stopped suddenly again. 'How did you get here, into the international terminal, without a ticket?'

Tom held up a boarding pass. 'I organised a ticket to Paris on my way here. I thought it would give me twenty-something hours to convince you to come home with me.'

Sara kissed him with tears streaming down her face.

Tom slipped her crystal keyring into her palm and closed her trembling fingers around them.

'Just promise me, Cinders, that you'll never leave me again.'

'Cinders?' she said, with eyes still bright from her tears. 'You knew about the keyring?'

'I've always known, Sara. It was another reason why I loved you. But I always felt I let my side of your crazy fairy-tale down.'

'You could never let me down,' she cried. 'Unless you let me go.' She met his kisses and melted into his arms.

'Then I promise you, Sara Fielding, you will never be let down again.'

\* \* \* \* \*

# WEDDING AT SUNDAY CREEK

BY
LEAH MARTYN

Published in Great Britain 2014
by Mills & Boon, an imprint of Harlequin (UK) Limited,
Eton House, 18-24 Paradise Road, Richmond, Surrey, TW9 1SR

© 2014 Leah Martyn

ISBN: 978 0 263 90773 5

Harlequin (UK) Limited's policy is to use papers that are natural,
renewable and recyclable products and made from wood grown in
sustainable forests. The logging and manufacturing processes conform
to the legal environmental regulations of the country of origin.

Printed and bound in Spain
by Blackprint CPI, Barcelona

**Jack scrubbed a hand roughly across his cheekbones, reminding himself to get some eye drops. His eyes felt as though a ton of shell grit had been dumped there.**

He hadn't slept well. His thoughts had spun endlessly—and always centred on this waif of a girl sitting opposite him: Darcie Drummond.

But she wasn't a waif at all. That was just his protectiveness coming into play. And she wouldn't thank him for that. She was capable of taking care of herself. More than. OK. He'd better smarten up.

'Darcie, I need you on board with all these changes. Otherwise nothing's going to work for us in any direction, is it?'

His plea came out low and persuasive and Darcie felt relief sweep through her. What he said made sense. They couldn't afford to be offside with one another. Professionally, they were doctors in isolation. It was simply down to her and Jack to make things work. Otherwise she'd have to leave. And she definitely didn't want that.

## Dedication

For Claire, for professional insight
and delicious bubbly as we celebrate
the launch of my *twentieth* book for Mills & Boon.

# CHAPTER ONE

Dr Jack Cassidy, trauma surgeon, part-time explorer sometimes lover, stood away from the aeroplane, slowly absorbing the rich, bold colours of the Australian outback. And thought, unlike England, there was no elegant restraint out here. The colours were in-your-face heart-stopping and glorious.

He breathed in deeply, his eyes picking out the silhouettes of a family of kangaroos grazing in a nearby paddock. Big reds, he decided, feeling exhilarated by the sight. It felt good to be *home*. Added to that, he'd finally stepped away from the train wreck of a long-term relationship and felt freer than he had in months. Riding the upbeat feeling, he wheeled back towards the plane, where his luggage was waiting on the airstrip, and bent to pick up his bags.

The hospital was only a short walk away. He understood from his telephone interview that presently there was only one doctor at the Sunday Creek hospital, Dr Darcie Drummond. And that's where his knowledge of her began and ended. He just hoped Dr Drummond wasn't into role demarcation in the practice. If she expected him to just sit in his office and *administrate*, then she'd have to change her thinking.

Jack Cassidy intended to be a hands-on boss.

With the merest glance at her watch, Darcie decided it was time to go home. The hospital would call her if she was needed. Rolling her chair away from the desk, she stood and moved across to the window, looking out.

It was still hazy towards the west and she knew the grey bank of cloud in the sky was caused by intermittent bush fires. Nothing to worry about, the locals had assured her. It was the regular burning off of long grass or bushfire fuel and the rural fire brigade would have everything under control.

Darcie just hoped they did…

'Knock, knock.'

She spun round, several fronds of dark hair zipping across her cheekbones as her gaze swivelled to the open doorway. A man, easily six feet if she was any judge, and someone she didn't recognise, lounged against the doorframe.

Out of nowhere, every nerve in her body jumped to attention. Darcie blinked, registering blue eyes, dark hair, knife-edge cheekbones and a mouth that had her instantly imagining fantasies that only existed in her dreams. She swallowed dryly. 'Can I help you?'

'I sure hope so.' He gave a cool imitation of a smile. 'I'm your new medical director.'

*He had to be kidding.*

Darcie's disbelieving gaze ran over him. She wouldn't have expected a suit and tie but this guy looked as though he'd just come down from a Himalayan trek. He was wearing combat trousers and a black

T-shirt, his feet enclosed in hiker's boots that came up over his ankles.

He didn't look like a senior doctor at all.

At least, not the ones she was used to.

'I came on the plane,' he enlightened her. 'You weren't expecting me?'

'No—I mean, yes. That is, we knew you were coming, we just didn't know when.'

He rumbled an admonishing *tsk*. 'Don't you read your emails? I sent my arrival details through a couple of days ago.'

Oh, help. This was going to sound totally lame. 'Our computer's anti-virus protection has turned a bit iffy lately. It's culling messages that should be coming through to the inbox. And a tree fell over some cables yesterday, bringing the internet down. We do the best we can...'

Jack caught her cut-glass English accent and frowned a bit. What kind of a hospital was she running here? Or *attempting* to run. Switching his gaze from her heated face to the sign on her door, he queried, 'You *are* Dr Darcie Drummond?'

Almost defensively, Darcie pulled back from the intensity of his gaze and cursed the zing of awareness that sizzled up her backbone. How totally inappropriate, she admonished herself. And grief! She'd forgotten his name! 'Yes, I'm Darcie Drummond.' Moving quickly from the window, she offered her hand.

'Jack Cassidy.' He took her hand, easily enfolding it within his own.

Darcie took her hand back, almost shocked at the warmth that travelled up her arm. 'You must think this is all terribly unprofessional,' she apologised.

One eyebrow quirked above Jack Cassidy's extraordinarily blue eyes. 'Thought of getting someone in to check your computer?'

Of course they had. 'We're rather isolated here,' she said thinly, as if that should explain everything. 'Technical help is never easy. You just have to wait until they get to you.'

He made a click of annoyance. 'The hospital should have priority. You should be out there, kicking butt.'

Darcie bristled. She knew whose butt she'd *like* to kick! And she was puzzled as well. She'd read Jack Cassidy's CV. That information *had* actually come through on her email. He'd been working in London for the past year. Surely he hadn't drifted so far from his Australian roots not to realise their rural hospitals were chronically under-resourced?

'I take it you do have running water?'

Darcie's hackles rose and refused to be tamped down.

OK—he was taking the mick. She got that. But enough was enough. 'We draw water from the well outside,' she deadpanned.

Jack's smile unfolded lazily, his eyes crinkling at the corners. *Nice one, Dr Drummond.* He felt his pulse tick over. The lady had spirit. And she was a real looker. Working with her should prove...interesting.

He lowered himself onto the corner of her desk. 'I need to make a couple of phone calls, check in with the hospital board. Landline working OK?'

She sent him a cool look. 'Yes, it is.' She indicated the phone on her desk. 'Make your calls and then we'll see about getting you settled in.' With that, she turned and fled to the nurses' station.

And female solidarity.

* * *

Darcie palmed open the swing door and went through to the desk. 'He's here!'

Nurse manager Maggie Neville and RN Lauren Walker paused in mid-handover and looked up.

'Who?' Maggie queried.

Darcie hissed out the breath she'd been holding. 'The new MD.'

'Cassidy?' Maggie's voice rose a fraction. 'I didn't see anyone come through here.'

'He must have cut through the paddock and come in the back way,' Darcie said. 'He's in my office, now.'

'Oh, my stars!' Lauren's eyebrows disappeared into her blonde fringe. 'It must have been him I passed in the corridor. Big guy in combats, flinty eyes, *out there* sexy?'

Darcie nodded, her teeth meshing against her bottom lip. Lauren's description was OTT but Darcie supposed Jack Cassidy had come across as very…masculine.

Lauren snickered. 'I thought he must have been an actor come in for some treatment!'

Darcie and Maggie looked blank until Maggie asked, 'Why on earth would you think that?'

'Keep up, guys!' Lauren said, making a 'duh' face. 'There's a reality series being shot out at Pelican Springs station. The film crew and cast are living in a kind of tent city. I can't believe you didn't know.'

'All news to me,' Maggie said cryptically. She flicked a hand. 'With you in a minute, Darc. We're just finishing up the report.' Maggie went on to tell Lauren, 'Keep an eye on Trevor Banda, please. If that old coot is up and walking—'

'I'll threaten him with a cold shower,' Lauren promised cheerfully. She slid off the high stool. '*Ciao*, then. Have a nice weekend, Maggie.'

'Chance would be a fine thing,' Maggie muttered, before returning her attention to Darcie. 'So, we have a new boss at last. Someone to take the flak. What's he like?'

*Absurdly good looking.* Darcie gave a one-shouldered shrug. 'He seemed a bit...*strutty.*'

'You mean stroppy?'

'No...' Darcie sought to explain. 'Strutting his authority.'

'Throwing his weight around,' Maggie interpreted with a little huff. 'Well, we'll soon sort him out.'

'Maybe it's just me,' Darcie reconsidered, thinking she had possibly said more than she should about their new boss. 'He caught me unawares. I looked up and he was just...there.'

Maggie's look was as old as time. 'Six feet plus of sex on legs, was it? That's if we can believe Lauren.'

Darcie rolled her eyes and gave a shortened version of the missing email containing Jack Cassidy's arrival details. 'He didn't seem too impressed with us,' she added bluntly.

Maggie made a soft expletive. 'Don't you dare wear any of that rubbish, Darcie. You've been here. Done the hard yards when no other doctor would come outback. And how challenging was that for someone straight out of England!'

Darcie felt guilt a mile wide engulf her. Coming to work here had had nothing to do with altruism, or challenge. It had been expediency in its rawest form that had brought her to Sunday Creek.

She'd more or less picked a place on the map, somewhere Aaron, the man she'd been within days of marrying, would never find her. She knew him well enough to know he'd *never* connect her with working in the Australian outback.

It was that certainty that helped her sleep at night.

'I couldn't have managed any of it without you and the rest of the nurses,' Darcie apportioned fairly.

'That's why we make a good team,' Maggie asserted, picking up her bag and rummaging for her keys. 'I can hang about for a bit if you'd like me to,' she offered.

'No, Maggie, but thanks.' Darcie waved the other's offer away. 'Go home to your boys.' Maggie was the sole parent of two adolescent sons and spent her time juggling work, home and family. In the time Darcie had been here, she and Maggie had become friends and confidantes.

Although it was usually Maggie who confided and she who listened, Darcie had to admit. Somehow she couldn't slip into the confidences other women seemed to share as easily as the name of their hairdresser. 'I'll be fine,' she said now. 'And it'll be good to have a senior doctor about the place,' she added with a bravado she was far from feeling.

Jack was just putting the phone down when Darcie arrived back in her office. 'All squared away?' she asked, flicking him a hardly-there smile.

'Thanks.' He uncurled to his feet.

Taking a cursory look around her office, she moved to close one of the blinds.

'So, what are the living arrangements here?' Jack asked.

'The house for the MD is being refurbished at present, so you'll have to bunk in with the rest of us in the communal residence for now. At the moment, there's just me and one of the nurses.'

'That doesn't seem like a hardship,' he said, giving a slow smile and a nod of satisfaction.

Darcie felt nerves criss-cross in her stomach, resolving to have a word with the decorators and ask them to get a wriggle on. The sooner Cassidy was in a place of his own where he could strut his alpha maleness to his heart's content, the better. 'The flying doctors stay over sometimes too,' she added, making it sound like some kind of buffer. 'And now and again we have students from overseas who just want to observe how we administer medicine in the outback.'

He nodded, taking the information on board.

Darcie's gaze flew over him. She'd waited so long for another doctor. Now Jack Cassidy's arrival, the unexpectedness of it, seemed almost surreal. 'Do you have luggage?'

'There didn't seem anyone about so I stashed it in what looked like a utility room on the way through.'

'We've a small team of permanent nurses who are the backbone of the place.' Darcie willed a businesslike tone into her voice. 'Ancillary staff come and go a bit.'

He sent her a brooding look. 'So, it's you and the nurses most of the time, then?'

She nodded. 'The flying doctors are invaluable, of course.'

'Whoops—sorry.' Lauren jerked to a stop in the doorway.

'Lauren.' Darcie managed a brief smile. 'This is Dr Cassidy, our new MD.'

'Jack.' He held out his hand.

'Oh, hi.' Lauren was all smiles. 'You arrived on the plane and there was no one to meet you,' she lamented.

'There was a mix-up with emails,' Darcie interrupted shortly, fed up with the whole fiasco. 'Did you need me for something, Lauren?'

'Oh, yes. I wondered if you'd mind having a word with young Mitchell Anderson.'

A frown touched Darcie's forehead. 'I've signed his release. He's going home tomorrow. What seems to be the problem?'

'Oh, nothing about his physical care,' Lauren hastily amended. 'But he seems a bit…out of sorts for someone who's going home tomorrow.'

'I'll look in on him.' Darcie sent out a contained little smile.

'Thanks.' Lauren gave a little eye flutter aimed mostly at Jack. 'I'm heading back to the station. Yell if you need me.'

'What was your patient admitted for?' Jack asked, standing aside for Darcie to precede him out of the office.

'Snakebite.'

'You know, he may just need to talk the experience through.'

Darcie shrugged. 'I'm aware of that. I tried to find a bit of common ground and initiate a discussion about snakes and their habits. I knew Mitch would be able to tell me more than I could possibly know but he didn't respond. I'd actually never seen a case of snakebite,' she admitted candidly. 'But I know the drill now. Compression, head for the nearest hospital and hope like mad they have antivenin on hand.'

'Mmm.' A dry smile nipped Jack's mouth. 'Much

more civilised than in the old days. They used to pack the bite puncture with gunpowder and light the fuse. You can imagine what that did to the affected part of the body,' he elaborated ghoulishly.

If he was hoping for her shocked reaction, he wasn't going to get it. 'Pretty drastic,' she said calmly. 'I read about it in the local history section of the library.'

Jack flashed a white grin. Oh, she'd do, this one. Clever, cool and disarmingly sure of her ground as well.

It was a real turn-on.

Uh-oh. Mentally, he dived for cover. He'd just untangled his emotions from one relationship. He'd have to be insane to go looking for a replacement so quickly. But as they began to walk along the corridor towards the wards, the flower-fresh drift of her shampoo awakened his senses with a swift stab of want as incisive and sharp as the first cut of a scalpel.

# CHAPTER TWO

JACK YANKED HIS thoughts up short with a barely discernible shake of his head. He needed to get back into professional mode and quickly. 'Give me the background on your patient.'

'Mitchell is sixteen.' Darcie spun her head to look at him and found herself staring into his eyes. They had the luminosity of an early morning seascape, she thought fancifully. She cleared her throat. 'He works on his parents' property about a hundred kilometres out. He was bitten on Monday last.'

'So he's been hospitalised all this week?'

'It seemed the best and safest option. I'm still getting my head around the distances folk have to travel out here. If I'd released him too early and he'd had a relapse and had to come back in—'

'So you erred on the side of caution. I'd have done the same. Where was he bitten?'

'On the calf muscle. Fortunately, he was near enough to the homestead to be found fairly quickly and he didn't panic. His parents were able to bring him straight in to the hospital.'

'You don't think he could possibly be suffering from some kind of PTSD?'

Darcie looked sceptical. 'That's a bit improbable, isn't it?'

'It can happen as a result of dog bites and shark attacks. How's he been sleeping?'

'Not all that well, actually. But I put it down to the strangeness of being in hospital for the first time.'

'Well, that's probably true. But there could be another reason why he's clammed up.' Jack's lips tweaked to a one-cornered grin. 'He's sixteen, Darcie. His testosterone has to be all over the place.'

Darcie's chin came up defensively. Same old sexist rubbish. 'Are you saying he's embarrassed around a female doctor? I was totally professional.'

'I'm sure you were.'

She swept a strand of hair behind her ear in agitation. 'Perhaps I should try talking to him again.'

'Why don't you let me?'

'You?'

'I'm on staff now,' he reminded her. 'And your Mitchell may just open up to another male. That's if you're agreeable?'

Darcie felt put on the spot. He'd given her the choice and she didn't want to be offside with him and appear pedantic. And he was, after all, the senior doctor here. 'Fine. Let's do it.'

Jack gave a nod of approval. 'Here's how we'll handle it, then.'

Mitchell was the only patient in the three-bed unit. Clad in sleep shorts and T-shirt, he was obviously bored, his gaze only intermittently on the television screen in front of him.

Following Jack's advice, Darcie went forward. 'Hi,

there, Mitchell.' Her greeting was low-key and cheerful. 'Just doing a final round.'

Colour stained the youth's face and he kept his gaze determinedly on the TV screen.

'This is Dr Cassidy.' Darcie whipped the blood-pressure cuff around the boy's arm and began to pump. 'He's going to be spending some time with us here in Sunday Creek.'

'Dr Drummond tells me you crash-tackled a snake recently, Mitch.' Casually, Jack parked himself on the end of the youngster's bed. 'What kind was it?'

The boy looked up sharply. 'A western brown. They're deadly.'

'They're different from an ordinary brown, then?'

Almost holding her breath, Darcie watched her young patient make faltering eye contact with Jack. 'The western is more highly coloured.'

Jack flicked a questioning hand. 'How's that?'

'These guys aren't brown at all,' Mitchell said knowledgeably. 'They're black with a really pale head and neck. They're evil-looking. The guy that got me was about a metre and a half long.'

'Hell's teeth…' Jack grimaced. 'That's about five feet.'

'Yeah, probably. I almost peed in my pants.'

'Well, lucky you didn't do that.' Jack's grin was slow and filled with male bonding. 'I heard you kept your cool pretty well.'

Mitch lifted a shoulder dismissively. 'Out here, you have to learn to take care of yourself from when you're a kid. Otherwise you're dead meat.'

Over their young patient's head, the doctors exchanged a guarded look. This response was just what they'd hoped for. And it seemed that once started, Mitch couldn't stop. Aided by Jack's subtle prompting, he relaxed like a coiled spring unwinding as he continued to regale them with what had happened.

Finally Jack flicked a glance at his watch. 'So, it's home tomorrow?'

'Yeah.' Mitch's smile flashed briefly.

'What time are your parents coming, Mitchell?' Darcie clipped the medical chart back on the end of the bed.

'About ten. Uh—thanks for looking after me.' He rushed the words out, his gaze catching Darcie's for the briefest second before he dipped his head in embarrassment.

'You're welcome, Mitch.' Darcie sent him a warm smile. 'And better wear long trousers out in the paddocks from now on, hmm?'

'And don't go hassling any more snakes,' Jack joked, pulling himself unhurriedly upright. 'Stay cool, champ.' He butted the kid's fist with his own.

'No worries, Doc. See ya.'

'You bet.' Jack raised a one-fingered salute.

'Thanks,' Darcie said when they were out in corridor. 'You were right,' she added magnanimously.

'It's what's called getting a second opinion,' Jack deflected quietly. 'I imagine they're a bit thin on the ground out here.'

'Awful to think I could have sent him home still all screwed up.'

'Let it go now.' Jack's tone was softly insistent. 'You've done a fine job. Physically, your patient is well again. He's young and resilient. He'd have sorted himself out—probably talked to his dad or a mate.'

She gave an off-centre smile. 'And we can't second-guess everything we do in medicine, can we?'

'Hell, no!' Jack pretended to shudder. 'If we did that, we'd all be barking mad. Now, do you need to check on any more patients?'

She shook her head. 'I'm only next door anyway if there's a problem.'

'Good.' In a faintly weary gesture he lifted his hands, running his fingers around his eye sockets and down over the roughness of new beard along his jaw. 'So, we can call it a day, then? I need a shower, a shave and a cold beer, in that order.'

'Oh, of course. I should have realised...' Darcie forced herself to take a dispassionate look at him. There was no mistaking the faint shadows beneath his eyes.

A sliver of raw awareness startled her. The fact that suddenly she wanted to reach up and smooth away those shadows, slowly and gently, startled her even more. Especially when she reminded herself that, for lots of reasons, her trust in men was still borderline.

The staff residence was next door to the hospital with a vacant block in between. Like the hospital, it was of weathered timber with wide verandas positioned to catch the morning sun and to offer shade during the hot summers.

'Here we are.' Darcie opened the gate and they went in, the heady scent of jasmine following them up the front path.

'Hello, who's this?' Jack asked, as a blue heeler cattle dog roused himself from under the steps and slowly came to meet them.

Darcie dimpled a smile. 'That's Capone.'

'Because…?' Jack bent and stroked the dog between his ears.

'He seems to get away with everything.'

Jack chuckled. 'Is that so, chum?' The dog's black button eyes looked back innocently. 'He's quite old, then?' Jack had seen the sprinkling of white hair mottling the dog's blue-grey coat. He went on stroking. 'What's his story?'

'Apparently, he belonged to one of the old-timers of the district.' Darcie recounted the information as she'd heard it. 'He died here at the hospital and his dog wouldn't leave, wouldn't eat and just hung around.'

'So the staff adopted him?'

'Something like that. Naturally, he couldn't be kept at the hospital so gradually they coaxed him over here and he's seems content enough to stay.'

'You're a great old boy, aren't you?' Jack gave a couple of hollow thumps to the bony ridge of the dog's shoulders. He was a sucker for cattle dogs. They'd had some beauties on the farm when he'd been growing up.

'Well, he seems to have taken to you.'

'Seems to.' Jack's expression softened for a moment.

Darcie took a shallow breath, all her nerve ends twanging. What a very compelling picture they made—a big man and his dog… She beat back the sudden urge to reach for her phone and take a picture. How absurd. How sentimental. Shooting her sensible thoughts back in place, she said briskly, 'Let's go in, shall we?

'There are six bedrooms, all quite large,' Darcie said as they made their along the wide hallway. 'Our funding allows for some domestic help. Meg McLeish keeps everything ticking over. She's a real gem.'

Jack managed a polite, 'Mmm.' He didn't need this kind of detail but it was a female thing. He got that.

'You should be comfortable in here.' Darcie opened the door on the freshness of lemon-scented furniture polish.

Jack's gaze tracked over the room, taking in the king-sized bed, fitted wardrobes and bedside tables. 'This is great, Darcie. Thanks. I'll manage from here.'

Darcie took a step back. Was he was trying to get rid of her? Tough. She hadn't finished. 'There's a linen cupboard at the end of the hall where you'll find sheets and towels. Sorry there's no en suite bathroom. I think the place was built long before they were in vogue. But there are two bathrooms for communal use.'

Jack plonked himself on the edge of the bed. 'Darcie—' he held down the thread of impatience '—it's all fine, thank you.'

'OK…' Her teeth bit softly into her bottom lip. 'I'll leave you to it, then.'

He looked up sharply with a frown. Had he offended her somehow? She'd tilted her chin in a gesture he was beginning to recognise. He pulled himself upright again. 'I'll just get cleaned up.' His mouth tweaked into a wry grin. 'I promise I'll be more sociable then.'

'Fine.' Darcie spread her hands in quick acceptance and began backing away. 'Come out to the kitchen when you're through and I'll find you that cold beer.'

Barely twenty minutes later Jack joined Darcie in the kitchen. She turned from the window. 'You were quick.' Her eyes flicked over him. Cleaned up and dressed in jeans and a pinstriped cotton shirt, he looked…well, more like a senior doctor should look, she concluded a bit primly. Crossing to the fridge, she took out a beer from a six-pack and handed it to him. 'You Aussies seem a bit territorial about your brands. I hope you like this one.'

Jack barely noticed the label and twisting open the top he took a long pull. 'Right at this moment I'd settle for any brand as long as it was cold.' He hooked out a chair. 'Are you joining me?'

She gave a stilted smile. 'I have a glass of wine here.'

'What do we do about meals?' Jack indicated she should sit at the table with him.

'At the moment there's just Lauren and me.' Darcie met his questioning look neutrally. 'So it's all been a bit haphazard, depending what shifts she's on. We tend to just grab something from the hospital kitchen. But now you're here, perhaps we should get a better system going. Do a regular shop.'

'Sounds good to me.' He rolled back his shoulders and stretched. 'What about right now? I'm starved. What can the fridge yield up?'

'There's some watermelon and fudge,' Darcie deadpanned.

'OK,' Jack said with studied calm. 'I see you've covered all the essential food groups.'

Her spontaneous laugh rippled out, the action bringing her whole face into vivid life.

Instinctively, Jack swayed forward, staring at the sweet curve of her laughing mouth. And feeling something else. *Oh, good grief.* Instantly, he took control of his wild thoughts, anchoring his feet more firmly under the table.

Darcie tilted her head to one side. 'If we'd known you were coming—'

'You'd have baked a cake,' Jack rejoined, sitting up straighter.

'Or cooked a roast.'

He chuckled. 'So, you're telling me there's nothing in the fridge we can make a meal with. No leftovers?'

She shook her head.

'A remnant of cheese? A couple of lonely eggs?'

'Sorry.'

'What about the pub, then? Food OK?'

'Pretty good. And it's steak night, if that's what you want to hear.'

'Excellent.' He downed the last of the beer and got to his feet. 'Let's go, then, Dr Drummond. I'm shouting dinner.'

'We'll take my vehicle,' Darcie said. 'It's a bit of a step up to the town centre.'

'What do I do about getting a vehicle?' Jack asked as they walked over to her car.

'The local Rotary Club bought a new Land Rover for the MD's use. It's presently garaged at the hospital. OK if we sort all that tomorrow?'

'Yup.' Jack opened the car door, sat down and leaned back against the headrest, deciding any further conversation about the practice could wait.

It was a typical country pub, Jack observed, with a bar, a billiard table and a scattering of tables and chairs.

'There's a beer garden through there.' Darcie indicated the softly lit outdoor area. 'We just have to order at the bar first.'

'So, what would you like to eat?' He guided her to the blackboard menu. 'Uh—big choice, I see,' he said dryly.

'Steak and vegetables or steak and chips and salad.'

'I'll have the steak and salad,' Darcie said. 'No chips.'

'You don't like chips?' Jack pretended outrage.

'I like chips,' she responded, 'just not with every-thing.'

They ordered and were told there might be a bit of a wait. 'Let's have a drink, then,' Jack said. 'Another wine?'

She shook her head. 'Mineral water, I think.'

'OK. Me as well. I don't want to fall asleep.'

Darcie sent him a cool look. Nice to know he found her conversation so scintillating. Being Friday evening, the beer garden was crowded. 'Most folk are friendly here,' she said, returning greetings from several of the locals.

'And you've made friends since you've been here?' Jack asked as they made their way to a vacant table.

'It's been good,' she evaded lightly. 'You're getting well looked over,' she added, taking the chair he held for her.

'I'd better behave myself, then.'

'Will that be difficult?'

'I'm not given to dancing on tables, if that's what you're worried about.'

Darcie propped her chin on her upturned hand. 'I've never actually seen anyone do that.'

'I tried it once.'

'Were you drunk?'

'Are you shocked?' Jack's teasing smile warmed the space between them. 'Final interviews were over and I knew they'd offer me a place on the surgical training programme.'

She raised an eyebrow. Oh, to have such confidence. But, then, she reasoned, Jack Cassidy seemed to be brimming with it. She took a deep breath and decided to find out more about this man who had literally dropped out of the sky and was now to all intents and purposes her boss. 'So—where have you come from today?'

His mouth tipped at the corner. 'You mean by the way I was dressed?'

And his tan. 'Well, I didn't imagine you'd just arrived from London.'

'No.' He picked up his glass unhurriedly and took a mouthful of his drink. 'I've been trekking in New Guinea for the past couple of weeks. I did part of the Kokoda track. I always promised my grandfather I'd walk it for him one day. His battalion was stationed there in the Second World War.'

'So, it has some significance for Australians, then?'

He nodded. 'Our lads were heroes in all kinds of ways. I got some good pics of the general area and managed to run off some film footage too. Next time I see Pa, he'll be able to see how it is now, although it's many years on, of course.'

Darcie felt her heartbeat quicken. She guessed this was her opportunity to extend their personal relationship a little further, ask about his family. But somehow it all felt a bit...intimate. And he'd probably feel compelled to reciprocate, enquire about her family. And as yet she hadn't been able to go there in any depth—not even with Maggie. While she was still cobbling her thoughts together, her attention was distracted by the sight of one of the hotel staff making his way swiftly between tables, almost running towards them. Darcie jumped to her feet.

'What's wrong?' Jack's head spun round, his eyes

following her gaze. He sensed an emergency and shoved his chair back as he stood. 'Do you know him?'

Darcie's eyes lit with concern. 'It's Warren Rowe. He's the manager—'

'Thank God you're here, Darcie.' Warren looked pale and shaken. 'The chef—young Nathan—he's had an electric shock. We need a doctor.'

'You've got two!' Jack turned urgently to Darcie. 'Grab your bag! I'll do what I can for the casualty.'

'How long has he been down?' Jack rapped out the question as the two men sped along the veranda to the kitchen.

'Not sure. Couple of minutes at most.' Warren palmed open the swing doors and jerked to a stop. He swallowed convulsively. 'It was the electric knife—'

Jack's breath hissed through his clenched teeth and in a few strides he was at the chef's side. The young man was glassily pale, blue around the lips and, worse, he was still gripping the electric knife that had obviously short-circuited and thrown him to the floor.

'I used an insulator and switched off the current at the power point,' Warren said helpfully. 'What do you need?'

'What emergency equipment do you have?' Jack had already kicked the knife away and begun CPR.

'Defibrillator and oxygen.'

'Grab them. We'll need both.'

'Oh, my God—Nathan!' Darcie burst in, her horri-fied look going to the young man on the floor. Drop-ping beside Jack, she shot open her medical case. 'Any response?'

'Not yet. Run the oxygen, please, Darcie. I need to get an airway in.'

'I can do CPR.' Warren dived in to help.

'Defib's charging.' Darcie watched as Jack positioned the tube carefully and attached it to the oxygen.

'Breathe,' he grated. 'Come on, sunshine. You can do it!'

Darcie bit her lips together. With sickening dread she waited for some movement from Nathan's chest. Waited. And watched as Jack checked for a pulse. Again and again. The nerves in Darcie's stomach tightened. 'Shocking?'

'Only option,' Jack said tersely. 'Everyone clear, please.'

Nathan's young, fit body jerked and fell. Darcie felt for a pulse and shook her head.

'Dammit! Shocking again. Clear, please.' Jack's controlled direction seemed to echo round the big old-fashioned kitchen.

Come on, Nathan. Come on! Darcie willed silently. And then…a faint jiggle that got stronger. 'We have output,' she confirmed, husky relief in her voice.

Jack's expression cleared. 'Good work. Now, let's get some fluids into this guy.' He looked up sharply. 'Has someone called an ambulance?'

'We're here, Doc.' Two paramedics stepped through with a stretcher.

Darcie looked up from inserting the cannula to receive the drip. 'Say hello to Dr Jack Cassidy, guys.' Relief was zinging through her and she gave rein to a muted smile. 'He's the new boss at the hospital—only been here a few hours.'

'And already saved a life, by the look of it. Zach Bayliss.' The senior paramedic held out his hand. 'My partner, Brett Carew.'

A flurry of handshakes ensued.

Nathan was loaded quickly. 'We'll see you across at the hospital, then, Doc?' Zach confirmed.

'We'll be over directly.' Jack turned to Warren. 'You should disconnect all power until it's been checked by the electrical authority. You might have other dodgy gear about the place.'

'Will do, Doc. Hell, I don't ever want to see a repetition of this…'

Jack looked around the kitchen. 'This will stuff up your meal preparation. Do you have a contingency plan?'

'We do. As it happens, we'd planned to put wood-fired pizzas on the menu tomorrow so we started up the brick oven for a trial run this afternoon. It's still going strong. We'll have a line of pizzas going in no time.'

Jack gave a rueful grin. 'You couldn't send a couple across to the residence, could you, mate? We still haven't have had dinner.'

'Yeah, absolutely. No worries.' Warren flicked a hand in compliance. 'On the house, of course. And thanks, Doc. Mighty job with Nathan.'

Jack waved away the thanks and they walked out together.

'Right to go, then?' Darcie had tidied up the medical debris and was waiting on the veranda.

Jack nodded and they went across to her car.

'Nathan didn't appear to have any fractures,' she said. 'But he must have landed with an almighty thump.'

'I'll check him thoroughly in Resus. Do you know if he has family to be notified?'

'Not sure. But Warren will have got onto that.'

Jack sent her a quick, narrow look. 'He said it was

your initiative to have both the defib and oxygen located at the pub. Well done, Dr Drummond.'

'I was just being proactive.' Darcie shrugged away his praise. 'There's always a crowd in the pub at the weekends. Accidents happen. The odd nasty punch-up. Even a couple of heart attacks while I've been here. Having the defibrillator and the oxygen on site seemed a no-brainer. And the staff at the pub all have first-aid knowledge.'

'Down to you as well?' Jack asked.

'And our nurse manager, Maggie Neville. You haven't met her yet.' Darcie gave a small chuckle. 'I think she could run the place if it came to it.'

'Good.' Jack stretched his legs out as far as they would go. 'Nice to have backup.'

A beat of silence.

'I was very glad to have *your* backup this evening, Jack.'

Jack felt an expectant throb in his veins. What was this? A tick of approval from the very reserved English doctor? And unless he was mistaken, her husky little compliment had come straight from her heart.

# CHAPTER THREE

WHEN THEY PULLED into the hospital car park, Jack said, 'I can take over from here, Darcie. Go home. I'm sure you've more than earned a night off.'

She made a small face. 'If you're sure?'

'More than sure. I'm pulling rank, Doctor. You're officially off duty.'

'Thanks, then.' Darcie felt the weight of responsibility drop from her. 'I'd actually kill for a leisurely bath.'

'And dinner's on its way,' Jack confirmed, as he swung out of the car. 'Warren's sending over pizzas.'

Lauren stood with Jack as he made notations on Nathan's chart. 'How's he doing?' she asked quietly.

'He has entry and exit burns on his left hand and right foot. It's obviously been a serious shock. We'll need him on a heart monitor for the next little while.'

'He's coming round.' Lauren looked down at her watch to check the young man's pulse. 'You're in hospital, Nathan,' she said as Nathan's eyes opened. 'You've had an electric shock. This is Dr Cassidy.'

'Take it easy, Nathan.' Jack was calmly reassuring. 'This contraption here is helping you breathe.'

Nathan's eyes squeezed shut and then opened.

'Pulse is fine,' Lauren reported.

'In that case, I think we can extubate.' Jack explained to their patient what he was about to do. 'You're recovering well, Nathan, and there's an excellent chance you'll be able to breathe on your own.' He turned to Lauren. 'Stand by with the oxygen, please, but let's hope he won't need it.'

Lauren noticed the surgeon's hands were gentle. Mentally, she gave him a vote of approval. In her time she'd seen extubations carried out with all the finesse of pulling nails with a claw hammer.

'I want you to cough now, Nathan,' Jack said as the tube was fully removed. 'Go for it,' he added, as Nathan looked confused. 'You won't damage anything.'

Nathan coughed obligingly.

'OK, let's have a listen to your chest now.' Jack dipped his head, his face impassive in concentration. 'Good lad.' He gave a guarded smile. 'You're breathing well.

'Thanks, Doc.' Nathan's voice was rusty. 'Guess I've been lucky. When can I get out of here?'

'Not so fast, mate.' Jack raised a staying hand. 'You've had a hell of a whack to every part of your body. We'll need to monitor you for a couple of days.'

Nathan looked anxious. 'My job—'

'Is safe,' Jack said firmly. 'Warren will be in to see you about that tomorrow. In the meantime, I want you to just rest and let the nurses take care of you.'

'And we do that very well.' Lauren gave the young man a cheeky smile. 'Fluids as a matter of course, Doctor?'

'Please.' Jack continued writing on Nathan's chart. 'Call if there's a problem, Lauren. I'll be right over.'

'Will do. Good to have you on board, Jack,' Lauren said as they walked out.

Jack pocketed his pen and then turned to the nurse. 'What time do the shops come alive here in the mornings?'

'Depends what you need.' A small evocative smile nipped Lauren's mouth. 'There's a truckers' café that opens about five-thirty, supermarket and bakery about six, everything else around eight-thirty-ish.'

'Thanks for the heads-up.' Jack acknowledged the information with a curt nod and strode off.

'This is fantastic!' They were eating pizza straight from the box and Jack pulled out a long curl of melted cheese and began eating it with exaggerated relish. 'Why the look, Dr Drummond?' He gave a folded-in grin. 'You didn't expect us to stand on ceremony and set the table for dinner, did you?'

Darcie took her time answering, obviously enjoying her own slice of the delicious wood-fired pizza. 'I thought the present state of the fridge would have proved I'm no domestic goddess.'

'Who needs *them*?' Jack wound out another curl of cheese. 'Do you want the last piece?'

Darcie waved his offer away and got to her feet. 'I found some raspberry ripple ice cream in the freezer. Fancy some?'

Jack shook his head. 'No, thanks.'

'Cup of tea, then?'

'Any decent coffee going, by any chance?'

'There's some good instant. Near as we get can to the real stuff out here.'

'Perfect.' Jack got up from the table and moved across to the sink to wash his hands. Drying them on a length of paper towel, he moved closer to look over her shoulder as she reached up to get mugs from the top cupboard. 'Turned out all right, then, didn't it?' His voice had a gruff quality. 'Our impromptu dinner, I mean.'

He was very close and Darcie felt warning signals clang all over her body. The zig-zag of awareness startled her, unnerved her. With her breathing shallower than usual, she said, 'It was great.' She took her time, placing the mugs carefully on the countertop as though they were fine china, instead of the cheerful, chunky variety from the supermarket.

'So, Darcie…' Jack about-turned, leaning against the bench of cupboards and folding his arms. 'Do you think we'll rub along all right?'

She blinked uncertainly. In just a few hours Jack Cassidy had brought a sense of stability and authority to the place, his presence like a rock she could hang onto for dear life.

Whoa, no! Those kinds of thoughts led to a road with no signposts and she wasn't going there. The water in the electric jug came to boiling point and she switched it off. 'We'd *better* rub along,' she replied, ignoring the flare of heat in his eyes and waving light-hearted banter like a flag. 'We're the only doctors for hundreds of miles. It won't do much for morale if either of us stomps off in a hissy fit.'

Jack gave a crack of laughter. 'Do male doctors have hissy fits?'

'Of course they do! Especially in theatres.' She made the coffee quickly and handed him his mug. 'They just call it something else.'

'Thanks.' Jack met her gaze and held it. She had the most amazing eyes, he thought. They were hazel, coppery brown near the pupils, shading to dark green at the rims. And they were looking at him with a kind of vivid expectancy. 'I suppose men might have a rant,' he suggested.

'Or a tirade?'

'A meltdown?'

'Ten out of ten. That's an excellent analogy.' She smiled, holding it for a few seconds, letting it ripen on her face and then throwing in a tiny nose crinkle for good measure.

*Hell.* Jack felt the vibes of awareness hissing like a live wire between them. Enough to shift his newly achieved stable world off its hinges.

But only if he let it.

Lifting his coffee, he took a mouthful and winced, deciding he'd probably given his throat full-thickness burns. He had to break this proximity before he did something entirely out of character.

*And kissed her.*

'Uh…' His jaw worked a bit. 'Let's grab what's left of the evening and take our coffee outside to the court-yard.'

Darcie looked surprised but nevertheless picked up her mug and followed him. 'I'll just turn on the outside light,' she said. 'We don't want to break our necks in the dark.'

'There's plenty of moonlight.' Jack looked around him as they sat at the old wooden table. The smell of jasmine was in the air. It twisted around a trellis at least six feet high. 'I guess this place would have a few stories to tell,' he surmised.

'Probably.' Darcie took a careful mouthful of her coffee.

Tipping his head back Jack looked up, his gaze widening in awe at the canopy of stars, some of which looked close enough to touch, while myriad others were scattered like so much fairy dust in the swept enormous heavens. So very different from London. 'You're a long way from home, Darcie.'

Darcie tensed. She'd expected the question or something similar but not quite so soon. For a heartbeat she was tempted to lower her guard and tell him the plain, unvarnished truth. But to do that would make her feel vulnerable. And perhaps make *him* feel uncomfortable, or worse even—sorry for her. And she so did not want that from any man. 'This is Australia.' She feigned nonchalance with an accompanying little shrug. 'So I imagine I must be a long way from home. But this is *home* now.'

Jack heard the almost fierce assertiveness in her voice. OK, he wouldn't trespass. Darcie Drummond obviously had her ghosts, the same as he did. But he liked to think he'd laid his to rest. On the other hand, he had a feeling young Dr Drummond here appeared to be still running from hers.

'So, tell me a bit about Sunday Creek,' he said evenly. 'No GP here, I take it?'

'Not for a long time. Anyone with a medical problem comes to the hospital.'

'So we take each day as it comes, then?'

'Yes.' She smiled into the softness of the night. 'I've treated a few characters.'

He chuckled. 'It's the outback. Of course you have.' With subtlety, he pressed a little further, determined to get to know her better. 'Any one instance stand out?'

'Oh, yes.' She smiled, activating a tiny dimple beside her mouth. 'Pretty soon after I'd arrived here I had a call out to one of the station properties. There'd been an accident in the shearing shed. I was still at the stage of being wide-eyed with wonder at the size and scope of everything.'

'That figures.' Jack tilted his head, listening.

'When I stepped inside the shearing shed I was thrown with the hive of activity. I'm sure I must have stood there gaping, wondering where to go or whom I should speak to. Then one of the men bellowed, "Ducks on the pond!" and suddenly there was this deathly kind of silence.'

Jack's laughter rippled.

Darcie pressed a finger to her lips, covering an upside-down smile. 'You know what it means, of course?'

'Yep.' He shot her a wry half-grin. 'It's simply short-hand for, "Mind your language, there's a lady present."'

'I had to ask Maggie when I got back to the hospital,' Darcie confessed. 'But the men were very kind to me and, fortunately, the emergency was only a case of a rather deep wound that needed suturing. I stayed for morning tea in the shed. I think I managed OK,' she added modestly.

'From the sound of it, I'd say you managed brilliantly.' In the moonlight, Jack's gaze softened over her. She was gutsy and no slouch as a doctor. He already had proof of that. He wondered what her story was. And why she'd felt the need to practise her skills so far from her roots.

Leaning back in his chair, he clasped his hands behind his head. 'I'll cover the weekend. I want you to have a break.'

'Oh.' Darcie looked uncertain. 'Shouldn't I hand over officially?'

'We can do that *officially* on Monday. Meanwhile, I'll get a feel for things in general, talk to a few faces.'

'I won't know what to do with myself...' The words were out before she could stop them.

'Have some fun,' Jack suggested. 'See your friends.'

He made it sound so simple—so normal. And it would look pathetic if she hung around the house for the entire weekend. Her brain quickly sorted through the possibilities. She supposed she did have a couple of friends she could visit—Louise and Max Alderton. They lived on a property, Willow Bend, only ten miles out. Louise was on the hospital board and somehow had sensed Darcie's need for a no-strings kind of friendship.

She could give Lou a call now. She'd still be up. See if it was OK to visit. Maybe they could go for a ride...

'OK. I'll do that. Thanks.'

Next morning, Darcie couldn't believe she'd slept in. If you called seven-thirty sleeping in, she thought wryly, sitting up to look out at the new day. The sun had risen, the temperature climbing already. Blocking a yawn, she stretched and threw herself out of bed. She had a holiday.

And she'd better remember there was a man in the house. Slipping into her short dressing gown, she sprinted along the hallway to the bathroom.

As she dressed, Darcie sensed something different about the place. A feeling of the house coming alive. And there was a delicious smell of grilling bacon coming from the kitchen.

And that could mean only one thing. Jack was up

and around and amazingly he must be cooking breakfast. She hoped he'd made enough for two because she intended joining him.

As she made her way along the hallway to the kitchen, her newly found confidence began faltering. Perhaps she was being presumptuous. She didn't expect Jack to feed her. She really didn't.

But already her preconceived ideas about him had begun falling like skittles. He wasn't *strutty*—just competent. And from what she'd observed, he seemed straightforward and she liked that. If he'd only made breakfast for one, then he'd tell her so.

She paused at the kitchen door, ran her tongue around the seam of her lips and said, 'You're up early.'

Busy at the cooker top, Jack turned his head and gave her a casual 'Morning. How do you like your eggs?'

'Um...' Darcie's mouth opened and closed. 'Scrambled, I think.' She joined him at the stove. He was turning sausages and the bacon was set aside in the warming oven.

'Me too.' He gave her a quick smile. 'Will you do that while I watch these guys?'

'Yes, sure.' She looked around and saw a pile of groceries had been unloaded onto the benchtop. 'Have you been to the supermarket already?'

'I was awake early,' he said. 'Thought I'd do a quick swoop. I borrowed your car. I hope that's all right?'

'Of course.' Darcie searched for a bowl and began cracking the eggs. 'You must let Lauren and me pay for our share of the groceries.'

'We can talk about that later,' Jack dismissed. 'Tomatoes for you?'

'Yes, please.' Darcie's mouth began to water. All

this home cooking was beginning to heighten her taste buds. 'And I'll make some toast. Did you get bread?'

'I did. The baker had his front door open a crack. I gave him a shout, introduced myself and he obligingly sold me a couple of loaves.'

'That'll be Jai.' Darcie found the wholemeal loaf and hacked off a couple of slices. 'He and his wife, Nikki, relocated from Thailand. He makes gorgeous bread.'

Jack piled the cooked sausages onto a plate. 'Should we keep some of this food for Lauren?'

'Uh-uh. She'll sleep for ages. And she's vegetarian anyway.'

'Oh—OK. Good for her,' Jack said, though he sounded doubtful. 'We won't have continuous tofu to look forward to, will we?'

Darcie chuckled. 'Tofu is the new meat. But she's more a risotto person. Although she does a great grilled halloumi and courgette salad.'

'You mean zucchini? Well, that sounds all right, as long as there's a nice T-bone steak to go with it,' he said with wry humour. 'This is about ready. Should we tuck in?'

'I'll get the plates.'

'I hope it's up to scratch,' he said.

'Oh, it will be.' Darcie was adamant. 'You seem like an amazingly good cook.'

'I was reared on a cattle property,' Jack said, as they settled over their meal. 'We all had to learn to throw a meal together, especially at mustering time. If you were given kitchen duties, you had to have something ready to feed the troops or risk getting a kick up the backside. Sorry...' His mouth pulled down. 'That sounded a bit crass.'

'Not at all.' Darcie dismissed his apology. 'So, are there a lot of you in the family?'

'I'm the eldest of five. Two brothers, two sisters. I recall some pretty rowdy mealtimes.'

And he made it sound so warm and wonderful. Darcie felt the weight of her own solitary childhood sit heavily on her shoulders. Meals on your own didn't have much going for them. But that was her *old* life. She shook her head as if to clear the debris and firmly closed the lid on that particular Pandora's box. She drummed up a quick smile. 'So, happy childhood, then?'

'Mmm.' Jack hadn't missed the subtlety of her mood change or her quickly shuttered look. But he didn't want to be stepping on any of her private landmines. One thing he did know, he'd shut up about his happy childhood.

'So, what are your plans for today?' He'd already noticed her boots, jeans and soft white shirt.

'I'm going riding.' She filled him in about the Aldertons and Willow Bend. 'You'll probably meet Lou sooner rather than later. She's on the hospital board and a great innovator.'

'Excellent. As the sole MOs for the entire district, we need all the help we can get.'

They batted light conversation around for the rest of the meal.

'You'll find a set of keys for your use at the nurses' station,' Darcie said, as they finished breakfast and began clearing the table. 'Including those for your vehicle.'

'Thanks.' He bent and began stacking the dishwasher.

Darcie blinked a bit. Heavens, he really was house-trained. 'Natalie Britten will be the RN on duty and with a bit of luck a couple of our ancillary staff should turn up as well. There's a list of numbers to call if there are any staffing problems.'

'You like all your ducks in a row, don't you?'

Darcie's chin came up. 'We're running a hospital,' she countered. 'We have to make some effort for things to be orderly.'

'That wasn't my first impression.' He smiled then, a little half-smile that seemed to flicker on one side of his lips before settling into place.

'A tiny glitch.' Darcie shrugged away his comment. 'I think you enjoyed surprising us.'

'Perhaps I did.' He considered her for a long moment. 'Will you be home tonight?' Oh, good grief! He squirmed inwardly. He'd sounded like her *father*!

Darcie looked up warily. Was he enquiring whether she had a boyfriend who might be wanting to keep her out all night? Well, let him wonder about that. 'Yes, I'll be home. But I may be late.'

Jack closed the door on the dishwasher and stood against it. 'Have a good day, then.'

'I shall.' She hovered for a moment, pushing her hands into the back pockets of her jeans. 'Thanks for this, Jack. The day off, I mean.'

He shrugged. 'You're probably owed a zillion.'

'If there's an emergency…'

He sent her a dry look. 'If I need you, I'll call you. Now scoot.' He flicked his fingers in a shooing motion. 'Before I reassign you.'

She scooted.

Jack wandered out onto the veranda, the better to take in the vibe of his new surroundings. Leaning on the timber railings, he looked down at the wildly flowering red bottlebrush. The hardiest of the natives, it simply produced more and more blossoms, regardless of the vagaries of the seasons.

Raising his gaze, he looked out towards the horizon. There was a ribbon of smoke-laden cloud along the ridge tops. So far it obviously wasn't a cause for concern. He hoped it stayed that way...

The clip of Darcie's footsteps along the veranda interrupted his train of thought. He swung round, a muscle tightening in his jaw, an instinct purely male sharpening every one of his senses. She'd gathered up her hair and tied it into a ponytail and she'd outlined her mouth with a sexy red lipstick.

His heart did a U-turn. His male antennae switched to high alert. Hell. This was right out of left field.

He fancied her.

Darcie stopped beside him, dangling her Akubra hat loosely between her fingers. 'Taking in the scenery?' Her quick smile sparkled white against the red lipstick.

'Just getting acquainted with the possibilities.' *And wasn't that the truth.*

'Good,' she said lightly, and proceeded down the steps. At the bottom she turned and looked back. 'Don't wait up.'

Cheeky monkey. Jack dipped his head to hide a burgeoning grin and countered, 'Don't fall off.'

Then, with something like wistfulness in his gaze, he watched as she reversed out of the driveway and took off.

His hands tightened their grip on the railings, some part of him wanting to rush after her, flag her down.

And spend the entire day with her.

# CHAPTER FOUR

DARCIE HALF WOKE to the sound of knocking on her bedroom door. For a few seconds she struggled to open her eyes, calling groggily, 'Who is it?'

'It's Jack. Can you come to the door, please? We have an emergency.'

Jack? Jack…? Darcie closed her eyes again.

Hell, what was she doing? Jack glanced at his watch. He rapped on the door again. 'Wake up, Darcie! I need to speak to you!'

Jack! Oh, good grief! Darcie sat bolt upright as reality struck. Throwing herself out of bed, she padded over to the door. 'What time is it?' She blinked up at him.

'Five o'clock—' He stopped abruptly. She was pulling on a gown over a short ruby-red nightie, her breasts moving gently beneath the silk. *Hell.* His breath jagged in his throat. He stepped back and blinked. 'Uh— we have an emergency out where some kind of film is being shot. Do you know about it?'

'Not really. Lauren mentioned it. What's happened?'

'Apparently two of the actors have fallen into a disused well. The message the ambulance got was pretty garbled. But they've asked for medical backup. I'm sorry to disrupt your sleep-in but I think this needs both of us.'

'OK…' Darcie pushed the heavy fall of hair back from her cheek. 'Give me a few minutes.'

'I'll meet you out front. Don't mess about.'

Darcie made a face at the closing door. She pulled on jeans and T-shirt and pushing her feet into sturdy trainers she sprinted to the bathroom.

Armed with a couple of trauma kits from the hospital, they travelled in Jack's Land Rover. 'I've spoken to Mal Duffy, the police sergeant,' Jack said. 'He's given me directions to the site. It's about forty Ks.'

'So, apart from the ambulance, who's in on this jaunt?'

'The state emergency service.'

Darcie nodded. She was well acquainted with the SES and their dedicated volunteers. 'Mal heads up the local SES. Their vehicle with the rescue gear is kept at the police station but he'll have to try to get a team together. At this early hour on a Sunday, it could be difficult.'

Jack raised an eyebrow, seeming impressed with her local knowledge. 'In that case, we'll just have to wing it until they get there.'

'Why on earth would they be filming so early?' she wondered aloud.

'Maybe they wanted to catch a special effect with the light.'

She glanced at him sharply. 'You know something about making films, then?'

'Oh, yeah.' He gave a hard, discordant laugh. 'My *ex* is an actress.'

For a moment his words formed an uncomfortable silence between them. Darcie glanced at his profile but it told her nothing. Was he sad or mad or both? 'Ex-*wife*?'

'No.' He paused infinitesimally. 'We didn't get that far. We'd been together for three years. But our jobs took us in different directions. In the end, the relationship proved unworkable.'

Of course, it hadn't helped that when he'd got to England, where Zoe had been filming, she'd found someone else. He swallowed the residue of bitterness. His ego had taken a hard kick, but life moved on. And thank heaven for that.

'I guess relationships are tricky at the best of times,' Darcie responded quietly. 'Do you have any idea what size this well might be?' She changed conversation lines tactfully.

'Going by my acquaintance with wells, I'd guess six by six in the old measurements.'

'So—the size of a small room,' she said consideringly.

Jack took his eyes off the road for a second to look at her. 'Any problems with confined spaces?'

'I've done a little caving…' Darcie recognised the flutter of uncertainty in her stomach. 'I don't know how that equates with going down into a well.'

'Only one way to find out,' Jack said. 'It'll be dark inside and there'll probably be rubble at the bottom. And I mean anything from rocks to old furniture. Usually, when a well is closed, some effort is extended to part fill the hole to make it less of a hazard. We'll need to look out for rats as well.'

'Rats?' Darcie suppressed a shudder. 'I hope they're dead ones and long gone.' A frown touched her forehead. 'It's daylight pretty early these days—how come they wouldn't have known the well was there?'

'I doubt it would have been used for years, and it's possible that some attempt would have been made to cover it over.'

'Well, whatever they did hasn't been good enough. Why wouldn't they build a roof or something?'

'A roof!' Jack hooted. 'You've still a lot to learn about life in the Australian bush, Darcie. Our graziers have to make the best use of their time to stay viable. They can't go around erecting a roof over every well they close. More than likely, they would have chucked some logs across the top. But with time they'll have become overgrown, which will have only served to camouflage the rotting wood beneath.'

'And there you have an accident waiting to happen,' Darcie concluded.

'By George, she's got it!'

Darcie gave an exaggerated eye roll. 'How much further, do you think?'

'Hmm...ten Ks possibly.'

'I hate this part of being a doctor out here,' she admitted candidly. 'Flying by the seat of your pants, not knowing what you'll find when you get there.'

'Comes with the territory, Darcie. You work as an outback doctor, you take on board the highs and lows.' And if she hadn't come to a realisation of that by now, then what the hell was she doing here?

'I understand all that, Jack,' she defended. 'It's just... medically, you can only do so much. And it's so *far* from everything.'

Jack felt his mood softening. 'Granted, we don't have the backup of a casualty department,' he conceded. 'So we make adjustments. In our heads as well as practically.' After a minute, he added, 'Whatever path we follow in life, we're probably conditioned by our backgrounds.'

'Perhaps we are.'

'I found working in London stressful.'

'Did you?' She sounded surprised.

'You bet. London is an amazing city, so many centuries of history, but I felt as isolated in the heart of its busyness as you possibly do here in these great open spaces. I'm human too, Doctor. Just like you...'

They turned to each other, eyes meeting. Seeing the slow warmth in his, Darcie's heart gave a little jiggle of recognition.

Suddenly, she felt a lift in her spirits, unexpectedly buoyed by his take on things. Perhaps they had, in quite different ways, quite a lot in common.

Within minutes they were at the location.

'OK, let's get cracking,' Jack snapped, as they alighted from the Land Rover. He moved to organise the gear they'd need, tossing Darcie one of the high-visibility vests the hospital had included.

Quickly, Darcie slid into the vest and secured the fastenings. 'We'd better find out who's in charge.'

'That looks like a site office.' Jack indicated the pre-fab building. 'We'll enquire there.'

A short, stocky man behind the desk shot to his feet as Jack rapped and stuck his head in. 'Blake Meadows,' he said, and held out his hand. 'I'm the film unit manager.' His gaze flicked to Darcie and back to Jack. 'You're the doctors?'

'Yes.' Jack made the introductions. 'What can you tell us?'

'Two of our young actors, Jessica and Lachlan, have fallen into the well. We've managed to gather a few details. Jess caught her arm on a piece of protruding metal on the way down.'

'So there's bleeding,' Darcie surmised.

The manager nodded. 'At the moment, she's been able to staunch it with her T-shirt.'

'And the other casualty?' Jack asked.

'Lachy hasn't been so fortunate.' Blake Meadows made a grimace. 'According to Jess, he landed on something hard—rocks maybe. Passed out. It's his leg…' He rubbed a hand across his face. 'If this gets out, we'll be in the news for all the wrong reasons. The company doesn't need this.'

'I don't imagine the young people needed it either.' Jack was tight-lipped. 'Can you direct us to the well?'

'I'll take you.' The manager hurried them from the office and towards an army-type Jeep parked nearby.

'We probably won't be able to do much until the SES gets here,' Jack said, as they scrambled aboard and took off.

'They should be right behind you,' Blake said. 'Frankly, I'm staggered with the promptness of everyone's response.'

Well, at least their attendance was appreciated, Darcie thought critically, hanging on for dear life as they rocked through the scrubby terrain towards the accident site.

To their surprise, Mal Duffy was already on the scene when they arrived. He greeted both doctors. 'Knew a short cut,' he explained in his slow drawl. 'This is my team for today. Meet Rod and Gez.'

With no time to waste, Mal and his team began erecting a tripod arrangement over the top of the well.

'Do we have any head torches?' Jack queried. 'It's going to be pretty dark down there.'

'Ah—unfortunately, we don't have any in stock,' Mal apologised. 'The lantern torches are high-powered and we'll place them to give you maximum light. Best we can do.'

'Put head torches on your list of priorities, then, please,' Jack countered thinly.

'Will do, Doc. Sorry for the glitch.'

'Has the air ambulance being notified?' Jack asked.

'CareFlight chopper is on its way,' Mal said. 'There's a helipad at Pelican Springs homestead. It's only about ten Ks from here. So once we get the casualties out, our ambos can shoot them across to meet the chopper.'

Jack's mouth compressed briefly. It all sounded straightforward enough but experience had taught him it probably wouldn't be. And if that was the case, then they'd just have to deal with any curve balls as they were thrown.

Mentally, Darcie began to prepare herself, watching as the SES team made their preparations.

'You OK?' Jack asked, shooting her a sideways glance.

'Fine.' She flicked a hand toward the SES team. 'I take it we're hooked up to this pulley thing and get lowered in?'

Jack nodded. 'We'll wear a safety harness. I'll drop in first and the SES guys will retrieve the rope and send you down. OK, looks like they're ready for us.'

Within seconds, Darcie found herself swinging down into the well. She gave a little gasp as she landed unevenly on some kind of rubble. Releasing herself from the guide rope, she began to take her bearings. It was darkish in the cavity, as Jack had predicted, and the place had a repulsive odour. 'Jack?'

'Right here.'

'Oh...' Darcie nudged in beside him, watching as he aimed his torch across to the other side of the well, locating their patients. She heard the girl's subdued whimper and said quietly, 'I'll take Jessica.'

'Thanks. I'll see what's happening with Lachlan.'

Swinging the trauma pack from her shoulders, Darcie hunkered down beside the injured girl. 'Hi, Jess,' she said softly. 'I'm Darcie. I'm a doctor. Can you tell me where you're hurt?'

'It's my arm. I've been so scared...' Her teeth began chattering,

'And you're cold.' Darcie unfolded a space blanket from her supplies and tucked it around the girl. 'Did you hit your head at all?' she asked, beginning to test Jessica's neuro responses.

'No. I've done some stuntwork. I know how to fall safely. But Lachy's really hurt, I think.' She squeezed her eyes shut. 'Please...' she whispered on a sob. 'Can you get us out of here?'

Darcie felt put on her mettle. Quickly, she sifted through her options.

Both Jess's neuro responses and pulse were fine but she needed to be got out of this hell-hole and into the fresh air. 'I'll just need to check your arm, Jess.' Gently, Darcie removed the bloodstained T-shirt. She pursed her lips. Jess had a deep gash from the point of her shoulder to her mid upper arm. The site was already swelling and dark blue with bruising. It was still oozing blood. Thankfully, there was no artery involved.

OK. Mentally, Darcie squared her shoulders. She needed to show some initiative here. She took the girl's uninjured hand and held it. 'Jess, we have trained people waiting up top. I'm going to signal for one of them to come down with a retrieval harness and take you up. The paramedics will take care of you until I can get up there and assess you properly. Is that OK?'

Jessica nodded. 'My arm's throbbing...'

'I'll give you something before you go. Do you feel sick at all?'

'Bit...'

Darcie nodded. 'I'll give you something to combat the nausea as well. You've been really brave, Jess,' Darcie said, shooting home the painkiller and anti-emetic. 'Now, let's get you up and out of here.'

It was all accomplished quickly and skilfully.

With Jessica safely out, Darcie concentrated on helping Jack with their other casualty. 'How's Lachlan?'

'Fractured NOF possibly. But we can't diagnose accurately without an MRI. His belly appears soft so it's safe to get a line in.'

'I think he's coming round.' Darcie felt a rush of relief.

'It's OK, Lachlan.' Jack's manner was calmly reassuring. 'You've fallen into a well, buddy. Knocked yourself out. I'm Jack and this is Darcie. We're doctors.'

Lachlan sucked air in through his lips. 'Leg...' he groaned. 'Pain's epic...'

'Yep. Hang in there, matey.' Jack gently lifted the youngster's head and applied the oxygen mask. 'Will you draw up morphine five and maxolon ten, please,

Darcie? We don't want him throwing up on us. As soon as we get him stable, we'll follow with fifty of pethidine. That should get him through transportation to the hospital.'

Darcie shot home the injections quickly.

'Let's start splinting now,' Jack said. 'The sooner we get this lad out of here the better.'

Darcie's eyes were on high alert for any changes in Lachlan's condition as she watched Jack place the supportive splints between the young man's legs. 'Bandages now?'

'Nice thick ones,' Jack confirmed.

'This shouldn't have happened, should it?' Darcie said, working swiftly to bind Lachlan's injured leg to his good one.

'Not if the location scouts were on top of their game,' Jack agreed gruffly. 'I think I'll be having a word to the Workplace Health and Safety people.'

'Report them?' Darcie felt a lick of unease.

'Just doing my job, Darcie.' Jack was unequivocal. He looked at Lachlan's still form. 'Whack him with the pethidine now, please. I'll make my way back over to the opening and give the guys a shout for the stretcher.'

As Jack moved away from her peripheral vision, Darcie felt the cave-like atmosphere close in on her, her hearing fixed on every tiny sound. A fragment of leaf-like debris floated down and landed on her shoulder. She gave an involuntary shudder, shaking it off, feeling the nerves in her stomach crawl. The conditions in the well were awful.

Darcie pulled herself up with a jerk. This wasn't the time to start losing it. She had a seriously ill patient depending on her skills as a doctor. About to draw up the drug, she stopped and froze. In a second everything had changed. Lachlan was gulping, his eyes rolling back in his head, his colour ashen.

'Jack!' Darcie's cry echoed off the earthen walls. Instinctively, she ripped open Lachlan's shirt and began chest compressions.

'What's happened?' Jack's bulk dropped beside her. 'He's arrested!'

Jack's expletive scorched the air. He would have to intubate.

With the speed of light, he began zipping open sections of the trauma pack, gathering equipment. Centring himself for a second, he prepared to carry out the emergency procedure. And drew back sharply. He cursed under his breath. This wasn't going to work. He needed more light…

But there was none. He'd have to make do, feel his way.

Slowly, slowly, he passed the tube down Lachlan's trachea, attaching it to the oxygen. 'Now, breathe for me, Lachy,' he grated. 'Come on!' He waited a second and then checked the carotid pulse in the young man's neck.

Nothing.

'We'll have to defib him.' Jack reached for the life pack. 'We are *not* losing this one, Darcie.' Jack's voice roughened. 'I'm counting on you.'

Darcie's expression was intense. Every compression meant life for Lachlan. Her heart began to pound against the walls of her chest, her pulse thumping in her wrists and throat. She began feeling light-headed, perspiration patching wetly across her forehead and in the small of her back. 'Jack, hurry…'

'This is a bloody nightmare,' Jack hissed between

clenched teeth. 'Be ready to take over the bag when I defib,' he snapped.

Darcie captured a rush of strength from somewhere. Whether Lachlan ever woke again could depend on their teamwork now.

'OK—do it!' Jack's command rang out.

Almost in slow motion Darcie reached out and took over the Air-Viva bag.

'And clear!'

Darcie dropped the bag and sprang back, willing the volts of electricity to do their work and kick-start Lachlan's heart.

A beat of silence.

'Jack?'

'Nothing. Let's go to two hundred. Clear!'

Darcie strove to keep panic at bay, aware only of its grip on her gut and the slow slide of sweat between her breasts.

'Start compressions again, Darcie.' Jack looked haunted. 'I'm giving him adrenaline.'

Darcie nodded, not capable of verbalising her reply.

Jack's mouth snapped into a thin line, his fingers curling round the mini-jet, which already contained the lifesaving drug. 'Come on, baby—do your job!' he implored, sending the needle neatly between Lachlan's ribs and into his heart. 'Clear!' He activated the charge.

A breathless hush as they waited.

Into the silence, the trace began bleeping and then shot into a steady rhythm. 'Yes...' Jack's relief was subdued.

Darcie slumped forward, her energy spent. She felt the threat of tears and held the heels of her hands against her eyes, gathering her composure. 'Oh, sweet heaven...'

Jack's arm came round her shoulders. 'Hey...'

'I'm OK...'

'You're not.' Jack turned her into his arms and held her.

Darcie allowed herself to be held, feeling the warmth of his body mingle with hers, melting into him, drawing strength from his strength and...the maleness of him. A need she hadn't known existed rose in her, but before she could wonder at its completeness she felt the swift stab of reality. She drew back sharply. What on earth had she been thinking of?

Lachlan was waking up, fear and confusion clouding his eyes.

'It's OK, Lachy.' Darcie beat back her own confusion. She took his hand and squeezed. 'You'll be fine.'

Jack swallowed, clearing the lump from his throat. He felt as though an invisible punch had landed in his solar plexus. She'd felt so right in his arms. And he'd so nearly kissed her. Taken that soft, beautiful mouth with his. And kissed her. Idiot. He drew in a quick, hard breath. 'Think a shot of midazolam is called for here, Dr Drummond?'

'I'd say so.' Darcie nodded, glad for the return to professionalism. The drug would act as a light anaesthetic and ease Lachy over the trauma of the next few hours. She turned away. 'Would you do it, please, Jack?' She wrapped her arms around her midriff, feeling hollowed out.

'Nice work, guys.' Zach Bayliss loomed out of the shadow, towing the collapsible stretcher. 'Could have been a whole different story, couldn't it?'

Darcie felt as though she'd been to hell and back. Swallowing hard on the tightness in her throat, she pulled herself upright. 'He's ready to move now, Zach. We've got him back into sinus rhythm but he'll have to be watched.'

'Understood, Doc.' Zach was a seasoned paramedic. He knew well the battle that had been fought here and, for the moment, won. 'Let's get this youngster on his way, then. If you're ready, Jack, on my count.'

In unison, they gently rolled Lachlan first on one side then the other, sliding each section of the supporting plinth under him and snapping the pieces together. A sturdy rope was attached to each end of the stretcher and almost immediately it was being winched safely to the top.

With Lachlan safely loaded into the ambulance, the emergency crew gathered around. It had already been decided Jess's care could be safely managed at Sunday Creek hospital.

'Where do you want Lachy sent, Jack?' Zach gave one last look inside the ambulance and closed the doors.

'The Royal in Brisbane is our best chance.' Jack was already pulling out his mobile phone. 'I'll alert the head of the trauma team, Nick Cavello. He'll coordinate everything from his end.'

'CareFlight chopper's landed at Pelican Springs.' Mal Duffy joined the group.

'We'll take off, then.' Zach sketched a farewell wave. 'You're OK with Jess travelling with you and Jack, Darcie?'

'I've already settled her in the back seat,' Darcie confirmed. 'Take care of Lachy.'

'Will do.' Zach threw himself into the driver's seat of the ambulance. 'Thanks, everyone,' he called, before starting the engine. Within seconds, the emergency vehicle was being manoeuvred carefully away down the bush track.

# CHAPTER FIVE

'JUST RELAX, JESS,' Darcie said, as they prepared for the trip back to Sunday Creek. 'We'll have you much more comfortable soon.'

'I'll try to minimise the bumps in the road.' Jack tried to inject some lightness into the situation and Jess gave a weak smile. 'Hang in there, kiddo,' he added gently. 'You're doing great.'

The return trip was covered mostly in silence as though each was busy with their own thoughts. As they reached the outskirts of the township, Jack said, 'It's still your day off, Darcie. I'll assume Jess's care if you like.'

'Thanks, but that's not necessary,' she answered firmly. 'Jess is my patient. I'd like to follow through.'

'Fine.' He glanced at her sharply with a frown. 'We'll need to debrief at some stage.'

Well, she knew that. Darcie rubbed at her collarbone through the thin material of her T-shirt. But if Jack had any thoughts of them *debriefing* about what had almost happened back there in the cave...

Soon they'd reached the hospital and Jack was reversing into the ambulance bay.

Dan Prentice, the hospital's only orderly, was waiting with a wheelchair and Jessica's transfer was made without fuss.

'Oh, hi, guys, you're back.' Natalie hurried forward.

'This is Jess, Nat.' Darcie kept her hand on her young patient's shoulder. 'Could you take her through to the treatment room, please? I'm just going to grab a quick shower and then I'll be back to suture Jess's arm.'

A quick shower meant just that. And years of practice meant Darcie had the logistics down pat. When she got back to the unit, Natalie had Jess ready in a gown, had drawn up lignocaine and opened the suture packs. 'Thanks, Nat. This all looks good.' Darcie gloved, pleased her patient was looking more relaxed. 'Little sting now, Jess,' she said, injecting the anaesthetic and infiltrating the wound. 'How's your tetanus status these days?'

'I had a top-up before I went on the film shoot.'

'Good.' Darcie smiled. 'That's one less jab we'll have to give you.' After several minutes she sought Jess's reaction and judged the anaesthetic had taken effect. 'Right, we're set to go. Nat, would you flush with normal saline, please? And, Jess, feel free to chill out, maybe have a little doze?'

Darcie's suturing was neat and painstakingly precise.

'You're so good at this,' Natalie murmured.

Darcie gave a half-laugh. 'I used to get hauled over the coals for being too slow.'

'I think suturing is an art,' Natalie maintained. 'In fact, everything about practising medicine is an art— at least, it should be.'

'Oh, if only that were true…'

Darcie inserted the final stitch. 'That's it.' She stripped off her gloves and stood back to enable Natalie to place a non-stick dressing over the wound. 'Jess, honey…' She roused her patient gently.

'Oh…' Jess's eyes fluttered open. She looked dazed for a second. 'Am I done?'

'Like a good roast.' Natalie chuckled. 'Dr Drummond's done a pretty fancy job with your stitches.'

'Thanks…' Jess blinked a bit. 'You've been really kind…' Two tears tracked down the youngster's cheeks and she wiped them away with the tips of her fingers.

Darcie pulled up a stool and sat down next to her patient. Poor kid. She'd been through a terrible ordeal. 'I want you put everything aside and just rest now, Jess. Think you can do that?'

Jessica bit her lip. 'I guess…'

'And I'd like to keep you here overnight.' And maybe for an extra one or two, Darcie thought. There could be residual effects from Jess's fall that would only become apparent later on. She gave her patient a reassuring smile. 'Now, can I call anyone for you—parents, perhaps?'

Jess shook her head. 'My parents live in Sydney. No need to alarm them. I'll call them when I'm up and around again. Mum would probably come racing out here and want to do my washing,' she added with a spark of humour. 'Where's Lachy?'

'We've sent him to Royal Brisbane. Dr Cassidy arranged that so I'm sure he'll get an update on Lachy's condition later today and let you know.' Darcie stood to her feet. 'Now, Nat will get you settled on the ward and I'll look in on you a bit later, all right? If you need a certificate for time off work, I'll take care of that as well.'

'I'm not going back there.' Jess shook her head firmly. 'They can shove their job.'

Mentally, Darcie stepped back. There was a raft of separate issues here and after what had happened to her, Jessica was probably not in the right frame of mind to be making snap decisions about her job. Obviously, she needed to talk things through but that could wait. Darcie picked up the notes. 'Your arm will probably ache a bit after the anaesthetic wears off,' she told her patient. 'I'll write up some pain relief for you.'

'And don't be a martyr,' Natalie chimed in with a grin. 'Just yell if you need something.'

Jack was taking his time about things. He'd hauled the trauma packs through to the utility room, repacking them and replacing the items they'd used. They were now ready for the next emergency.

Strictly, it wasn't his responsibility, he conceded, but Sunday Creek wasn't a big city hospital and everyone had to pull their weight wherever it was needed. Even senior doctors. Besides, he admitted a bit ruefully, he'd wanted to be a hands-on boss. Well, now he had that here. In spades.

Job done, he went back to the residence, showered and changed and made his way back to do a ward round. There were only four patients and it wasn't an involved process. Returning the charts to the nurses' station, he paused for a moment and then looked at his watch. A second later, he was striding towards the treatment room. Pulling the curtain aside, he poked his head in. Nothing.

'Are you looking for me?'

Jack arched back. 'Darcie...' He blinked a bit. She stood there in pale blue scrubs, her hair twisted up into a topknot, her face scrubbed clean. She looked...

wholesome and…gorgeous. He ordered his pulse to slow down. 'I wondered if you needed a hand.'

'All finished.' Darcie gave a guarded smile. 'We've put Jess on the little veranda ward. It's cool and quiet. Hopefully, she'll get some natural sleep.'

'Good.' He gave an approving nod. 'I was just on my way to get some food. Care to join me?'

'I'd kill for a cup of tea.'

Jack snorted. 'You need something more substantial than that, Dr Drummond. Come on.' He put out a hand in an ushering movement. 'Let's raid the hospital kitchen. They're bound to have a few scraps left over from breakfast.'

A short while later they were tucking into the crisp bacon and fluffy scrambled eggs Carole, the hospital's long-time cook, had whipped up.

'More toast, doctors?' Carole called from the servery window. 'I've made plenty.'

'Thanks, Carole. You're a star.' Darcie sent the older woman a warm smile and made to rise to her feet.

'I'll get it.' Jack's hand landed briefly on Darcie's forearm. 'Finish your food.'

Later, as they sat over big mugs of tea, Darcie said, 'I could sleep for a week.'

'Why don't you, then?' Jack saw her eyes were faintly shadowed. 'At least for the rest of today. I gave you the weekend off, if you recall.'

'I promised to look in on Jess later.'

Jack's mouth gave a mocking twist. 'I think I can just about manage that. Go home to bed, Darcie.'

'You mentioned a debrief.'

'That can wait.'

Darcie's heart began hammering. 'I'd…rather get it over with.'

A beat of silence.

OK. Jack drew in a long breath and let it go. It didn't need rocket science to fathom what was going on here. She was feeling guilty about what had happened in the well when, in reality, if there was any fault to be laid it was down to his actions, not her response. That he'd almost kissed her was beside the point. And she was wound up. He could imagine what her heartbeat was doing under the thin cotton of her scrubs.

And he was technically her boss. That point probably mattered to her. Plus they were sharing job space and home space. There was no room for awkwardness. He had to sort things. 'What happened was a pretty normal reaction,' he said evenly. 'Hell, we saved a life!'

She bit her lip. 'I…suppose.'

'It was just a hug, Darcie.'

Did he really believe that? Darcie fought for control of her wildly see-sawing heart. 'I…don't usually act that way with a senior colleague,' she countered, the set of her small chin almost defiant.

'But, then, I'd imagine you're not *usually* practising emergency medicine at the bottom of a stinking well, are you?'

'No.' She managed a small smile that was almost a grimace. He was spinning things to save her feelings. Well, if that's the way he wanted to play it… But he had to know she'd clung to him and he'd responded by holding her more tightly. He *had* to know that.

But it was his call. For now.

Jack laced his hands around his tea mug. 'If we'd

won the lottery and I'd gathered you up in a hug, you wouldn't have thought it odd, would you?'

Her breath caught and fire flooded her cheeks. But they hadn't won the lottery and it hadn't been *that* kind of hug.

And they both knew it.

She couldn't answer. Instead, she lifted a shoulder in a shrug. Jack Cassidy could make of it what he liked.

Darcie slept well into the afternoon. When she woke, she checked her phone for messages and found one from Maggie. She promptly called back.

'Hi, Maggie. What's up?'

'Can you come to my place for a barbecue this evening?'

'Um, yes, I probably could. Something special going on?'

'I wish I knew.' Maggie forced an off-key laugh. 'I've invited Sam Gibson.'

'The new vet in town,' Darcie said.

'I think I must be sick in the head to have started any of this.'

Darcie rearranged her pillows and made herself comfortable. Maggie was usually very much in charge but now she sounded rattled. 'So, what's with you and Sam?'

'He's come round for coffee a couple of times.'

'How did you meet?'

'We had to take our Staffy for his shot. It kind of went from there. He took the boys trail-bike riding yesterday so I thought I should ask him for a meal. A barbecue sounded, well, more casual, I suppose. Only I feel a bit weird just inviting Sam.'

Darcie chuckled. 'You want me there as a buffer?'

'I want you there as a friend! I'm so out of practice with this relationship stuff, Darc.'

'Oh, rubbish! You just need to chill out and enjoy this new friendship that's come your way. Flirt a bit.'

'Flirt!' Maggie squawked. 'How does one flirt again? Remind me. I vaguely remember something about fluttering eyelashes. If I did that, I'd look demented.'

'For heaven's sake, relax and go with the flow. If Sam asks you out on a date, accept nicely.'

'So says the woman who makes a career of not dating *anyone*.'

'I have so been on dates,' Darcie defended.

'Oh, when was that? I'll bet it was so long ago you can't even remember who you went out with.'

'I went out with one of the flying doctors only recently.'

'Brad Kitto?' Maggie dismissed. 'Fly in, fly out. Nice guy but he's a Canadian on a three months' exchange. How was that ever going to amount to anything?'

'OK, OK.' Darcie shrugged off a feeling of discomfort. She didn't need an inquiry into her dating habits, even from someone as well meaning as Maggie. 'But could I remind you this began as a discussion about your love life, not mine.'

'Point taken. So, will you come?'

'Of course…' Darcie gave an exaggerated sigh of acceptance.

'Oh, and invite the big guy.'

'Jack?' Darcie felt her mouth dry.

'Might be a nice chance for him to mix a bit with the locals. And I haven't met him yet.'

Darcie swallowed. She only hoped she and Jack could revert to being at ease with one another. Perhaps going out among a few friendly folk would help. That's if he agreed to it, of course. 'Well, I'll ask,' she said carefully, 'but he's quite likely pretty tired. We had a call-out at five this morning and he's been over at the hospital all day.'

'Mmm, I heard about the emergency from Karen Bayliss. By the way, I've invited her and Zach.'

'Oh, good. They're a nice couple. Would you like me to make a cake for dessert?'

'Oh, would you, Darce? I've spent most of the day trying to get my hair to look less like the ends of a straw broom.'

Darcie's soft laugh rippled. Maggie's colourful take on things always lightened her spirits. 'Shall I come round about five, then? Help you set up?'

'Thanks. And ask Jack,' Maggie reinforced, before she ended the call.

Jack was offhand when Darcie relayed Maggie's invitation.

'Sure. What time?'

'I'm going about five.'

Jack's mouth drew in as if he was considering his options.

'Is that too early for you?' Darcie's gaze was a little uncertain.

'Maybe a bit. Give me the address,' he added, his shoulder half-turned as if he was about to walk away. 'I'll follow on later.'

Information imparted, Darcie watched as he walked out of the kitchen as though he couldn't leave fast enough. As though he was distancing himself from her. Or from the situation they'd found themselves in. That was more likely, she decided.

Swiping up the scattering of flour from her baking, she gave an impatient little tut. This unease was her fault. Why couldn't she have been cool about everything? Laughed it off as the adrenaline rush after having saved a life?

Because she couldn't.

Jack went back to his bedroom. He hated this…distance between them. And he didn't really feel like socialising. God, he just wanted sleep. But he had to show his face. Part of the job. Get to know the locals.

Ignoring what were probably house rules, he flung himself down on the patchwork quilt, boots and all, and stared at the ceiling.

Darcie Drummond.

She'd got to him. He snorted a self-derisive laugh. Perhaps he should just kiss her and get it out of his system. Get *her* out of his system. Yeah, like that was going to help. It would just muddy the atmosphere even further.

He pressed his fingers across his eyelids. He needed to lighten up.

It was early evening when Jack arrived at Maggie's place. The buzz of conversation interspersed with laughter and the mouth-watering smell of steaks cooking drew him along the side path and towards the back garden where he guessed the barbecue was happening.

Maggie saw him the moment he poked his head around the lattice screen. *Wow! Now, there was seri-*

*ous talent.* She smiled and went forward to greet him. 'Jack?' She rolled her eyes in a wry gesture. 'Of course you must be. I'm Maggie. Come and meet everyone.'

Maggie introduced Jack to Sam Gibson, who was officiating at the barbecue. 'Welcome to Sunday Creek, Doc.' Sam's handshake was firm. 'I'm new here myself. Animal doctor,' he enlightened with a grin.

'We're bound to cross paths, then.' Jack laughed.

'But not instruments.' The dry irony in Sam's tone made Jack laugh again. It was going to be OK, he thought. He looked forward to relaxing and enjoying the down time.

'Zach you know, of course.' Maggie was pressing on in her role of hostess. 'And this is Karen, Zach's wife.'

'Hi.' Karen Bayliss gave a friendly little wave. 'And this is our daughter, Molly.' The pride in her voice was unmistakable as she tucked the baby onto her hip.

'How old is she?' Jack ran the tip of his finger along the plump little arm.

'Ten months.'

Jack's mouth crimped at the corners as the little one gave back a haughty look. He felt a twist inside him and the oddest feeling ripped through him. He could have been a father by now if things between him and Zoe had worked out. But for crying out loud! He was thirty-seven. As far as fertility went, he still had oceans of time to find the right woman to have a child with. He shook his head, wondering where the mad rush of introspection had come from.

'She's giving you *the look*,' Karen said with a chuckle.

'She's a princess,' Jack murmured. 'You're very lucky, Karen.'

'Yes, we know.' Karen sent a soft look at her husband. 'We'd almost given up hope when this one trotted into our lives. That's why we chose the name Molly. It means *longed-for* child.'

Out of nowhere, Jack felt drenched in emotion. Hell's bells. He blinked a bit, seizing the escape route with relief when Maggie said, 'And these are my sons, Josh and Ethan.'

'Hey, guys.' Jack shook hands with the two. 'I saw the trail bikes as I came through the carport. You ride a bit?'

'Yep,' Josh, the elder, said. 'Sam took us over to some tracks yesterday. It was awesome.'

'I like skateboarding best,' Ethan chimed in, sensing an interested audience in Jack.

'I used to do that when I was about your age,' Jack said. 'Do you have a bowl here?'

Ethan looked blank.

'Duh.' His brother dug him in the ribs. 'A skate bowl?'

Ethan coloured. 'I just use the concrete paths at the park. But some of the kids use the footpath outside the shops.'

'And you know you're not allowed to do that,' his mother intervened. 'It's illegal.'

'Yeah, I know, Mum.' Ethan gave Maggie a long-suffering look.

'Always good to obey the rules, champ.' Jack grinned, giving support to Maggie's parental role.

'Thanks,' she said, as the boys turned and went off about their own business. 'They're a challenge.'

'They seem like great kids, Maggie. Uh...' Jack

raised an eyebrow in query. 'I've brought wine. Where can I stash it? Fridge?'

'Oh, yes.' For the first time Maggie noticed the carry bag he'd parked on the outdoor table. 'Sorry for rabbiting on. Just go up onto the deck. Kitchen's straight through. Darcie's there. She'll organise it for you.'

Head bent, Darcie was busy at the countertop. She looked up, flustered when Jack walked in. 'Hi…' It was no more than a breath of sound.

He gave a tight smile. 'I brought some wine.' He hoisted the carry bag onto the bench. 'Maggie said you'd find a home for it.'

'Oh—OK.' Just looking at him caused a well of emotion to rise in her chest and lodge in her throat.

He was wearing faded jeans and a simple white polo shirt that showed the tanned strength of his upper arms. The arms that had held her with such caring. Such… tenderness.

She took in a breath that almost hurt and her gaze dropped to his mouth. Desire leached through her. The image of her leaning across the counter to kiss him sent her heart dancing a wild flutter in her chest. A jagged breath snatched at her throat. She didn't do this. Lust after men. And Jack was not some random male. He was a senior colleague. Her boss. She swallowed dryly. 'I'll find some space in the fridge.'

Jack's gaze stayed riveted to her. She was like a sprite in her black sleeveless top and long skirt that dipped round her ankles. He felt like jumping the counter that separated them, whirling her into a mad dance. And then slowly closing in on her so that their bodies were separated only by a whisper of air. And finally…

Darcie closed the fridge and turned back to face him. She gave him a smile that was gone before it could take shape. 'Have you met everyone?'

'Mmm, think so. Not too many faces to remember.'

'That's always a help.' She picked up a flat-bladed knife to finish off the frosting on her cake. 'Um, would you like a drink? Maggie left instructions for everyone to help themselves.'

'Thanks. I'll get something later.'

Jack propped himself against the countertop, leaning slightly towards her and catching the drift of her light-as-air shampoo for his trouble. 'Cake looks good.'

Tipping her head back, Darcie smiled. 'My contribution towards dessert. I once shared a flat with a pastry chef.' Darcie set the finished cake aside. 'She gave me a few tips along the way.'

'So chocolate cake is your signature dish?'

'It is.' She scooped out a tiny drizzle of frosting with the tip of her finger and pushed the bowl towards him, her gesture inviting him to help her lick the bowl.

He gave a huff of laughter. 'I haven't done this since I was about six.'

'Some catching up to do, then,' she suggested, and he chuckled.

'So, I guess you did this with your mother?' Jack asked.

She gave an off-key laugh. 'My mother doesn't cook. We had a housekeeper. I spent lots of time in the kitchen with her. My parents are history professors. Away on the lecturing circuit a lot. They missed most of my significant milestones when I was at school,' she added as a kind of resigned afterthought.

And wasn't that a crappy way to spend your child-hood. 'Were you an only child?' Jack asked evenly.

'Mmm-hmm.' She dragged in a breath and let it out in a whoosh. 'Don't feel sorry for me, Jack.'

'Sorry for you is the last thing I feel,' he countered gruffly.

Their eyes locked and her tongue flicked a tiny dab of frosting from her bottom lip. Jack's throat closed un-comfortably. And for just a moment, a blink of time, there was a connection of shared awareness. Sharp. Intense.

'Hey, you two!' Maggie called, and suddenly their eye contact retracted as quickly as turning off a light switch.

# CHAPTER SIX

MONDAY MORNING AND already the barbecue felt like a lifetime ago.

'Thanks for your input, Darcie.' Jack relaxed back in his chair, legs stretched out under his desk. They'd officially completed handover.

'If that's it, I'll do a ward round.' Darcie half rose.

'Hang on a minute.' He flicked a hand in a delaying motion. 'I've arranged for the theatre to be thoroughly cleaned and made sterile. I'm aware it's small but everything's there. If we can keep it ready for emergencies, it will save having to call out the flying doctors, which will in turn save them time and money.'

A beat of silence.

'You're the surgeon and the boss.' Darcie's gaze fluttered down and then up to meet his piercing blue eyes. 'It's obviously your call.'

'But?' Jack's dark brows rose interrogatively.

'We don't have much backup for major trauma.'

Jack all but rolled his eyes. Did she think he was a complete novice at this? He tapped his pen end to end on the desk. 'I'm talking relatively straightforward emergency procedures, Darcie, not heart transplants.'

Stung by his air of arrogance, Darcie said coolly,

'What about anaesthetics? I have a little knowledge but I'm not qualified.'

'I can guide you.'

Well, he obviously thought he had the answer to *everything*. But far from reassuring her, it only added to Darcie's uncertainty. 'I...just don't want us to start playing God every time there's an emergency and think we can automatically sort it here.'

'You don't like me taking over,' Jack interpreted flatly.

Darcie brushed a fingertip between her brows. That wasn't it at all. She wasn't making herself clear. But she'd woken with a headache that morning, her thoughts muddled, her concentration shot to pieces. And all because she couldn't seem to get a grip on her feelings about Jack. She felt very out of her depth but the last thing she needed was her personal feelings spilling over into their professional involvement.

A soft breath gusted from her mouth. Had it been only yesterday they'd been in cahoots like kids, licking frosting from a bowl?

'Didn't you sleep well?' Jack tilted his head, his eyes narrowing. The faint shadows were still there. Her light olive complexion was a dead giveaway.

She lifted her chin. Whether she slept well or not was none of his business.

For a second tension crackled between them, as brittle as spun sugar.

'Could we get back to the point?' Darcie said stiffly. 'I'm more than accepting of your appointment here, Dr Cassidy. The place needs a senior doctor. You're it. Obviously my protocols don't work for you, so change them!'

Jack clicked his tongue. 'It's about trying to get the

hospital up and running to its full potential, Darcie. So work with me here, please.'

He scrubbed a hand roughly across his cheekbones, reminding himself to get some eye drops. His eyes felt as though a ton of shell grit had been dumped there. *He* hadn't slept well. His thoughts had spun endlessly and always centred on this waif of a girl sitting opposite him.

But she wasn't a waif at all. That was just his protectiveness coming into play. And she wouldn't thank him for that. She was capable of taking care of herself. More than. OK. He'd better smarten up. 'Darcie, I need you on board with all these changes, otherwise nothing's going to work for us in any direction, is it?'

His plea came out low and persuasive and Darcie felt relief sweep through her. What he said made sense. They couldn't afford to be offside with one another. Professionally, they were doctors in isolation. It was simply down to her and Jack to make things work. Otherwise she'd have to leave. And she definitely didn't want that.

Where would she go?

'I guess we're both on a bit of a learning curve right now,' she admitted throatily.

'And medically it's been a draining couple of days.' Jack was more than willing to be conciliatory.

Darcie looked at him warily, meshing her teeth against her bottom lip. 'You'll have my support, Jack.'

He let out a long breath. 'Thank you.'

Darcie blinked a bit as he sent her a fence-mending kind of smile. *We'll be OK*, it seemed to imply. Well, she could live with that.

Rolling back his chair, he went to stand with his back

against the window. 'The board will be here at eleven for a meeting.'

'Oh—OK.' Darcie rose. She flicked him a wide-eyed query. 'Do you want me there?'

'Silly question.' He paused deliberately, his eyes capturing hers, darkened by the slanting light from the window. 'Of course I *want* you.'

Darcie was still feeling the weight of Jack's parting words knocking against her chest as she finished her ward round.

She'd purposefully left Jessica until last.

'How are you feeling?'

Jess lifted her head from the glossy magazine she'd been reading. 'Much better, thanks.'

Darcie smiled. 'I can see that.' Jess was sitting in the easy chair beside her bed. The hospital gown was gone and she was dressed in a very cute pair of hot pink pyjamas.

'Are you going to release me, Dr Drummond?'

'Let's see what Dr Cassidy has to say, shall we?' Darcie plucked the chart from the end of the bed. She read Jack's notes swiftly. After an initial dose early yesterday afternoon, Jess had needed no further pain relief. Her neuro responses were normal and she'd slept well without a sedative. 'You've bounced back remarkably well, Jess.' Darcie replaced the chart. 'I guess I'm going to have to let you go.'

'Now?' Grinning, Jess threw her magazine aside. 'Cool.'

'Got time for a quick chat first?' Darcie propped herself on the edge of the bed. 'You're quite sure you don't want to go back to your job?'

'Quite sure.' Jess gave a small grimace. 'Too late anyway. I've already resigned and had a friend collect my stuff and bring it in.'

'No problem with contracts and things?'

'It was open-ended,' Jess explained. 'A get-out clause for both parties. They could get rid of me or vice versa.'

'It doesn't sound very secure.'

Jess flapped a hand. 'That's the business I'm in. It doesn't worry me.'

I must be getting old, then, Darcie decided. Because it would worry me. A lot. 'So, what are your plans?'

'Maggie checked to see if there were any flights out of Sunday Creek today. Apparently, one of the local graziers is flying his own plane to a conference in Brisbane this afternoon. He's kindly offered me a seat. I'll go and visit Lachy at the Royal. Then I'll head home to Sydney and start looking for a new job. There are a couple of films happening soon. I'll shoot my CV out. I'll be offered something,' she added with youthful confidence.

'So—obviously, you weren't happy with the film company at Pelican Springs?'

'They took short cuts with safety.' Jess was unequivocal. 'That doesn't work for me.'

Darcie looked thoughtful. So Jack had been right. But, of course, to make charges stick, you had to have people to back up your convictions. And if those same people needed their jobs…?

'I'm OK to go, then?'

Her patient's slightly anxious query jolted Darcie back to her role as Jessica's doctor. 'Just a couple of loose ends to tie up. I'll give you a note for your GP in Sydney and a script for some antibiotics just to be on the safe side. You'll probably be able to have the stitches out in a week or so. And I'll give you a leaflet explaining what's necessary for the care of your wound. This will be an essential part of its healing,' Darcie emphasised. 'Don't neglect it, Jess, all right?'

'I won't,' Jessica promised. 'Mum'll be on my case anyway. But that's what mums do, isn't it?' she added with a philosophical little shrug of her shoulders.

'Yes, I suppose they do.' Darcie's eyes were faintly wistful. She blew out a controlled breath. 'Now, I'll leave your paperwork at the nurses' station. See Maggie before you go. And, Jess, good luck with everything.'

'Oh, thanks, Dr Drummond.' Jess got to her feet, obviously keen to gather her things and get going. 'And thanks for looking after me,' she added with a very sweet smile.

'You're welcome and it's Darcie. We went through a lot together, didn't we?'

Jess nodded. 'I was never so pleased to see anyone as I was to see you at the bottom of that well…' The youngster suppressed a shiver. 'But we did good.'

Darcie smiled. 'Well, make sure you keep *doing good* when you leave here.' She went to the door. Pausing, as if a thought had just occurred to her, she turned back. 'Just to put your mind at ease, Jess, there should be minimal scarring on your arm. Well, nothing the camera will pick up.'

'I'm not a bit worried.' Happy, back in charge of her life, Jess grinned. 'Dr Cassidy said you did a brilliant job.'

Sunday morning, two weeks later, Darcie rose earlier than usual but it was obvious Jack had risen earlier still. She found him in the kitchen, his hands wrapped round a mug of tea. 'Morning,' she said, helping herself from the pot he'd made.

'Louise Alderton called last night,' Jack said. 'She invited us out to Willow Bend today. I accepted for both of us. I hope that's all right.'

A dimple appeared briefly as Darcie smiled. 'We're taking the day off, then?'

'We've earned it, don't you agree?'

'Well, you certainly have,' Darcie apportioned fairly. 'You've hardly drawn breath since you arrived.' But she wasn't about to question Jack's motives or his workload. He was the boss. He could do what he liked. 'A day out at Willow Bend sounds wonderful,' she said instead. 'What time do they want us?'

'As soon as we'd like. Max will yard a couple of horses for us. Fancy a ride with me?' His gaze lifted, straying momentarily to the sweet curve of her mouth.

'Should be fun,' she said lightly, but if she'd looked in the mirror at that moment she would have seen her flushed image reflecting a wide-eyed vulnerability.

They left for Willow Bend just after nine. As they drove, Darcie said, 'The colours are really something special out here, aren't they? The landscape seems so pure and clean and everything seems so incredibly *still*. The vastness takes my breath away.'

'You're not alone there,' Jack responded quietly, wondering whether this time away from the hospital confines would allow him to get to know her better. He wanted to. So much. But he couldn't rush her. He knew that as well. Perhaps they were destined never to be more than medical colleagues.

Perhaps today would be the day he'd find out.

* * *

'I've saddled the horses for you,' Max Alderton said. 'I hope you'll be happy with Hot Shot, Jack. He's fairly spirited.' They were sitting on the homestead veranda in comfortable wicker chairs, enjoying the morning tea Louise had prepared.

'Can't wait.' Jack's look was keen. 'Although it's been a while since I actually did any riding.'

'Hot Shot is a former racehorse,' Louise joined in. 'Nice mouth. Let him stretch out on the flats. Darcie will show you the trails we use.'

'I'll be riding Jewel as usual?' Darcie helped herself to a scone topped with jam and cream.

'Of course.' Louise smiled. 'I think she's missed you. You haven't been out for a while.'

Darcie lifted a shoulder. 'Busy at the hospital. Not that Jack's a slave-driver or anything.' She looked across at him and her breath caught in her throat. Those blue eyes were far too knowing. And suddenly she was afraid. Afraid of what seemed to be happening between them, and whether she wanted it or not.

After morning tea, Jack and Darcie made their way across to the horses. It was a beautiful day, not too hot, with a slight breeze.

A good day just to be alive, Jack thought a bit later, admiration flickering in his eyes as he watched Darcie swing lightly to her mare's saddle, her Akubra tipped rakishly forward and her hair cascading from under it to her shoulders. 'Where are we aiming for?' he asked, deftly circling his own mount to steady the frisky stallion.

Darcie flicked a hand towards a line of lacy willows.

'Louise and I usually cross the creek and head on up to the plateau. The view's amazing from there.'

They took off at a leisurely pace.

'Enjoying it?' Darcie asked after they'd been riding for a while.

'Fantastic.' Jack couldn't believe the sheer exhilaration he felt.

'Oh, Jack, look!' Darcie pointed to a mob of grey wallabies. Alerted to the presence of humans, the quaint little animals were suddenly all flying legs and tails, almost colliding with each other in their haste to leap away to the safety of the scrub.

'Silly beggars.' Jack laughed. Spurred on by the lightness of his mood, he gathered up the reins. 'Fancy a gallop?'

'You're on!' Darcie gave a whoop of delight and took up the challenge.

In perfect rhythm they took off across the paddock, their horses' hooves churning a wake of green through the tall grasses.

Leaving the flat country behind, they climbed higher and higher, until Darcie signalled she was about to stop and wheeled Jewel to a halt halfway up the slope. Her eyes alight with pleasure, she looked down. 'Isn't that something?' she said softly.

Jack reined in Hot Shot beside her, his gaze following hers to the expanse of the valley below, across the faint shimmer of the creek and beyond to the homestead nestling far away on the natural rise of the land.

'Yes, it is…' He closed his eyes, breathing in the woodsy tang of the morning air, tasting it, almost hearing it.

Watching him, Darcie took a long breath, loath to

disturb what she perceived as a very private moment. She felt so in tune with him. So, what had happened? Had some fundamental change taken place within herself? And why suddenly today did *everything* about him seem to call to her? As if to clear her thoughts, she raised her gaze to the eastern rim of the cloudless sky. 'Should we head back now?'

'Uh…OK.' Jack blinked a bit, as if reconnecting with the world around him. 'Perhaps we could stop at the creek, spell the horses for a bit?'

The horses were surefooted, picking their way carefully down the track to the creek. Dismounting, Jack looped the reins around Hot Shot's neck, setting him free to graze.

Somewhat guardedly, Darcie followed his example. 'Are you sure they won't take off and leave us stranded?' she asked.

'Not when they have one another for company.' Bending down to the stream, he scooped up a handful of water and drank it thirstily.

'Is that safe?' Darcie bobbed down beside him, her head very close to his.

Jack scoffed a laugh. 'Of course it's safe, Darcie. It's running water! And see over there…' He pointed to where the creek trickled over some rocks. 'That's watercress. And it's lush and green, a sure sign there's no pollution.'

'If you say so, Dr Cassidy.'

Jack chuckled. 'Go on, try it,' he urged, and watched as she dipped her hand into the water and gingerly tasted it.

'It's quite nice.' She gave qualified approval.

'*Quite nice?*' Jack imitated her crisp little accent to a T. 'It's beautiful.'

She made a face. 'And you're the ultimate authority, I suppose. Jack—' She broke off, laughing. 'What do you think you're doing?'

'Nothing.' He grinned innocently, in the same instant showering her with a spray of water he'd scooped up from the creek.

Darcie shrieked. 'You are such rubbish!' Recklessly, she showered him back until it was a free-for-all battle between them.

'Enough!' Jack finally called a halt, the last of his ammunition slipping between his fingers in a silver rainbow of trickles.

'I'm drenched,' Darcie wailed, peeling her wet shirt away from the waistband of her jeans. 'And cold.'

'Poor baby.' Jack grinned, quite unabashed. 'Want me to warm you up?' He wasn't waiting for her answer. Instead, he reached out and gently drew her towards him, his intent obvious.

'Jack…?'

'Darcie…? Jack looked down at her. A stiff breeze had whipped up, separating tendrils of her hair from around her face and fluffing them out. She looked so vulnerable. And so desirable.

'Should we be doing this…?' Her voice faded to a whisper.

He made a dismissive sound in his throat. 'I've given up trying to find reasons why we shouldn't.'

Darcie swallowed; her heart tripped. He was bending towards her, the deep blue of his eyes capturing hers with an almost magnetic pull. And the sun felt intoxicatingly warm against her back. There was no urgency in the air.

Just a languid kind of sweetness.

Jack was so close to her now she could see the faint shadow across his jaw, the slight smudges under his eyes. Yet his face reflected a toughness, a strength.

'Sweet…' Jack took her face in his hands, his need materialising in the softest sigh before his mouth found hers. The kiss rolled through his blood and raw need slammed into him like nothing he had ever known. Her lips parted and her own longing seemed to match his, overwhelming him like the heady aroma of some dark heated wine.

Applying a barely-there pressure through his hands, he whispered the tips of his fingers down the sides of her throat, then in a sweep across her breastbone to her shoulders, gathering her in.

Darcie clung to him. And the kiss deepened, turned wrenching and wild. She felt a need inside her, an over-whelming need to be touched like this, held like this.

And *stroked* to the point of ecstasy by this man.

But it wasn't going to go that far. At least, not today. She felt Jack pulling back, breaking the kiss slowly, gently, his lips leaving a shivering sweetness like trails of insubstantial gossamer.

A long beat of silence while they collected them-selves.

'Oh, help…' Darcie turned away, sinking onto the ground and pulling her knees up to her chin. 'What was that all about, do you suppose?'

Jack settled beside her. 'Does there have to be a reason?' His voice was muted, slightly gravelly. 'We kissed. It's been waiting to happen almost since we met.'

Darcie inhaled a ragged little breath. 'I suppose…'

'I could say you were irresistible, if that will help.'

In a quick, protective movement, Darcie put her hand to her mouth, feeling his kiss return in a wash of quivering nerve-ends. OK, they'd kissed, she owned. But as a result had they opened another set of problems? And where was any of it leading?

'Hey…' Jack turned her head a fraction, tipping her chin up with a finger. 'Don't tell me you didn't enjoy it, Darcie. Because I won't believe you.'

She breathed in and out, a soft little breath through her slightly parted lips. 'It's not that.'

'What is it, then? Surely you know you can trust me.'

'I know…'

'Well, then…'

As if in a dream, she went with him as he gently lowered them to the grassy bank of the creek.

'Darcie…you're beautiful…' Jack buried his face in her throat, his hand sliding beneath her shirt to roam restlessly along her back and then to her midriff, half circling her ribcage, driving upwards until his thumbs, let free, began stroking the underswell of her breast.

With a passion she hardly knew she possessed, Darcie took the initiative, opening her mouth on his, tasting him all over again. And again.

How long they stayed wrapped in their own world she had no idea, but when he drew back and they moved apart to lie side by side, she could tell the sun had shifted, shedding light on the face of the river gums. Her chest lifted in a long steadying sigh. 'How long have we been here?'

Jack shook his head. He felt poleaxed, set adrift without a lifeline. 'Does it matter?' When she didn't answer, he turned to look at her. 'Are you OK?'

What was OK any more? Darcie wondered, pulling herself into a sitting position.

Jack half rose, leaning back on his elbows and surveying her. He didn't like what he saw. Her shoulders looked tightly held, almost shutting him out. 'Talk to me, Darcie.'

For answer, she plucked off a blade of grass and began shredding it. 'I don't know what to say...'

'About what?'

'This—us.'

Jack wrenched himself forward and sat next to her. He held up his hand as if to study it. 'Well, I'm real and as far as I know you're real. We're without ties and single. So where's the problem?' His dark brows hitched briefly. 'You *are* single, aren't you?'

'Yes!' There was a weight of feeling in her voice.

'So I'll ask again. What's the problem?'

She shook her head.

In the silence that followed, Jack reached across and took her hands, brought them to his mouth and kissed each palm. Then, while his eyes said, *Trust me*, he flattened them on his chest. The action brought Darcie very near the edge. Suddenly, without warning, she felt surrounded by him, his masculine strength and the wild pull he exerted on every one of her senses.

'Darcie...?'

'I was engaged, Jack.' Her voice was fainter than air.

'And?'

She swallowed dryly. 'I ran away and came to Australia.'

'So you broke it off. There's no shame in that. I'm sure you had your reasons.'

She pulled in a slow, painful breath. 'Oh, I did.'

Looping out an arm, he gathered her in. 'Going to tell me?' he pressed gently.

Darcie felt the weight of indecision weigh heavily. But if ever there was a time for honesty between them, then it was now. 'His name was Aaron,' she began slowly. 'He was a doctor where I worked at St Faith's in London. A bit older than I. We seemed well suited. We got along. He looked out for me. When he asked me to marry him, I didn't hesitate.'

'But later you began to second-guess your engagement,' Jack suggested quietly.

'Once he'd put the ring on my finger, he changed. Small ways at first so that I thought I'd been mistaken. But then…his caring turned into…control. Control in all kinds of bizarre ways…like how I wore my hair and make-up. He began choosing my clothes, insisting I wear what he'd bought…and that was just the beginning.'

Jack felt the tiny shudder go through her and swore under his breath. 'He wasn't physically abusive, was he?'

'Oh, no.' She shook her head decisively. 'I'd have been gone in two minutes. But, no…his behaviour was the problem. So…manipulative.'

'You did the right thing to get out.'

'You think so?'

'And fast.' Jack frowned a bit. 'What about your parents? Couldn't you have gone to them?'

She shook her head. 'My relationship with them is a bit complex. Sometimes I feel as though I don't know them at all. And they don't know me,' she added in a kind of quiet resignation.

Jack thought long and hard. Something was eating away at her. Whatever else, they couldn't leave things like this. 'Do you want to talk about it?' he offered. 'It goes without saying anything you tell me will be confidential.'

Darcie felt her mouth dry, her breathing become tight. 'Are you being my doctor here, Jack?'

'No, Darcie.' His voice was soft, intense. 'I'm trying to be your *friend*.' When she didn't respond, he took the initiative. Carefully. 'At what part of your growing up did you begin to feel alienated from your parents?'

'From when I was about twelve,' she faltered, after the longest pause.

'You mentioned a housekeeper so I'm guessing you weren't sent away to school?'

'No, but perhaps it would have been better. At least I'd have had company of my own age. I was lonely a lot of the time.'

Jack heard the pain in her voice and a silent oath lodged in his throat. 'Go on,' he encouraged gently, touching her lightly on the shoulder.

Darcie turned to look at him. It had been a feather touch of reassurance, and why it had the capacity to make her reassured she had no idea. But, unaccountably, it did. Words began to tumble out.

'My parents had reached the peak in their careers. They had invitations to speak all over the UK. In between speaking engagements they'd swoop home and gather me up like I was the most important thing in their lives. But in a few days they'd be gone again.'

'Pretty erratic parenting, then,' he said.

She tried a half-laugh. 'I guess you'd say so. And maybe...' she added, as if the thought had suddenly occurred to her, 'that's why I took Aaron at face value. He was always there for me. Something my parents hadn't been.'

'So, gravitating towards Aaron was a fairly natural reaction on your part,' Jack said. Cautious.

Darcie released her breath on a shuddering sigh. 'I think I was extremely gullible. So easily duped...'

'Hey, don't beat up on yourself. Foresight is a bit scarce on the ground when you really need it.' Concern showed in his gaze as it locked with hers. 'Did your parents ever get to meet Aaron?'

'Of course. We were engaged, planning a wedding. They liked him. If I'd tried telling them what I suspected about him, they'd have thought I was overreacting.'

'But they know where you are now? And reasons why you left England?'

'Yes.'

It seemed a long time until she continued. 'When I began to realise what my life would be like if I married Aaron, I knew I had to get away. I didn't trust myself to confront him because I knew how persuasive he could be. He'd have tried to talk me round.'

Jack rubbed a hand across his cheekbones. He couldn't bear the thought of her being the brunt of such subtle, despicable behaviour. 'Survival is an instinct,' he said quietly. 'So what did you do to survive?'

'I'd become friends with a doctor who'd come over to St Faith's on an exchange, an Aussie girl. When she left to continue her travels she told me if ever I found myself in Australia to let her know, and if I wanted a job she'd see if there was anything going in her old hospital in Brisbane. I called her and explained my difficulty. Within twenty-four hours I was on a flight. I left a note for Aaron, making sure he wouldn't get it until I was airborne.' She paused and then continued, 'I worked in Brisbane for a couple of months but it wasn't the right fit for me.'

'You were still looking over your shoulder.'

She hesitated. 'Perhaps.'

Jack held her more closely. He could imagine her desperation. *Her fear...*

She turned up her face to his. 'I decided to do a bit of a job search on line. I saw the Sunday Creek vacancy...'

'And one year later, here you are.'

'Yes.' She took one slow breath and then a deeper one, feeling her lungs fill and stretch. It had been such a relief to tell Jack and have him believe in her.

He searched her face for an endless moment. 'Sometimes you look a bit...*haunted* for want of a better word. Do you worry that cretin will find you?'

'Not so much now. It's been ages and he'd never think I'd do something as bold as this.'

Jack snorted. 'He didn't know you very well, then, did he? You are one gutsy lady.'

'Me?'

His eyes caressed her tenderly. 'Yes, you, Darcie Drummond. Thank you for telling me. For trusting me with your confidence.'

Was what they'd done going to change things between them? Darcie wondered as they rode leisurely back to the homestead. It didn't have to, the sensible part of her reasoned. They could still be professional colleagues.

But out of hours—what? Best friends? Friends with chemistry? Lovers? At the thought, butterflies rose and somersaulted in her stomach. Now, *that* was a bridge too far. Should she talk to Jack about how they'd handle things? Or not...?

*Not*, she decided, but her thoughts kept spinning this way and that.

Back at the stables, they unsaddled the horses and gave them a quick rub-down. 'Thank you for a lovely ride, sweetheart.' Darcie looped her arms around Jewel's neck and held her cheek to the mare's smooth coat.

'Are you talking to me?' Jack's mouth quirked into a crooked grin.

'Perhaps I was,' she said, and saw his eyes darken. 'Indirectly,' she added, and laughingly dodged the handful of chaff he threw at her.

# CHAPTER SEVEN

IT WAS A week later when Darcie made her way along the corridor to Jack's office. They hadn't seen much of one another recently.

Jack had been away setting up what he called an outreach clinic. But at least he was at the hospital today and Darcie meant to make the most of it.

She knocked and popped her head in. 'Got a minute?'

'Good morning.' Jack heaved his chair away from the desk and beckoned her in. 'Haven't seen you much this week,' he said, as she took the chair opposite.

'No.' Her smile was quick and gone in a flash. She looked across at him. He looked serious and she wondered for the umpteenth time whether he was regretting their kisses and the shift even for a few hours from professional to personal. Maybe he hadn't thought about it at all.

The possibility left her feeling hollow inside.

'How are preparations for the clinic going?' she asked.

'So far, so good. The board members are enthusiastic and the owners of Warrawee station have offered space we can utilise. And it will be a central point and closer for some of the patients than having to travel in here to the hospital. Would you and Maggie have time to put your heads together and work out the basics of what we'll need for the start-up?'

'Of course.' Darcie looked enthusiastic. 'So—starting from scratch, we should think about furnishings for a treatment room and some kind of reception area? Bed, chairs, desk and so on. We can take patient files and laptop on the day. Maybe the whole area will need a lick of paint. And what about a water cooler, tea-making facilities…?'

'Hang on, Darcie.' Jack injected a note of caution. 'Let's just do the basics until we see whether patient numbers indicate it's viable. And it goes without saying all emergencies will still have to come here to the hospital.'

'I realise that. But I think a less clinical environment should work well for our indigenous folk, at least. Some of the elders in particular still have a fear of actual hospitals.'

'You've really got a handle on Sunday Creek and its people, haven't you?'

Darcie's gaze tangled with his as his gentle words soothed all the lonely places in her heart. Breaking eye contact, she said quietly, 'Everyone here has shown me the kind of respect a doctor can only dream about. And I've felt incredibly welcome.'

Jack rubbed absently at his jaw. 'You've obviously earned every bit of trust people have placed in you.'

Darcie coloured faintly, shrugging away his compliment. 'How often would you visualise running the clinic?'

'Perhaps every couple of weeks.' Jack's mouth turned down. 'Depends if folk warm to the idea.'

Darcie sent him an old-fashioned look. 'Establish it and they will come.'

'Let's hope so.'

'Am I going to get a turn or are you intending to keep it to yourself?'

His mouth puckered briefly. 'You may have a turn, Dr Drummond. Now…' Jack placed his hands palms down on the desk '…what did you want to see me about?'

'I'd like a second opinion about a patient, David Campion, age twenty-seven. He's an artist, lives fairly basically in a shack in the bush, according to Maggie. Rather eccentric, I suppose. He wanders in when life gets a bit beyond him.'

The leather creaked, as Jack leaned back in his chair. 'He's not using us as a hostel, is he?'

'No, I'd say not. He seems genuinely under the weather but I can't get a handle on whatever it is.'

'Drug use?'

'I've never detected any sign.'

Jack steepled his fingers under his chin. 'So, what does he live on—the sale of his paintings?'

'They're exceptional.' Darcie warmed to her subject. 'Wonderful outback images. He had a showing at the library not so long ago. I bought two of his smaller prints. They're on my bedroom wall.'

'Is that so…?' Jack's blue gaze ran across her face and down to where the open neck of her shirt ended in creamy shadow. 'I must look in some time.'

Darcie's heart revved at his cheeky remark. She moistened lips that had suddenly gone dry. Did he mean that? More to the point, did she want him to mean it? She swallowed. Was she brave enough to force the issue now, this minute? Go after what her heart was telling her she wanted, needed?

Jack hadn't missed her startled look, or the way her gaze fluttered down. Then back. He gave himself a mental kick. He shouldn't go around making facetious remarks like the one he'd just made. Look into her bedroom? What the hell had he been thinking of? But the remarks had just…slipped out. *Darcie*. Every time he looked at her, he came alive inside.

Wanting her.

But she was vulnerable.

So he shouldn't rush things.

It took him barely seconds to come to that conclusion.

'We'll talk soon, Darcie…'

Darcie caught her breath. The promise in his words was like a husky whisper over her skin, warming her.

For a second she looked at him like a deer caught in the headlights. She waited until her body regained its centre. Then she nodded. She knew what he meant. No explanations were needed.

Abruptly, Jack pulled his feet back and stood. 'Let's have a look at your patient, then, shall we?'

Jack's examination of David Campion was thorough. He ran his stethoscope over the man's chest and back, his mouth tightening. 'Cough for me now, please, David. And again. You've a few rattles in there. When did you last eat?' Folding his stethoscope, he parked himself on the end of the treatment couch.

'Dunno.' David shrugged his thin shoulders. 'Haven't felt hungry.'

'I'm going to keep you in.' Decisively, Jack began scribbling on the chart. 'You've a chest infection. We'll try to zap it before it turns nasty. I'd like to run a few tests as well, see if we can turn anything else up. Is that OK with you?'

The man blinked owlishly. 'I guess so.'

'We'll get you settled in the ward shortly, David.' Darcie sent her patient an encouraging smile. 'It was good you came in today.'

'A word, please, Darcie.' Jack clicked his pen shut and slid it into his shirt pocket. He stepped outside the cubicle and pulled the screens closed. 'Ask Maggie to get things rolling for David's admission, would you, please?'

'As soon as he's settled, I'll take the bloods,' Darcie said. 'What are we testing for?'

Jack reeled off what he wanted. 'Oh, add hypothroidism as well.'

Darcie frowned. Under-activity of the thyroid gland. 'That's more common in women, isn't it?'

'Perhaps.' Jack lifted a shoulder. 'But we can't take a gender-based view and not test for it. As a case in point, a couple of years ago at Mercy in Melbourne, they had a young *man* of twenty with breast cancer.'

'I guess it would explain David's continued lethargy to some extent,' she conceded.

'There were other pointers,' Jack expanded as they began to walk along the corridor. 'His heart rate was quite slow, plus his skin was as dry as old bones.'

'That could be because of a less than adequate diet and his iffy living conditions.'

Jack's mouth pleated at the corners. 'Well, we'll see when the bloods come back. Ask the lab to email the results, will you? We'll do a CT scan as well. We're equipped to do that here, aren't we?'

'Yes, but the technician is also the chemist, so I'll have to give her a call to come in.'

'Do that, then, please. Interesting case,' he said, as he handed her the chart and continued on his way.

It was a week before David's test results were back. Jack went to find Darcie and together they went along into his office.

When they were seated, she looked at him expectantly. 'So, was it the thyroid, as you suspected?'

'Mmm. Plus his iron stores are abysmally low. But we can treat him.'

'If we can find him,' Darcie warned. 'As you know, he discharged himself after only a day and went bush again.'

'You don't think he'll be at his shack?'

'Unlikely. He told me he has to get several paintings ready for a gallery in Melbourne a.s.a.p. He's possibly taken his swag and easel and gone somewhere to paint.'

Jack tugged thoughtfully at his bottom lip. 'Then we'd better find him and get him started on some medication. See if Maggie can draw us some kind of mud map for the general location where he might be. Fancy a ramble?'

Darcie looked torn. 'Should we both be away from the hospital?'

'It's quiet and it's not as though we're disappearing for the rest of the day.' He curved her a brief smile. 'I'm the boss and I'll take the flak if there's any. Look on it as doing a house call. If we can find David promptly, I'm hoping we may be able to persuade him to come back to the hospital with us.'

'That would be so helpful,' Darcie agreed. 'The sooner his condition is treated, the better.'

Jack got to his feet. 'That's why we need him here where we can monitor him and get his dose of thyroxine right.'

'That could be David's place through there.' Darcie pointed ahead to where a timber shack was just visible through the belt of spindly she-oaks. They'd been driving for about thirty minutes and Maggie's map had been spot on.

'Well, let's just hope he's home.' Jack brought the Land Rover to a stop.

Picking their way carefully, they climbed the rickety steps, stepping through a fringe of trailing vine to the landing. Raising his hand, Jack knocked and called out but there was no response and no sound from within. He placed his hand on the doorknob. 'Shall we?'

Darcie looked uncertain. 'Perhaps we're being a bit intrusive, Jack.'

'He could be ill and not able to answer the door.'

Jack's logic held up and Darcie nodded her assent.

The door was stuck hard and it needed extra impetus from Jack's knee to get it open. They stepped into the cool interior, which had light coming in from a glass panel at the rear of the building.

They stood there in complete silence until Darcie breathed, 'Oh, my goodness…'

'Wow,' Jack added, clearly awestruck.

The place was filled with artwork, unframed pictures of varying sizes and subjects, ranging from the simplicity of a handful of wildflowers in a jar to the dramatic wildness of a gathering storm.

Darcie's hand went to her throat. 'He's so talented.'

'Amazingly so.' Jack took a step backwards. 'We're treading on very private space, Darcie. I think we should go.'

They left quietly. Descending the steps, they stood for a moment and looked around.

'It's so still, isn't it?' Darcie sounded awed by the silence.

Jack's mouth folded in. 'Might be if the cicadas shut up for two seconds. But I know what you mean.'

It was the middle of the day, the sun high in the heavens, the feathery foliage of bush wattle trees clumping as far as the eye could see. Jack turned his gaze upwards, following the height of the eucalyptus that towered over a hundred feet into the sky. Then out to where the boulders rose up in uneven humps, their reddish-yellow tints like polished brass in the sun. He exhaled a long breath that turned into a sigh. 'David could be anywhere.'

'What should we do, then?'

'I guess we could try a coo-ee and see if we get any answer.'

Darcie knew he was referring to the Australian bush call. 'Go on, then,' she urged.

Jack needed no encouragement. Cupping his hands around his mouth, he called, 'Coo-ee-ee-ee.' The sound, high-pitched, reverberated and echoed back. And back.

They waited.

Nothing.

'Like to try one with me?' Jack's clear blue gaze suggested a challenge. 'Two of us might make a bit more of an impact.'

'Me?' Darcie wavered for a second. 'I've never…'

'Come on,' Jack encouraged. 'It's easy. Follow me.' She did and made a sound between a squawk and an out-of-tune trumpet.

Jack shook his head in disbelief. 'That wouldn't wake a baby! Let's go again. Ready?'

This time she did much better. 'Now I'm getting the hang of it,' she said, clearly delighted with her progress. 'Shall we try again?'

'Third time lucky?' His mouth quirked. 'Let's go.'

But there was still no answering call. Darcie turned away, disappointed. 'I hope he's not lying injured somewhere, Jack.'

'That's not likely. I'd guess he knows this part of the bush like the back of his hand. If he's heard us, he might simply have chosen not to respond.'

Darcie's gaze followed the myriad little bush tracks that ran off into the distance. 'Should we start looking then?'

'No.' Jack vetoed that idea. 'That's not our brief.'

'But David is ill, Jack. He needs treatment.'

'Yes, he does. I'll leave a note for him and shove it under his door.'

'Stress the urgency for him to come into the hospital, won't you?' Darcie looked concerned.

'Why don't you do it, then?' Jack flipped a spiral notebook and pen from his shirt pocket. 'Since David knows you, he might take more notice. While you're doing that, I'll give Maggie a call and check on things there.' Jack began moving to a spot from where he could get a signal for his mobile.

'Did you get on to Maggie?' Darcie asked when he returned.

'Nothing urgent on.'

'So we'll head back to town, then?'

'I think we could hang around a bit longer. David might show and it'd be a shame if we missed him. Let's give ourselves a break and find a shady spot where we can have our lunch.'

'Lunch? You brought lunch?'

He shrugged. 'I threw a bit of stuff together. It's always a good idea to carry food and water when you set out anywhere in this kind of country. Your vehicle can let you down, you can get lost, have an accident. Any number of unforeseen circumstances can see you stranded and waiting hours for help to come. And you don't venture out *anywhere* without telling someone where you're going.'

Darcie made a tsk. 'I *know* all that, Jack.'

'Just reinforcing the message,' he replied evenly. 'Can't have you getting lax.'

'As if!' she huffed, and set about helping him organise their picnic.

'That looks like a good spot over there.' He pointed towards some dappled shade provided by one of the gum trees. 'Bring the blanket from the back seat, will you, please? I'll just check there are no ants.' After a quick inspection he stated that it was OK.

'I see you've raided the hospital linen,' Darcie said, helping him spread the blanket on the grass.

He sent her a rakish grin. 'Are you going to report me?'

'Report you to *you*? Don't think I'll bother. Think of all the paperwork.'

He chuckled. It was brilliant to see her relaxed, upbeat and...happy. And he vowed to keep it that way. If he could. 'I'll just get the cooler.'

* * *

'I feel a bit guilty sitting here having lunch while our patient is missing,' Darcie said.

They'd eaten crusty bread rolls stuffed with cheese and cherry tomatoes and were finishing with coffee, from the flask Carole had thoughtfully provided, and some chocolate biscuits.

'We're just making the best use of our time,' Jack rationalised.

Darcie began gathering up the remains of their picnic. 'How long are we going to wait, Jack?'

'Darcie, it's been barely twenty minutes. Do you want us screaming with indigestion? We're entitled to time off but how often do we get it?'

'Not often...' Darcie made a small face. 'Well, not on a regular basis, I suppose...'

'So all the more reason to take it when the opportunity presents itself. And after all we could be considered working,' he said with a grin. 'We're waiting for a patient. Meanwhile, let's get more comfortable.'

When they'd settled themselves against the broad base of the gum tree, Jack turned to her. Raising his hand, he brushed the backs of his fingers gently across her cheek. 'This is good, isn't it?' he murmured.

'It's good...' Darcie voice faded to nothing. Almost without her noticing, he'd moved closer and gathered her in.

And in a second Darcie felt caught in a bubble. The world faded away and there was just the two of them. Her lips suddenly felt parched and she moistened them, her tongue flicking out to wet them.

Jack followed the darting movement and exhaled a long, slow breath. Leaning into her, he claimed her

mouth. He tasted coffee and chocolate and was instantly
addicted. A shot of adrenaline buzzed through his system. She opened her mouth on his, inviting him in. But
he wanted more. Much more. He wanted to lay her back
gently on the blanket. Make love to her here with nothing but the deep, rich smell of the earth and the sighs
and sounds of the bush around them. His hand shook
as it slid beneath her shirt and smoothed the softness of
her skin where her waist curved into her hip.

At last the kiss ended. But not their closeness. Jack
lowered his mouth to her throat, his lips on the tiny
pulse point that beat frantically beneath her chin.

Darcie felt her throat tighten, fluttering her eyes
closed as his fingertips idled, taking their time, delicate, like the finest strands of silk.

'Darcie...open your eyes for me...'

She did, every part of her aware of the heat of his
body against hers, of that fathomless blue gaze and of a
need as basic as her own. Lifting her hands to the back
of his neck, she gusted a tiny sigh. 'I wish we could
stay here for ever.'

They looked at each other for a long moment, un-
moving until Jack reached out a finger and began to
twine a silky lock of her hair around it. His gaze softened over her. 'Our time will come, Darcie.'

But obviously not today, she thought resignedly a
second later as his mobile rang.

Jack swore under his breath. 'Whoever invented cell-
phones should be sectioned.'

'Then what would we rely on?' Half-amused, Darcie drew herself to a sitting position. 'Coo-ee calls?'

'Well, not yours.' He grinned, mock-swiping her with
the offending phone and scrambling upright.

Activating the call, Jack said, 'Hi, Maggie, what's up?'

'Max Alderton's been injured. Severe neck wound.'

'What happened?'

'Apparently he was out on his motorbike, mustering. He ran into a single-strand wire placed across the track. Louise said it was put there deliberately.'

Jack whistled. 'What's the damage?'

'Profuse bleeding to the right side of his neck.'

'Can we expect arterial damage?'

'Lou isn't sure. Fortunately, Max had his mobile with him. He was able to alert Louise. She's bringing him straight in. I've told her to keep Max sitting up. But he should go straight to Theatre, Jack.'

'Yes.' *In a perfect world.* Jack was thinking fast. 'What staff do we have, available, Maggie?'

'Well, I can scrub in. And providentially Brad Kitto, one of the flying doctors, has just arrived, returning a patient from chemo in Brisbane. He'll gas for you.'

'He's qualified?'

'Extremely.'

'Good.' Jack felt relief wash through him. 'Ask him to scrub and get himself set up, please, Maggie. We'll cane it back now.'

Jack filled Darcie in on the way back to Sunday Creek.

'Oh, how dreadful for Max! And Louise thinks it was sabotage?'

'Seems so. Max has worked Willow Bend for over twenty years. You'd think he'd know if there were any single-strand fences about the place.'

Darcie shook her head. 'He could have been—'

'Decapitated.' Jack didn't mince words. 'If someone was out to injure him, it's an appalling situation.'

'You'll take him straight to Theatre?'

'Yes. Maggie's on it. And fortunately we have an anaesthetist. A contingent from the flying doctors arrived, returning a chemo patient.'

'Oh, that will be Heather Young. We like to keep her overnight and make sure everything's OK before she travels home.'

'And where's *home*?' Jack was concentrating on his driving, keeping the Land Rover at a swift but steady pace.

'Loganlea. About two hundred Ks out. Her family will be in to collect her tomorrow, I imagine.'

'What's Heather's prognosis?' Jack asked.

'Quite hopeful. But with cancer you never know.'

'Obviously you've been managing her care extremely well,' Jack said. 'I'll read the notes when I get a chance.' He glanced down at his watch. 'Another ten minutes should get us there.'

Darcie suppressed a sigh overlaying her concern for Max. In reality they were never off duty.

Already the enchantment of their magical time away from the hospital seemed light years away.

# CHAPTER EIGHT

THEY ARRIVED AT the hospital almost simultaneously with the Aldertons. Max was groggy but conscious. In no time at all they were all inside.

'Didn't need this...Doc,' he slurred.

'Save your strength, Max,' Jack said gently. 'We'll do the best we can for you.' He whipped out a stethoscope, listening intently, checking his patient's breathing. 'Seems OK.'

Tossing the stethoscope aside, he very carefully removed the thick towel from around Max's throat, examining the wound with a clinical eye. 'Main aorta is intact. You've been very lucky, mate. Clamps, please, Darcie.'

Darcie handed him the instrument resembling a cross between a pair of scissors and a pair of pliers. Systematically, he began a temporary closure of the wound. 'Would you dress it now, please?'

Darcie was ready with several thick pads to staunch any residual bleeding. 'He's ready for oxygen.' She looked sharply at Jack. 'What capacity do you want it?'

He made a moue. 'Make it eight litres a minute. We'll see what that tells us.'

Darcie worked automatically, dovetailing with Jack

as they carried out the emergency procedures. The probe was in place on Max's finger, allowing them to monitor the degree of oxygen saturation in his blood.

'We'll need a cross-match,' Jack said.

Natalie, who had been called in, said quietly, 'I'll sort that.'

'Thanks, Nat,' Jack acknowledged. He began preparing an IV line. 'How's the wound, Darcie?'

'Some seepage, but it's holding. Oxygen sats ninety per cent.' She gave a rundown of the BP and pulse readings. 'I'll get him some pain relief.'

When Darcie returned with the drugs, she could see Jack wasn't taking any chances. Max had been placed on a heart monitor.

Darcie shot the pethidine and anti-emetic home. 'He should begin stabilising fairly quickly. You should get to Theatre, Jack. Go,' she insisted, when he hesitated. 'I can monitor things here.'

'OK.' Jack ripped off his gloves and tossed them aside. 'And find Louise, Darcie. Give her as much support as you can.'

'Of course.' Darcie tamped down a prickle of annoyance. She'd have done that anyway.

Darcie found Louise standing beside the window in the patients' lounge, looking out as if fixed on a spot in the distance.

'Lou?'

Louise spun round. 'How is he?' she asked without preamble.

'He's stabilised. Natalie's just taken him along to Theatre. Come and sit down,' Darcie urged. 'I've asked Carole to bring us a pot of tea.'

'Ironic, isn't it?' Louise sent a distracted glance around the room. 'I never thought when I organised for this lounge to be refurbished that I'd be one of the first making use of it. Max will be all right, won't he, Darcie?'

Darcie hesitated. In emergency situations no result was ever guaranteed. 'Jack is a fine surgeon.'

'Thank God we have him here.' Louise's statement was heartfelt. 'Otherwise Max would have had to wait hours for the flying doctor to come and then be transported miles away for surgery. How long will the operation take?'

'We can't know that until Jack assesses the extent of Max's injury. Oh, here's Carole with the tea.'

'I've made a few little sandwiches as well,' Carole said. 'Wasn't sure if you'd managed a bite to eat before Mr Alderton had his accident.'

'That's very kind of you, Carole.' Louise gave a trapped smile. 'Thank you.'

'You're welcome, dear.' Carole went on her way.

Darcie poured the tea. 'How did all this happen? Jack mentioned something about sabotage.'

'Something like this makes my blood run cold.' Louise shook her head as if in disbelief. 'Max is a generous and fair employer. I can't think why anyone would want to hurt him.'

Darcie frowned. 'So, you think it was someone who worked for you?'

'A couple of young farm labourers. Max caught them stealing petrol. We keep large quantities of fuel for the farm vehicles and machinery. Max gave them a warning and they told him they were sorry and they'd only wanted to top up their ute to go to a dance over at Barclay.'

'And Max believed them?'

'He put it down to them being young and wanting a night out. And they offered to pay for it but Max said he'd let it go this time.' Louise took a nibble of her sandwich. 'Then two days ago he caught them at it again. But this time they were filling drums—obviously to sell. As far as Max was concerned, that was the end of their employment. He sacked them then and there and gave them an hour to be off the property.'

'Oh, lord.' Darcie gave her a wide-eyed look. 'So, they've got back at him in this awful way...'

'Looks like it. They knew his daily routine, knew where he'd be and when. They'd seen it often enough. They obviously set up the wire during the night.'

'That's so calculated. And so frightfully scary. Have you spoken to the police?'

'I've given them what information I had and what I surmised had happened. They'll take it from there. My concern has to be for Max and his recovery.' Louise rubbed a hand across her temple as if staving off a headache. 'You'll have to keep him in, won't you?'

'For a few days at least,' Darcie said. 'And Max will have to put up with his food being puréed for a little while. But as soon as he's able to swallow comfortably and if everything else checks out, he should be as right as rain again.'

Louise blinked rapidly. 'You can't imagine the relief to know you and Jack are in charge of our hospital, Darcie. And to have the theatre up and running. That hasn't happened in years.'

'Well, that was mainly Jack's initiative,' Darcie said fairly.

'But you supported it, surely?'

'Of course.' *Eventually.* 'Jack has far more experience than I do,' Darcie said carefully.

Nodding almost absently, Louise glanced at her watch.

'It'll be a while yet, Lou,' Darcie said gently. 'Would you feel more comfortable over at the residence? I'd come and get you when Max is back from Theatre.'

'No, I'm fine here. But thanks.' Louise managed a small smile, looking around her at the array of up-to-date magazines, the colourful mugs and facilities for making a hot drink. She flicked hand. 'Your little touches, I'd guess. Am I right?'

'Nothing worse than sitting in a dreary hospital lounge, waiting for news of a loved one.' Darcie offloaded the praise with a shrug.

'You feel in tune here in Sunday Creek, don't you.'

It was more a statement than a question. Darcie took a moment to answer. 'Yes, I do,' she said simply. And *safer* than she'd felt in her whole life. 'The outback has touched something deep down inside me.' Her downcast lashes fanned darkly across her cheekbones. 'That must sound a bit...odd.'

'Not odd at all.' Louise's green eyes grew soft. 'It's why most of us continue to live out here, through good times and bad. But don't let me keep you, Darcie.' Louise picked up one of the glossy magazines. 'I'll be fine. And you must have a hundred things to do.'

It was late afternoon. At the nurses' station Darcie began writing up her notes on Emma Tynan. The thirteen-year-old had been admitted the previous night with an asthma attack. Thank heaven she was stabilising, Darcie noted, but not as quickly as she would have hoped. 'You know, Nat,' she said thoughtfully, 'I have a feeling Kristy Tynan is still smoking around her daughter. But as usual Emma is totally loyal and noncommittal.'

Natalie shook her head. 'I sometimes wonder who exactly *is* the mother in that family.'

'Kristy works those awful shifts in the truckers' café,' Darcie said. 'It can't be easy for either of them. Do you know if there's a dad anywhere about?'

'Sorry, can't help you there. Kristy and her daughter landed here a couple of years ago. They live in that block of flats near the bowls club.'

Darcie replaced the file. 'Do you think Emma has to fend for herself, then?'

'Well, she'd certainly be on her own a bit with her mother's shiftwork.'

'Poor little thing.'

Natalie gave a frustrated click. 'I can't understand why Kristy can't just ditch the smokes and be done with them.'

'Some folk find it very difficult,' Darcie came in diplomatically. 'It's simply the drug they cling to when they're constantly under stress.'

'I guess so.' Natalie's sympathy showed. 'I could up the percussion on Emma's back if you think it would help. Just to keep an eye on how she's recovering.'

'Yes, it would, thanks, Nat.'

'Oh, look…thank goodness…' The nurse exhaled a relieved breath. 'Here come the guys at last.'

Darcie swung round. Although neither she nor Natalie had voiced their thoughts, she knew they'd been waiting for news of Max's surgery for the past hour. 'Oh, Brad's here!' Darcie was smiling.

'I thought you knew.'

Darcie shook her head. 'Jack just said one of the flying doctors was going to gas for him.'

Natalie leaned forward confidentially. 'Brad fancies you.'

'Brad's in love with life,' Darcie dismissed, feeling her nerves tense slightly, her cheeks grow warm, as the doctors crossed to the station.

'Hey, *Dee-Dee*!' Brad almost quickstepped to Darcie's side, flinging his arms around her in a bear hug. 'Good to see you, babe.'

*Dee-Dee?* Arms folded, Jack's gaze narrowed in speculation. What the hell was that about?

Feeling pink and flustered, Darcie disengaged herself from Brad's arms. 'I didn't realise you were the escort bringing Heather back to us.'

'You bet. I had to bribe someone to get the gig.' Brad's white smile flashed briefly. 'Couldn't miss the chance of seeing you. Harry's here too.'

Darcie nodded. 'I saw Harry earlier.' Harry Liston was one of the regular pilots for the flying doctors. 'Are you on turn-around or can you stay with us tonight?'

'Counting on it.' Brad did an impressive little drumroll with his fingers on the countertop. 'Let's have a party, huh? We've brought seafood. Maybe we could gas up the barbecue?'

'Maybe…' Darcie gave a breathless little laugh.

'Natalie, you in?' Brad turned teasing blue eyes on the RN.

'Sorry, I'll have to pass.' Natalie propped her chin on her upturned hand and looked on amusedly. 'I'll be sharing dinner with my two-year-old.'

'That's too bad—'

'Where's Louise?' Jack cut in, his voice tripwire-tight.

Darcie blinked uncertainly. 'She's here, in the lounge.'

'Wouldn't she have been more comfortable over at the residence?'

Darcie's chin came up. He'd said it brusquely enough to sound like a reprimand. 'I offered,' she replied coolly. 'Louise preferred to wait here. I gather Max's surgery went well?'

'Brad will fill you in. I need to speak with Louise,' he muttered, before striding off.

Watching his retreating back, Darcie fancied she was dodging the invisible bullets he'd fired. But dropping innuendos was not Jack's style. If he had an issue with anyone or anything, he was upfront about it. So what was suddenly bugging him? She turned to Brad for enlightenment. 'There wasn't a problem in surgery, was there?'

Brad pursed his lips as if reluctant to get into it. 'Bit of a glitch when we were halfway through. But we were on it. Max will be just fine,' he confirmed.

Darcie couldn't help the relief she felt, both for Max and Louise but for Jack as well.

A beat of silence, until Brad continued quietly, 'It seems today's surgery was something of a litmus test for the viability of the OR.' He saw her tight little nod and added, 'Jack knows what he's doing, Dee. Trust me. I know a good surgeon when I see one.'

\* \* \*

Jack swore silently and darkly as he headed towards the hospital lounge. Did Darcie have something going with Kitto?

Was she sleeping with him?'

He tried the shattering thought on for size. Did it fit?

He hissed a rebuttal through tight lips. That seemed inconceivable. Only a few hours ago *they'd* been as close as any two people could be without actually making love.

Something in Jack's heart scrunched tight.

Surely she wasn't playing him…

Pausing outside the door of the lounge, he took a deep breath, knocked and went in. It took a herculean effort to force his lips into a smile. But his eyes were unable to hide the mixed emotions that stalked him.

Deep in thought, Jack almost collided with Darcie as they made their way from opposite ends of the corridor some time later. He pulled up short. 'What are you still doing here?'

Darcie all but rolled her eyes. What did he think she was doing there? 'Maggie has to get off. We were just ensuring cover is in place for the night shift.'

'Shouldn't you be over at the residence, looking after our visitors?'

Darcie took a calming breath. There was that innuendo again. She had to be professional here. It was obvious *he* wasn't capable of it. 'They're well able to look after themselves. Lauren's there anyway and I imagine a few more folk will turn up if a party's in the offing. You look like you could do with an evening off yourself.'

Two frown lines jumped into sharp relief between his eyes. 'I need to be here to keep an eye on Max post-op.'

'If you're needed, you're two minutes away at the house.'

'It's fine.' His mouth drew in. 'I'd like to stick around for Louise as well.'

Darcie took a step back as if to regain her space. This was getting too petty for words. 'Why are you being like this?'

Jack folded his arms, leaning back against the wall, challenge like a gathering storm sending his eyes to darkest blue. 'Like what?'

She raised a shoulder uncertainly. 'So...cross.'

'Cross?' The storm broke into harmless little showers and he looked amused.

Darcie sucked in her breath. 'You know what I mean. You're offside with me and with Brad as well. Surely, you should be thanking him for stepping up today.'

'We've debriefed,' Jack said shortly. 'I have no problem with Brad's medical skills.'

Darcie's thoughts were churning but this conversation was going nowhere. 'Lou will want to stay in town tonight. We're a bit full up at the residence...'

'She's made arrangements to stay at the motel. She knows the managers. They'll make her comfortable. In any event, she'll want to stay here with Max for a while longer.'

'Then what?' Darcie pressed determinedly. 'You'll come home and share a meal with the rest of us?'

In other words, pretend to be sociable? Pretend he was oblivious? 'No offence, Darcie, but as the senior doctor I should be here. Today's circumstances were... unusual to put it mildly. But we coped.'

But at what cost? Darcie wondered. Already there was an air of tension emanating from him. Her mouth thinned. If he'd allow her, she could massage his stress away in a second. But the way he was acting around her, he'd probably prefer a one-way conversation with Capone than let *her* anywhere near him. Instead, she held her head high and said clearly, so there would be no mistake, 'Since you've elected to remain on duty, I'll be here first thing in the morning to check on Max. Feel free to catch up on some sleep.'

Jack completed a final ward round and found nothing untoward with any of the patients. Max's status was stable and he'd been placed in the hospital's only private room. Ursula Cabot was a competent night sister so why wasn't he over at the residence, partying with the rest of the team?

Because he was being plain stubborn, wallowing in a pool of self-induced jealousy.

Jack passed sentence on himself, ploughing a hand through his hair in frustration as he made his way along to the hospital kitchen. Ten minutes later he was half-heartedly forking his way through yesterday's casserole, trying to ignore the tantalising aroma of garlic prawns wafting through the window. The seafood barbecue was obviously in full swing.

'Fool,' he muttered, giving up on the casserole and consigning it to the waste bin. He'd acted like a jerk towards Darcie earlier. But the fact was he'd hated to see her wrapped in another man's arms *Hated it*.

He wandered back to the nurses' station, realising the soft hush of night had crept over the hospital without him even noticing.

Ursula Cabot sat under the subdued lighting at the station, her blonde-grey head bent over a crossword puzzle. She looked up as Jack leaned across the counter.

'Would you like a cup of tea, Ursula?'

'No, thanks.' The senior nurse shook her head. 'I've already had several since I came on duty. And you're wearing out the floorboards, Jack. Go home. Isn't there a party going on at the residence?'

Jack lifted a shoulder indifferently. 'I'm just here to keep an eye on things. Max Alderton had major surgery today.'

'And that's why *I'm* here,' Ursula said dryly. 'I checked Max only five minutes ago and I'll keep monitoring him regularly.' She sent Jack a reproving look over the rims of her smart black-framed glasses. 'There's no need for you to keep hovering, Dr Cassidy. I'll call you if I need you.'

Jack's mouth flattened in a thin smile. 'You're chucking me out.'

'Seems like it. Now, scoot. There's dancing happening, by the sound of it. Go and join the fun. Have a twirl around the floor with Darcie. I'll bet that girl's light on her feet.'

Oh, she was. As light as air. At least, that's how she'd felt in his arms.

Jack's thoughts were spinning as he made his way slowly across to the residence. Would he look in on the party? Perhaps. Perhaps not. As he opened the front gate, Capone stirred from his special place under the steps and came to meet him. 'Hello, boy.' Putting out a hand, Jack rubbed the dog's neck as he pushed in against his legs. Then, seemingly satisfied with the small show of attention, Capone gave a feeble wag of his tail, breaking the contact and wandering back to his hidey-hole.

Jack mounted the steps, hearing the music in the form of Norah Jones's husky voice urging someone to 'come away with me'. He dragged in a shallow breath, his normal good sense shattering by the second. Was Brad Kitto even now urging Darcie to do just that? And would she be tempted?

He didn't want to know.

Instead, he bypassed the rec room, where the party was happening, and made his way along the hall to his bedroom.

Minutes later, he was lying in bed, arms wishboned behind his head, staring at the ceiling. But all he saw was the hurt puzzlement in Darcie's eyes staring back at him. She hadn't understood his stubbornness earlier. Hell, he hardly understood it himself.

How could he have acted like that? As though he was some kind of martyred soul? Had what happened with Zoe destroyed his trust in women so thoroughly? God, he hoped not. Rolling over, he buried his face in the pillow. He had to try to keep his trust in what he and Darcie shared.

Somehow.

# CHAPTER NINE

DARCIE CAME THROUGH the silent house, looking for Jack. She finally located him outside, where the morning's soft rays were illuminating the courtyard. He was sitting at the wooden table, nursing a mug of tea, Capone at his side.

'Morning.' She went briskly down the steps.

Jack looked up and felt something shift in his chest. She was dressed in cotton trousers and a pinstriped shirt that moulded every one of her curves. She was femininity in motion.

'I thought you were going to sleep in.' She pulled out a chair and sat down. It was barely seven.

'I did sleep in. How are things at the hospital?'

'Max was in some pain. Brad upped his meds. Otherwise he'd had a reasonable night.'

Jack sent her a mocking kind of look. 'Has our fly-boy gone?'

'He left a while ago.' Darcie kept her cool. 'He and Harry wanted to be on their way. We were up before five.'

*We?* Jack's mouth tightened. Hearing the inclusive pronoun, his worst fear seemed validated.

'So…' Darcie blinked a bit. He seemed suddenly

distant, locked down. 'What are you going to do with your day off?'

'I wasn't aware I was having one,' he growled.

Darcie took a deep breath and threw caution to the winds. 'You're acting like a grumpy teen, Jack. I know you're the boss but you need a change of scene. And I'm quite capable of running things at the hospital. There's fishing tackle in the garage. Go and make use of it. Bunbilla Crossing is a good place to start.'

Jack moved his lips in a mocking little twist. 'So says the girl from England.'

Darcie refused to be drawn. 'Take Capone. You seem to prefer his company to that of the rest of us.' She stood and pushed her chair in. 'And I'll expect some decent-sized river perch for dinner tonight.'

Darcie inspected Max's wound. 'You're looking good, Max.' She smiled. 'We'll review your swallow in a day or so. But so far everything's textbook.'

Max managed a husky 'Thanks'.

She placed a hand on his forearm and squeezed. 'Lauren will replace your dressing now and Jack will see you first thing tomorrow.' At least, she hoped he would.

Darcie was thoughtful as she made her way back to the station.

'Jack for you.' Maggie held up the landline phone.

Darcie's heart skipped. She put the receiver to her ear. 'Jack?'

'Dinner in fifteen,' he said. 'Can you be here?'

'Just about to clock off.'

'Good. See you in a bit.'

'Wait…' Darcie sensed he was about to hang up. 'Did you catch my fish?'

He snorted. 'Of course I caught your fish. Hurry up.'

A trapped smile edged Jack's mouth as he put the phone down. She'd been right. He had needed to get away from the hospital, if only for a few hours. The break had re-energised him. He'd swum in the river, baked in the sun for a bit.

And caught her fish.

All things considered, he'd fulfilled all the requirements for a satisfactory day off.

Darcie had guessed what he'd needed and that had to mean something.

He couldn't wait to see her.

Darcie's feet had wings as she made her way across to the residence. A sense of relief washed through her. She'd been afraid she might have overstepped the mark, but it sounded as though Jack had accepted her suggestion without rancour and had taken himself off for the day. There'd been a lightness back in his voice. Suddenly life felt good again.

Making her way across the back deck, she popped her head in the kitchen. 'Hi.'

Jack looked up from preparing the fish. 'Hi, yourself.'

She smiled. 'Can you hold dinner for a few more minutes? I need to jump in the shower.'

He waved her away. 'I won't start cooking until you get here.'

Darcie was in and out of the shower in record time, the sweet sting of anticipation slithering up her spine. Bypassing her usual casual cargos and T-shirt, she pulled on a sundress in a pretty floral print, admitting she wanted to look special for Jack. They needed to re-connect. She knew that instinctively.

Taking a moment to look in the long mirror, she decided she'd do. The top of the dress was held up by shoestring straps, showing off the light tan she'd ac-quired. And just wearing the dress made her feel cool and feminine—and something else.

Desirable?

She stopped for a moment and took a deep breath. There was so much going on between her and Jack. So many undercurrents. He hadn't spelled anything out. Neither had she.

She scooped her hair away from her neck and let it fall loosely to her shoulders. This evening was to be about relaxing. Not supposition. Closing her bedroom door quietly, she went along the hallway, passing the dining room on the way. Stopping, she peered in. Her hand went to her throat. 'Wow...'

'Darcie, you ready?' Jack's voice came from the kitchen.

'I'm here.' She stepped through the doorway into the kitchen.

Jack's eyes swept her from head to toe.

'We're eating in the dining room, I gather?'

'Well, a portion of it,' he countered with a dry smile. He'd set one end of the long refectory table after finding rather elegant placemats and cutlery in a drawer of the big old-fashioned sideboard and had thought, Why not?

'Can I give you a hand?' Darcie's eyes flicked over him, her gaze almost hungry. By now she knew all his features by heart—the clear blue eyes that spelled honesty, the dark hair, always a bit unruly, springing back from his temples, the strength of his facial features, honed to an almost hawk-like leanness. And his mouth—the gateway to the fulfilment of all her private dreams…

'You could pour us a glass of wine,' Jack said. 'There's a Riesling in the fridge. I thought it would go well with our fish. And Lauren's left some kind of salad.'

'Oh, that was sweet of her.' Darcie brought out the wine and the salad from the fridge. 'How are you cooking the fish?'

'I'll pan-fry it.' Jack raised a dark brow. And then let it rest in the oven for a minute or two. 'Is that all right with you?'

'Perfectly. I'm sure it'll be wonderful.'

It was.

Jack had prepared the fish into chunky fillets, leaving the skin on. Pan-fried quickly, the flesh was crisp, full of flavour and delicious.

'That's the best meal I've eaten in weeks,' Darcie said, replete.

Jack swirled the last of his wine in his glass. 'What about your seafood last night?'

'It was nice,' Darcie allowed, with a little shrug. 'But this was much more special.'

'In what way?' His dark head at an angle, Jack looked broodingly at her.

She swallowed dryly. Even in the subdued light from the candles they'd lit, she could feel the intensity of his gaze. 'Because you cooked it especially for me.' A beat of silence. 'Didn't you?' She felt her eyes drawn helplessly to his.

'I *needed* to do something for you.' He threw back

his head and finished his wine in a gulp. 'After my boorish behaviour recently, I thought you might walk,' he admitted candidly.

'Leave?' Darcie almost squawked. 'Why would I do that? Anyway, I have a contract. So unless you're booting me out, Dr Cassidy, I'm not going anywhere.'

Jack couldn't believe the relief he felt. 'So…when will you be seeing Brad again?'

'I have no idea. But he's extended his time here for a couple of months so I imagine he'll be back and forth a bit.'

'You seemed pretty *cosy* with him.'

'And you couldn't wait to make a snap judgement.' Two spots of colour glazed Darcie's cheeks. She knew where he was going with this and felt like thumping him. 'I don't creep around keeping men on a string. That's not my style at all. And if you know anything about me, Jack, you should *know* that.'

'OK…' Jack held up his hand in acceptance. 'I admit to a streak of jealousy a mile wide. I'm sorry for thinking what I did. Deep down I knew it wasn't like you. I—just couldn't seem to get past the possibility…'

Darcie gave a sharp glance at the sudden tight set of his shoulders. So, someone, somewhere had stuffed up his ability to trust. It didn't take much imagination to know where the blame lay. She pressed forward gently. 'What kind of relationship did you have with your former girlfriend? You gave the impression it was just a mutual parting of the ways. But I have to wonder if it was as simple as that…'

'I don't want to talk about it.'

Darcie *tsked* and gave a little toss of her head. 'So,

it's OK to have me spilling the facts of my messed-up love-life but not you. How is that fair, Jack?'

It wasn't fair at all, Jack had to admit. But he'd been left feeling such a fool and worse. He dragged air in and expelled it. 'You want me to talk about this here? Now?'

'The place doesn't matter.' Her voice was soft, intense. 'The telling does. Begin with her name, Jack. And go from there.'

'Zoe,' he said after the longest pause. 'You already know some of the rest of it.'

'Some but not all,' Darcie said calmly. 'Go on.'

He rubbed a hand across his eyes. 'We met in Sydney through mutual friends. We hit it off. Pretty soon we were a couple. Our lives were busy, different, and that's probably what kept everything fresh.'

'But you had such diverse callings,' Darcie stressed.

'Yes.' Jack eased back in his chair, unaware his eyes had taken on a bleak look. 'Back then, Zoe had stage roles so she was working mostly at night. I worked mostly in the day. At first it didn't seem to matter. We grabbed what time we had. Made the most of it.'

Mostly in bed, Darcie interpreted, and felt a spasm of dislike for this woman who had obviously led Jack a merry dance and then for whatever reason had dumped their relationship and him along with it.

'Zoe wanted to try her chances for work in England.' Jack picked up the thread of the conversation reluctantly. 'It seemed feasible and obviously I didn't want us to be separated so I applied for an exchange. It took a while to organise and Zoe was over there for three months before I could join her.'

'But surely you kept in touch?'

'Of course, but, looking back now, I see it was mostly

at my instigation. Zoe just said she was doing the rounds of the casting agents and I understood how much time and effort that took. Then, almost simultaneously, she landed a film part and my exchange came through. I texted her to let her know I was on my way. Told her what flight I was on.'

And he would have been full of expectation and excitement at the prospect of reuniting with his lover. Darcie's heart ached for him. She felt a moment of doubt. Perhaps she shouldn't have started any of this... She held out her hand to him across the table and he took it, clasped it and looked her squarely in the eyes.

She blinked. 'Stop now, if you want to, Jack. I think I know what happened.'

'I arrived in London a day earlier than scheduled.' Jack went on as though she hadn't spoken. 'I went straight to her flat. Zoe opened the door. It was obvious my arrival was unexpected, to say the least.'

Darcie took a dry swallow and tried gently to fill in the picture he was painting. 'She was there with someone else?'

He gave a hard laugh. 'Well, they weren't in bed but near as dammit. She was in a dressing gown and he was parked against the bedroom door, smoking one of those filthy cheroots. I wanted to smash the place up and him along with it.'

Oh, lord. Darcie took a breath so deep it hurt. 'So, it ended then and there? Did you not...talk?' Yet *she* hadn't, Darcie had to admit. She'd just cut and run...

'At that moment there didn't seem much point.' Jack gave a hollow laugh. 'But we did meet up some time later. Zoe simply said she'd moved on. That *Simon* was an actor, that he gave her what she needed. What I obviously hadn't been able to.'

Darcie heard the pain in his voice. 'You must have been gutted.'

His jaw worked a bit before he answered. 'I just got on with things. I had to. And I am *over* her.'

But there was still a residue of hurt there, Darcie decided. She ran her tongue over her bottom lip. 'That's probably why you didn't enjoy your time in England as much as you should have.'

'Possibly.'

'If you'd been with me, I could have shown you the most wonderful time, the magical places that make England so special.'

A beat of silence.

'I'm sorry you had to leave your country,' he said softly, his gaze, blue, clear and caressing, locking with hers.

'Don't be. Life happens, as they say.' Her smile was a little forced as she got to her feet. 'Now, what about a cup of tea?'

Jack felt his throat thicken. The need to hold her and kiss her was so urgent he almost jumped up from the table to make it happen. Instead, he let the avalanche of emotion wash over him. 'Tea sounds good.' His jaw tightened for a moment. 'And, Darcie?'

'Jack?' She turned back.

'Thanks for the talk. And the day off.'

They took their tea and some chocolate mints Darcie found and went outside to the courtyard. 'We seem to make a habit of this,' she said, as they made themselves comfortable.

'It's a good place to relax, listen to the night sounds. Are you used to them yet?'

'Mostly.' Darcie made a small downturn of her mouth. 'But the dingoes' howling at night still scares the life out of me. Thankfully, they don't come too close.'

'They're carnivores, for the most part,' Jack said. 'They hunt smaller animals. They only venture closer to civilisation when they can't find food.'

'So I wouldn't find one waiting for me on the back deck, then?

He chuckled. 'Unlikely. And even if you did, the dingo would be more scared of you than you of it.'

'Well, I hope so.' Darcie didn't sound convinced.

'Darcie, they're native dogs, not wolves,' Jack's eyes crinkled in soft amusement. 'The rangers keep tabs on their whereabouts so stop worrying.'

They lapsed into easy silence until Jack said, 'Would you mind if we talked shop a for a bit?'

Darcie gave a throaty laugh. 'I'd be amazed if we didn't. I've held off so you'd feel you'd had a *real* day off.'

'It was good.' Jack lifted his arms to half-mast and stretched. 'Very good.'

'So, where do you want to start?' Darcie said.

'How's Max's recovery?'

'So far, he's checking out well. Pain-free for most of today. I told him we'll review his swallow quite soon.'

Jack made a moue of conjecture. 'I'd like to leave it for a bit longer.' He paused and stroked his thumb across the handle of his tea mug. 'Brad filled you in about Max's surgery?'

'Yes, he did,' Darcie said slowly. 'He said it was your skill as a surgeon that got him through.'

'Generous of him.' Jack's mouth tightened. 'It was a joint effort. Brad's an instinctive clinician.'

'That's what makes him such a good fit for the flying doctors.'

'Mmm.' Jack's mouth curled into a noncommittal moue. He didn't want the obvious warmth she felt towards Kitto burning a hole in his skull. So, move on. 'The whole episode relating to Max's surgery got me thinking, though.'

'In what way?'

'We need to re-evaluate what kinds of surgery can be safely carried out here. And I want you to know I'd never have attempted Max's surgery without knowing there was a qualified anaesthetist on board. I'd have had Max flown out. You were right to be cautious about opening the theatre.' He held her gaze steadily. 'On the other hand, I was pretty arrogant about what could be accomplished here.'

Darcie's quick glance was very perceptive. As a proud man, she guessed it had cost him something to have admitted his lapse. 'But there was no harm done, Jack.'

'This time.' He gave a jaded laugh. 'I want you to know I would never put you in any position where you felt medically compromised, Darcie. In other words, only the very basic surgical procedures will be done here in future. And whether or not we decide to do them at all will in turn be a joint decision.'

'That's more than fair. Thank you.' After a moment, she continued. 'But I think we need to get this across to the board. And where Louise is concerned, gently, of course. But she took it as read that Max's surgery would happen here. She was grateful and relieved that he wouldn't have to be flown miles away.'

Jack gave a philosophical shrug. 'Well, I'll talk to her privately about that. As for the rest of the board, they'll have to be made aware that we call the shots about medical protocols.'

Which was what she'd tried to convey in the first place, Darcie thought. But she didn't bear grudges. She was just infinitely glad that the matter had been settled and that Jack had been the one to call it.

'Sunday Creek hospital is very lucky to have you, Darcie Drummond.'

'Pft!' Darcie dismissed the earnest look in his eyes and said lightly, 'It's a team effort between the doctors and the nurses. The practice only functions because of the efforts of both.'

His lips tweaked to a one-cornered grin. 'Well, that seems that matter dealt with. Any news of David Campion?'

Darcie shook her head. 'I'm still hoping he'll make his own way in to us.'

'If he feels grotty enough, he may,' Jack conceded. 'Let's hope your intuition is right.'

'Oh, it will be.' Darcie's lips turned up prettily. She got to her feet. 'Now, I'm going to do the dishes.'

'I'll help you.' Jack was on his feet as well.

'Uh-uh.' Darcie waved away his offer. 'You got dinner.'

'Oh, let's just leave it. I'll bung it all in the dishwasher later,' Jack declared, moving around the table toward her.

In a second she was in his arms.

'About before…' Darcie's look was contrite, her eyes glistening in the muted light. 'I didn't mean to pry.'

'It's fine,' he answered, meaning it. 'And you know what, Dr Drummond?'

She shook her head.

'You're a very good listener.'

'Oh. But I only—'

He kissed her into silence.

'You have the sexiest lips,' he said gruffly, looking down at her.

'Do I?' Her gaze widened and she saw the heat flare in his.

'You do,' he murmured, just before he claimed her mouth again.

Darcie made a tiny sound like a purr and felt a strange lightness, as if love and desire had rolled into one high-voltage surge, sweeping through her body and out to the tips of her fingers and toes. And with a half-formed decision of whatever would be would be, she curled her body into his, each curve and hollow finding a home, a placement, as though they'd been carved out and had been waiting to be filled.

When he pulled back, she felt empty, bereft. She looked up at him, warm honey flecks of uncertainty chasing through her eyes.

Looking at her, Jack felt all his senses go into free-fall. Was this the moment he asked her to go to bed with him? If not now, then when? He agonised for a few seconds, waiting for the words to form. In the almost dark the night air around them began snapping with cicada clicks and simmering with the sharp scent of lemon tea-trees.

'We could take this inside…' he murmured tautly.

Jack's meaning was clear and Darcie felt the nerves grab in her stomach, her mind zeroing in on the fact that they had the house to themselves and there was no one to disturb them. Whatever they chose to do...

'I want to be with you, Darcie. Let me...' His hands stroked up her arms before he gathered her in again, holding her to him so that she felt the solid imprint of him from thigh to breast.

'Jack...' She drew in breath, feeling his hands on her lower back, tilting her closer still, and the wild sting of anticipation pin-pricked up her spine.

'Just say the word.' His plea was muffled against her hair.

Darcie's arms went round his neck, images she'd dreamt about chasing sensible thoughts away. She longed to tell him what he so wanted to hear. But a little voice in her head told her that once they had taken that step, there was no going back. Nothing between them would be simple again.

And there'd be nowhere to hide if it all went wrong. Nowhere.

Wordlessly, she stepped away from him, wrapping her arms around her midriff. 'Jack—there's a thousand reasons why we shouldn't go rushing into things.'

'Who's rushing?' He made a sound of dissension. 'This has been waiting to happen for weeks. You *know* we'd be good together.' His voice was husky with gentle persuasion.

Darcie kept her gaze lowered, unwilling to let him see her fears, her vulnerability.

'You're scared, aren't you?'

She licked suddenly dry lips. 'Can you blame me?'

'No.' Jack thrust back against the lattice wall. 'But

I blame that piece of work in England who took away your ability to trust your own judgement. But you have to trust again, Darcie. You have to trust *me*!'

Her heart scrunched tight and she shut her eyes against the surge of desire. This was what she wanted, wasn't it? To be a *real* part of Jack's life. Yet something pulled her back from the edge. 'Just give me a little space, Jack. A little more time.'

'Time for what, Darcie?' Jack's voice was without rancour but he was clearly frustrated. 'To start over-thinking things. Imagining worst-case scenarios? Come on…'

'Come on, what?' She spun away when he would have contained her. 'You want instant solutions.' Her heart began beating with an uncomfortable swiftness. 'Well, sorry, Jack. I can't give you any.'

Suddenly the atmosphere between them was thick and uncomfortable.

'We have to work together,' she said without much conviction. 'Day in, day out.'

'So what?' He huffed a jaded laugh. 'Are you saying we can't have a personal life outside the hospital?' He pushed a hand roughly through his hair in irritation.

'I'm not being difficult for the sake of it, Jack.'

He shrugged.

Her eyes searched his face. 'We can't leave things like this.'

'I know.'

'How can we go forward, then?'

'I'll back off,' he said, as if coming to a decision.

'I— Thank you.' She forced the words past the dryness in her throat.

His mouth tightened for a second. An intensity of

emotion he'd never felt before gnawed at his insides. God, she was so brave and beautiful. He curled his hands into fists to stop them reaching for her. 'The last thing I want is to be offside with you, Darcie. What can we do to make things right again?'

Her uncertainty wavered and waned. She couldn't doubt his sincerity. And she should remember that this was Jack Cassidy, proud and purposeful. And if it came down to it, she'd trust him with her life.

'I suppose we could kiss and make up,' she said softly.

Jack needed no second invitation. Keeping his hands off her by sheer strength of will, he bent towards her, letting his tongue just touch her lower lip as lightly as he could manage when every cell in his body wanted to devour the sweet mouth that opened for him so enticingly. Slowly, slowly, he drew back. 'Sweet dreams, then...' he murmured, and touched his forehead to hers. 'Just make them all about me, hmm?'

Darcie felt the smile on her skin as he touched his mouth to her throat. 'As long as you reciprocate, hmm?'

'Done.' He leaned forward and placed a quick, precise kiss on her lips. Hell, when the time was right, and they'd be able to make dreams into reality, he'd make her feel so *loved*, she wouldn't be able to see straight for a week.

# CHAPTER TEN

WITHIN TWO WEEKS Max had been discharged and was doing well. David Campion had come to the hospital and been treated and was now following a health regime Jack had set out for him.

Life was good, Darcie thought reflectively as she updated Emma Tynan's chart at the nurses' station. And although they hadn't actually spelled it out, she felt as though she and Jack had reached a plateau in their personal relationship.

Everything was possible. And the thought lit her up from inside. She made a reflective moue, bringing her thoughts back to Emma. Was there something more she could be doing for the child's wellbeing? She was such a plucky little thing...

'Excuse me, Darcie...'

'Oh, Carole.' Darcie's head came up and she smiled. 'Sorry, I didn't see you there. I was away with the fairies.'

'That's all right.' Carole looked apologetic. 'I wondered, while it's a bit quiet, whether I could have a word?'

'Of course you can. Let's pop along to my office,

shall we?' Darcie led the way, hoping Carole wasn't ill and needing medical advice.

'I won't beat about the bush,' Carole said in her practical way when they were seated. 'I'd like to give in my notice.'

'Oh…' Darcie looked pained. 'There's nothing wrong, is there? I mean, you're not ill or anything?'

'No, no.' The older woman waved away Darcie's concern. 'My daughter and son-in-law have asked me to go and live with them in Brisbane. Ben's just got one of these fly-in, fly-out jobs and he's away a lot. Nicole's feeling lonely and finding it hard to cope with the two little ones on her own.'

'So you're going to help out?' Darcie surmised.

'Well, I'd like to and I do miss the grandchildren. They're lovely little things.'

'Of course they are.' Darcie's tender heart was touched. 'When would you like to go?'

'Well…as soon as you can replace me. But I won't leave you in the lurch,' Carole hastened to add.

'We'll be sorry to lose you, Carole. But I realise things change and family should always come first if possible.'

'That's what I think too,' Carole said, getting to her feet. 'But I'll miss Sunday Creek and all you folk here at the hospital.'

'We must have a little send-off for you.' Darcie smiled, as they walked back to the station. 'And *we'll* do the cooking.'

'Oh—I never expected…' Carole looked suddenly embarrassed. 'But that'd be lovely, Darcie. Thank you.'

Darcie went straight along to Jack's office. As well

as Carole's news, she had something else to tell him. She knocked and popped her head in.

'Hey.' He looked up, sending her a quick smile and beckoning her in.

'You were late home last night,' Darcie said. 'I just wanted to check in and ask how things went.' Yesterday had been the opening of their outreach clinic.

'Word had got out apparently.' He leaned back in his chair and stretched his legs out under the desk. 'We were swamped. Lots of follow-up to do. Thank heavens for Maggie's all-round skills. I couldn't have managed without her.'

'So we'll take her each time, then?'

'For the moment.' He rubbed a hand across his forehead. 'I imagine the other nurses would like a turn as well.'

'And me,' Darcie reminded him.

His gaze slid softly over her. 'Of course you, Dr Drummond. Maggie has a list of what else needs to be done to make the space more patient-friendly at the clinic.'

'Excellent. She's on shortly. I'll have a chat to her when she gets in. By the way, Carole's just told me she's leaving. We'll have to find someone to replace her.'

'Oh, no.' Jack made a face. 'I love Carole's spaghetti and meatballs.'

Darcie sent an eye-roll towards the ceiling. 'And on a lighter note, we had news yesterday the MD's house is finished.'

'Mmm,' Jack said absently. 'I know. Louise left me a set of keys.'

'Well, then.' Darcie's look was expectant. 'You should make a time to move in.'

He lifted a shoulder in a tight shrug. 'I'll think about it.' In fact, he had no real desire to move at all. He was quite happy to be living in the communal residence. The MD's house was meant for a family man, wife, kids, dog, the whole box and dice. He'd rattle around like a lost soul. He couldn't think why a needy family in the town couldn't be offered the place instead of him. But he was sure the board would have none of that.

'Meg McLeish will look after the domestic side of things for you,' Darcie said, 'so you only need to gather up your personal stuff and move in.'

One dark brow lifted. 'Keen to get rid of me, Dr Drummond?'

She flushed. 'Your moving doesn't mean we can't see something of one another outside work.'

He hadn't thought of that. 'Are you saying it could offer us a few *possibilities*?'

Darcie felt the slow build-up of heat inside her. 'Might.'

'We've unfinished business between us, Darcie,' he reminded her softly. 'Don't we?'

She gave a little restive shake of her head, her mind conjuring up a vivid image his evocative words had produced.

She got to her feet. 'If you need a hand with the move, I'm around.'

Darcie was thoughtful as she made her way back to the nurses' station. She found Maggie settling in for her shift. After the two had exchanged greetings, Maggie said, 'Jack tell you we need to organise a few more amenities for the outreach clinic?'

'Leave that for the moment, please, Maggie. I wanted

to talk to you about something else.' Darcie swung onto one of the high stools next to the senior nurse, realising without her even knowing it that a possible solution for Emma and her mother had begun crystallising inside her head. 'Do you know anything about Kristy Tynan's personal situation?'

'I know she's a hard worker,' Maggie said. 'Been here a couple of years. Divorced. No man about the place. Keeps to herself.'

Darcie bit down on her bottom lip. 'I don't mean to be nosy here, Maggie but something's cropped up staff-wise.'

Maggie raised a well-defined dark brow. 'Someone leaving?'

'Carole. Relocating for family reasons.'

'And you're wondering whether Kristy would fit the bill?'

'My, you're quick!' Darcie grinned.

Maggie smirked. 'Just ask my boys. But, seriously, I think Kristy would jump at the chance to get out of that truckers' café. The hours she has to work are horrendous.'

Darcie looked at her watch. 'I think I'll go and have a chat to her now. The sooner we can get someone for the job, the sooner Carole can go to her family.'

'Working here would certainly be a nicer environment for Kristy,' Maggie reflected. 'And as we're supposed to be a caring profession, I don't imagine the board would object to Emma tagging along when necessary. And we could quietly work on a quit-smoking campaign for Kristy,' Maggie finished with a sly grin.

'You should be running the country,' Darcie quipped. 'But you've read my mind exactly. I'll see you in a bit.'

At the roadhouse, Darcie looked around and then made her way across to what looked like the dining area.

'Can I help you?' a young man, who was wiping down tables, asked.

'I was hoping to have a word with Kristy Tynan,' Darcie said.

'No worries. I'll give her a shout.'

Moments later, Kristy batted her way through the swing doors that led from the kitchen. Recognising Darcie, her hand went to her throat. 'It's not Emma, is it?'

'No, nothing like that, Kristy. Sorry if I startled you,' Darcie apologised. 'But I've come about a job at the hospital. I thought you might be interested in making a change.'

Kristy wiped her hands down the sides of her striped apron, agitation in her jerky movements. 'I don't understand...'

'Could you spare a few minutes?' Darcie looked around hopefully. 'Somewhere we could have a private chat?'

'I'm due a break.' Kristy pulled off her apron and placed it over the back of a chair. 'Let's go outside. There's a bit of a deck where we can sit.'

Quickly and concisely Darcie explained the nature of the job at the hospital. 'You'd be required to plan a menu but it would be nothing complicated, except now and again a patient might have special dietary needs.'

'Well, I could handle that,' Kristy said, looking almost eager. 'I actually did two years of a chef's apprenticeship in Sydney but then I got married and we moved away and I had Emma…' She paused and chewed her lip. 'You probably know I'm divorced now, Dr Drummond. There's just Emma and me.'

Darcie nodded. 'We could offer you more reasonable hours at the hospital, Kristy. And if Emma needed to come with you, that would be fine.' Darcie smiled. 'You could have your meals together and I believe the school bus stops outside the hospital as well.'

Kristy blinked rapidly. 'It seems too good to be true…'

'It's true,' Darcie said. 'Carole, our present cook, is leaving. We need someone just as capable to replace her. And as soon as possible.'

Kristy's mouth trembled. 'So, would I have to come in for an interview or something…?'

'You've just had it,' Darcie said warmly. 'I'll run everything past the board and you'll need a couple of referees.'

'I can manage that.'

'Good. And if everything checks out, then the job is yours.'

'Oh…' Suddenly Kristy's eyes overflowed and she swiped at them with the backs of her hands. 'You can't know what this will mean to Emma and me, Dr Drummond. And thank you for thinking of me.'

'Folk in Sunday Creek have been very kind to me,' Darcie said earnestly. 'I'm just passing it along.'

Later that afternoon, Jack tracked Darcie down in the treatment room. She was suturing the hand of a local carrier who had received a deep wound when unloading roofing iron at a building site. 'Could I have a word when you're finished here, please, Dr Drummond?'

Darcie turned her head. 'Almost done. I'll come along to your office, all right?'

Jack merely nodded. 'Thanks.'

'So, what's up?' Darcie asked, having sent her patient on his way with a tetanus jab and a script for an antibiotic.

Jack stood up from his desk, his expression a bit sheepish. 'I—uh—thought, if you're not busy, we could go across to the house and take a look.'

Darcie's gaze widened in disbelief. 'You haven't been near the place since you arrived here, have you?'

'Didn't see the need.' He came round from behind his desk and began to usher her out. 'Want to come with me, then?'

She shrugged in compliance. 'I'll just tell Maggie where we'll be. By the way, I think I've found us a new cook. I've approached Kristy Tynan. She's keen and I think she'll do a wonderful job.'

Jack whistled. 'Well done, you. Nice footwork there, Dr Drummond.'

'So you approve?'

'Of course. It'll be an excellent move for the Tynan ladies.'

'It will,' Darcie agreed. 'I'll pass the whole thing along to Louise, and she can sort out Kristy's terms of employment and so on. And Carole can get on her way.'

'Oh, we're here already!' Darcie sent him an encouraging look as they pulled up outside the house. 'They've painted the outside as well.'

'Aw, gee,' Jack deadpanned.

'Stop that. It'll be fine,' Darcie said bracingly. 'Let's go inside and see what they've done.'

Inside, the house smelled of new paint and it was obvious the renovation was complete. They wandered from room to room, peered into the master bedroom with its king-sized bed and en suite bathroom, down the hall to two smaller bedrooms, both with their own en suites, and then on to the living room and kitchen.

'It's obvious Lou has had a hand in the furnishings.' Darcie was enthusiastic. 'It's wonderful, Jack, so clean and bright.'

Jack merely looked unimpressed. 'What am I supposed to do with all this space?'

'Live here, one assumes.'

'I suppose I could offer it to the old woman who lived in a shoe,' he grumbled, and sent Darcie a pained look. 'I won't be expected to *entertain*, will I? Give a drinks party before the mayor's ball or something?'

Darcie gave an inelegant snort. 'Don't be pathetic. And as far as I know, Sunday Creek doesn't have a mayoral ball. And look…' she went forward and opened the pantry cupboard '…Meg's already stocked up for you.'

'I just don't need this,' Jack insisted.

'Well, it comes with the MD's position,' Darcie pointed out. 'The board is just fulfilling its part of your employment contract. You have a certain position in the town, Jack,' she reminded him. 'You don't want to be remembered as the rogue medico who wouldn't live in the doctor's residence.'

Jack dredged up a jaded smile. 'Do you think I could coax Capone across to live with me?'

Darcie sent him a look of resignation. She imagined Jack Cassidy could coax a herd of kangaroos to come and live with him if he chose. Her heart dipped. Even *her.* One day. 'I imagine Capone will probably opt to settle here if you offer him a few treats. Oops, that's me.'

Reaching back, she pulled her phone out of the back pocket of her cargos. 'Oh, hi, Lou,' she said brightly. 'Jack and I are just over at the house. It's lovely— Sorry, what did you say?' As she listened, Darcie began making her way slowly along the hallway and out onto the front veranda.

Hearing her abrupt change of tone, and fearing something untoward, Jack followed and waited until she ended the call. 'Darcie?'

She turned from the railings, her expression strained. She licked her lips. 'That was Louise…'

'I gathered that.' Jack went to her. 'Is someone hurt?'

'It's Jewel.' Darcie's throat pinched as she swallowed. 'She's stumbled into some kind of rabbit hole. They've only just found her. Her front leg's shattered. Sam Gibson's on his way…' She stopped and blinked.

'Oh, baby…I'm so sorry.' Jack hooked an arm around her shoulders and felt her shaking. 'Do you want to go out to Willow Bend?'

She nodded. 'Lou thought I might want to…' She bit her lips together to stop them trembling. 'My poor little Jewel.'

'Come on,' Jack said gently. 'I'll take you. Just give me a minute to lock up here and let Maggie know what's happening.'

'Do we have some idea where we have to go when we get there?' Jack asked quietly as they drove.

'Not far from the homestead. Louise said she'll keep a lookout for us,' Darcie answered throatily.

Jack put out a hand, found hers and squeezed.

* * *

A shadecloth had been erected over the little mare. Jack pulled to a stop a short distance away. 'Go ahead,' he urged gently. 'I won't be far behind.'

Darcie almost ran to where Max and Sam were standing just outside the shelter. Their body language told her everything she'd feared.

Max looked grim. 'Sad day for us, Darcie.'

Darcie turned to Sam, a tiny ray of hope lingering in her questioning eyes.

The vet shook his head.

'C-could I spend a few minutes with her?' Darcie's mouth trembled out of shape.

'Take as long as you need.' Sam's look was kind. 'And Jewel's not in pain, Darcie,' he stressed. 'I've sedated her.'

The little mare was resting on her side. Darcie knelt next to her. 'I'm here, sweetheart,' she murmured, touching her hand to the horse's neck, feeling the soft coat, the already fading warmth. Jewel's big dark eyes opened and Darcie knew she'd been waiting for her.

She touched the velvet ears, rubbed gently along the white blaze on the mare's forehead, her every action rooted in preserving life, until Sam returned to do what he had to do.

Darcie's goodbye was silent. Instead, she held Jewel's head for a moment before burying her face in her soft, shiny coat.

'Time to go, Darcie…' Max looked drawn.

Unable to speak, Darcie raised a hand in farewell and turned blindly into Jack's waiting arms.

He hurried her towards the Land Rover. Making sure they were belted in, he took off swiftly down the track. If there was a shot, he didn't hear it, and silently thanked Sam for his sensitivity. Darcie didn't need that last wrenching finality.

When they hit the main road back to town, he spoke. 'It hurts like hell, doesn't it?'

'Yes, it does.' Her voice broke. Tears made slow rivulets down her cheeks and she wiped them away with the tips of her fingers. Her thoughts spun and became muddled. It wasn't like her to be so emotional. Perhaps it was just past history and other losses, she thought bleakly.

When they neared Sunday Creek township, she asked, 'Could I come home with you, Jack?'

Jack felt his pulse tick over. 'To the new house?'

'If you wouldn't mind...' She didn't look at him, just stared straight ahead.

Jack placed his hand on her thigh. 'Of course I don't mind. I'll just swing by the residence and grab some whisky. I think we could both use a drink.' He flicked a glance at her and saw a solitary tear fall down her cheek. He tightened his fingers in a gesture of empathy. 'I know how bad it feels when you lose a favourite animal.'

'I...don't usually fall apart like this...' Her voice was low, throaty, the admission sounding as if it was wrenched from deep within her. 'I became so attached to Jewel.' She managed a jagged, self-deprecating laugh. 'Perhaps it was just wanting desperately something to love.'

*Sweet God.* Jack could feel the fine tremor running through her skin beneath his hand. '*I'm* here! he wanted to yell to the treetops. 'Love *me*!' But of course he couldn't.

* * *

Jack took down two whisky tumblers from the wall cupboard. 'I can have this neat,' he said. 'But what about you?'

'Is there any ice?' Darcie sat at the breakfast bar on a high stool.

He opened the freezer door. 'There is. Our Meg's a legend.' He shook out ice cubes from the tray and dropped several into her drink. Picking up the glasses, he joined Darcie at the counter.

'Here's to Jewel,' he said softly.

Darcie managed a small smile. She took a mouthful of her drink and blinked a bit. 'It's probably crazy to get so emotional over an animal, isn't?'

'It's not crazy.' Jack stroked her hand, which was curled into a fist on the countertop. 'Animals are wonderful, with hearts as big as the sky. And they're everlastingly faithful. Something humans could learn from.'

A little while later Darcie felt the liquor begin to warm her insides. The trembling had stopped. 'You really get me, don't you, Jack?'

Jack paused giving weight to his answer. 'I think we get each other.' He looked into her face and saw the honesty there. But he also saw the passion. So, what was she telling him? What was she asking him here?

She lifted her glass and took the last mouthful of her drink. 'I don't want to be anywhere else other than here with you.'

Jack's mouth tightened fractionally. 'Are you sure?'

For answer, she leaned across and pressed her lips against his, asking a silent question. She felt his resistance for a second and then he exhaled a breath and his mouth softened. Then it opened and his tongue stroked against her lips and she sighed as he lifted her off the stool and gathered her in. Her whole body quivered and she pressed herself in against him, snaking her arms around his neck and opening her mouth, surrendering it to his.

Passion like she'd never known flared inside her. She pushed her hands into his hair, wanting more than anything to touch him. All of him. Her hands fell to the buttons on his shirt, pulling at them impatiently, almost desperate to feel his naked skin, absorb his heat and craving to get closer.

Jack was momentarily taken aback. This was a Darcie he didn't know. Yet hadn't he always known this was the woman inside the contained little shell she exhibited to the outside world? He could sense her loss of control but, on the other hand, he didn't want her to regret what they were about to do. Pulling away from her mouth, he kissed her throat, trying to slow their ardour. If they were going to make love, he didn't want it to be a hurried affair, over in seconds. He wanted them to *know* each other in the finest way possible.

'Come with me,' he murmured, taking her hands and bringing them to his mouth, pressing a kiss into each palm. He twitched a Jack-like smile. 'Let's try out my new bed, shall we?'

Jack closed the bedroom door softly and for a long moment they looked at each other.

Darcie couldn't believe this was really happening. Yet she knew she'd wanted him for the longest time. Wanted him as much as her next breath. 'Undress me,' she breathed, a tide of need overcoming her, shocking her in its intensity.

'I want this to be about us, Darcie,' he said with a

rich huskiness that rippled along her skin. 'You and me. In the truest sense...'

Darcie gasped, feeling his urgency match her own as he flicked open her shirt, bending to put his mouth to the hollow between her breasts, peeling back the lace of her bra, tracing each tiny exposure of skin with his tongue.

With the last item of their clothing peeled away, Darcie couldn't wait a moment longer to burrow in against him. To hold him and be held in return.

'I can hardly believe you've come to me at last...' Jack's voice was rough-edged with passion held in check.

The softest smile edged her mouth. 'But you always knew I would, didn't you?' She reached out to carry his hand to her breast, standing full and proud as she straightened back.

'Feel. My heart's going wild.'

Jack's mouth dried. She was...magnificent. And soon they would be as one.

Lovers at last.

Darcie had never been so aware of her own sensuality. Leaning down, she patted the clean sweep of the bed. The invitation was in her eyes, her husky feminine laugh almost daring him.

Jack took her challenge, encircling her wrist and twirling her round so she landed on the bed on her back. In a second he was there beside her. Reaching for her, he gathered her close so that they were looking into each other's eyes, their mouths a breath apart.

'God—' Jack brought his head up sharply. 'I don't have anything with me.'

'I'm covered,' she whispered, dazed with emotion. 'Don't hold back, Jack.'

He didn't.

Darcie let all her emotions come to the surface. Soul-destroying scars from the past fell away and she felt as though she'd crossed to another time zone. Jack's touch was instinctive, seeking responses from her she hadn't known existed, touching her deepest senses, sculpting her body from head to toe.

'Let me now,' she whispered, deep in thrall, aching to discover him. His groan of pleasure pushed them closer to the edge and finally, irrevocably, they were lost in the taste and texture of each other, moving in perfect rhythm, climbing even higher where they met in the wild storm of their shared release, drenched in a million stars.

For a long time after, they stayed entwined. Quiet. Even a little amazed that they were there.

In his bed.

Lovers.

'You're smiling,' Darcie said.

'How do you know?'

She brought her head up from where it was buried against his chest. 'Because I am too.' Lifting a hand, she ran a finger along the shadow already darkening his jaw. And stared into his eyes and let her fingers drift into his hair.

Jack touched a finger to her lips, his gaze devouring her. 'No words?'

'No words,' she echoed, feeling her lips tingle where he'd touched them. She burrowed in against him once more.

'Hungry?' Jack asked after a while.

'Lazy, I think. But perhaps a bit hungry too. You?'

'I wouldn't mind a feed,' he admitted. 'But let's have a shower first.'

Darcie raised her head slightly and blinked. 'Together?'

'Of course together.' Laughing softly, he spanned her waist with his hand. 'I'm not letting you out of my sight.

'I'd rather not go out to eat,' Darcie said when they were dressed again and on their way to the kitchen.

'Me neither.' Jack placed a hand protectively at the back of her neck. Going out would somehow break the spell they were under. And that would come sooner rather than later, he decided realistically. 'Let's see what Meg's left us.'

'Left *you*, you mean.' She sent him an indulgent, half-amused look. 'Meg wouldn't know I'd be here.'

They found bread in the freezer, eggs and cheese in the fridge and a can of peaches in the pantry. 'Enough for a feast,' Jack declared. 'Cheese on toast, peaches for dessert.'

'And lashings of tea,' Darcie requested.

'Of course.' Tilting her face towards him, Jack kissed her gently on the mouth. 'English tea for my English rose.'

Cocooned in happiness, Darcie marvelled, 'I can't believe the phone hasn't rung.'

'I can.' Jack flexed a shoulder and grinned. 'I told Maggie we were not to be disturbed for anything less than a multi-trauma.'

'Oh, Jack...' A flood of colour washed over her cheeks. 'Does she know—about us?'

'She'd talked to Sam.' Jack seemed unfazed. 'Maggie got the picture. She said, and I quote, "I'm so glad Darcie has you, Jack."'

'Oh, heavens.' Darcie pressed a hand to her heart. 'Next thing she'll have us engaged.'

'No, she won't.' His mouth worked for a moment. But he thought the idea had real possibilities for all that.

'Will you take me home now?' Darcie asked, when they'd tidied up after their impromptu dinner.

'I'm coming with you,' Jack said. 'I'll move in here by degrees. When it feels right.'

'Oh…' Darcie felt a funny lump in her throat. She wasn't quite ready to share a bed with him on a permanent basis. And she guessed Jack understood that. *Even though I love him.* The realisation nearly tipped her sideways. She wrestled the startling thought back. Instead, reaching up, she placed her palm against his cheek.

Jack nodded. Message received and understood. Turning his head a fraction, he kissed the soft hollow of her palm. 'Let's go home,' he said, his blue eyes steady. 'It's late and I haven't said goodnight to Capone.'

# CHAPTER ELEVEN

A WEEK LATER, Darcie and Maggie were sitting at the nurses' station, batting light conversation around, when the phone rang. Maggie turned aside to answer it. 'Bleep Jack,' she mouthed urgently, and began taking details quickly.

Jack came at speed to the station. 'What's up?'

'Another accident out at that movie site at Pelican Springs,' Maggie relayed. 'A stuntman hanging upside down from a tree. Apparently he's caught and they can't release him. They're in a panic.'

Jack swore pithily. 'Still no nurse on the set?'

'Apparently not.' Maggie spun off her chair. 'Let's grab some trauma packs, guys. You need to be gone.'

There was no use surmising anything, Jack decided grimly as they drove. But a few probable scenarios leapt into dangerous possibilities.

'If our patient has been upside down for any length of time, he's quite likely lapsed into unconsciousness,' Darcie said. 'It's going to be tricky, isn't it?'

Jack snorted. 'That's the understatement of the year. We could have a death on our hands, Darcie. Those bastards are obviously still ignoring normal safety protocols. But this time I'll nail them.'

Darcie felt the tense nature of the situation engulf her. Every crisis they faced out here meant delivering medicine in its rawest form. 'Should we run over what we might find? We're going to have to think on our feet from the moment we land there.'

'I've spoken to Mal Duffy.' Jack's response was clipped. 'The SES are on their way, likewise the ambulance and police. Mal's wearing both hats. He's gone ahead and contacted the folk at Pelican Springs. By sheer good luck, the telephone company is doing some work at the property. The phone techs have been using a cherry picker to connect new wiring to the poles. They're on their way to the accident site as we speak.'

'A cherry picker works like a crane, doesn't it?' Darcie's unease was mirrored in her questioning look.

'Mmm. It'll be mounted on the back of a truck,' Jack explained. 'Usually, the operator stands at the control panel at the side of the truck and directs the crane to wherever it's needed. There's a cage-like platform at the top of the crane, of course,' he added. 'The rescue team will ride up in that.'

And that meant Jack himself would go up, Darcie thought tightly. 'I hate this!' she said with feeling. 'We're doctors—not monkeys!'

That brought a glimmer of a grim smile to his mouth. 'It offends me too, Darcie, that these morons think they can get away with treating their workers with such disrespect. Let alone the people who have to come and rescue them from their folly.'

Darcie bit down on her bottom lip. She could tell, even without looking at him, that Jack was strung tight, focused…almost driven. She only hoped he'd keep a cool head. But, of course, he would. They both would.

Because there was no other choice.

The accident site was in chaos when they got there. Automatically, the doctors donned their high-visibility vests and hard hats. 'Here's Mal,' Darcie said with something like relief. 'Perhaps he can tell us what's going on.'

Jack grunted. 'More than that clown Meadows, by the look of it.' Even as he spoke, the unit manager was screaming at the grips—the unskilled workers on the set—to do *something*.

Mal didn't bother with greetings. Instead, he cut to the chase. 'The flying doctors are within a two-hundred-mile radius. We managed to catch them at Harborough station before they turned round to head back to base. If they cane it, they should be here within the hour.'

'Thanks, Mal.'

'Cherry picker's just arrived,' the policeman said. 'Two of the SES guys will go up with you. While you see what can be done medically, they'll start cutting him away.'

'Do we have a name?' Jack's gut clenched. This was a nightmare.

'Wayne Carmody. Sixtyish.'

'Oh, hell…' Jack shook his head. 'What's he think-ing of, doing stunt work at his age?' Well, he already knew the answer. This whole set-up was nothing short of illegal. Understaffed and unsafe. Only people des-perate for work would consider risking their lives here. 'Right, I'm ready.' Jack creased his eyes against the sudden glare as he looked up at the skeletal outline of the crane. 'Let's get that contraption moving.'

'I'm coming with you.' Darcie's voice showed quiet determination.

'You're not!' Jack's response was immediate and unequivocal.

'We're a team, Jack,' she reminded him, pushing down her own fears. 'We combine our skills.'

For a fleeting moment they challenged each other and Jack's mouth pulled tight. She was as pale as parchment. But as plucky as all get-out. There was no way she'd be left out of this. 'Just do what I tell you, then,' he stipulated, the edges of his teeth grating.

Darcie felt the nerves in her stomach pitch and fall as they were hoisted upwards. Nausea began gathering at the back of her throat and she almost made a grab for Jack. But she fought back the impulse. Instead, she anchored her panic by breathing deeply and holding onto the metal bars of the cage for dear life.

As they reached their target, Jack took in what they had to deal with. Trauma with a capital T. Poor guy. Wayne Carmody was hopelessly entangled, hanging onto consciousness by a thread, his face and arms almost purple with the pressure from his upside-down position.

The crane's operator directed the platform in as close as it would go. 'Best I can do, Doc,' he called from below.

'Thanks—just keep it steady,' Jack yelled back. 'Wayne,' he addressed the rapidly failing stuntman, 'can you hear me?'

The man's response was a bubble of sound.

'Don't lose it, mate,' Jack said. 'We'll have you down soon.' He turned to Darcie. 'Let's get a non-rebreathing mask on him. It's the only way we can manage the oxygen flow. His BP has to be off the wall. And getting an IV in nigh impossible.'

'I'll get an aspirin under his tongue.' Darcie steadied her position, delving into the trauma kit. It wasn't the ideal solution but the aspirin would begin lowering the injured man's blood pressure and at least alleviate some of the shock his body was undergoing. 'I think there's a possible femur fracture, Jack.' Her worried eyes took in Wayne's right leg, which was hanging at a very odd angle.

'Maybe not. But his circulation has to be critically impaired. We can't tell what we're dealing with until we get him down.' Jack looked up to where the SES team was vainly trying to separate and cut through the thick ropes. 'Come on, guys!' he exhorted. 'Lean on it! What's keeping you?'

'Doin' our best, Doc.' The hard-breathed reply came back. 'Five more minutes.'

The doctors exchanged a swift, tight look, both acknowledging that the time for a successful rescue was running out.

Darcie kept her gaze focused on their patient until her eyes burned. If they didn't reverse Wayne's upside-down position in the next couple of minutes...

Fear and anguish pooled in her stomach and froze the sunny afternoon, stretching the moments into a chasm of waiting.

'OK—we're about to cut the last of the ropes!' Chris, from the SES, yelled. 'He's all yours, Doc!'

Jack reached up, the muscles in his throat and around

his mouth locked in a grimace as he took the brunt of the injured man's weight.

Darcie pitched in, her slender frame almost doubled as Wayne's body descended heavily and fast into their waiting arms and they were able to guide him down onto the floor of the platform.

There were plenty of hands to help them once they were safely on the ground. 'I want the patient treated as a spinal injury,' Jack said tersely. And God knew what else. 'How's the BP, Darcie?'

'Coming down, one sixty over ninety.'

Jack hissed out a breath. He bent closer to their patient. Wayne was dazed and confused, babbling he couldn't feel his legs. Jack brought his head up. 'Will you do a set of spinal obs, please, Darcie?' he asked. As soon as she'd finished, he asked, 'Anything?'

She shook her head. There had been no feeling or sensation in either leg.

'Right, let's give Hartmann's IV, one litre. Stat, please.'

Darcie complied. Did Jack suspect internal bleeding? If he did, then they were hedging their bets here. It was better and safer to give a fluid expander if there was any doubt.

'Flying doctor's landed,' someone said, waving a phone.

'Almost ready for us, Jack?' Zach Bayliss hovered anxiously. This guy looked very bad. The sooner they got him loaded and away the better.

'Just give us a minute to get some morphine into him, Zach.' Jack brought up the dose. 'I'll come with you for the handover.'

'Right, good.' The paramedic looked relieved. 'Where are the flying docs taking him?'

'The Princess Alexandra in Brisbane.'

'It's the best place for him,' Zach agreed.

Jack nodded, proud of his old teaching hospital. The PA was outstanding. The leaders in immediate post-trauma care. And for Wayne it could mean the difference between life and death, or full or partial paraplegia.

'Darcie.' Jack touched her shoulder briefly. 'Check there are no minor injuries to be dealt with, please. I'll be back as soon as I can.'

Good luck, Wayne. The silent wish came from Darcie's heart as she watched the ambulance move away. She felt a shiver of unease up her backbone. This place was beginning to give her the creeps, the tree where the stuntman had been caught rising like some kind of grotesque giant. No, not a nice place at all, she decided. And the sooner they were shot of it, the better...

'I take it you've put in a call to Workplace Health and Safety?' Darcie said much later, as they drove back to town.

'And the local MP.' The tension in Jack's face had eased remarkably. 'If Meadows and his cronies haven't had their dodgy operations closed down by tonight, I'll raise hell.'

'Mal and his constables took statements from the film crew,' Darcie said. 'Blake Meadows had the hide to say that time meant money and that he wasn't going to hang about.'

Jack snorted. 'I'll bet that went down well with Mal.'

'He told Meadows that if he ignored a police directive, he'd be arrested,' Darcie said with satisfaction. 'Mal was brilliant.'

'So were you, Dr Drummond.' Jack reached across and found her hand, sliding his fingers through hers. 'I—uh—finished moving into the house this morning.'

'Oh—I hadn't realised...' Silence seemed to hang between them, a great curve of it, until Darcie gave an off-key laugh edged with uncertainty. 'Are you going to have a house-warming, then?'

The sides of his mouth pleated in a dry smile. 'I thought we'd already done that.'

Darcie lowered her gaze, at the same time feeling her skin heat up.

'What about coming for dinner?' Jack increased the pressure on her fingers.

Darcie tried to ignore the sudden leap in her pulse as his thigh brushed against hers. 'I think I can manage that,' she said slowly. 'Shall I bring something towards the meal?'

'Not necessary. Just come prepared to stay, Darcie.' Jack's voice had dropped to a deep huskiness. 'I want to hold you all night.'

The following morning Darcie asked if they could debrief.

Jack's dark brows flicked up. 'About Wayne?' They were sitting side by side at the breakfast bar, their mugs of tea in front of them.

'Have you heard anything?'

'I got on to the surgical registrar a while ago,' Jack said. 'Wayne's still with us.'

'Oh, thank heavens. Was it a fractured NOF?'

'Herniated L one, two and three.'

Lumbar vertebrae prolapse, Darcie interpreted. 'It must have happened in the initial fall when the rigging collapsed and left him hanging. Poor man. He must have been in such agony.'

'He's been put on a Fentanyl protocol IV. It's a strong narcotic so I guess his pain is manageable.'

'What about spinal damage? Do we know?'

'He's had MRI and CT scans. Seems OK. I'll check with the surgeon in charge later today.'

Darcie's eyes went straight to his face and slid away. 'Do you ever wish you were back there in the thick of it again?'

A small silence bled inwards, until Jack lifted his mug and drank the last of his tea. 'No, I don't,' he said. 'Why would I, when I can be here with you?'

'Same here...' She looked past Jack to the open window and beyond it, her eyes soft and dreamy.

Watching her expression, Jack took stock. I don't *ever* want to be away from her, he thought, unbelieving of the avalanche of emotion that arrowed into him. And recognising with stark reality that what he'd had with Zoe now seemed a pale imitation of what Darcie had brought to his life.

Jack Cassidy had fallen headlong in love. The thought scared him, delighted him, amazed him. 'Why don't we get married?'

Darcie's mouth opened and closed. She blinked rapidly. 'Married?' Her voice was hardly there.

'I love you,' he said for the first time.

She took a shuddery little breath. 'I know...'

'And you love me.' His jaw worked. 'You couldn't be with me the way you are, unless you did.'

'Marriage, though…' she countered inadequately. 'We're from such different backgrounds, different countries…'

'Happens all the time,' he drawled, his tone careful and hard to read. 'Just please don't say we hardly know each other, Darcie.'

'No.' She gave a forced laugh. 'That would be silly. Marriage is an enormous commitment, though, Jack. Doesn't it scare you?'

'Not at all. We're perfect together and I love everything about you.'

'Oh, Jack…' She shook her head. 'I have so much baggage.'

'No, Darcie. You don't.' He lifted her hand and rubbed the knuckles against his cheek. 'You left it all behind at the creek, when we kissed for the first time.'

But it's still there, she thought silently, and carefully reclaimed her hand. 'I need some time to process all this.'

'In other words, you're going to tie yourself in knots.'

Self-preservation hardened her response. 'Well, I'm sorry I can't see everything in black and white like *you*.'

'You're taking this to extremes, Darcie. Hell! I've asked you marry me, not jump off London Bridge!'

Maybe that would have been easier.

'Why do we even have to talk about marriage?' Sheer panic sharpened her words. 'We're all right the way we are.'

He gave a snort of derision. '*Sometimes* lovers. Would you be happy with that?'

Meaning that he wouldn't. 'I'm just grateful for what we have.'

'But it could be so much more!' Sliding off the stool, he strode to the window and turned back. 'So, what do you need from me, Darcie? Just tell me.'

Her eyes clouded. 'I just need you to give me some more space. And no pressure.' She swallowed thickly. 'I don't want to hurt you, Jack, but I won't be pressured into making a life-changing decision.'

'On the other hand, if you could bring yourself to trust me, we could have something amazing together.'

Or broken hearts for ever if it didn't work. She got to her feet. 'I need your word about this, Jack.'

Jack stared at her for a long moment, his jaw clenched, a tiny muscle jumping. He flicked an open-handed shrug. 'If that's what you want…'

What *did* she want? In a moment of self-doubt she wanted to ditch her scruples and accept Jack's proposal. Make a life with him far from everything that had driven her here. But deep down she knew she couldn't make the leap. Not yet. *Perhaps not ever.* She swallowed the razor-sharp emotion clogging her throat. 'That's what I want.'

Three days later at the nurses' station Maggie asked Darcie if she was OK.

'Fine.' Darcie looked up from the computer. 'Why?'

'You seem a bit…distracted.'

The nerves in Darcie's stomach did a tumble turn. 'You're imagining things, Maggie.'

'I'm not,' Maggie insisted.

Darcie huffed a laugh. 'That carry-on the other day out at the film site would make anyone distracted,' she offered by way of explanation. 'I hate administering medicine on the trot like that.'

'Well, Meadows and his lot have left the district,' Maggie said. 'Packed up and gone apparently. And there's an investigation pending. You and Jack will likely be called as witnesses.'

That's if she was still here in Sunday Creek. Darcie felt her throat tighten. 'I thought you were going with Jack to the outreach clinic today,' she said, changing lanes swiftly.

'I cried off. Ethan's not feeling so well.'

'Oh, poor kid,' Darcie commiserated. 'Would you like me to check him over?'

'Thanks, Darce, but he'll be fine. It's just a tummy upset. I'll pop home at lunchtime and take him some new DVDs. Lauren was keen to get a turn at the clinic so it worked out all right. Hey, great news Jack's organised for an ophthalmologist to take a regular clinic out here, isn't it? Quite a few eye problems among our indigenous folk, from all accounts.'

Darcie felt taken aback. 'He didn't mention any of that to me.'

The two looked at each other awkwardly. And then Maggie took the initiative. 'He's got a lot on his plate. Probably slipped his mind.'

Or perhaps he was just taking her request for space to extremes. Darcie felt her stomach dive. It was all such a mess.

And it couldn't go on indefinitely.

It was early evening the same day and Jack was sitting on his front veranda. Since Darcie's standoff, he'd felt like throwing things. He'd even considered howling at the moon once or twice but that wouldn't have solved anything.

Why the hell had he mentioned the M word to Darcie? Just because it had seemed a good idea at the time. He hated the panic he'd seen on her face. And knowing he'd been the cause of it made it even worse. Idiot! His heart lurched. He should be renamed *Crass* Cassidy.

He had to talk with her. Keeping this ridiculous *space* between them was crazy. 'What do you think, mate?' Reaching down, he ruffled Capone's rough coat. Capone laid his head on his front paws and gave a feeble wag of his tail, before settling. Jack thought about it for one second. 'I guess that's a yes, then.'

Decision made, he got to his feet swiftly and went inside to locate his car keys. He'd go across to the residence now before he could change his mind. Making sure the house was secure, he pocketed his keys and walked back along the hallway to the front veranda.

About to close the front door, he stopped. Headlights lit up the street and a car stopped outside his house. He muttered a curse. Who wanted him now? Was it one of the board members? If it was, why couldn't they come to the hospital in daylight hours like normal people?

He blew out a resigned breath and waited. It was no use pretending he wasn't home as his silhouette was backlit from the sensor light on the veranda. As he waited, the driver's door opened and a figure got out. He blinked a bit. There were no streetlights but unless his eyes deceived him, it was…Darcie?

'Hi,' she called throatily, as she opened the gate and came up the path.

'I didn't recognise the car.' Jack winced at the mundane greeting.

Darcie reached the steps. 'My car wouldn't start. The guys from the garage lent me this one.'

Jack beckoned her up the steps. 'Any clue what's wrong with your car?'

She shrugged. 'One of the mechanics will sort it.' And why on earth were they talking about dumb cars? The nerves in Darcie's stomach twisted. Already, the tension between them was as sticky as toffee. Her shoulders rose in a steadying breath. She had to do what she'd come to do. 'Could we talk?'

Jack felt relief with the force of a tsunami sweep through him. 'Of course we can talk.' He swallowed the sudden constriction in his throat. 'As a matter of fact, I was almost out the door myself. I was coming to talk to *you*.'

'Oh…'

They looked at each other helplessly, unable to bridge the gap.

'OK if we sit here?' Jack waved her to one of the cane chairs on the veranda. 'Or we can go inside.' *Or I can take you in my arms and hold you.*

She shook her head. 'Here's fine.' She took the chair he offered.

'So…' His mouth tightened for a second before he hooked out a chair and sat. 'What did you want to say to me?'

Darcie ground her lip. 'I have some leave due. I'd like to take it.'

Jack sat back as if he'd been stung. This was *not* what he'd been hoping to hear. In the ensuing silence he scraped a hand across his cheekbones, took a long breath and released it. 'When do you want to go? In other words, do you need to make plans?'

'I've made them.' In fact, she'd spent the last couple of hours online, doing just that.

'OK...' He digested that for a minute. 'So, when?'

'There's a flight out tomorrow. I'd like to be on it.'

'To Brisbane?'

She nodded.

Jack suspected he should leave it there but couldn't. 'Well, that's probably a good call. Being in Brisbane will give you easy access to the coast.'

She met his gaze, startled. 'I'm not going to the coast.' She swallowed past the lump in her throat. 'I'm flying home.'

*Home?*' Jack emphasised, feeling as though his heart had been cut from its moorings and was flailing all over the place. 'To England?'

She gave a tight shrug, wishing she'd used another word. But it was out there now. Front and centre.

'I thought you said Australia was home for you now?' A latent prickle of anger sharpened his response.

'I don't want to start playing semantics, Jack.' Suddenly Darcie felt apart and alone. 'This is something I have to do.'

'Why, Darcie?'

'You know why...' She met his gaze unflinchingly, although inside she was quivering. 'I hate the term but I have to say it. I need *closure*.'

'You're going to see *him*, aren't you?' Jack's eyes burned like polished sapphires. 'What, precisely, is the point of doing that?'

'Because I let him get away with everything! I should have stood my ground! Called Aaron on his despicable behaviour. Instead...' She paused painfully. 'I folded like an empty crisp packet. And bolted.'

'Which is what you should have done. God, Darcie...' Jack shook his head in disbelief. 'The cretin isn't worth the plane fare to England. Do you even know if he's still at the same hospital?'

'He's still there. I checked.'

Suddenly the atmosphere between them was crackling with instability.

Darcie felt the quick rise of desire, watching the play of his muscles under his dark T-shirt as he leant back in his chair and planted his hands on his hips. 'Here's another scenario,' he said. 'If you could delay your departure for a couple of days, I could arrange to come with you.'

Her teeth worried at her bottom lip. She felt guilty for not wanting him to accompany her. But he had to understand this was something she had to do on her own. 'Jack—my travel arrangements are locked in. Besides, the board would hardly approve your leave, would they?'

'The board can mind their own business.'

She gave a fleeting smile. 'The running of the hospital *is* their business, Jack. And, honestly, you don't need to feel responsible for me. I know what I'm doing.'

'Have you considered *he* might talk you into giving him a second chance?' Jack didn't look at her because he couldn't. The question he'd posed was too important. Just spelling it out opened a door on a future— their future—that was suddenly treacherous with deep, dark chasms and the crippling effect of stepping into a minefield.

Agitatedly, Darcie began stroking the edge of the table. Jack watched her hands, fine, delicate with short neat nails; doctor's hands.

'He won't, Jack.'

Jack looked up.

She brought her hands together and locked her fingers.

'Loving you has made me strong.' For a long moment she returned his gaze, her intent never wavering. 'He won't talk me round.'

# CHAPTER TWELVE

AND THAT HAD been supposed to reassure him? The question ran endlessly through Jack's head for the umpteenth time as he scrubbed his hands vigorously at the basin. Well, he wasn't reassured. Far from it.

'Which one do you want to do first?' Beside him, Natalie began opening a suture pack. She was referring to the twelve-year-old boys who'd been brought in after crashing into each other while skateboarding. Neither had been wearing protective headgear. Both were bloody with split eyebrows and pale with shock at finding themselves in Casualty.

'Doesn't matter. Either one. Idiot kids,' he growled. 'And why weren't they at school?'

Natalie sent him a long-suffering look. 'It's Saturday, Jack.'

'Oh—is it?' he replied edgily. 'I've lost track.' But he hadn't lost track of the number of days Darcie had been gone. She'd been gone ten days and each had seem to last longer than the one before it.

'Perhaps I'd better take the kid with the egg on his forehead,' Jack reconsidered.

'Matthew,' Natalie supplied. 'Are you concerned he might be concussed?'

Jack shrugged. 'As far as we know, he didn't pass out but I'd like his neuro obs monitored for a couple of hours just to be on the safe side.'

'Need an extra hand?'

Jack spun round from the basin as if his body had been zapped by a ricocheting bullet. His dark brows snapped together. 'You're back.'

Darcie coloured faintly. He didn't seem very pleased to see her and it wasn't the welcome she'd orchestrated in her mind at all. 'I'm back,' she echoed.

'Good trip?' Jack's gaze narrowed.

'Wonderful.'

She looked fantastic. *Shining.* It was the only word Jack could think of to describe her. And she had a new hairstyle. A spike of resentment startled him. But surely it was justified? He'd been here worrying his guts out about her wellbeing, when she'd been off, obviously having a fine old time in merry England.

'Darcie, hi!' Diplomatically, Natalie jumped in to fill the yawning gap. 'Welcome back. It's good to see you.'

'And you, Nat. And I have presents for everyone,' Darcie singsonged.

'Oh, my stars!' Natalie's hand went to her heart. 'From London?'

'Of course.' Darcie was smiling.

'That's so cool.'

'Could we get on?' Jack yanked his gloves on. He'd had enough of the small talk.

'What do we have?' Darcie directed her question to Natalie.

'Two youngsters, two split eyebrows, two suturing jobs.'

'I'll do one.' Darcie looked directly at Jack. 'Is that OK?'

'If you have the time.' Jack elbowed his way out of the door.

Natalie looked helplessly after him. 'I don't think Jack's been sleeping very well.'

And that was supposedly her fault? Darcie went to the basin. Suddenly her legs felt like jelly. 'Nat, if you've arranged to assist Jack, go ahead. I'm sure I can manage a few sutures.'

'Oh, OK…' Natalie's voice faltered. 'It's so great to have you back, Darcie.'

'Thanks, Nat…' Darcie blew out a calming breath. She'd been buoyed up by excitement, coming back. Now jet lag was suddenly beginning to catch up with her, leaving her flat. She'd sought to surprise Jack but that had obviously backfired. She gave vent to a sigh. Why was nothing in life ever simple? Drying her hands, she shook out a pair of sterile gloves from their packet and went to find her patient.

Darcie did her usual careful job, nevertheless. Placing four stitches in her young patient's wound didn't take long. She completed his treatment chart and handed him over to his mother with instructions to come back in a week to have the stitches removed.

Oh, boy. She wiggled her fingers stiffly. She must be more tired than she'd thought. But she was determined to wait for Jack. She looked at her watch. It was already late afternoon. Perhaps a cup of tea would revive her. Decision made, she went along to the hospital kitchen.

It was there Jack found her.

'You look like hell,' he said bluntly.

She brought her chin up. 'Fancy that.'

Jack's mouth crimped around a reluctant smile. He put out a hand towards her. 'Let's get you home.'

Outside the air was clear and sharp. Darcie felt a slight dizziness overtake her, the ground coming up to meet her. 'Oh…'

'You're out on your feet,' he growled, wrapping a supporting arm around her shoulders. 'When did you fly in?'

'Very early this morning,' she said, wondering why her eyelids felt weighted down. 'But then I had to coordinate two flights to get home to Sunday Creek.'

'No wonder your body clock's out of whack. You need sleep.' He stopped at his Land Rover and opened the passenger door. Scooping her up, he lifted her in.

'Did you miss me?' She mumbled the words against his shoulder as he settled in beside her.

'You bet I did.' His gaze softened. 'I should never have let you go without me. Did you miss me?' He turned his head, waiting for her answer, but she was already asleep.

Darcie woke to silence and the gentlest breeze wafting through the partly open window. Blinking uncertainly, she half raised her head. Where was she? She looked around at the unfamiliar prints on the walls, the white linen blinds. And then reality struck. She was in one of the guest bedrooms in Jack's house.

She muffled a groan into the pillow. He must have got her to bed after they'd left the hospital. What else had he done? Cautiously, she put a hand under the duvet and touched the softness of the jersey pants she'd worn on the flight. Except for her shoes, he hadn't attempted to undress her. 'Oh, Jack…' A smile curved gently around her mouth. 'You are such an honourable man.'

The sharp click of the front door closing had her sitting boldly upright, pulling her knees up to her chin. 'Jack?' Her voice came out throatily. 'Is that you?'

'Ah…' Jack's dark head came round the door. 'Sleeping Beauty's awake, I see.'

Darcie blushed, watching him amble into the bedroom, his powerful masculinity making the space appear to shrink to doll's-house proportions. 'Good sleep?' he asked.

'It was. Sorry I passed out on you,' she said ruefully. 'What time is it?'

'Five-ish.'

Darcie frowned. 'Five-ish when?'

'Sunday afternoon.'

'You mean I've slept the clock round?'

He looked at her with steady eyes. 'Jet lag will do that to you every time. How about some dinner? Hungry?'

'Starving.' She smiled a bit uncertainly. 'But at the moment I need the bathroom more than I need food.'

A wry smile nipped his mouth. 'See you in a bit, then. Oh, I swung by the residence and picked up your suitcase.'

'Oh—thanks for that.' She watched as he slipped out and retrieved it from the hallway.

'I've made minestrone.' He hefted her case onto the end of the bed. 'Hurry up.'

Darcie threw herself out of bed and into the en suite. Were they back together? Properly back together? She ground her lip in consternation, letting the rose-scented gel drift silkily over her body and puddle around her feet. They hadn't parted on the best of terms. Jack had clearly not been happy about her reasons for going to England. But surely he wouldn't have brought her here to his home if he was still offside with her?

Air whistled out of her lungs, ending in an explosive little sigh as she dressed quickly. Conjecture was getting her nowhere. She left the bedroom, an odd flutter of shyness assailing her as she made her way along the short length of the hallway to the kitchen.

Jack had set places at the table. Standing for a moment, she watched him, her gaze lingering, drinking in his maleness. He was wearing a black T-shirt that delineated the tight group of muscles beneath and a pair of washed-out jeans. 'Something smells good.'

He turned from the stove, eyeing with obvious approval her sleek black leggings and pearl-grey top. 'Feeling better?'

'Much.' She joined him at the stove. 'Anything I can do to help?'

He turned off the heat and gave the minestrone a final stir. 'Couple of bowls might be a good idea. And there's some multigrain rolls in that bag there. Then we'll be in business.'

'Another?' Jack's look was softly indulgent a little later as Darcie neared the end of her second bowl of soup.

'Heavens, no!' She gave an embarrassed laugh. 'But that was truly delicious, Jack. Thank you.'

His mouth pulled at the corner. 'You're more than welcome, Darcie.' He looked at her guardedly. 'Coffee?'

She shook her head. 'Perhaps later.'

He shifted awkwardly in his chair. 'Sorry for acting like a prat when you arrived yesterday.'

Eyes cast down, she made a little circle with her finger on the tabletop. 'Do you want to hear about my trip?'

Jack's heart was beating like a tom-tom. Lord, how he'd missed her! And now she was back, barely centimetres away from him, her faint, delicate fragrance teasing his senses, making a mockery of his control. 'I suppose we should get it out of the way.' Standing to his feet, he collected their used dishes and took them across to the sink.

Darcie had the feeling of being dismissed. But not for long. She rose from the table, moving purposefully across to join him at the window, peering out. 'The reason I went, Jack, was to come to you whole. If you want us back together, the least you can do is listen.'

Something in Jack's heart scrunched tight. He blinked and turned his head a fraction. Her eyes were cast down, her long gold-tipped lashes fanning across her cheeks. He felt a lump the size of a lemon in his throat as he swallowed. 'You're right. But let's get more comfortable, shall we?'

They went through to the lounge room. Darcie switched on the two table lamps and a gentle glow of light flooded the room. Jack held out his hand and guided her to the big, squishy sofa. Once they were seated, he looped out an arm and gathered her closely. 'OK.' He took a deep breath and let it go. 'Fire away.'

Darcie's heart quickened and she edged back so she could look him in the eye. 'I saw Aaron.'

His jaw tightened for a moment. 'How long did you spend with him?'

'Not long. Needless to say, he was stunned to see

me. I didn't bother with small talk. I just hit him with everything. I let him have it all—everything I'd been feeling. How his behaviour had been reprehensible, how he'd sapped my self-worth and a whole lot more.'

Jack's eyes burned with a strange intensity. 'How did he react?'

'He folded. Apologised. Several times, in fact.' Her eyes clouded briefly. 'I suggested he should get some specialist psychiatric help. It's obvious he's deeply unhappy.'

Jack sent her a guarded look. 'How did he respond to that?'

'He said he's already in therapy.' A breath of silence. 'I…said I hoped it worked. Then I got up and left.'

'Were you upset?' Jack asked carefully.

'Maybe a bit. But I felt free. It was a fantastic feeling.'

'My gutsy, brave girl.' Jack pulled her close again. 'I'm so proud of you.'

'Wait until you hear what else I did.'

'Good grief.' Jack shook his head. 'Better hit me with it then.'

'I went to see my parents. They were actually home for once.'

'And?'

'I had a very frank talk with them.' She sent him a dazzling smile. 'On the flight over to England the thought came to me that they hadn't shaped up very well as parents. There was you and your big loving family and you obviously had a happy childhood. Maggie doing so well as a single parent, and Nat with her husband working away so much, managing to keep her little girl safe and happy. And my parents took none of the responsibility that comes with parenthood. They're bright people. They *should* have known.'

Jack blinked and blinked again. Sweet heaven, she was lovely. His gaze slid softly over her. 'So, what was the outcome?'

'For the first time we sat together like a family. And we talked. Really talked.' Darcie's mouth wobbled a bit. 'They both apologised for their lack of involvement but assured me over and over that they'd always loved me. And Mum cried. And Dad called me his *darling girl*.'

Jack's throat constricted. 'You continue to amaze me, Darcie.' He held her more closely, his lips making feathery kisses over her temple. 'So you had your big talk. Then what? Dare I ask?'

'They're coming to our wedding!'

Jack looked at her, startled.

Her breath caught. 'That's if you still want to marry me…?'

'Oh, God, yes!' he said hoarsely. 'With bells on.' In one liquid movement he hauled them both upright. In a second their bodies were surging together like breakers dashing to the shore.

They kissed once, fiercely, possessively. And again. This time slowly, languidly, taking all the time in the world to savour each other. To reconnect.

On a little whimper Darcie burrowed closer, drinking him in, feeling the absorption of his scent in her nostrils, through her skin.

When they drew apart, they stared at one another, the moment almost surreal. 'We're getting married,' Jack said.

'Yes.' She reached up and drew her finger along his throat and into the hollow at its base. 'And I want everything, Jack. A real outback wedding. I want our little bush church decorated with masses of flowers, big bows on the seats and the church filled with family and friends.'

Jack looked bemused. 'And after?'

'We'll hire a marquee and find somewhere special to put it. And we'll have fairy-lights and maybe a dance floor and glorious food.'

Jack's eyes went wide in alarm. 'I won't have to cook, will I?'

Darcie snickered. 'Of course not. We'll fly caterers out from Brisbane if we have to. And don't look like that,' she chided gently. 'My parents are paying for everything. I bought a wedding dress in London,' she added shyly. 'I hope you'll like me in it.'

'Of course I'll like you in it.' There was a gleam in his blue eyes. 'And out of it too.'

Darcie laughed, feeling the warm flood of desire ripple through her body. 'We just have to make a date, then.'

'Let's leave that for tomorrow. Right now, we need to be doing other things. Don't you agree…?'

'I agree, Jack.' The catch in his voice told her everything she needed to hear. A slow, radiant smile lit her face as she slipped her hands under his T-shirt, loving the smooth sweep of his skin against her palms. Loving *him*. 'Now,' she enticed coyly, 'come and unwrap your present.'

# CHAPTER THIRTEEN

IT WAS A perfect day for a wedding.

'Darcie, could you possibly stand still for a half a second?' Maggie did a slow inspection around the now dressed bride. They were at the residence with barely fifteen minutes left before they were to leave for the church.

'I'm so happy I could burst, Maggie.'

'Don't do that,' Maggie pleaded. 'I'd have to fasten these tiny buttons all over again.'

'What do you think of the dress?' Darcie posed in front of the full-length mirror. 'Does it look OK?'

'OK?' Maggie's voice went up an octave. The dress was a stylish combination of silk and hand-made lace with a fitted bodice, tiny cap sleeves and slim-cut skirt. 'Honey, you look stunning.' Maggie's gaze had a misty look. 'Jack's eyes will be out on stalks.'

'That's if he can see at all,' Darcie said dryly. 'I can't believe his brothers hauled him off to the pub for a buck's do the night before the wedding!'

'Well, boys will be boys,' Maggie countered practically. 'And, anyway, Jack stuck to the soft stuff mostly, according to Sam.'

'Mmm.' Darcie didn't seem convinced.

'Oh, Darce.' Maggie laughed. 'Relax, would you? Even if Jack ended up a bit tipsy, he's had all day to sleep it off.'

Darcie gave a reluctant chuckle. 'Then it's lucky we decided to have the wedding in the late afternoon, wasn't it? For everyone's sake.' She paused and sobered. 'Maggie, thank you so much for standing up with me and for your endless kindness and friendship.'

'Oh, tosh.' Maggie shook her dark head. 'Friendship is a two-way street. And yours has been invaluable to me as well. Now, hush up.' She gave an off-key laugh. 'Or we'll both be bawling and ruining our make-up. Shame you're not getting a honeymoon, though.'

'Price of being doctors in the outback.' Darcie looked philosophical. 'But we're getting a couple of nights away. Jack's arranged for someone to fly us across to the coast. Posh hotel and all the trimmings.'

'Oh, yes…' Maggie waggled her eyebrows. 'Breakfast in bed?'

Darcie's face went pink. 'All that. I'm so happy, Maggie.'

'Sweetie, you deserve it.' Maggie's look turned soft. 'Oh, I meant to ask, how are your parents enjoying Sunday Creek?'

'They're loving it.' Darcie picked up their bouquets of red roses and handed one to Maggie. 'It was so sweet of Louise to invite them to stay at Willow Bend.'

'Willow Bend is such a beautiful property,' Maggie agreed. 'And they'll get a real taste of station life as well.'

'Your transport's here.' Lauren stuck her head in the door. 'Oh, my stars! Darcie, you look incredible!'

'Oh…thanks, Lauren.' Darcie gave a shaky laugh.

Suddenly she was all butterflies. What if Jack didn't turn up? What if his brother, Dom, forgot the rings? What if they both messed up their vows? With trembling fingers she reached up to touch the delicate silver heart at her throat. Jack's gift to his bride. She blinked back the sudden possibility of tears. 'Do we have time for a glass of wine?'

'No, we don't,' Maggie said firmly. 'It might be fashionable to be late but personally I think it's plain bad manners. Besides which, Jack will be wearing out the carpet and the priest will be getting tetchy.'

'Oh, he won't,' Darcie remonstrated. 'He's been lovely to us.'

'Come on, guys.' Lauren began to usher them out into the hallway. 'Your chariot awaits.'

'Do you have all our stuff, Lauren?' Maggie raised a quick hand in question.

Lauren held up her big purple holdall. 'Spares of everything and the bride's pashmina in case it gets chilly later.'

'Thanks. You're a star.'

'Happy to be your lady-in-waiting,' Lauren said cheerfully, and the little party began to move forward to the front veranda.

'Wh-what's that?' Darcie's voice squeaked with shock. She pointed to the buggy and two handsome grey horses that were drawn up outside.

'It's your transport,' Maggie said. 'Isn't it fabulous?'

Darcie's mouth opened and closed. 'But Louise promised to lend us their Mercedes!'

'She did.' Maggie grinned. 'And it's for Lauren and me. You, my dear, are travelling in style by horse and coach.'

'You wanted a real outback wedding,' Lauren reminded the bride.

'But horses!' Darcie looked helplessly between the two women.

'Aren't they a picture?' Maggie looked so pleased. 'Sam found them for us. And they're accustomed to this kind of thing, so you'll be quite safe.'

'Besides, the locals will want to wave to you along the way,' Lauren put in. 'You'll be like a princess.'

Darcie began to laugh. 'I can't believe you've all done this to me!'

'Oh, we're not devoid of innovation out here,' Maggie said innocently. 'Now, here's your dad come to escort you.'

'Good afternoon, ladies.' Professor Drummond greeted the little group and then took his daughter's hands, holding her at arm's length, his gaze suspiciously moist. 'Darcie...you look radiant. And so grown-up...'

'Oh, Dad...' Darcie choked back a slight lump in her throat and thought this was how it should be on her wedding day. It would have been unthinkable if her father had not been here.

'You look very lovely, Maggie.' The professor took his eyes off his daughter for a moment.

'Thank you, Richard.' Maggie acknowledged his compliment with a dignified little nod.

'Richard!' Lauren hissed in a shocked stage whisper. 'Isn't that a bit disrespectful? Isn't he a *lord* or something?'

'No.' Maggie snickered behind her hand. 'He asked us to call him Richard when he and Darcie's mum hosted a pre-wedding do a few days ago.'

'Now, are we ready, ladies?' Professor Drummond

tucked Darcie's arm through his and proceeded to walk her carefully down the flight of shallow steps.

Darcie aimed her bouquet towards the horses and buggy. 'Are you all right about this, Dad?'

'It's really quite comfortable.' He turned his head and smiled at her. 'And our driver, Jay, is a very interesting chap. We had a most pleasant journey in from Willow Bend.'

'You came all that way in a buggy?' Darcie was astounded at her usually conservative father's easy acceptance of the rather *out-there* mode of transport for her wedding.

'Here, Darcie, give me your flowers while you hop aboard,' Maggie instructed. 'And don't panic. The seat is well sprung and it's spotlessly clean. You'll arrive in perfect order.'

'I'm just grateful I'm not wearing a hooped skirt,' Darcie vented as she placed her foot gingerly on the buggy's running board.

'Then we might have had a problem,' Maggie conceded, watching as Darcie settled back in the red leather seat and reclaimed her bouquet. 'Safe journey.' Maggie gave a jaunty finger wave and stepped back. 'See you at the church.'

Darcie's heart was cartwheeling as she stood in the church porch beside her father.

'You look beautiful, darling,' he said. 'Jack is a very lucky man. And a fine one,' he added with obvious approval.

Darcie took a steadying breath. 'Is he here, Dad? Can you see him?'

Maggie, who had arrived seconds earlier, said briskly,

'Of course he's here!' Lifting a hand, she brushed a tiny tendril of hair from Darcie's cheek. 'Now, are we ready?' she whispered.

Darcie nodded and swallowed.

'Good.' Maggie gave a smile of encouragement. 'Then let's do it.'

Standing in front of the altar, Jack felt his chest rise in a long steadying breath. She was here at last, his English bride, his Darcie, his love. She had almost reached him when he turned, lifting a dark brow in admiration.

Seeing the familiar broad sweep of her bridegroom's shoulders, the proud set of his head, Darcie stifled a whirlpool of nerves and found the impetus to walk the last few paces to his side.

'OK?' he murmured, reaching for her hand. Darcie nodded, and clung for dear life.

'Welcome, guys.' Standing in front of them, Father Tom Corelli beamed across at the bride and groom. 'Now, before we get on to the real business, I believe you have something personal you wish to say to each other.'

'Thank you, Father.' Darcie struggled with her prickling eyes and turned to face Jack. He smiled encouragingly at her and they took hands. Darcie drew in a steadying breath and began.

'Jack, you are my rock. You have listened to me and supported me both personally and professionally. My love for you is as wide and deep as the outback sky. You are my true north. And I will love you always and for ever.'

Raw emotion carved Jack's face and he wished he'd

thought of something so poetic. But he'd do the best he could.

'Darcie, you are my true love. You are as strong and brave as the finest trees of our forests, yet as tender and beautiful as our most delicate wildflower. And I will love you always and for ever.'

Darcie made the rest of their formal vows in a haze of happiness, hardly registering when she and Jack exchanged rings. When Father Tom pronounced them husband and wife, they kissed. And kissed again to a ripple of applause and a few whistles from one or two daring members of the Cassidy clan.

Smiling broadly, the priest ushered them to an especially prepared table at the side of the altar. And as they sat to sign the register, Lauren delighted them by singing a huskily sweet rendition of 'The First Time Ever I Saw Your Face'.

'I had no idea!' Darcie's whisper was shot with amazement.

'Just our little surprise for you.' Jack's expression was tender. 'And I have another for you as well, Mrs Darcie Cassidy.'

'Oh?' Darcie blinked and tried to speak and wondered if it was possible to overdose on sheer happiness.

Jack's smile began slowly and then widened. 'We're having a proper honeymoon,' he said. 'A whole week to ourselves. We've got us a locum.'

Darcie looked fascinated. 'Who?'

There was a gleam in Jack's blue eyes. 'One of the flying doctors.'

Darcie's eyes flashed wide in disbelief. 'Are we talking about Brad Kitto here?' she whispered.

Jack nodded. 'As a wedding present, he's kindly offered to give up a week of his leave for us.'

Darcie was dumbfounded. 'But Brad?' she emphasised in a stage whisper. 'You always looked on him as something of a rival.'

'That was then.' Jack seemed unfazed.

'But didn't you feel uncomfortable about accepting his offer?'

'Why would I?' Jack looked at his bride, his entire heart in his gaze. 'After all, my love, you'd chosen *me*.'

\* \* \* \* \*

*A sneaky peek at next month...*

## MEDICAL ROMANCE™

**THE ULTIMATE IN ROMANTIC MEDICAL DRAMA**

### *My wish list for next month's titles...*

In stores from 4th July 2014:

❑ 200 Harley Street: The Shameless Maverick
  — Louisa George

& 200 Harley Street: The Tortured Hero — Amy Andrews

❑ A Home for the Hot-Shot Doc

& A Doctor's Confession — Dianne Drake

❑ The Accidental Daddy — Meredith Webber

& Pregnant with the Soldier's Son — Amy Ruttan

**Available at WHSmith, Tesco, Asda, Eason, Amazon and Apple**

### *Just can't wait?*

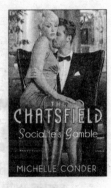

# Join our *EXCLUSIVE* eBook club

## FROM JUST £1.99 A MONTH!

*Never miss a book again with our hassle-free eBook subscription.*

★ Pick how many titles you want from each series with our flexible subscription

★ Your titles are delivered to your device on the first of every month

★ Zero risk, zero obligation!

*There really is nothing standing in the way of you and your favourite books!*

**Start your eBook subscription today at www.millsandboon.co.uk/subscribe**

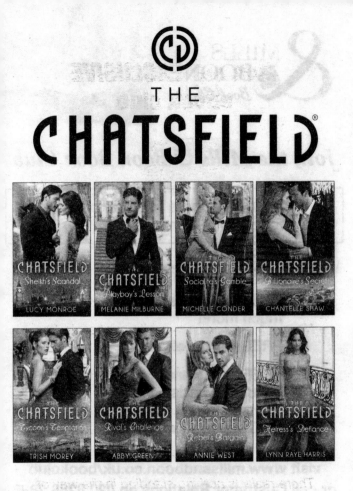

**MILLS & BOON®**
*Book Club*

## *Join the Mills & Boon Book Club*

Want to read more **Medical** books?
We're offering you **2 more** absolutely **FREE!**

We'll also treat you to these fabulous extras:

-  **Exclusive offers and much more!**

- **FREE home delivery**

- **FREE books and gifts with our special rewards scheme**

*Get your free books now!*

**visit www.millsandboon.co.uk/bookclub**
**or call Customer Relations on 020 8288 2888**